A TIMELESS SPELL

Colin cradled the back of her head in his broad palm, pressing her face to his chest. One squeak from her or the cat and they would be trapped at the mercy of Brisbane's men.

Their forced intimacy should have been awkward. But there was something disarmingly natural about standing in Colin's arms, feeling the powerful throb of his heart. An inexplicable languor melted through Tabitha, making her feel warm and cherished and safe from all harm for the first time in her life.

Until the menacing hoofbeats receded and the tension failed to melt from Colin's body.

His hand crept around to cup her cheek, alerting her to a more subtle danger. But the warning came too late. He didn't even have to tilt her face upward to find her lips with his own. They were already there—tingling, moist, and parted in an invitation Tabitha hadn't even realized she'd extended until it was too late to rescind it.

His mouth brushed hers, his bottom lip too persuasively soft to belong to such a hard man. Lost in a daze of pleasure, Tabitha considered calling back Brisbane's guards. From a practical viewpoint, she'd be better off losing her head in this century than her heart . . .

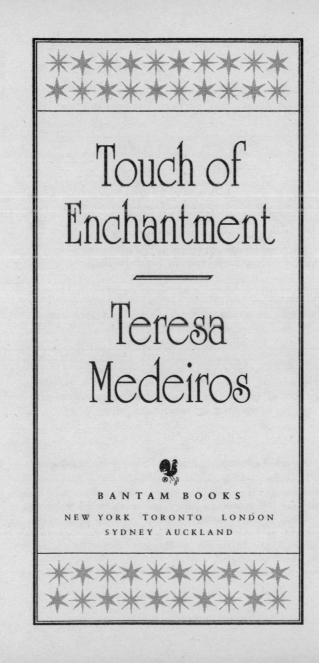

Touch of Enchantment

Teresa Medeiros

BANTAM BOOKS

NEW YORK TORONTO LONDON
SYDNEY AUCKLAND

TOUCH OF ENCHANTMENT
A Bantam Book/July 1997

ISBN 0-553-57500-7

Published simultaneously in the United States and Canada

Bantam Books are published by Bantam Books, a division of Bantam
Doubleday Dell Publishing Group, Inc. Its trademark, consisting of
the words "Bantam Books" and the portrayal of a rooster, is
Registered in U.S. Patent and Trademark Office and in other
countries. Marca Registrada. Bantam Books, 1540 Broadway, New
York, New York 10036.

PRINTED IN THE UNITED STATES OF AMERICA

OPM 10 9 8 7 6 5 4 3 2 1

To the memory of Suzanne Wages, a shining star who blazed brightly, but all too briefly, through our lives. See you on the other side, sweetheart.

To Jack and Berta Pitzer and Patricia Ramsden, who shone the light so brightly I could not help but follow.

To Wendy McCurdy, who was generous enough to give me the keys to the kingdom without even realizing it.

And to Michael, whose steadfast love makes every home we live in a castle of dreams.

Prologue

Tabitha Lennox hated being a witch. The only thing she hated more than being a witch was being a rich witch. But she had little or no say in the matter, having been born the sole heir of both her father's multibillion-dollar empire and her mother's rather unpredictable paranormal talents.

Her mama had named her Tabitha, pronouncing it a good solid Puritan name. Her daddy had smoothly agreed, but the reason for his wry chuckle had not become readily apparent until a *Bewitched* marathon on Nick at Nite had choked a scandalized gasp from her mother.

"Did you know that cheeky little brat was named Tabitha?" she asked, referring to Darrin and Samantha Stevenses' precocious progeny.

Her daddy lowered his *Wall Street Journal* and blinked behind his reading glasses, his gray eyes disarmingly innocent. "Sorry, darling. It must have slipped my mind."

But a hint of a smirk betrayed him. Tabitha's mama launched herself across the cozy great room, pummeling him with one of the fluffy couch pillows until they both collapsed over the ottoman in a giggling heap.

"You really can't blame me," her daddy gasped, tickling her mama into submission. "Your second choice was *Chastity*!"

As their playful tussle dissolved into a tender kiss, seven-year-old Tabitha had rolled her eyes at the plump black cat lazing on the hearth and returned her attention to her laptop computer, wondering why her parents couldn't communicate through E-mail or their lawyers like the parents of all the other children in her Montessori school.

From an early age, Tabitha had craved the soothing boredom of routine the way other children craved toys and candy. Although her parents made a convincing show of normalcy with their Victorian house nestled in the Connecticut countryside, far more than her father's wealth set her apart from her playmates.

Several of her peers rode to school behind the smoked-glass windows of stretch limousines or hosted birthday parties at The Four Seasons, but none of them ever came home from school to find the family cat quoting Shakespeare to a shelf of engrossed plants or a trio of elves peering at them from beneath the shrubbery. Tabitha's mama didn't just bake cookies. She baked dancing cookies that had the unnerving habit of popping themselves into Tabitha's mouth every time she opened it to complain. Tabitha would proudly display her completed homework only to have it vanish into thin air the night before it was due.

Her father would frantically help her duplicate her fractions while her mother conjugated French verbs and apologized profusely for her lack of control over her magic. Although her dismay at causing her daughter distress was genuine, her mama could never quite hide the pride she took in her unusual gift.

Tabitha didn't consider it a gift. She considered it a

curse. Which explained why on her thirteenth birthday, when her casual wish for purple icing on her birthday cake sent sugary globs of it coursing over her stunned head, she experienced no wonder, but only frigid horror.

Trailing purple goo, she fled up the stairs and threw herself on her ruffled bed, weeping as if her little heart would break.

Her parents followed, sinking down on each side of her to exchange a helpless glance over her sobbing form. Her daddy patted her heaving shoulder while her mama stroked her sticky hair.

"Don't cry, *ma petite*," her mama murmured. "You must think of your talents as a gift from God. You'll soon get used to the idea of being special."

Struggling to catch her breath, Tabitha blurted out, "You don't understand! I don't want to be special! I want to be normal." She snuffled into the *Snow White* comforter she had always detested. "I want you two to yell at each other instead of kissing all the time. I want my toys to stop talking and the dishes to stop running away with all the spoons. I want to live in a trailer park and wear clothes off the rack and," her voice broke before rising to a wail, "eat my birthday dinner at McDonald's!"

This startling declaration provoked an even more puzzled glance and a shudder of distaste from her father.

Despite her frequent and often disastrous brushes with the supernatural since that day, Tabitha continued to turn up her rather plain little nose at Disney movies with their talking teapots and singing mice, much preferring the stolid gloom of Ingmar Bergman festivals to those silly princesses always yearning for Prince Charming to swoop down off his stallion and carry them away.

Tabitha Lennox had no choice but to believe in magic.

But she didn't believe in fairy tales.

Or happy endings.

Or Prince Charming.

Yet.

PART ONE

Beguiled

> *'Tis the strumpet's plague to beguile
> many and be beguil'd by one.*
>
> —WILLIAM SHAKESPEARE

> *Yet she wish'd that heaven had
> made her such a man.*
>
> —WILLIAM SHAKESPEARE

CHAPTER 1

NEW YORK CITY

It was at moments like this that Michael Copperfield keenly missed his ponytail. Since he could no longer tug on it when faced with an insurmountable frustration, he was forced to snap a pencil in two to relieve his tension. "You don't seem to understand the gravity of the situation. Your parents have vanished."

The young woman slumped in the leather chair opposite his desk didn't even bother to look up from the reports she was studying. "That's hardly an unusual occurrence, Uncle Cop. My parents vanish all the time. At parties. From taxicabs. During stockholder meetings. They once disappeared into thin air for the entire second act of my senior play." She spared him a brief, mocking glance before flipping a page of the report. "You should try explaining *that* to your high school drama teacher."

Her lackadaisical acceptance of his news only increased Copperfield's sense of urgency. He rose and came around the desk, forcing her to shift her attention from the software configurations to his troubled face. "It's different this time, Tabitha. They didn't just wink out of focus for a few minutes or wish themselves to

Paris for lunch. This time their entire plane disappeared. Over the Bermuda Triangle."

Tabitha blinked owlishly at him from behind her glasses.

Copperfield pressed his advantage. "The company jet vanished over sixteen hours ago without so much as a blip on the radar. The Navy's sent out search planes and ships to comb the site, but they haven't found even a trace of wreckage. Of course, that's not unusual in that area. I'm trying to hold the media at bay for a few days, at least until the Navy's completed their search. But I can assure you the disappearance of one of the richest men in the world isn't going to go unnoticed for long."

Tabitha's skeptical chuckle sounded forced. "So what's your theory, Uncle Cop? Have they been seized by a foreign government? Kidnapped by a terrorist organization?" She whistled a few notes of the theme from *The X-Files.* "Abducted by aliens?"

He retreated to his chair, feeling far older than his fifty-five years. "I'm afraid their plane may have gone down."

Silence permeated the office for an entire sweep of the second hand on the brass desk clock before Tabitha burst out laughing. "Don't be ridiculous! This is just another one of Mama's little paranormal hiccups. The jet will probably reappear exactly where it vanished or pop into the landing pattern at La Guardia just in time to give one of their air traffic controllers another nervous breakdown." As if to escape his pitying scrutiny, Tabitha rose and went to the window, shoving a listless strand of blond hair out of her eyes. "You forget that Tristan and Arian Lennox have an uncanny way of wiggling out of trouble. Remember when the Lamborghini crashed? They walked away without a scratch. And wasn't it you who told me how they once traveled back in time to 1689 to defeat my evil grandfather, proving once again that true love conquers all?"

The note of cynicism in her voice disturbed him. "A theory you don't concur with?"

"It's a charming hypothesis, Uncle Cop, but you have to remember that this is the twenty-first century. True love is no longer in vogue. Romance has been replaced by cybersex with nameless, faceless strangers or holograms of your favorite video stars."

Cop snorted quizzically. "And you find that preferable?"

Tabitha shrugged. "The advantages are obvious." The window reflected her pensive expression, making her appear less convinced than she sounded. "No connection, no commitment . . . no risk."

Copperfield shuddered, but reminded himself that his rebuttal would have to wait. He had more pressing business at hand. "Your parents may have been lucky enough to find true love, sweetheart," he said gently. "But that doesn't make them immortal."

Tabitha swung around to face him, thrusting her hands in the pockets of her baggy tweed trousers. "Have you forgotten that my mother was born in 1669? She may not be immortal, but she looks damn good for a woman approaching her three hundred and fifty-first birthday."

Copperfield sighed, having learned from long and bitter experience that the only thing you got out of arguing with a Lennox was a pounding headache.

Recognizing that more drastic measures would be necessary, he withdrew a manila envelope from his desk drawer and held it out to her. "Your mother asked me to give this to you in the event of her . . ." His fingers tightened on the envelope. It was almost as if handing it over would make it true.

Tabitha stared at the envelope for a long moment before blithely snatching it from his hand. "You're going to be embarrassed by your melodramatics when my parents come popping out of a heating duct at the next Lennox Enterprises board meeting." She started to flip open the metal clasp, but Copperfield closed his hand over hers.

"Arian said you might want to wait until you were alone to open it."

Tabitha frowned down at the envelope. Although she kept her voice light, her bravado appeared to be wearing thin. "What is it? My adoption records? I always told Mama and Daddy that I was too imagination-impaired to possibly be their natural child."

Copperfield cupped Tabitha's chin in his hand and gently drew off her glasses. Her somber gray eyes surveyed him uncertainly. Her thick mop of blond hair had been cut in an efficient shoulder-length bob, but her feathery bangs persisted in drifting over her eyes whenever she relaxed her guard. At twenty-three, Tabitha was nearly as tall as he was and twice as awkward, her gracelessness oddly endearing. Her even features revealed the keen intelligence that had allowed her to enter M.I.T. at the tender age of fifteen, earn her doctorate in Virtual Technology before she turned twenty, and achieve the status of department head in the Lennox Enterprises Virtual Reality Division in less than three years. But beneath the cool competence lurked a disarming hint of wistfulness, of dreams unfulfilled and wishes unvoiced.

As Copperfield studied the face of the child he loved nearly as well as his own daughters, he was seized by a pang of nostalgia. Tristan Lennox had become far more than just his blood brother when, as two lonely little boys, they had exchanged a solemn oath in that Boston orphanage all those years ago. He had become his friend.

"Oh, you're your parents' child all right," he murmured. "Have I ever told you how very much you remind me of your father?"

Dodging his affectionate caress, Tabitha retrieved her glasses and slid them on with a tight smile. "You shouldn't tease me, Uncle Cop. My mother used to say the same thing and I always thought it was a little cruel." Before he could protest, she swept her shapeless lab coat from the back of the chair. "You knew—" She faltered, betrayed by her hesitation. "You *know* Daddy better than anyone. He's always smiling and laughing, finding pleasure in the simplest things. He's graceful and still drop-dead gorgeous, even at fifty-six. He's loved and respected by everyone who's ever had the pleasure of working with him. He's *nothing* like me."

She tucked the envelope beneath her arm and flashed him a brittle smile. Then she threw open the door, revealing the brass plaque that read MICHAEL COPPERFIELD, EXECUTIVE VICE PRESIDENT. "Give Aunt Cherie my love. I'll call you if . . ." She shot him a defiant look. "*When* I hear from my parents."

After the door had slammed in his face, Cop returned to his desk and sank into his chair, torn between laughter and tears. "You didn't let me finish, Tabitha," he muttered, rubbing his burning eyes. "You remind me of your father . . . *before* he met your mother."

As she stepped from the shower, a dripping Tabitha Lennox groped for her glasses even before she reached for the towel. Most of her coworkers poked fun at her behind her back for clinging to the archaic devices when corneal molding had been perfected nearly a decade ago, but she preferred the cool solidity of wire frames to having her eyeballs manipulated by a stranger. Her eyesight wasn't really that bad. Sometimes she suspected she wore them more out of habit than need.

She towel-dried her thick hair and slathered cold cream on her face, then wiggled into a pair of cotton panties and the sturdy L.L. Bean pajamas she'd draped over the towel warmer before entering the shower. The heated flannel enfolded her like an invisible hug. A contented sigh escaped her as she slid her feet into a pair of plush slippers designed to resemble giant chipmunks— her one concession to whimsy.

She padded through the penthouse living room to the efficiency kitchen, pointedly ignoring the manila envelope she'd tossed on the couch after returning from her meeting with Uncle Cop.

She opened the freezer. Her hand wavered between a Lean Tureen frozen dinner that promised zero calories due to the addition of *Phat!*—the dramatic new fat substitute—and a frosty tub of Häagen-Dazs. After several seconds of agonizing, she defiantly chose the ice cream.

So what if she had a few extra pounds clinging to her midriff? Her baggy slacks and lab coat would hide a multitude of sins. And it certainly wasn't as if anyone was going to be seeing her without them.

As she fished a tablespoon from the silverware drawer, a furry head butted her in the ankle.

"Well, hello, little Lucy," Tabitha crooned, squatting to spoon a dab of ice cream into the kitten's bowl. "Did you miss Mommy while she was at work?"

The tiny black cat had been a twenty-third birthday gift from her parents. Fearing that Tabitha would be inconsolable after family cat Lucifer expired at the crotchety old age of twenty-two, her father had arranged for Lucifer's sperm to be frozen until it was needed. With the animal overpopulation crisis finally resolved, test tube kittens were becoming all the rage.

Still skirting the couch, Tabitha paused at the wall keypad to choose a musical selection from the digitalized menu, finally settling on Nina Simone's "I Want a Little Sugar In My Bowl." The sultry warble coaxed a wry smile from Tabitha's lips. She already had a little sugar in her bowl.

She savored a mouthful of ice cream as she watched the lacy snowflakes drift past the glass expanse of the north wall. How pleasant it was to be warm and cozy with a winter storm raging right outside the window! In the past few months, the penthouse had become her haven—the only place where she truly felt safe.

She knew it had hurt her parents' feelings when she'd retreated there after her graduation from M.I.T. They had rejected the spacious suite located at the pinnacle of Lennox Tower years ago in favor of a sprawling Victorian mansion with no climate control system and windows that swung open to beckon in both sunshine and rain.

Tabitha had always felt like an intruder there. Although her parents had made every effort to draw her into their charmed circle, she chose to remain standing outside, too shy to accept their invitation. She would never break their hearts by confessing that she felt more at home with the anonymous strangers battling their way through the snow-clogged city streets below.

She set the empty bowl on the carpet and Lucy materialized to lick it clean. Hugging back a chill, Tabitha frowned into the deepening darkness. It was one thing to reject her parents' idyllic lifestyle when she knew they were out there somewhere, loving her from a distance. But the possibility of a world without their laughter, their tenderness toward one another and toward her,

added a bleak edge to her loneliness. An edge dangerously near panic.

Tabitha slowly turned to face the couch. The envelope
lay where she had abandoned it.

As Tabitha picked it up, a thrill of dread coursed
through her. She understood Uncle Cop's reluctance to
hand it over. His words still haunted her.

*Your mother asked me to give this to you in the event
of her . . .*

"Stop being so superstitious," Tabitha muttered. "It's
an envelope, for God's sake, not Pandora's box." Determined to face her fears, she tore open the clasp and
dumped the contents.

A silvery disk skittered across the glass coffee table.
Tabitha instantly recognized it as a video disk. She took
it to her modular workstation and popped it into the
appropriate drive, praying it wouldn't be one of those
maudlin presentations favored by funeral directors in
which sobbing violins nearly drowned out the dearly
departed's last words.

The forty-five-inch wall screen winked to life.

Tabitha found herself gazing up at an image of her
mother seated on a stool with the impish grace of an elf
perched on a mushroom. She wore a vintage Chanel
suit, red to match her lipstick.

Before she'd been forced to so ruthlessly curb her
imagination, Tabitha had fancied her mama a fairy princess. Delicate and petite, Arian Lennox possessed an
otherworldly quality that even age couldn't tarnish. The
wiry threads of silver she stubbornly refused to color
only enhanced the lustrous beauty of her dark hair.
Shallow laugh lines bracketed her lush mouth and sparkling eyes.

It wasn't her mother's fault that Tabitha had always
felt like an ungainly elephant next to her. Or that she

secretly wished she'd inherited her mama's looks and her daddy's talents, instead of the other way around.

Suppressing a wistful sigh, Tabitha stabbed the button that would activate the video.

"Hello, my darling Tabby-Cat."

Her mother's husky voice actually seemed to warm the room. Tabitha felt a rush of nostalgia at the sound of that Gallic lilt. Her mother hadn't called her by that particular endearment in years—not since Tabitha pronounced it too undignified for a mature young lady of seven years. Tabitha's eyes stung. Too many hours spent gazing at a video screen, she told herself, blinking hard. Lucy hopped into her lap, demanding to be stroked.

Her mother looked guiltily over her shoulder before placating the camera with a mischievous smile. *"Your father would never forgive me if he knew I was doing this."*

"That's where you're wrong, Mama," Tabitha murmured. "Daddy would forgive you anything."

But as her mother's dazzling smile faltered to a pensive frown, even Tabitha felt a chill of doubt.

The invisible camera seemed to disappear as her mother fixed her with a penetrating gaze. *"Parents have very little control over which traits they pass on to their children, my dear. Sometimes it's gray eyes, or big feet, or an insatiable fondness for ice cream."*

Tabitha gave the empty bowl a rueful glance.

"Or, as your father would say"—Arian sat up straighter and adjusted a pair of imaginary reading glasses in a dead-on imitation of Tristan Lennox—*"the ability to manipulate the space-time continuum and convert thought energy into matter."* A conspiratorial wink. *"I prefer to simply call it 'magic.' "*

Tabitha's smile faded along with her mother's.

"I'd be lying if I told you it didn't distress me that

you've always considered that particular trait more a nuisance than a gift. But I suppose I can't really blame you. You tried so hard to be a good little girl. I'll never forget how hard you cried the day the principal sent you home from school because he believed you'd set off all the sprinklers out of spite. I thought my own heart would break."

Tabitha's cheeks burned with remembered mortification from that incident and a hundred more like it. Like the time she'd innocently admired a dress displayed in a store window only to find herself standing stark naked in the middle of the mall, surrounded by laughing classmates. Or the time the boy she adored had finally asked her out only to be turned into a frog during their very first kiss. He'd taken Viveca Winslow to the senior prom and Tabitha hadn't dared kiss a boy since.

As if anticipating her thoughts, her mother leaned toward the camera. *"Your father and I are deeply concerned about the way you've withdrawn from the world. Neither one of us can stand to see you lock yourself away in that penthouse like a princess in a tower."*

Tabitha snorted and wiggled her feet, discomfited by the guilt in her mother's big brown eyes. "Yeah, Mom. A princess wearing chipmunk slippers and cold cream. You always were an incurable romantic."

"After much soul-searching, I've concluded that you might not view your talent as such a curse if you could only achieve some small measure of control over it."

It was Tabitha's turn to lean forward in her chair, riveted by that single seductive word.

Control.

"That's why I've decided to share with you the only secret I ever kept from your father."

Her mouth fell open. Good grief! Was she about to learn she'd been sired by the mailman?

The story that followed was even more inexplicable. Lapsing into occasional French, Arian rambled on about magic charms, warlocks, corrupt ministers, microprocessors, and wicked magicians until Tabitha's head began to reel with the effort it took to follow her dizzying flights of logic. Her mother's talent for circumventing a point had always been one of her less endearing traits. By the time Arian paused for breath, Tabitha had decided she was either poking fun at her or in desperate need of psychotherapy.

But the look Arian gave her was so tender, Tabitha could not help but be transfixed by it. *"So now you understand why I let your father believe I destroyed the amulet all those years ago."*

Tabitha frowned, more clueless than before.

"I trust you will use it wisely, my dear, to focus and restrain your remarkable powers." Her mother touched two fingers to her lips and blew the camera a kiss, bittersweet longing in her eyes. *"No matter what your future may hold, you have already made me very proud. Au revoir, ma chérie."*

The image froze.

Tabitha sank back in the chair, clutching Lucy without realizing it. The kitten squirmed in protest.

Until we meet again, my darling, her mother had said. Not farewell. Not good-bye. *Until we meet again.*

Tabitha found scant comfort in the words. Her parents had begged her to accompany them on their Caribbean vacation, but as always, she'd insisted she was too busy, her presence too vital to her department. Had she accepted their invitation, she might have been on that plane with them.

Dear God, what if they were really gone? Her sweet, charming mama? Her beloved daddy—the man she had always regarded with a wistful mix of adoration and hero worship?

Blinded by tears she could no longer blame on eyestrain, Tabitha stretched a hand toward her mother's image. "Oh, Mama," she whispered. "I wish . . ."

The word died in her throat, smothered by bitterness. She must never wish. It was the one thing denied her. Because neither money nor magic could protect her from the disastrous consequences of her longing.

Tabitha tapped the escape key. She had forgotten to cancel her audio selection, so as her mother's image faded to black, the first haunting strains of Nina Simone's "Wild Is the Wind" drifted through the room.

CHAPTER 2

Sleep eluded Tabitha. She thrashed in her Laura Ashley sheets for nearly three hours, hoping her parents would get a good laugh out of all her wasted angst when they returned from the Caribbean. She tried to occupy her mind by sorting through her mother's babblings about warlocks and magical talismans. Three words kept emerging from the incoherent tangle.

Control. Restraint. Focus. Irresistible concepts to a woman who'd spent her entire life feeling like the butt of some dismal cosmic joke.

The digital clock on her bedside table read 3:02 when she finally groaned her defeat and tossed back the covers. The kitten draped over her feet mewed in protest.

"Don't worry, Lucy," Tabitha whispered as she reached for her glasses. "It's past the witching hour." Fatigue was definitely making her punchy.

She donned her slippers and shuffled into the bathroom, starting when she caught a glimpse of herself in the mirror. With her tousled hair and cold-cream mask, she looked like a wild-eyed mime. She rinsed her face, then surveyed the elegant bathroom, trying to see it through her mother's eyes. Arian had protested vehemently when Tabitha had suggested redecorating it. Maybe she'd had another motivation besides sentimentality—considering the object she claimed to have hidden there over twenty-four years ago?

Feeling more than a little ridiculous, Tabitha got down on her hands and knees to peer under the towel warmer. Nothing. Feeling even sillier, she lifted the porcelain lid and peeked into the commode tank. It would be just her luck to find a family heirloom in the toilet, she thought ruefully. More nothing.

As Tabitha studied the room, a wistful pang reminded her why she'd been so desperate to redecorate. The penthouse bathroom with its sunken whirlpool tub and array of plush towels had been designed with sensual pleasure in mind. Its twin pedestal sinks were nothing but a cruel reminder of all the small but significant intimacies she could never allow anyone to share. And she certainly had no need for twin showerheads, especially when one of them was perpetually clogged.

Tabitha stiffened. Acting on a hunch, she swept open the door of the frosted-glass enclosure and unscrewed the offending showerhead. She gasped in astonishment as a length of chain unfurled into her waiting hand.

"Well, I'll be damned," she whispered.

She cupped the tarnished treasure in her palm. Although moisture had corroded the delicate chain, the emerald nestled in the antique setting showed remarkably little sign of wear. Tabitha recoiled. Was it her imagination or had the brilliant gem winked at her?

"You don't have any imagination," she reminded herself sternly, although the day she was having was enough to make her see pink elephants.

Thinking it might make her feel better to wear something of her mother's next to her heart, she started to slip the necklace over her head. A tingle of apprehension made her hesitate. Hadn't Arian called the necklace an amulet, a talisman, a magical charm?

Should she wish? Tabitha wondered. And if so, what should she wish for? Freedom from the temptation to wish? A shrill giggle escaped her, warning her that she was dangerously near exhaustion.

Determined to start behaving like a sane scientist instead of a mad one, Tabitha marched into the living room and voice-activated her computer and mini-monitor. Thanks to the wonders of modern technology, she wouldn't have to wait until tomorrow to prove the emerald was nothing more than a pretty rock. Her modem connected her to the Lennox Enterprises laboratory computer network with a chirp of agreement.

She arranged the necklace on an analysis pad. Her fingers flew over the keyboard, commanding the sophisticated software to analyze the structural composition of the emerald. Lucy hopped up on her lap and began to bat at the white plastic mouse that controlled the blinking cursor. Tabitha doubted the kitten would know what to do with a real mouse.

The necklace's image appeared on the screen, each segment divided into color-coded cross-sections. Tabitha leaned forward until her nose almost touched the screen as she beheld the wondrous secret contained within the emerald.

"Magnify," she croaked.

The computer obeyed, highlighting the gem itself. Tabitha drew off her glasses, rubbed her weary eyes, then slid them back on. The stunning image on the screen was still there.

The emerald encased a tangled maze of microcircuitry, incredibly complex by today's standards, utterly impossible when measured against the crude technology available nearly a quarter of a century ago. Her mother had not exaggerated. This was magic indeed and to Tabitha's methodical mind, it was a magic far more profound than that of blundered wishes or spilled fairy dust. The miraculous web of wires and nodes represented sheer wizardry, conceived and executed by the most ingenious of intellects. During her lifetime, Tabitha had met only one man capable of such incandescent brilliance.

"Daddy?" she whispered.

She touched one fingertip to the screen, almost as if she could absorb her father's invisible presence. But the cold glass only reminded her that she had no idea where her father was, or if he was still alive.

Sighing heavily, she settled back in the chair. Her own brain was nothing to scoff at and she was determined to use it to solve the puzzle of the emerald. The scanning abilities of the Lennox Enterprises virtual reality software rendered physical dissection obsolete. She would simply magnify and magnify again until she could catalogue and study each node of the tiny microprocessor.

She squinted at the screen before tapping out a *1* on the numerical keypad. The emerald's image doubled in size.

An odd rumbling sounded overhead. Tabitha cast a distracted glance toward the window. Thunder? She'd never heard of it thundering in New York in January. Especially during a snowstorm.

She decided to magnify the image again. Her finger punched the *2,* quadrupling the original image.

A warm draft poured through the room. Still gazing at the screen, Tabitha made a mental note to call maintenance in the morning. The central heating unit must be malfunctioning.

Perhaps she should enhance the current magnification

to the fifth power. Without a heartbeat of hesitation, she chose the 5.

Lucy's fur crackled beneath her hand, charged with a burst of static electricity. If Tabitha had glanced over at the emerald at that moment, she would have seen that it was lit from within by a fierce glow.

Ignoring the kitten's alarmed meow, Tabitha yawned. Perhaps she should steal a few hours sleep and resume her investigation in the morning. She was due in the lab at seven, but it wouldn't matter if she was late. That was one of the perks of being a department head. And the boss's daughter.

Unable to resist one last peek at the workings of her newfound treasure, she studied the keypad. Her finger hovered indecisively over the numbers, wavering between the 1 and the 2.

A mischievous smile curved Tabitha's lips. "And to think you've always accused me of having no sense of adventure," she murmured to her absent mother before gleefully stabbing the 4.

The screen exploded in a burst of white-hot light. Tabitha recoiled, but her finger remained riveted to the keypad, galvanized by the dazzling arc of electricity that darted between computer and amulet and back again. Lucy yowled her fright and crawled up Tabitha's pajama sleeve.

Tabitha felt her entire body start to vibrate like the overtuned strings of a Stradivarius. Her scalp tingled as each individual hair began a quivering ascent. A scream built in her throat. Thinking only to break the arc, she stretched her other hand toward the necklace, forcing her fingers through the crackling veil of resistance.

At the moment her hand closed on the emerald, the artificial lightning cracked like a whip, sending her flying backward into the arms of darkness.

CHAPTER 3

"That was one hell of a power surge," Tabitha murmured, still too numb to move more than her lips.

Her eyelids refused to budge and an ineffectual twitch was all she could coax from her fingers. Her mouth tasted as if someone had been soldering inside of it. She sincerely hoped the singed smell in her nostrils wasn't coming from her hair. Or her eyelashes.

A strange radiance bathed her in warmth. The heating unit must have been in worse shape than she realized. Its malfunction must have caused the surge protector on her computer to fail, leaving her vulnerable to a dangerous influx of electricity. But it wasn't until the peculiar light flickered against her eyelids that she began to wonder if the penthouse was on fire.

Refusing to panic, Tabitha pried open her eyes and blinked up at the ceiling. Or where the ceiling should have been. In its place was a vault of dazzling blue, unsullied by even a trace of smog. She shaded her eyes against the ball of sunlight dangling directly over her head.

There must have been a fire, she thought dazedly. The penthouse had burned, but some hunky fireman had carried her down ninety-five flights of stairs and laid her on the sidewalk in front of Lennox Tower.

But where were the piles of grimy snow? The sirens? The rude gawkers who always materialized at the first sign of any disaster? Tabitha sat up, gingerly rotating her neck to see if it would support the weight of her aching head.

The surrounding landscape slowly came into focus. She was sitting in the middle of a meadow carpeted in minty green grass and springy clover. Its vast expanse was broken only by a sparse scattering of oaks. An array of colorful wildflowers sprinkled the field, dancing in the sultry embrace of the breeze. Tabitha ducked as a fat brown grasshopper whirred past her nose. The musical chirps of a nearby songbird drifted to her ears.

After months of bitingly cold temperatures and snow-laden skies, Tabitha's senses were overwhelmed. It was like being dropped smack-dab in the middle of some eternal summer.

Her breath caught. What if this wasn't eternal summer, but eternity? With a capital *E*. Perhaps there really had been a fire, but no hunky fireman.

"Don't be silly," Tabitha muttered. "God wouldn't be spiteful enough to let you die a virgin. You're simply in a coma. Or having an out-of-body experience."

She spotted her glasses lying in a nearby patch of clover. She reached for them, but was distracted by the sight of Lucy hopping through the grass in pursuit of a bright yellow butterfly.

Kittens in heaven? It was a darling concept, but as Tabitha surveyed the pastoral paradise, a far less charming suspicion was beginning to dawn in her mind. What if this was nothing more than her parents' elaborate little scheme to get her to take that vacation they'd been nagging her about for years? What if they'd arranged the entire thing—the faux plane crash, Uncle Cop's doleful performance, her mother's poignant video? That would explain why the mysterious "amulet" appeared to contain technology far beyond anything that should have been possible.

Tabitha uncurled her stiff fingers, realizing that she was still clutching the necklace. Sunlight struck the emerald, splintering into fragments. The gem's mischievous sparkle seemed to taunt her.

It wouldn't be the first time her mother had tried to manipulate her with magic. All for her own good, of course, like the time Arian had cast a love spell on Brent Vondervan when Tabitha was seven. The poor besotted boy had followed Tabitha everywhere after that, fawning over her with such drooling adoration that she could no longer respect him, much less like him. Her own mother had believed she could only win a boy's heart with charms of the supernatural variety. The humiliation still stung.

Tabitha's sense of betrayal flourished. Why, her parents and Uncle Cop were probably back at the Tower right now, toasting their cunning and sharing a hearty laugh at her expense! She started to toss the counterfeit heirloom away, but a pang of doubt stopped her. What if it was her only ticket back to her cozy penthouse?

Seething with anger, she slipped the necklace on and scrambled to her feet. "Mo-ther," she yelled at the sky. "I am *not* amused."

Lucy paused in batting around a cricket to blink at her, and Tabitha realized she was standing in the middle of a meadow wearing nothing but an antique necklace, her L.L. Bean flannel pajamas, and a pair of chipmunk slippers.

"You couldn't just buy me a ticket to Club Med, could you?" she muttered.

She stuffed her glasses into her pajama shirt pocket and tried to figure out which way she should march. Her parents never left anything to chance and she doubted it was a coincidence that the meadow was bordered by a forest primeval identical to the ones in all of those silly fairy tales her mother had always insisted on reading to her.

The trees were taller than any Tabitha had ever seen, their trunks nearly as broad as California redwoods. Shafts of sunlight pierced the leafy canopy woven from their boughs, transforming the forest floor into a dappled cathedral. Motes of pollen drifted through the air like fairy dust, but Tabitha was too disgruntled to be charmed by their sparkle. Only her mother could have conjured up such an idyllic setting. She wouldn't have been surprised to see Bambi and Thumper come bounding out of the forest, followed by Snow White trilling "Someday My Prince Will Come."

"Oh, no," Tabitha whispered, her spirits plummeting even lower as a dreadful new possibility dawned in her mind. There was only one thing her hopelessly old-fashioned mama might want her to have more than a vacation.

A man.

Despite Tabitha's flawless arguments, she had never managed to convince her mother that a modern woman no longer needed a man to achieve happiness and fulfillment. Perhaps somewhere in the most secret corner of her heart, she'd never quite convinced herself either.

Tabitha glared at the forest. She had far more to fear from Prince Charming than Snow White. If this was her mother's misguided attempt to set her up with a blind date, it should be only a matter of minutes before some simpering oaf came prancing out from the trees on his white horse.

She frowned. Was it her imagination or had the bird-songs dwindled to silence? A waiting stillness seemed to have fallen over both forest and meadow. Even Lucy crouched in the grass. The sun ducked behind a wisp of cloud, sending an odd chill—half anticipation, half fore-boding—down Tabitha's spine.

She cocked her head, listening intently. Instead of the dainty clip-clop of silver-shod hooves, she heard a low-pitched roar, like the rumble of distant thunder. The earth beneath her feet began to shake.

The roar swelled, sweeping toward Tabitha like an inevitable tide. Stricken by primitive terror, she backed away from the woods. She would have fled, but there was nowhere to hide. Her chipmunk slippers were not made for the uneven terrain. She stumbled and fell to her back just as a snorting black monster came thunder-ing out of the forest.

Before she could unleash the scream from her throat, the monster reared over her, deadly forelegs slicing at the air, nostrils flaring. Tabitha squeezed her eyes shut and waited to be trampled.

She didn't open them until she felt the blade at her throat. Her bewildered gaze traced the length of the shimmering sword up to a gauntleted hand, then higher still to an implacable face haloed by an unruly mane of dark hair. Golden eyes, as voracious and pitiless as a tiger's, surveyed her unblinkingly.

This was no prince, she thought dazedly, but more of a beast than the nightmarish creature he was riding.

Making a valiant attempt to swallow around the knot of terror in her throat, Tabitha timidly croaked, "Ex-cuse me, sir, but have you seen my mother?"

CHAPTER 4

He thought the creature was female, but he couldn't be sure. Any hint of its sex was buried beneath a shapeless tunic and a pair of loose leggings. It blinked up at him, its gray eyes startlingly large in its pallid face.

"Who the hell are you?" he growled. "Did that murdering bastard send you to ambush me?"

It lifted its cupped hands a few inches off the ground. "Do I look like someone sent to ambush you?"

The thing had a point. It wore no armor and carried no weapon that he could see unless you counted those beseeching gray eyes. Definitely female, he decided with a grunt of mingled relief and pain. He might have been too long without a woman, but he'd yet to be swayed by any of the pretty young lads a few of his more jaded comrades favored.

He steadied his grip on the sword, hoping the woman hadn't seen it waver. His chest heaved with exhaustion and he was forced to shake the sweat from his eyes before stealing a desperate glance over his shoulder.

The forest betrayed no sign of pursuit, freeing him to return his attention to his trembling captive. "Have you no answer for my question? Who the hell are you?"

To his surprise, the surly demand ignited a spark of spirit in the wench's eyes. "Wait just a minute! Maybe the question should be who the hell are *you*?" Her eyes narrowed in a suspicious glare. "Don't I know you?" She began to mutter beneath her breath as she studied his face, making him wonder if he hadn't snared a lunatic. "Trim the hair. Give him a shave and a bath. Spritz him with Brut and slip him into an off-the-rack suit. Ah-ha!" she crowed. "You're George, aren't you? George . . . George . . . ?" She snapped her fingers. "George Ruggles from Accounting!" She slanted him a glance that was almost coy. " 'Fess up now, Georgie boy. Did Daddy offer you a raise to play knight in shining armor to my damsel in distress?"

His jaw went slack with shock as she swatted his sword aside and scrambled to her feet, brushing the grass from her shapely rump with both hands. "You can confide in me, you know. I promise it won't affect your Yearly Performance Evaluation."

She was taller than he had expected, taller than any woman of his acquaintance. But far more disconcerting than her height was her brash attitude. Since he'd been old enough to wield a sword, he'd never met anyone, man or woman, who wasn't afraid of him.

The sun was beating down on his head like an anvil. He clenched his teeth against a fresh wave of pain. "You may call me George if it pleases you, my lady, but 'tis *not* my name."

She paced around him, making the horse prance and shy away from her. "Should I call you Prince then? Or will Mr. Charming do? And what would you like to call me? Guenevere perhaps?" She touched a hand to her rumpled hair and batted her sandy eyelashes at him. "Or would you prefer Rapunzel?"

His ears burned beneath her incomprehensible taunts.

He could think of several names he'd like to call her, none of them flattering. A small black cat appeared out of nowhere to scamper at her heels, forcing him to rein his stallion in tighter or risk trampling them both. Each nervous shuffle of the horse's hooves jarred his aching bones.

She eyed his cracked leather gauntlets and tarnished chain mail with blatant derision. "So where's your shining armor, Lancelot? Is it back at the condo being polished or did you send it out to the dry cleaners?"

She paced behind him again. All the better to slide a blade between his ribs, he thought dourly. Resisting the urge to clutch his shoulder, he wheeled the horse around to face her. The simple motion made his ears ring and his head spin.

"Cease your infernal pacing, woman!" he bellowed. "Or I'll—" He hesitated, at a loss to come up with a threat vile enough to stifle this chattering harpy.

She flinched, but the cowed look in her eyes was quickly replaced by defiance. "Or you'll what?" she demanded, resting her hands on her hips. "Carry me off to your castle and ravish me? Chop my saucy little head off?" She shook that head in disgust. "I can't believe Mama thought I'd fall for this chauvinistic crap. Why didn't she just hire a mugger to knock me over the head and steal my purse?"

She marched away from him. Ignoring the warning throb of his muscles, he drove the horse into her path. Before she could change course again, he hefted his sword and nudged aside the fabric of her tunic, bringing the blade's tip to bear against the swell of her left breast. Her eyes widened and she took several hasty steps backward. He urged the stallion forward, pinioning her against the trunk of a slender oak. As her gaze met his, he would have almost sworn he could feel her heart thundering beneath the blade's dangerous caress.

A mixture of fear and doubt flickered through her eyes. "This isn't funny anymore, Mr. Ruggles," she said softly. "I hope you've kept your résumé current, because after I tell my father about this little incident, you'll probably be needing it."

She reached for his blade with a trembling hand, stirring reluctant admiration in him. But when she jerked her hand back, her fingertips were smeared with blood.

At first he feared he had pricked her in his clumsiness. An old shame quickened in his gut, no less keen for its familiarity. He'd striven not to harm any woman since he'd sworn off breaking hearts.

She did not yelp in distress or melt into a swoon. She simply stared at her hand as if seeing it for the first time. "Doesn't feel like ketchup," she muttered, her words even more inexplicable than her actions. She sniffed at her fingers. "Or smell like cherry cough syrup."

She glanced down at her chest. A thin thread of blood trickled between her breasts, affirming his fears. But as her bewildered gaze met his and the ringing in his ears deepened to an inescapable roaring, he realized what she had already discovered. 'Twas not her blood staining her breast, but his own. His blood seeping from his body in welling drops that were rapidly becoming a steady trickle down the blade of his sword. Horror buffeted him as he realized it was he, and not she, who was in danger of swooning. The sword slipped from his numb fingers, tumbling harmlessly to the grass.

He slumped over the horse's neck, clutching at the coarse mane. He could feel his powerful legs weakening, betrayed by the weight of the chain mail that was supposed to protect him. Sweat trickled into his eyes, its relentless sting blinding him.

"Go," he gritted out. "Leave me be."

At first he thought she would obey. He heard her skitter sideways, then hesitate, poised on the brink of flight.

His flesh felt as if it were tearing from his bones as he summoned one last burst of strength to roar, "I bid you to leave my sight, woman. Now!"

The effort shredded the tatters of his will. He could almost feel his pride crumbling along with his resolve, forcing him to choke out the one word he detested above all others. "Please . . ."

Swaying in the saddle, he pried open his eyes to cast her a beseeching glance. Sir Colin of Ravenshaw had never fallen before anyone, especially not a woman.

And in the end he didn't fall before this one either.

He fell on her.

CHAPTER 5

Tabitha lay utterly still, afraid to breathe. In her most daring fantasies, she had wondered what it might feel like to have a man on top of her. To lay hip to hip, thigh to thigh, her tender breasts crushed against his brawny chest, his face nuzzled in her freshly washed hair.

She sniffed lightly, unable to resist satisfying her clinical curiosity. Her father always walked around in a cloud of expensive aftershave and the handful of men she'd dared to date showered and shaved twice a day. She'd never before smelled the sweat of honest toil, tempered with the mingled musk of horse, woodsmoke, and leather. She found the combination earthy, yet as undeniably beguiling as the prickle of the stranger's unshaven jaw against her cheek. She half expected him to murmur some husky endearment.

He groaned. Tabitha's eyes flew open. The poor man probably wouldn't be inclined to whisper sweet nothings in her ear while bleeding to death. As much as she wanted to believe he was just some flunky hired by her parents to woo her, the blood soaking the front of her pajama shirt felt alarmingly real.

She tugged one hand free and shoved at his shoulder. "Mr. Ruggles?" she hissed. "George?"

He groaned again and settled his body more firmly against hers. Tabitha squirmed at the increasing intimacy, but that only made things worse.

This was frustrating. And it was her own fault. When he'd fixed her with that puppy-dog stare and started to tumble off the horse, she'd had every opportunity to hop out of harm's way. Instead, she'd given in to the inexplicable urge to break his fall. All she'd gotten for her heroic effort was to be pinned under his weight. She was afraid he'd crush her, but it was as if he'd deliberately landed so as to do her the least harm. Even the glasses in her shirt pocket seemed to have survived the impact.

She turned her head, looking around for help. The horse stood a few feet away, placidly munching on a patch of clover as if he hadn't threatened to trample her to death only minutes before. Lucy had draped her small, furry body over a sun-drenched hillock and was blissfully napping.

A butterfly perched briefly on Tabitha's nose, making her eyes cross, then fluttered away with blithe abandon. She sighed, wondering if she was destined to spend eternity trapped beneath this ill-tempered stranger.

When she turned back, he was gazing down at her, his golden eyes more quizzical than threatening. Tabitha's breath stalled in her throat. He looked like a sleepy tiger trying to decide if he should eat his prey or simply toy with it.

Tabitha did not need her glasses to see him clearly. She was nearsighted and he was very near indeed. She could feel the pounding of his heart as if it were her own.

His face loomed in her vision—angry slashes of eyebrows over deep-set eyes; a strong, blunt nose; a mouth that had lost its smile, but not its winsome quirk; a stubborn jaw armored with dark stubble. The faint bags beneath his eyes hinted at exhaustion, but did not detract from the dangerous appeal of his thick, stubby lashes.

Tabitha blinked. She'd never been the sort of woman to fall for a pair of bedroom eyes. His gruff words reminded her why.

"Whose woman are you?"

Her dismay erupted in outrage. "Why, of all the arrogant, politically incorrect, blatantly chauvinistic—"

He behaved exactly as she would have expected an arrogant, politically incorrect, blatantly chauvinistic male to behave. He clapped a gauntleted hand over her mouth, stifling her words. She glared at him, tasting leather against her lips.

"I asked you a simple question, lass. Do you belong to any man?"

She shook her head furiously, but it wasn't until his gaze softened, becoming both tender and predatory, that she remembered she had practically invited him to ravish her before he'd come tumbling into her arms.

She was being ridiculous. Surely no man who'd lost that much blood could—

A faint shift of his hips brought a warm and fulsome weight to bear against the softness of her belly. Apparently, he hadn't lost *that* much blood.

She gazed at him, the two of them suddenly reduced to something more elemental than the sum of their parts. Man. Woman. Power. Vulnerability. She felt a flicker of doubt. Her mother might bemoan the fact that Tabitha spent most of her Saturday nights at home watching reruns of *The X-Files* on the Sci-Fi network, but she wouldn't have set her up on a blind date with a rapist.

Would she?

As he freed her mouth and lowered his parted lips to hers, a fresh realization struck terror in Tabitha's heart. He wasn't going to rape her. He was going to kiss her. Struck by a vision of this mighty warrior squatting on her chest croaking "rbbit, rbbit," she turned her face away and gave his chest a panicked shove.

He rolled off of her with less resistance than she expected, groaning as if in mortal agony.

Tabitha sprang to her feet. "You were going to kiss me!"

"I know," he muttered, eyeing her warily. "Delirium must be setting in."

She rested her hands on her hips, trying to decide whether to be relieved or insulted. "You can whine and moan all you like, you bogus Beowulf, but I'm not going to feel sorry for you." She pulled the sticky flannel from her skin, grimacing in distaste. "Why look what you've done! Ruined my very favorite pair of pajamas!"

"Do forgive me. I'll take more care where I spill my heart's blood in the future."

She flinched. As he lay there propped up on his elbows in the grass, those golden eyes burning with pride over his pinched, pale mouth, she discovered to her dismay that she did feel sorry for him.

She dropped to her knees at his side. He eyed her with sullen suspicion, but allowed her to gently pry away the hand he'd cupped protectively over his shoulder.

" 'Tis naught but a scratch," he muttered.

Tabitha winced. Something had slashed through his armor, carving an ugly furrow just above his armpit. "If that's a scratch, I'd hate to see what you consider a laceration." She began to tear the hem from her pajama shirt.

He nodded toward her straining hands. "I thought that was your favorite garment."

"At the moment it's my only garment," she mumbled ruefully, using her teeth to rip free a broad strip of the flannel.

He surprised her by cupping her throat in his hand, his grip somewhere between a caress and a threat. "I might not live to regret this if you turn out to be one of them."

The ruthless glitter of his eyes convinced her that this man's enemy was not something she should ever aspire to be.

She forced a cool smile. "You won't live to regret it if you bleed to death either."

Conceding her point, he allowed her to proceed. After she'd torn another strip from her pajamas, she peeled back the soft leather shirt beneath his armor to reveal the sort of chest one couldn't buy from a personal trainer or expensive gym. Oddly enough, the numerous nicks and scars seemed as much a part of him as the crisp whorls of dark hair that fanned across the dusky expanse. Tabitha bit her bottom lip, struggling to concentrate on the task at hand.

As she wound the fabric around his shoulder, she glanced up to find him transfixed by her feet. He nodded toward her slippers with their bright plastic eyes and cheerfully bobbing whiskers. "What manner of creature did you kill for those?"

This time her smile was genuine. "The dreaded polyester." She was securing the bandage with a tasteful bow when his head snapped upright.

"What is it?" Tabitha whispered. She heard nothing.

Nothing but the eerie silence that had preceded his own arrival.

She sincerely hoped his tense posture was simply psychotic paranoia or overwrought acting. "What is it?" she repeated. "I don't hear anything."

He held up a hand for silence. Lucy crouched on the hillock, fully alert now, hackles rising. The horse tossed his head, whickering a warning. Then she heard it, far off in the distance like an echo from a nightmare.

The thunder of hoofbeats. The baying of hounds. The excited clamor of male voices.

The stranger grabbed her hand. "Flee, woman! I'm too weak to ride and if they find you here with me, 'twill not go well for you."

"If those are the same men who stabbed you, then I doubt it'll go very well for you either," she pointed out with irrefutable logic.

Bitterness darkened his eyes. "I'm a man. They'll only string me up from the nearest oak or cut my throat. But you're a woman. If Brisbane's dogs don't tear you to shreds, his men will."

Suddenly Tabitha didn't want to play this particular game anymore. She wanted to snatch Lucy into her arms and sprint for the far side of the meadow. She wanted to tip her face to the sky and wail, "I want my mommy!"

But her mother was nowhere in sight and this man's urgency was real, as real as the blood still seeping through the clumsy flannel bandage, as real as the bite of his fingers into her flesh, the desperate entreaty in his eyes.

"Take my mount and go," he commanded. "Before 'tis too late."

The forest no longer looked cheerful and welcoming, but dark and sinister—just right for Snow White's wicked stepmother and an entire orchard of poison apples. The baying of the hounds was growing louder and more relentless with each passing second.

Tabitha looked uncertainly at the horse. "I've never ridden before. Is it anything like riding in the back of a limousine?"

Her captor softened his grip, caressing her knuckles with his gauntleted thumb. "Go, lass," he said gently. "We'll have no more of your dallying."

Oddly enough, it was that tender rebuke that decided her.

Tabitha would never know where she found the strength to try and get him astride the horse. He cursed the entire time, colorful indictments of the fair sex in general and herself in particular. Her shortcomings were described in meticulous detail, down to her wretched stubbornness, disobedient nature, and deplorable lack of wit. When he tumbled off the horse for the third time while reaching to give her ears a halfhearted cuff, she was finally forced to admit defeat.

They lay on their backs in the grass, Tabitha gasping for breath, the knight glowering at her through the dark locks of hair that spilled over his forehead. She felt a familiar vibration shimmy up her spine, a thousand times worse than it had been before. The ground trembled as if a herd of elephants was stampeding straight for them. Not elephants, she realized in panic, but horses.

She scrambled to her feet.

"Now will you go?" the stranger bit off, his eyes glazed with a blend of fury and pain.

Sunlight glinted off steel, catching Tabitha's frantic eye. She snatched up Lucy and thrust the kitten into the man's hands. His sputters deepened to oaths when she bent to retrieve his fallen sword. It strained every muscle in her shoulders to lift the massive weapon, but lift it she did, staggering around to face the invisible threat.

If these men were ruthless enough to cut down a wounded man, they would have to come through her first.

Tabitha had never thought of herself as being particularly brave. Somehow she found the courage to stand her ground when the horses came pouring out of the forest, led by a pack of baying hounds. The riders reined in their mounts less than a foot from her outstretched blade, fanning out in a circle to surround them. The hounds bared their teeth and snapped at her pajama legs. Tabitha bit her bottom lip until she tasted blood to keep from crying out in terror.

The man mounted at the head of the party shouted some incomprehensible command and the dogs fell back, slinking away with flagging tails and reproachful looks.

"I can hardly blame them," their master drawled, "I'd sulk, too, if I'd been deprived of such a tasty morsel."

Tabitha slowly lifted her gaze to the face of the man who held their fates in his velvet-gloved hands. She expected to find a ruthless sneer, not the sort of urbane smile so prevalent at company cocktail parties. A rush of confusion dizzied her. Surely *this* was the man her mother had chosen to star in her fantasy.

He rode a snow-white charger with a profusion of ribbons and bells braided into its silky mane. They tinkled a winsome melody each time the spirited beast tossed its head. Tabitha wouldn't have been surprised to see a golden horn sprout from its milky brow.

The horse's master was no less a creature of myth. A honeyed mantle of hair brushed his shoulders, framing a face that might have been considered effeminate in its elfin beauty were it not for the determined jut of his clean-shaven chin. He wore a forest-green cloak trimmed in cloth-of-gold draped over his cream-colored tunic and leggings. Despite the grueling ride, he looked as fresh as if he'd just stepped from a hot shower. Tart lemon perfumed the air around him.

The man's green eyes glittered beneath arched brows a shade darker than his hair. "I've never known you to let a woman wield your precious blade, Ravenshaw." Tabitha's arms had began to droop with exhaustion; all it took was a nudge of his booted foot to drop the sword another six inches. "Perhaps you're growing soft in defeat."

The men burst into raucous laughter.

"Go to hell, Brisbane," her companion said, his voice soft, yet sharp enough to slice through their mockery.

Following Tabitha's gaze to the fallen knight, Prince Charming smiled. "And what were you going to do if this fair maiden failed to behead me? Sic your pussycat on me?"

In his effort to rise, the knight had made it only as far as his knees. Frightened by the smell of the dogs, Lucy was clinging to his brawny shoulder. A sudden thought struck her. If the man on the white horse was Prince Charming, then who the hell was he? Prince Surly? What if she'd inadvertently been aiding and abetting the villain of the piece?

She decided to test her theory. Wishing she'd paid more attention to the dialogue in those Disney movies, she tilted her head back and offered Prince Charming her sweetest smile. "Forsooth, kind sir, methinks it most fortuitous thou hast stumbled upon this damsel in distress."

One of his men nudged the other. "What'd she say?"

"Hell if I know. She's got good teeth though." The

squat man grinned, revealing a mouthful of cracked and blackened stumps.

The knight was staring at her as if she'd lost her mind. But his opinion was not the one that mattered.

Prince Charming favored her with such a loving smile that she dared to lower the sword and lightly touch his knee. "I beseech you, my lord, should we not retire posthaste to your castle?"

She could not help but be slightly dazzled when he brought her grubby hand to his lips and gazed deep into her eyes. "Aye, my lady. Your wish is my command."

Your wish . . .

His words gave her a chill, even in this enchanted setting. But not nearly as much of a chill as his next words did.

"Take Ravenshaw and his whore back to the castle," he commanded, his smile curling into a sneer. "Cast them into the deepest, darkest dungeon. They can rot there just as well as they can in hell."

Tabitha snatched back her hand, but the sword was torn from her grasp before she could hoist it. Prince Charming wheeled his charger in a circle, abandoning her to the fate he had decreed. As the tinkle of bells faded in the distance, his men dropped from their mounts.

They wrenched her arms behind her and bound her wrists before swarming over Ravenshaw. He only got one lick in, but it was a good one. One of Prince Charming's minions stumbled backward, blood gushing from his broken nose.

Tabitha cringed at the thud of fists against flesh.

"Raven's naught but a craven!" someone bellowed.

"Ravenshaw's a boor!" another man shouted. "Defended by a whore!"

As they forced him to his feet and dragged him

toward a packhorse, the others took up the singsong chant, repeating it until Tabitha's head rang. If her hands hadn't been bound, she would have covered her ears. She remembered only too well how it felt to be mocked and taunted.

She looked helplessly at the knight, but he turned his face away from her, his mouth tightened in a contemptuous line. She didn't know why it should bother her, but her spirits plunged even further as she realized her foolish daring had earned her his eternal loathing.

CHAPTER 6

"Excuse me!" Tabitha shouted, rattling the iron grate set in the thick wooden door. "Excuse me, sir! Don't you have room service in this establishment?"

The only answer from the shadowy corridor beyond was the whisper of water trickling down the dank stone walls. Tabitha licked her lips, more thirsty than she'd realized.

"I should've run you through when I had the chance."

The voice came from behind her—lilting, conversational, almost tender. Tabitha swung around to shoot its owner a wounded glare. He was seated on the floor of the cell, his back to the stone wall, one lean leg drawn to his chest. Fresh blood stained his bandage and his lower lip was slightly swollen, making him look even more sullen than when she'd first encountered him.

If that were possible.

"I would think you'd be grateful," she retorted in the tone she used with insubordinate employees. "After all, I did risk my own life to save yours."

He snorted. " 'Twasn't your life you were risking, but your virtue. You were drooling over Brisbane as if he were a sweetmeat. For a moment there, I thought you were going to lick his fancy boots. Or his . . ." He trailed off, mumbling something beneath his breath she assumed she was better off not hearing.

Embarrassed to be reminded of how dazzled she'd been by Brisbane, Tabitha quickly changed the subject. "I wonder what happened to poor Lucy. I hate to think of her lost in that meadow. She must think I went off and abandoned her."

"If Lucy's your accursed cat, I saw one of the men stuff her into his knapsack. Going to take her home and eat her, I'd wager." At Tabitha's horrified cry, he rolled his eyes. " 'Twas only a jest, lass. He'll probably just carry the wee beastie back to the village for his bratlings to play with."

Tabitha sighed forlornly. "If only she were here."

"Why? So *we* could eat her?"

Tabitha started to protest, but she couldn't tell if his eyes were sparkling with mischief or malice. "Do you have a name?"

"Colin," he said, all traces of humor disappearing from his face. "Sir Colin of Ravenshaw."

"Colin." She rolled the name around on her tongue to savor the taste of it. She'd always thought Colin a very dignified name, the sort that ought to belong to a pale English lord sipping tea in front of the hearth with his hunting dogs napping at his feet.

"Colin the Barbarian," she tried, smiling at him.

He was not amused.

"I'm Tabitha," she volunteered. When he maintained his stony silence, she added a mocking curtsy. "Lady Lennox."

He grunted, making her wish she'd introduced herself as the *Princess* Tabitha. She sighed and turned back to the door. Poking her nose through the bars, she yelled,

"Hey! Couldn't you at least send down some mints for our pillows? Or some pillows for our mints? If this abominable service persists, I'm going to have to insist on speaking with the concierge."

This time she was rewarded by the clang of a distant door and the shuffle of booted feet. She shot Colin a triumphant look. "See. You just have to know how to address the help."

She was forced to jump backward when a wooden bowl and a rusty cup were shoved through a metal flap at the base of the door. The footsteps receded as she picked up the bowl and poked at its contents with the wooden spoon. "Mmmm," she murmured. "Gruel. How yummy."

"You'd best eat up," Colin said quietly. " 'Tis the only food you're likely to be getting for a while."

Praying she hadn't actually seen something wiggle in its depths, she held out the bowl to him. "I'm not really very hungry. You can have my portion."

Shrugging, he took the bowl and dug into the watery mush as if it were a filet mignon from Peter Luger's. "A body can survive without food, you know, but not without water."

Tabitha took the hint, lifting the cup to her lips for a hearty swallow. A searing cough exploded from her lungs.

"Christ, woman, don't go wasting perfectly good ale."

"Ale?" she wheezed. "I thought you said it was water."

He shrugged. "Ale. Water. What's the difference?"

"About fifty proof," she ventured, swiping the back of her hand across her lips in a futile attempt to quench their burning. The beverage was nothing like the fulsome German lagers she'd sipped at the Twenty-One

Club. She handed it to Colin. He downed it in one swallow.

Tabitha was becoming aware of another more pressing urge. While Colin polished off the gruel, she circled the cell, exploring the shadowy corners and giving several of the stone blocks timid pushes in the hopes that one of them would slide open to reveal a secret passageway. She found nothing but a splintery wooden bucket and several rat-sized holes in the crumbling mortar.

Colin finally erupted in a baffled oath. "What in God's blood are you looking for, woman?"

Tabitha spun around, embarrassed. "The bathroom."

He fixed her with that unblinking golden stare. "From the smell of you, I wouldn't say you were in want of a bath. Yet."

It discomfited her to realize he'd even noticed her scent. She hadn't dabbed on any perfume after her shower, so she doubted she smelled of anything more enticing than baby shampoo and Ivory soap. She resisted the urge to tuck her nose into her pajama shirt and steal a whiff.

"I don't need a bath. I need to . . ." She trailed off, seeking the appropriate euphemism.

"If it's a piss you're after . . ." He nodded toward the bucket.

Tabitha hated herself for blushing.

The knight arched one of his dark eyebrows, challenging her to trot right over to the corner, drop her drawers, and plop down on the rickety bucket.

At the thought of this indignity, Tabitha slid down the wall to a sitting position and hugged her knees to her chest. Her parents never stayed at any accommodation less luxurious than a five-star hotel. While it might be conceivable that they had decided a weekend in a dungeon might prove a character-building experience, she doubted they would have chosen a dungeon with no maid service or bathroom facilities.

For the first time, she was forced to confront the possibility that this might not be her mother's idea of a romantic fantasy, but bitter reality.

She lifted her hollow gaze, really seeing the murky cell for the first time. A flimsy torch sputtered high on the wall. It didn't take much imagination to envision what might come creeping out of those holes in the mortar once the torch burned to darkness. A chill damp saturated the air, seeping through the tattered flannel of her pajamas. She hugged her knees tighter, suppressing a shiver.

"Where are we?" she whispered.

"Brisbane's dungeon," the knight whispered back.

Tabitha sighed. She didn't feel up to getting the answers she wanted out of the laconic barbarian at the moment. Given both the terrain and the speech patterns, they could be anywhere in the United Kingdom— Wales, England, Ireland, perhaps even Scotland. That would explain Sir Colin's lilting burr and his endearing tendency to drop the occasional *g*.

But if this was Scotland, why wasn't he dressed like some Catholic schoolgirl in plaid skirt and stockings? She wracked her brain, wishing she'd paid more attention in history class. She'd always excelled at math and science, but disdained literature and history as frivolous indulgences for the less pragmatic. Her quirky brain would store complex mathematical and scientific equations and song lyrics from the 1950s, but she could never remember exactly what year Benedict Arnold wrote the Declaration of Independence.

She vaguely remembered that the short kilt was of less ancient origin than most assumed, its modern popularity heightened by Queen Victoria's obsession with all things Scottish and the heather-drenched romanticism of Sir Walter Scott. The farther one traveled back in time, the more likely one was to encounter a civilization that was more muck than myth and more grit than glory.

Her matter-of-fact musings made her head throb. She could too easily imagine the knight's sarcastic response to *When are we?*

What if she had actually breached the time continuum? It wasn't completely inconceivable. According to Uncle Cop's bedtime stories, her mother had jumped time streams on three separate occasions, once with Cop and her father in tow.

Tabitha drew the emerald amulet from her shirt and studied it, wondering if it had been the catalyst for this entire disaster.

Sir Colin's attention sharpened. "And what would that be?"

She started guiltily before dropping the necklace back down her shirt and faking a bland smile. "Just a gift from my mother. A good-luck charm." One that had brought her the worst luck of her life.

Feeling Colin's predatory gaze on her, she thought of something else. If this man wasn't her mother's twisted idea of a blind date, then he was a dangerous stranger. A stranger who might have committed some terrible crime to deserve this imprisonment. She stole a glance at his face from beneath her lashes. Its baby-faced charm was offset by his brooding expression and the fresh stubble that shaded his jaw. What if he was a robber or a serial killer? Or even a rapist? With his fierce eyes and wild hair, he looked capable of committing all three felonies before breakfast without so much as breaking a sweat.

"How were you wounded?" she asked, nodding toward his bandage.

"Escaping."

He certainly wouldn't win any congeniality awards. "Escaping from where?"

She thought his expression couldn't become any more murderous. She was wrong. "From this dungeon."

Tabitha winced, suddenly comprehending the enormity of what she'd done. If she hadn't intercepted him, he would be well on his way to freedom by now.

"This Brisbane fellow doesn't seem to be terribly fond of you. What did you do to him?"

"What did I do to him?" he repeated, the soft rasp somehow more alarming than a full-throated roar. "What did I do to him?"

Before Tabitha could take it back, he rose and staggered toward her. She scrambled to her feet. But he didn't touch her; he didn't have to. He simply backed her against the wall with the sheer force of his will, leaving her helpless to do anything but look into those smoldering eyes.

She remembered learning long ago that the men of previous generations had rarely achieved the heights of her contemporaries. Her classmates had giggled, envisioning an army of dwarves riding Shetland ponies. She realized now how naive they had been.

This man might be no more than half an inch taller than she was, but he exuded raw virility. There was something unnerving yet exhilarating about standing toe-to-toe with such a man.

She tried to lower her gaze, but he caught her chin in his hand and tilted her face upward, his grip as steely as his voice was soft. "Why don't I tell you what Brisbane did to me?"

"If you'd like," she offered timidly.

"While I was defending the cause of Christ against the infidels in Egypt, he laid siege to my father's castle. After he'd starved several of the inhabitants of the castle to death, including my stepmother and infant sister, he stormed the keep and torched the village. His henchmen slaughtered all the men of fighting age and raped the women, from the oldest crone to the most innocent child."

The blood drained from Tabitha's face. He went on.

"When I set foot on Scottish soil for the first time in six years, Brisbane's men ambushed me and carted me off to this dungeon where their lord was gracious enough to inform me of the fate of my family."

Not really wanting to know the answer, she whispered, "Your father?"

"Died of apoplexy before the castle surrendered. 'Twas most likely the shock of my stepmother's death that killed him."

Tabitha swallowed. Hard. "No wonder you're in such a bad mood. You're probably suffering from post-traumatic stress syndrome or unresolved grief. Perhaps a good psychotherapist . . . ?" She stammered to a halt. His unflinching gaze made her psychobabble sound unbearably trivial.

For some inexplicable reason, his grip on her chin gentled. "Brisbane took my home. He took my family. He took my freedom. He left me with nothing but my honor. And you, my lady, handed that to him on a silver platter when you defended me with my own sword and allowed his men to make mock of me."

Raven's a craven!
Ravenshaw's a boor! Defended by a whore!

"What was I supposed to do?" Tabitha protested. "Let him cut you down in cold blood?"

"Aye," he replied without hesitation. "At least I would have died with my honor intact."

She wanted to denounce his archaic reasoning, but the image of this proud knight driven to his knees at his enemy's feet was too fresh in her memory.

She was horrified to feel her throat closing. "I'm sorry," she said fiercely, returning his glare, trying to hold back tears.

Sir Colin of Ravenshaw was not a man to be melted by heartfelt apologies. He stilled the trembling of her lower lip with his thumb before turning away from her. "Not half as sorry as I, my lady."

Tabitha huddled in a corner of the cell, transfixed by the waning torch flame. She'd been watching it burn for a long time and knew it would be only a matter of minutes before it smoldered to ash, leaving them in darkness. She thought longingly of the contents of the Gucci purse she'd left in her apartment—a travel flashlight, a half-eaten Twinkie, a pack of sugar-free gum. Although only hours had passed since Brisbane had locked them away, she could no longer remember the last time she'd eaten or drank or slept.

Probably because it had been several centuries in the future.

What would Uncle Cop make of her disappearance? Would he call the police or would he assume the envelope he'd given her had contained some crucial information about her parents' whereabouts? He had no way of knowing she'd discovered her mother's amulet. It saddened her to realize that it might be days before anyone even noticed she was missing. She had no close friends and her coworkers at the lab were probably celebrating the absence of their perfectionist boss.

Sir Colin hadn't spoken a single word to her since their earlier confrontation. His silence only deepened the frigid chill until Tabitha could feel it sinking into her very bones along with the icy fear she could no longer ignore. If her parents hadn't arranged this bizarre encounter, then that meant they weren't safe at home, chuckling at her predicament. They were still missing, perhaps even . . . She shuddered away the possibility, refusing to consider what she couldn't accept.

It wasn't until Sir Colin's soft snores pierced the eerie hush that she dared to creep over and make use of the bucket, her cheeks burning the entire time.

She shuffled back to her corner to find the torch fading. No longer able to stifle her shivers, she inched closer to the knight's shadowy form. She'd felt lonely most of her life, but she'd never felt quite so alone. She couldn't blame Colin for hating her. It had taken her only a few careless minutes in this century to destroy a reputation he'd labored on for a lifetime.

The torch sputtered. She bit her lip, willing it to keep burning. With a hissed sigh, the flame collapsed, losing the battle against the darkness.

Tabitha froze. She'd survived New York blackouts before, but she'd never endured a darkness so palpable. It pressed down like a lead weight. It seemed to her that they weren't so much imprisoned as buried alive. She forgot to breathe, so paralyzed with fear she didn't even realize the rhythmic snores had also ceased.

Then it came. The dreaded skitter of claws on stone.

Forgetting courage and pride, Tabitha launched herself in the general direction of Sir Colin, coming up hard against his side. She cowered against his broad, warm body, waiting for him to yell at her or push her away or make fun of her fear.

For a long moment, he didn't move or say a word,

every muscle in his body as rigid as stone. Then with a labored sigh, he drew her into his arms and rested his chin on her head.

"Don't be afraid, lass," he murmured. "I'm too tough for the rats to eat and you're too scrawny."

No one had ever called her scrawny before. Tabitha rested her cheek against his chest, marveling at how quickly her teeth stopped chattering. His chain mail should have been cold, but the body beneath radiated heat like a furnace.

As the tension began to melt from her muscles, she wondered if Brisbane would leave them to die in this place. Would someone unearth this cell centuries from now to find their bones seemingly entwined in a lover's embrace? Somehow that seemed the unfairest cut of all since the man holding her so tenderly was nothing more than a stranger who despised her.

Sighing wistfully, she reached into her pajama shirt and closed her hand around her mother's amulet. "I wish . . ." she whispered, just before drifting into sleep.

CHAPTER ✳ 7

Tabitha's mother had warned her more than once about eating chocolate before bedtime.

She should have listened, Tabitha thought, as she snuggled deeper into her fat, fluffy pillow. Her dreams had been populated by a cast of bizarre characters, including a brimstone-snorting stallion, a fey sadist dressed like Elvis in his rhinestone-cape period, and a surly knight with bedroom eyes and a brooding smirk, who'd spent most of her dream waving an enormous sword at her. She found the latter by far the most disturbing. She'd never relished being dominated, yet who could this provocative satyr be but the Freudian embodiment of her most primal sexual desires?

Groaning, she tossed back the eiderdown quilt and fumbled for the alarm, hoping to mute it before Vivaldi could blare in her ear. Her reach was thwarted by something tangled around her waist.

She glanced down, expecting to find a cotton sheet wound around her midriff. Instead, she discovered a well-muscled forearm dusted with crisp, black hairs. Tabitha stared at it in fascination, dumbfounded by the novel experience of having a warm male body nestled against her backside. He arched his back and mumbled something into her hair, molding himself even more firmly to her rump. She gasped with fresh shock. A very warm, very male body.

Since she wasn't in the habit of surfing bars for one-night stands, there could be only one conclusion.

She hadn't been dreaming. She was actually imprisoned in a medieval dungeon with a surly barbarian.

Doubly confused, she blinked at the water-pocked walls. If this was a dungeon, then why were they snuggled in an Ethan Allen cherry sleigh bed? Why was the air warm and toasty instead of chill and damp? She tried to wiggle out of Colin's embrace, but his possessive grip only tightened. He finally grunted a sleepy surrender and rolled to his back, an intriguing hint of a sulk playing around his stoic mouth.

Tabitha sat up on her knees on the plush mattress, her eyes widening as she surveyed the transformed cell. Wall-to-wall Berber carpet covered the mottled flagstones. A ceramic heater roosted in the corner, merrily radiating heat although its cord was plugged into thin air. A Tiffany lamp cast a burnished glow over the knight's slumbering form.

She clapped a hand over her mouth, her initial wonder eclipsed by an all-too-familiar dread. "Oh, hell," she whispered. "What have I done now?"

Her nose twitched in an involuntary response to the enticing aromas drifting up from the satin-draped table at the foot of the bed. A table laden with all of her favorite foods from the restaurants where she so frequently lunched, brunched, and dined. There were Hungarian tortes drizzled with strawberries from the Café Des Artistes, browned sea scallops in a creamy risotto from 44, juicy fried chicken from Sylvia's in Harlem, crème brûlée from Le Cirque, blinis from the Russian Tea Room, and an entire pyramid of her guilty little lunch secret—steaming Big Macs. Tabitha moaned as her empty stomach contracted.

She buried her face in her hands, trying to figure out how she could have authored such a disaster. She remembered drifting toward sleep in Colin's arms, succumbing to her vague and dreamy longings for warmth and light and food. Closing her hand around her mother's amulet . . .

Before she could pursue that thought, Colin stirred in his sleep. She looked frantically around the tiny cell, seeking somewhere to hide the result of her fantasies. She even leaned over and peered under the bed, as if she might actually be able to stuff everything under it and distract him from noticing the bed itself.

When Tabitha righted herself, she found Colin propped up on the pillows, eyeing her rump appraisingly.

She glanced down, suddenly afraid she'd wished herself into a skimpy Victoria's Secret teddy. She was relieved to find she was still wearing her frumpy flannel pajamas, though they didn't stop Colin's drowsy scrutiny. His heavy-lidded gaze drifted lazily downward, then up again, finally coming to rest on her puzzled face.

The corner of his mouth lifted in a sheepish curl and Tabitha thought for a moment he might actually smile at her.

But his attention was caught by the scents wafting up from the table at the foot of the bed. As he surveyed the feast, his habitual scowl reappeared, only to be slowly replaced by an expression of terror.

He scrambled out of the bed in a blind panic, jerking the flowered sheet around his waist as if he were naked instead of fully clothed and partially armored.

"What manner of trickery is this?" he demanded,

backing away from her until his shoulders struck the cell wall.

Forced to improvise, Tabitha shrugged. "I don't know. It was all here when I woke up. Maybe you have an ally in Brisbane's court who wanted to make your captivity more comfortable."

She inched toward the table, prodded by her empty stomach. Now that the jig was up, she didn't see any point in depriving herself.

She chose a plump chicken breast. But before she could bring it to her lips, Colin crossed the cell and smacked it out of her hand. It landed on the carpet with a juicy plop.

She dolefully looked at the fallen morsel. "Do you think it might be poisoned?"

"Worse," he said, signing a cross on his breast. "Enchanted."

Tabitha managed to smile weakly. "Enchanted?"

"Aye." The husky timbre of his voice sent a strange shiver through her. "I've heard many a tale of bold and true knights who partook of enchanted food only to fall under the spell of the enchanter for all eternity."

She wasn't hypocrite enough to chide him for being superstitious. "Well, since we're probably going to be spending eternity right here in this dungeon . . ." She snatched a Big Mac and bounded off the opposite side of the bed, cramming a bite into her mouth before he could stop her. A moan of sheer delight escaped her. Processed cheese had never tasted so delicious.

Colin watched her devour the steaming hunk of beef, hunger obvious in his eyes. She held out the remainder of the burger. "Go on. I think it's safe. I don't feel the least bit beguiled."

After a moment of hesitation, he reached across the bed to accept her offer. He peeked under the sesame-seed bun and scowled at the pickles, then tore into the burger. Tabitha admired the flash of his delighted grin, thinking he didn't have bad teeth himself for a man with no access to a Long Island orthodontist or twice a year cleanings.

While she settled cross-legged on the bed to feast on fried chicken, Hungarian tortes, and a stack of crisp, succulent blinis, Colin polished off that Big Mac and two more. His wound no longer seemed to be troubling him and she was beginning to think his collapse the day before was due to dehydration and lack of food rather than blood loss.

She hadn't considered the consequences of introducing a medieval knight to American junk food. Suppose Colin gave up slaying dragons to open the world's first fast-food restaurant chain? What if she had changed the course of history by hardening the arteries of her great-great-great-great-great-great-great-great-great-great-great-grandfather?

"You're no relation to the McDonalds, are you?" she asked, eyeing him warily.

"I should say not," he replied through a mouthful of burger. "My great-grandfather fought against Clan MacDonald when they tried to steal Malcolm's crown."

"Good." She celebrated by downing an egg cream from Rumpelmayer's ice cream parlor.

Still chewing, Colin resumed his suspicious examination of the cell. "No man could have done such mischief as this while I was sleeping. An Egyptian in Mansourah tried to slit my throat once when I was napping in the sun and I had his heart in my hand before it had even ceased beating."

Tabitha licked away her egg cream mustache, her appetite deserting her. "I'm sure whoever's responsible didn't mean you any harm."

"Harm or no, that doesn't explain how they lifted me from the floor to the bed without arousing me."

She averted her eyes, trying not to remember precisely how *aroused* he'd been when she'd awakened. "I know how they could have done it," she said with what she hoped was conviction. "They probably drugged us. We did both drink the ale, you know."

Her attempt to divert Colin's suspicions failed miserably. He turned his narrowed gaze on her. "Aye, but you refused the pottage, didn't you? You insisted I eat your portion as well as my own."

"I wasn't very hungry," Tabitha lied, realizing too late that he'd just watched her polish off half a chicken.

He took a step toward the bed, pointing an accusing finger at her. " 'Tis past time you told me what you were doing in that meadow. Did Brisbane use you to bait his trap?" To her relief, he swung away from her to pace around the bed, dragging a hand through his unruly hair. "He'd rather toy with me than kill me, wouldn't he? Perhaps he even allowed me to escape from the dungeon the first time. That would explain the ease with which I retrieved my armor and sword. He knew I'd never break under torture, so he set a woman in my path, thinking to prey on my weakness."

Tabitha might have laughed at being cast in the role of temptress, but her amusement fled when he knelt on the bed next to her.

He cupped her cheek in his hand, gazing deep into her eyes. "Is that what Brisbane believed? That I wouldn't have the strength to resist your big gray eyes? That I'd be swayed by the freshness of your scent?" He ran his thumb across her lips, its callused tip parting them to evoke a primal shiver. "The softness of your lips?"

Tabitha's mouth went dry. She couldn't manage even a squeak of protest.

Colin's hand slid around to her nape, tightening even as his voice softened. "If I find out you're one of Brisbane's whores . . ."

At that moment the door crashed open, and Colin jumped to his feet.

A squat guard stood well back from the cell, as if fearing an ambush from the man within. His disembodied voice grated like iron on stone. "Follow me, Ravenshaw. My lord demands your presence in the bailey. And bring the whore," he added as if in afterthought.

"I am not a whore," Tabitha snapped for both of their benefits as she scrambled out of the bed and followed Colin from the cell. "I'm a Ph.D."

A second guard was gripping a haggard old man by the elbow. While his companion clapped a pair of iron manacles on Colin's wrists, he thrust the toothless fellow into their abandoned cell and slammed the door.

As the crossbar fell, Tabitha heard the old man exclaim, "Praise be to God! I've died and gone to paradise!"

The guard shook his grizzled head. "Batty old fool. He'll be dead soon enough with nothin' but gruel and rats to eat."

Tabitha smiled a small, secret smile, hoping the old man liked fried chicken and crème brûlée. But her smile faded when she realized Colin was still eyeing her with suspicion.

"Maybe this Brisbane fellow is going to free us," Tabitha hissed as she and Colin marched through the dank maze of tunnels beneath the castle.

"Or execute us."

Tabitha nervously touched her throat as they trotted

up a steep incline at the prodding of the guards. "I've always considered myself something of a cynic, Mr. Ravenshaw, but you really should examine your own attitude. A positive outlook on life has been known to ward off illness and extend the life span by a number of years."

"Death!" boomed a jovial male voice. "Death to the Scot and his strumpet!"

As they emerged from the gloom into blinding sunshine to the catcalls and hisses of an enthusiastic mob, Tabitha feared it might take more than just a positive attitude to extend their life span. She shaded her eyes against the sun, feeling exposed with her rumpled pajamas and tousled hair. Even her chipmunk slippers seemed to be losing their irrepressible joie de vivre.

"Ravenshaw's a boor! Defended by a whore!"

Tabitha cringed, expecting Colin to shoot her a reproachful look, but he stood tall and straight, wearing his manacles as if they were twin Rolexes. A thrill of pride caught her off guard.

As the sun's glare abated, Tabitha realized they were standing at the foot of a broad ribbon of straw-sprinkled sand. The ribbon unfurled between a wooden platform and a colorful flock of tents topped with scarlet, green, and buttercup-yellow flags that rippled and snapped in the warm summer breeze. It was as if they'd stumbled into a remake of *Prince Valiant*.

She might have been charmed by the pageantry if the invisible director hadn't borrowed his cast from *Monty Python and the Holy Grail*. A mob of peasants dressed in the grunge equivalent of medieval garb swelled against the fence surrounding the sandy belt, their grimy faces distorted by toothless sneers and feral snarls. As the guards shoved Tabitha toward the platform, Colin nudged her sideways to keep her from being spit on. A rotten onion sailed past his own ear.

The occupants of the platform looked somewhat neater, if not much cleaner. While the peasants had been dressed in dull shades of brown and rust, their noble counterparts wore rich reds, dazzling purples, and apple-greens and yellows.

Tabitha blinked, overwhelmed by their brilliance. She'd somehow expected the past to be etched in grainy black and white or washed in sepia. The vibrancy of the scene made their predicament feel even more immediate.

The mocking chants subsided as a man lounging on a massive throne used the advantage of the platform's height to sneer down his nose at them. Sunlight glinted off his golden hair, but Tabitha saw only the tarnish of corruption.

Brisbane had traded his hose and tunic for a brocade bathrobe similar to the one she'd bought for Arian last Mother's Day. Its forest-green hue had probably been carefully chosen to match the shade of his eyes. Tabitha felt a flare of rage when she realized his milk-white hands were stroking Lucy's smoky fur. He had fastened a ruby-encrusted collar around the kitten's tiny throat, making her look more like a prisoner than a pampered pet.

Tabitha didn't realize she had bared her teeth at him until he drawled, "If it's not the lady with the comely teeth and her bold champion."

Several of the veiled and wimpled women seated on benches behind him giggled. From the plainest to the prettiest, their smiles revealed startling gaps where teeth should have been.

"I'll have you know these teeth cost my father a pretty penny," Tabitha retorted. "If you'd like, I can give you my orthodontist's number. Maybe he could whittle down your fangs."

Brisbane didn't have to understand all of her words to know he was being mocked. "Comely teeth and a sharp tongue. Perhaps I should pull the one and cut out the other."

Tabitha didn't remember inching closer to Colin, but suddenly he was there, his presence at her shoulder a palpable comfort. "Your quarrel is with me, Roger. Not with her."

Brisbane handed Lucy off to one of his ladies and glided down the platform stairs. When he reached the ground, Tabitha realized that she towered over him by almost two inches. He hastily retreated to the last step, but not before an amused smirk had touched Colin's lips.

"Where did you find such a treasure, Colin?" Sarcasm dripped from Brisbane's beautifully modulated voice. "In the brothels of Egypt?"

"Look at her shoes!" shouted a bell-capped fool. "Mayhaps she was traveling with a band of mummers!" He topped off his joke with a jingling somersault.

When the laughter had died down, Brisbane snorted. "A band of camp followers more likely."

"Perhaps 'tis your tongue that needs the trimming," Colin said, his eyes hinting at the fury smoldering just beneath his implacable facade.

"Do forgive me," Brisbane murmured without a trace of remorse. "Have I offended you by impugning the honor of your lady?"

Tabitha waited for Colin to say, "She's not my lady," or some other, more insulting variation of "She's no lady! She's my wife."

But he simply stared Brisbane down until the man's thin lips curled in a petulant sneer. Brisbane gestured toward the platform, his gem-encrusted fingers glinting in the sunlight. "My guests and I are in dire need of amusement so I've decided to give you one last chance to defend your lady's honor and your own."

"I thought your taste in amusement ran to defiling children and baiting bears," Colin said.

"Ah, but baiting you, my friend, is so much more gratifying."

The peculiar mixture of contempt and familiarity simmering beneath their banter caught Tabitha off guard. She had assumed they were simply rival barons battling over land.

His cold grin undaunted, Brisbane borrowed a leather glove from a nearby knight and whipped it across Colin's face, leaving an angry welt. Tabitha flinched. Colin did not. "Do you accept my challenge, sir?"

"With pleasure," Colin replied.

"Very well. If you win the joust, you and your lady may go free. If you lose . . ." Brisbane paced up the steps, then down again, tapping his pursed lips as if deep in thought. "I suppose I could ransom you to your family, but oh, I forgot . . . they're all dead."

Tabitha knew her outrage could only be a shadow of the hatred Colin must be feeling.

Brisbane shrugged with mock regret. "If you lose, I suppose I'll just have to take both your heads."

CHAPTER 8

The world shimmered before Tabitha's eyes as the crowd erupted with bloodthirsty cries of approval. She expected a smug "I told you so" from Colin, but as her knees threatened to buckle, he braced himself against her to keep her from falling. Thank God she had eaten. She didn't think she could tolerate being beheaded on an empty stomach.

Colin seemed to agree. "That repast in the dungeon must have been Roger's twisted idea of a last meal."

Terror spoiled Tabitha's relief at being excused from his suspicions. "Don't accept his challenge," she whispered fiercely. "Tell him you've changed your mind."

He cast her an incredulous look. "And forever lose the chance to redeem my honor?"

"Would you rather lose your honor or your head?"

Before he could give her an answer she didn't want to hear, he was torn from her side by half a dozen guards. She might have fallen had a mob of Brisbane's women not swooped down from the platform to seize her by the arms and drag her up the narrow stairs. Tabitha struggled, but it was like battling a fleshy dragon with an infinite number of limbs and a dozen tittering heads. She had to hold her breath to keep from choking. Not even several layers of spicy perfumes could disguise the sour taint of body odor. No wonder Colin had noticed her fresh-from-the-shower scent.

As they dragged her past a tonsured priest filling out what she assumed was a medieval coroner's report, she craned her neck to peer over the bobbing feather of his quill. Her glasses were still tucked away in her pajama pocket so she had to squint to make out the date etched in his flowery script—*Year of Our Lord Twelve Hundred and Fifty-Four.*

"Twelve Fifty-Four. Twelve Fifty-Four," she muttered.

There was something naggingly familiar about that particular sequence of numbers. One. Two. Five. Four. She groaned as she remembered magnifying the amulet's image within those precise parameters. Why couldn't she have chosen one, nine, seven, and six? Then she wouldn't have had to face any challenge more daunting than the advent of disco.

As they thrust her into the chair next to Brisbane's throne, Lucy's plaintive mew sounded from somewhere behind her.

She leveled a steely glare at her assailants. "Let go of me, you bullying cows, or I'll . . . I'll . . ."

Sue for assault?

Dial 911?

Give you a verbal reprimand?

Tabitha sputtered to a frustrated halt.

"You can't blame the wench for being vexed," crooned one of the women as she forced a coronet of flowers over Tabitha's tousled hair. "After all, she'll soon be losing more than her temper." Clucking in mock sympathy, she ran a finger across Tabitha's throat.

Another woman fanned herself with her pudgy hand.

"One night with Ravenshaw may cost her both her head and her virtue." She offered her companions an impish wink. " 'Twas well worth it, no doubt. The rogue's prowess in bed surely exceeds even his prowess on the battlefield."

The women tittered. Tabitha stiffened. They'd have probably been laughing louder had they known she'd failed to incite even the most perfunctory lust in Sir Colin. At least while he was conscious.

Her tormentors put the finishing touches on her humiliation by draping an ermine-trimmed cloak over her shoulders. She was beginning to feel like Miss America—without the scholarships. Still whispering and giggling among themselves, the women withdrew to their benches. Tabitha barely had time to steal a breath of fresh air before Brisbane drifted back to his throne on a cloud of tart fragrance that smelled vaguely like Lemon Pledge.

"Shouldn't you be down on the field?" Tabitha snapped. "Defending your honor . . . or your lack of it."

Brisbane's nonchalant shrug was enhanced by the ripple of his robe. "Every man and woman has the right to choose their own champion. I've chosen mine and ah . . . here's yours now."

Malice oozed from his voice, but Tabitha still couldn't resist leaning forward and gripping the rail that encircled the gallery.

Jeers and hoots of derision assailed her ears as Colin was led onto the field riding a shaggy pony. They'd stripped him of both armor and shirt, leaving him wearing nothing but his boots and a pair of loose black breeches. He should have looked ridiculous, but even half-horsed and half-naked, he still looked like a man capable of slaying a dragon or two. Robbing him of his shirt only revealed the powerful ripple of muscles honed by warfare and bronzed by the Egyptian sun.

As one of Brisbane's smirking squires paraded him past the platform, the knight's indomitable dignity shamed the crowd to silence.

Tabitha was relieved to note that his wound still showed no sign of fresh bleeding. She'd learned from experience never to discount the restorative powers of a Big Mac. And Colin had wolfed down three of them.

She expected Brisbane to hurl a taunt, but it was the priest who rose from his bench, raised his arms, and piously intoned, "Go with God, my son, and—"

"I've no need of your blessing, Father," Colin called out, his voice ringing in the shocked silence. "The Church may have failed to protect my property and family as they vowed to do while I was on Crusade, but God always fights on the side of right."

The priest retreated, muttering something about arrogant whelps and heresy. Tabitha covered her mouth with her hand, both touched and horrified by Colin's naivete.

"Cocky bastard," Brisbane muttered. "Let the priest save his blessing for the wretch's burial."

Tabitha slanted him a rueful glance. If this man called Colin "friend," she would hate to meet his enemies.

She gasped in unison with the crowd as a monstrous ogre of a man appeared at the far end of the field, his chain mail glinting in the sunlight. He wore a metal helm molded to resemble the snout of a mighty boar. Steel plates protected his elbows and knees, making Colin look painfully vulnerable in contrast.

"Scot-Killer! Scot-Killer!" the crowd chanted with renewed vigor.

Brisbane leaned over and whispered, "King Henry knighted Sir Orrick for valor after he killed over thirty

Scots during a border skirmish. He brought their heads home in a bloody sack and piked them on his bailey walls like rotten melons."

She refused to give him the satisfaction of glancing up at the jagged spikes adorning his own castle walls. "Did he also strip them of their armor first? Or were they defenseless women and children?"

Brisbane settled back in his chair, a pout pinching his lips. "I can assure you, my lady, that Colin has never been defenseless."

Tabitha found that difficult to believe as Sir Orrick's squire led his master toward the platform. Orrick's magnificent sable stallion dwarfed Sir Colin's pony. She sucked in a breath as she realized Brisbane had added insult to injury by giving Colin's own horse to his opponent. The stallion shied sideways, unaccustomed to the bulk of his new rider. The Scot-Killer drew back his golden-spurred heels and drove them into the horse's flanks, laughing heartily when the squire's tenacious grip on the reins kept the terrified horse from bolting.

It was the first time Tabitha had ever seen Colin flinch.

After the horse had stopped bucking and stood trembling in submission, Sir Orrick bowed his head and humbly accepted the priest's blessing. The crowd murmured its approval. Tabitha watched with mounting horror as the ham-handed knight was outfitted with an iron-studded shield and an enormous lance. Delicate ribbons laced its length, but not even their festive splash of purple and yellow could disguise the deadly point at its tip. She feared the ribbons would soon be stained with Colin's blood.

The crowd burst into laughter as Brisbane's squire handed Colin a lance that was little more than a tree branch whittled to a blunt tip. He accepted the crude weapon without complaint, handling it with the same care Arthur would have given Excalibur. He was not offered a shield.

Tabitha sprang to her feet. "You should be ashamed of yourself. This isn't a joust. It's a joke."

Brisbane's lips curved in a feral grin. "One I'm sure Colin will appreciate. He always did have a droll sense of humor."

She found it hard to imagine the dour Scot having any sense of humor at all.

"I should think you'd be flattered," her host crooned. "'Tis an honor to be crowned Queen of the Tournament."

"In that dress you're wearing, you should have crowned yourself Queen," Tabitha retorted. The effect of her jibe was spoiled when her makeshift crown slid over one eye. Two of Brisbane's women clapped their hands on her shoulders, shoving her back into her seat.

The combatants were led to opposite ends of the field. A fat little man who looked as if he'd just waddled off the back of a deck of playing cards lifted a golden trumpet and blew a flourish of brassy notes, signaling the riders to commence battle.

As the armored giant bore down on Sir Colin, the stallion taking two strides to every one of the pony's, the crowd roared their approval. Tabitha clapped a hand over her eyes, but couldn't resist peeking through her fingers.

Colin used the giant's size against him, ducking neatly beneath the lance's first thrust. The gallant effort coaxed a smattering of applause from the audience, but it was quickly quelled by Brisbane's sullen glare.

Sir Orrick howled with rage inside his helm. Tabitha feared Colin would not be so lucky on the next pass. The Scot-Killer reached the end of the field and wheeled the stallion in a taut circle. He seemed to be having more trouble controlling the unruly beast. Perhaps the horse had caught a whiff of his master's scent.

Brisbane clutched the rail with white-knuckled anticipation as he prepared to give the signal for the second pass.

Determined to win Colin a few precious seconds to recover, Tabitha leaned forward. "I gather that you and Sir Colin were once friends. What turned you into such bitter enemies?"

He cast her a contemptuous glance. "You should ask my twin sister Regan."

"And what would she tell me?"

Brisbane snorted. "That her precious Colin could do no wrong. Regan was content to spend hours listening to him boast about winning his spurs, encouraging him to prattle on and on about his eagerness to serve both God and king." His voice rose to a shout. " 'Twas disgusting!"

The priest cleared his throat. Brisbane recovered from his bout of jealousy only to realize that all eyes were gaping at him. He cast Tabitha a furious look before shooting to his feet.

"To the death," he shouted, sealing both Colin's fate and her own.

Tabitha's breath lodged in her throat as the Scot-Killer came thundering down the stretch, leveling his lance at Colin's unprotected heart. Colin never blinked, never faltered, and Tabitha discovered she couldn't dishonor him by burying her own face in her hands. As death raced toward him in the guise of a monstrous boar, she grabbed the amulet from her pajama shirt.

"I wish . . ." she whispered.

Brisbane shot her a look, his sharp gaze tracing the length of the chain to her clenched fist.

"I wish . . ." she repeated fiercely.

But she'd spent too much of her life biting back her wishes. Now, when she needed the words the most, they wouldn't come soon enough. Her cowardice was going to cost this courageous young knight his life.

But Sir Colin of Ravenshaw had no need of magic, only might.

As the stallion bore down on him, he stood up in the stirrups—his broad chest glistening with sweat, his dark hair flying behind him—and roared a battle cry that made every hair on Tabitha's nape stand up. Sir Orrick struck low, missing his target completely. Colin struck high, ramming his own stunted lance into the vulnerable gap between chain mail and helm. The Scot-Killer collapsed in the sand, the soft tissue beneath his jaw gushing blood.

The onlookers surged to their feet as Colin emitted a shrill whistle. The stallion wheeled from its mad flight, heeding his master's irresistible summons. Colin easily vaulted from pony to stallion, then swooped low to snatch Sir Orrick's dagger from its sheath. The horse reared, its nostrils flaring at the scent of blood, but Colin calmed the terrified beast with a stroke of its satiny neck and a soothing murmur.

He shoved the dagger into his waistband and nudged the stallion into a gallop. Brisbane pounded on the rail and howled, "Stop him, you imbeciles!"

His guards either stood gaping, paralyzed with shock, or ran in ineffectual circles, stumbling over one another in their efforts to gather both their gear and their wits. Colin bent low over the stallion's neck, clearing the fence with magnificent ease.

Tabitha was on her feet, cheering as wildly as she ever had at a New York Giants game, when she realized he was abandoning her to her death. She gripped the railing, the chaos around her fading to a dull roar. Unexpected tears stung her eyes, but she frantically blinked them back. She didn't have any right to be disillusioned. This was no fairy tale and even a knight's gallantry must have its limits. She could hardly expect Colin to sacrifice his own life for a woman he barely knew and didn't even trust.

But none of those rational arguments eased the desolate ache in her heart as she watched him race across the meadow and up the grassy slope toward freedom.

At the crest of the hill, he wheeled the horse around and sat silhouetted against the sky, his dark hair billowing in the wind.

Brisbane paled. An eerie hush fell over the crowd, as if they were all holding their breaths.

Although she knew it was impossible from that distance, Tabitha would have almost sworn Colin was gazing right into her eyes. Her heart began to pound in her throat. She clenched the rail, wanting to hope, but knowing she would hate herself for it when he turned his back and rode out of her life forever.

This time he didn't bother with a battle cry. He simply drove the stallion straight down the hill, his thundering charge scattering the panicked guards.

Tabitha's heart sang with exultation.

"He's mad," Brisbane breathed, the strangled note of admiration in his voice unmistakable. "The bastard is utterly mad."

Sir Colin added credence to that assessment by aiming his horse straight for the gallery stairs. The admiring cries from the ladies behind Tabitha erupted into squeals of terror. As the horse lunged up the stairs, rocking the entire platform, several of them dove over the rail, their veils rippling behind them like colorful kite tails.

Brisbane shot Tabitha a murderous look, plainly torn between breaking her neck before Colin could reach her or diving to safety himself. Tabitha helped him make his decision by planting a foot firmly in the middle of his solar plexus. He crashed *through* the rail instead of over it, hurtling through the air to land in the sand with a satisfying thud. She tore off the coronet of flowers and tossed it on his chest, thankful for the self-defense lessons Uncle Sven, Lennox Enterprises's towering Chief of Security, had given her.

Then Colin was there, his hand extended, his golden eyes blazing brighter than the sun. Tabitha had no time to ponder her fear of horses, no time to do anything but seize his hand and allow him to drag her up and astride the horse behind him. She wrapped her arms around his waist, clinging for dear life.

He guided the horse around only to discover that several of Brisbane's more foolhardy guards had blocked the stairs, their swords drawn for battle. Tabitha had no idea what he intended to do until he urged the horse to prance backward, leaving a clear shot between them and the splintered rail.

"Hang on," he shouted.

"Oh, God," she whispered, squeezing her eyes shut and burying her face against the feverish warmth of his back.

Beneath Colin's gentle mastery, the stallion soared off the platform as if winged. The sensation of weightlessness might have actually been exhilarating if Tabitha hadn't been convinced they were about to crash in a heap of torn flesh and shattered bone.

They hit the ground with an impact that jarred her teeth, but the horse miraculously kept its feet, stretching its powerful limbs into a canter.

They were racing up the hill when a terrible thought

struck Tabitha. She pounded on Colin's shoulder, oblivious to his grunt of pain. "We have to go back! I forgot Lucy. I can't abandon her a second time. Brisbane will eat her for sure!"

"Are you mad, woman?" Colin shouted over his shoulder. He made no attempt to slow the horse's flight until she reached around him and tried to grab the reins.

He wrenched the horse to a shuddering halt and twisted around to glare at her. "I should have let Brisbane have your pretty head. 'Tis plainly of no use to you."

Tabitha didn't even notice he'd called her pretty. She was too embarrassed by her clogged throat and the pink she could feel creeping into her nose. In less than twenty-four hours, she'd traveled over seven hundred years into the past, been captured by a sadistic madman, thrown into a rat-infested dungeon, and threatened with decapitation. She didn't think she could bear losing Lucy as well.

"Oh, please," she said, dabbing at her nose with the ermine-trimmed hem of Brisbane's cloak. "You're a knight, aren't you? Rescuing damsels in distress is supposed to be part of your job description."

He gazed into her pleading eyes for several seconds, a muscle in his jaw working savagely, before biting off an oath she hadn't even realized existed yet and swinging the horse back around.

She clung to him as much out of gratitude as desperation as they charged back into the fray.

"There she is," Tabitha shouted when she spotted the bell-capped jester sprinting for cover, the yowling kitten tucked beneath his arm like a football.

Colin never even slowed the stallion. He simply leaned sideways in the saddle and plucked the kitten from the jester's grip, leaving him staring after them in blank astonishment. Lucy immediately clawed her way up Colin's wounded shoulder and glared at Tabitha as if to say, "What the hell took you so long?"

Tabitha laughed through her tears, even as Brisbane's archers sent a cascade of arrows whizzing past their heads.

As they galloped toward the distant horizon, leaving the shouting and chaos far behind, she rested her cheek against Colin's back, going limp with relief.

"My hero," she murmured, sobered to realize she was only half joking.

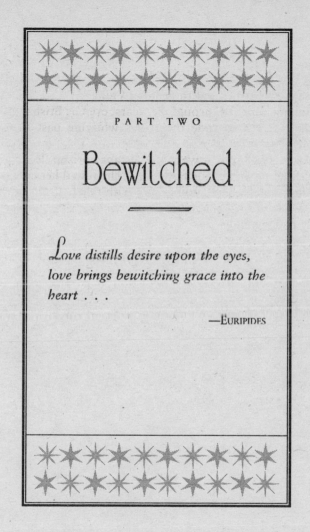

PART TWO

Bewitched

*Love distills desire upon the eyes,
love brings bewitching grace into the
heart . . .*

—EURIPIDES

Tabitha kept her arms twined trustingly around Colin's waist as he drove the stallion deep into the winding maze of the forest. The canopy of branches laced together like the ribs of some mighty dragon, weaving an illusion of eternal twilight. The hoofbeats and frustrated curses of their pursuers would fade, then swell, then fade again as Colin led them on a merry chase through copse and thicket. Lucy huddled in the cup of Tabitha's hand, cradled securely against Colin's taut stomach.

The roar of a waterfall nearly masked a triumphant shout as one of Brisbane's men spotted their trail.

"Duck!" Colin shouted.

When Tabitha's frantic gaze encountered no sign of a woodland fowl, she obeyed just in time to keep her head from being lopped off by an overhanging ledge. Cool spray drenched her skin as Colin drove the stallion into the yawning mouth of the cave tucked behind the screen of rushing water.

Colin gave her little time to adjust to the hazy half-light. He flung himself off the horse without a word of explanation, dragging her with him. He wrapped his arms around her as he slammed his back against the cavern wall, draping them both in shadows. The stallion stood motionless, as if he'd been trained to do so by an infinitely patient master.

Tabitha held her breath as two men passed so close to the mouth of the cave that even the spill of water failed to muffle their disgruntled voices.

"Bastard couldn't have just disappeared."

"You'd best pray not 'cause the master'll have our heads if we go back without 'im."

Tabitha bit back a cry of pain as Lucy dug her claws into her arm.

Colin cradled the back of her head in his broad palm, pressing her face to his chest. Her first absurd notion that he was trying to cop a feel collapsed when she realized that one squeak from her or the cat and they would be trapped at the mercy of Brisbane's men.

Their forced intimacy should have been awkward. But there was something disarmingly natural about standing in Colin's arms, feeling the powerful throb of his heart beneath her lips. His crisp chest hairs tickled her nose, forcing her to swallow a sneeze. His well-muscled frame could have been modeled from tensile steel, but an inexplicable languor melted through Tabitha, making her feel warm and cherished and safe from all harm for the first time in her life.

The menacing hoofbeats receded, but the tension failed to melt from Colin's body.

His hand crept around to cup her cheek, alerting her to a more subtle danger. But the warning came too late. He didn't even have to tilt her face upward to find her lips with his own. They were already there—tingling, moist, and parted in an invitation Tabitha hadn't even realized she'd extended until it was too late to rescind it.

His mouth brushed hers in a dry, chaste caress, his bottom lip too persuasively soft to belong to such a hard man. Lost in a daze of pleasure, Tabitha considered calling back Brisbane's guards. From a practical viewpoint, she'd be better off losing her head in this century than her heart.

Lucy must have agreed, for she scrambled out of Tabitha's grip, yowling at the top of her tiny lungs. Tabitha and Colin sprang apart, the curious spell that had bound them broken.

Colin glared at her, his chest heaving, his hands clenched into fists. She felt a brief pang of regret that her kiss *hadn't* turned him into a frog. A frog might have been easier to deal with than a hundred eighty pounds of disgruntled male.

She scrambled to fill the awkward silence. "There's really no need for alarm or apologies. A false sense of intimacy is a completely normal psychological reaction to the stress of sharing a life-threatening experience." She smoothed her hair back from her burning cheeks, laughing shakily. "The relatively common phenomenon explains why traditionally during wartime, so many hasty marriages are made and babies conceived—"

He crossed his arms over his chest and arched one eyebrow, challenging her to continue. She snapped her mouth shut, wishing she'd kept it that way.

His scowl darkened. "You talk much, lass, but say little. How is it that you have a glib answer for everything except where you came from in the first place?"

Tabitha's mouth fell open. He'd taken up the threads of their earlier conversation as if they'd never been interrupted by a joust, the threat of decapitation, or a headlong flight from disaster. She'd dealt with I.R.S. tax attorneys who were less focused.

This time there was no dungeon guard to blunder to her rescue and no escaping Colin's bright, fierce gaze.

Suspecting this wasn't the opportune moment to confess she was a time-traveling witch, Tabitha seized upon something Brisbane's jester had said. "I was traveling with a band of mummies."

Colin blinked at her. "Mummers?"

"Yes, mummers," she echoed.

"Ah." He nodded, not looking the least bit convinced. "And what did you do with these mummers? Perform the pantomime? Rope dance?" His gaze strayed ever so briefly to lips that were still tingling from his kiss. "Swallow swords?"

Tabitha felt as if she were swallowing an entire lance as she struggled to come up with some diversion she might actually perform if pressed. Her ballet lessons had ended in disgrace when she'd gotten her oversized foot stuck in the barre and she'd been kicked out of the girls' chorus at her private school when she fell through the risers during a Christmas recital.

"Magic," she finally blurted out in desperation. "I did magic."

Colin cocked his head to the side. "Indeed. And might I entreat you to perform one of your tricks?"

"I really couldn't." She shook her head as she backed away from him, hoping her panic would be perceived as modesty. "I wouldn't want to bore you."

"You've yet to bore me, my lady."

Unsettled by his frank gaze, Tabitha backed right into the horse, who shied away from her. She didn't trust her mother's amulet enough to risk a genuine wish. She doubted she'd survive an hour in this wilderness if she accidentally turned Sir Colin into a waffle iron.

Remembering a simple trick her daddy had taught her when she was a little girl, she extended her hand. "Do you have a coin?"

Colin made a great show of patting his bare chest.

"I'm afraid I haven't a farthing to my name at the moment."

Tabitha chose a small, flat rock from the cave floor as a substitute. "Watch my hand," she intoned in what she hoped was a mesmerizing approximation of her mother's husky voice. "No matter what happens, don't take your eyes off my hand."

He dutifully complied as she rolled the rock between the fingers of her right hand, dropping it twice before establishing a respectable rhythm. "Watch closely, sir, and you'll see this magical stone disappear before your very eyes." She opened her hand with a flourish. "Abra cadabra!"

The rock flew out of her grip, hitting him squarely in the temple.

Tabitha winced. "Sorry. Let me try again."

Colin rubbed his head, eyeing her warily. "Perhaps we should wait until I can retrieve my helm."

She found another rock and repeated the procedure, stage fright making her fingers even more stiff and clumsy than usual. This time when she extended her hand and shouted, "Abracadabra!" the rock had vanished.

Flushed with pride, she swept Colin a triumphant bow. He caught her wrist and turned her hand palm-down to reveal the stone wedged firmly between her thumb and forefinger. Up went that infuriating eyebrow again; down went Tabitha's spirits.

"Spoilsport," she muttered, jerking her wrist free of his grip.

"You're not very gifted, are you?"

She was surprised by how much his gentle observation stung. Resisting the temptation to grab the amulet and show him just how gifted she could be, she decided to turn his pity to her advantage.

She conjured up a wistful sigh. "That's why the mummers kicked me out of their troupe. Because I was such a terrible embarrassment to them."

His eyes narrowed, his speculative gaze warning her that Sir Colin of Ravenshaw was not a man to be fooled by either illusion or deceit. But before he could challenge her fable, a distant shout forced them to round up kitten and horse and seek a new hiding place to prevent the cave from becoming their tomb.

Roger Basil Henry Joseph Maximillian, Baron Brisbane, strode through the winding passages beneath his castle, affecting a swagger to disguise the limp bestowed upon him by Colin's treacherous whore. He despised revealing any sign of weakness to his inferiors.

"This had best be good," he snapped. "If you've summoned me from my bath for naught, I'll have Cook boil you in tomorrow's pudding."

The two dungeon guards quickened their pace until they were almost skipping, eager to stay out of striking reach. They'd learned from harsh experience that their lord's angelic countenance hid a devilish temper. A temper worsened by Ravenshaw's spectacular triumph on the jousting field and daring escape. Over half of their master's guards had already come crawling back, trembling in their boots and vowing their quarry had vanished into thin air. Accusing them of blaming their own ineptitude on fairies and "haints," Brisbane had ordered the lot of them flogged.

Less than eager to join their groaning comrades in the gatehouse, the guards rushed forward, one sweeping open a cell door while the other tugged at the greasy forelock creeping out from beneath his helm.

"I've never before seen the like, my lord."

"Aye, master, 'tis a riddle only you can solve."

Brisbane swept into the cell, took one look at its occupant, and said, "He's dead. What else do you need to know?"

The corpse lay on his back in the bed, his toes turned outward and a blissful expression on his wizened face. Brisbane poked the old man's bloated belly with one fingertip, his aristocratic nostrils flaring in distaste.

"Who is this fellow? What was his crime?" Roger had had enough on his mind with Colin's return. He could hardly be expected to keep track of all the mewling peasants he sentenced to death or lifelong imprisonment.

"Poachin', my lord," chirped one of the guards. "He claimed to be starvin'. Et one of the castle rats, he did."

Brisbane shook his head sadly. "Poor sot would have done well to remember that gluttony is one of the seven deadly sins."

The guards exchanged a wary look. "Precisely our point, my lord," the bolder one said.

They gestured as one to the table at the foot of the bed. Brisbane's eyes widened, his jaded attention finally engaged. Although it was obvious a sizable dent had been made in the feast, the table still contained enough food to feed an entire garrison of soldiers. He glanced back at the corpse, realizing for the first time that the object clutched in the old man's gnarled hand was a chicken bone, sucked clean of its tender flesh.

Baffled, he peeled back a hunk of bread to reveal a cold patty of meat. He swiped a finger through its creamy orange glaze and brought it to his lips. "Mmmm," he murmured thoughtfully. " 'Tis a special sauce."

One of the guards drew off his conical helm, elbowing the other into sheepishly following suit. " 'Twas more than the old wretch's gullet could take."

Brisbane's troubled gaze wandered from the beaming corpse to the stained-glass lamp shade, the plush rug, the opulent bed. "Aren't these appointments a trifle bit luxurious? When I had the stonemason design the dungeon, I had something a bit more . . . stygian in mind. You know—iron manacles, piles of rotting bones, slavering rats."

One of the guards marched into the corridor and flung open the door of the opposite cell to reveal the exact scene his lord had just described. A herd of squealing rats raced for the walls, their feral eyes gleaming bloodred in the gloom.

Brisbane grinned. "Ah, now that's much better."

The guard returned to his companion's side. " 'Twas this very cell Ravenshaw and his lady shared before we locked up the old man in their place."

Their master's smile slowly faded. "So how did Colin cajole you into providing him with these luxuries? He never lacked for charm, you know, even as a lad. He stole my own sister's heart away from me with nothing more than a grubby fistful of weeds. Did he bribe you? Offer you some bauble he acquired in the Holy Land?"

The men exchanged another panicked glance, knowing their very survival depended on their answer. " 'Twas not our doing, but theirs, my lord." He traced a cross on his mail hauberk with a trembling finger. "We were naught but the victims of some dark enchantment."

Brisbane's upper lip curled in an ominous sneer. "I'm warning you. I've already heard enough superstitious drivel for one day. Ravenshaw may be sickeningly pious, but he's no saint. He can't work miracles or conjure roasted chickens out of thin air." Disgusted by their blithering, Brisbane turned and marched from the cell.

"Not Sir Colin, but *her*," one of them called after him. "We believe *she's* the one who did all this."

"Aye," blurted out the other, clearing his throat when his voice cracked with terror. "The woman."

"The woman?" Brisbane slowly pivoted on his heel in the doorway. "The woman," he repeated, frowning.

The woman who had appeared out of nowhere. The woman who had dared to taunt him with no visible fear of retaliation. The woman who had clutched the strange amulet she wore as if it possessed the power to grant her most passionate desire.

He fingered his chin thoughtfully. He'd always been inclined to dismiss such nonsense. After all, he wouldn't have hesitated to barter his soul for personal gain and Satan had never bothered to approach him.

Yet the woman had touched the amulet and Sir Orrick had fallen beneath Colin's lance as if struck by an invisible foe.

Heartened by the flush of delight slowly spreading over their master's face, one of the guards asked, "Shall we rouse the rest of the garrison to rejoin the hunt, my lord?"

"Aye," said the other. "The witch must be captured and put to death. We'd hoped you might allow us to captain the expedition as reward for our discovery." The two men stood shoulder to shoulder, all but panting with eagerness.

Brisbane shook his head. 'Twould never do to allow these two simpletons to rush from the dungeon, braying about witches and stirring his villeins to panic.

He favored them with a benevolent smile. "You mustn't be so greedy. You should always remember that virtue is its own reward."

Still smiling, he slammed the door in their stunned faces. Ignoring their hoarse cries, he bolted the door behind him, leaving them to rot along with the old man's corpse.

He strode through the dank corridors, nearly chortling aloud at the delicious irony. His only virtue was patience, but he possessed it in abundance when it served his needs. Patience enough to call off his own dogs and give the toothsome bitch ample time to tear out Colin's heart.

The godly fool would never knowingly consort with a witch. If this woman was truly a daughter of Satan, Colin's alliance with her could very well cost him something he valued even more highly than his life—his immortal soul.

"What are you doing?" Tabitha whispered.

"Praying," Colin replied without opening his eyes.

She sighed and withdrew to the opposite side of the campfire. Colin had been on his knees for nearly an hour, head bowed and hands clasped before him. She'd had ample opportunity to study him in the flickering firelight. Although his posture appeared to be penitent, his expression was as unrelenting as ever, its fierceness softened only by the silky, dark crescents of his lashes resting against his cheeks.

An inhuman screech pierced the night. Tabitha shivered and drew her ragged pajama top tighter around her. She almost regretted offering Brisbane's cloak to the shirtless knight. But as a breeze caught the woolen folds of the garment, whipping them back to reveal the swarthy expanse of his chest, she remembered that she'd made the gesture more for her protection than his own.

She averted her eyes with a disdainful sniff. She'd

never had much taste for beefcake. She'd always preferred cerebral men. Men content to admire her mind, not her body. Men so intimidated by her father's wealth and her own frigid reputation that they would never presume to do more than shake her hand at her door, much less steal a tender kiss in a moment of weakness.

She jumped as a predatory scream was followed by a choked gurgle, as if the voice of some small, helpless creature had been forever silenced. Colin's horse whickered uneasily. Lucy glanced up from the feast of fish Colin had speared in a nearby stream and roasted over the fire, then went back to devouring the flaky white morsels with a feline shrug.

Tabitha's fearful gaze searched the shadows cast by the ancient trees. By night, the forest primeval appeared more cursed than enchanted. She'd never had a problem embracing the survival-of-the-fittest theory in the safety of her cozy penthouse. But here in this alien time and place, it was too easy to imagine a fearsome dragon prowling the night, looking to make a meal of some poor succulent virgin.

She edged nearer to Colin, desperate for some human comfort, even that of her own voice. "Who are you praying for?"

He opened one eye to glower at her, before dismissing her by closing it again. "My enemies."

Even a devout cynic such as herself had to be impressed. "How very noble of you."

"I'm praying that God will deliver them into my hands so I can destroy them."

"Oh." Tabitha was somewhat taken aback. "So you're an Old Testament kind of guy, eh?"

A long-suffering sigh escaped him. "Perhaps I should be praying for the patience of Job."

"Sorry," she muttered. "I didn't mean to interrupt."

Both of his eyes flew open, their suspicious gleam reignited. "You're not a heretic, are you? We burn heretics, you know."

"Oh, no," she said hastily, inching away from the fire. "I prefer to think of myself as sort of an Emersonian transcendentalist."

He didn't seem to know what to make of that so he simply rose to tether his grazing horse to a nearby tree.

"Does he have a name?" Tabitha asked, watching Colin stroke the stallion's velvety nose, his rough hands gentled by affection.

"Nay, my lady. Chargers die by the thousands in battle and 'tis a wee bit harder to bid farewell to a creature with a name. Most mothers don't even name their bairns until they're of an age where they're likely to survive."

Listening to the wind sigh through the creaking boughs, Tabitha was chilled anew by the fragility of life in this era. Colin's profile was pensive and she wondered if he was thinking of the infant sister he'd never known. Would the child be remembered by name or simply forgotten as if she'd never existed? Her own sense of urgency mounted. She had to find a way home. If she didn't, she might never learn if her own parents were dead or alive.

An owl hooted overhead, startling her anew. "Are you sure we're safe here? How do you know Brisbane's men won't find us?"

Colin squatted to throw another handful of sticks on the fire. "We've crossed the border into Scotland, lass." He flashed her a less than pious grin that made her heart do an odd little flip. "Roger's men couldn't find their arses with a map in these hills."

Tabitha nibbled on her bottom lip to hide a smile. Sir Colin certainly wasn't a man to mince words. "When I asked Brisbane why the two of you hated each other, he told me I should ask his sister."

Colin's grin faded. Although his eyes reflected the leaping flames, their utter absence of expression chilled her. " 'Twould be an amazing feat considering Regan's been dead for nigh on seven years."

Tabitha frowned. "How did she die?"

"I killed her."

Tabitha weaved imperceptibly beneath the blow, then waited for him to elaborate. Waited for him to explain how his horse had accidentally trampled the poor girl while she was picking wildflowers in a meadow. Or how she'd tumbled out a tower window while waving good-bye to him.

Colin just sat there, letting her twist in the wind.

"Well, *how* did you kill her? Did you push her off a cliff? Chop her into pieces with your sword? Poison her with hemlock? If we're going to be spending the night out here in the middle of nowhere, I'd really like to know your preferred method of murder."

The dangerous glint in Colin's eyes warned her that he wasn't oblivious to her sarcasm. But when he spoke, his voice was as dispassionate as if he were recounting a tragedy that had happened long ago to another man. "Roger, Regan, and I were childhood friends. I was young and foolish. Regan was sweet and willing. When we were both seventeen, I got her with child. She begged me to marry her, but I'd been promised to another since I was a lad. Breaking the betrothal contract would mean war for my father. I hadn't the courage to defy his wishes until 'twas too late. When I finally went to the cottage where we trysted to tell Regan I would make her my wife, I found her hanging from the rafters, my unborn child dead in her womb." He shrugged. " 'Tis simple enough. Regan loved me. I killed her."

"She killed herself," Tabitha said softly, refusing to yield before his fierce gaze. "It's not fair for her brother to blame you for her death and it's not fair for you to blame yourself."

His shield slipped for an elusive instant, giving her a glimpse of old wounds and bittersweet regrets. " 'Tis unfortunate, my lady, that absolution isn't yours to grant." He stretched out on the ground, rolling into the cloak. "We'd best get some sleep. We'll proceed to my castle on the morrow."

Tabitha was alarmed by a new thought. "Won't your castle be the first place Brisbane comes looking for you?"

His eyes drifted shut, but a ruthless smirk flirted with his lips. "God willing."

Tabitha reclined on her side and pillowed her head on her hands. The fire crackled and snapped, creating a disarming aura of intimacy.

"Why did you come back for me?" she asked softly, finally daring to ask the other question that had haunted her since their wild flight from Brisbane's castle.

Colin's hesitation was nearly imperceptible. "Because honor demanded it."

"Oh, of course. Honor."

His words left her feeling cold. She eyed the woolen cloak, hoping his precious honor would goad him into offering it back to her. Although it was the heart of summer, a fallow chill still clung to the forest floor.

His contented snores ended her hopes. Sighing, she drew Lucy's warm, furry body into her arms. Before she could even close her eyes, the kitten had squirmed out of her grip and sauntered boldly over to Sir Colin. The little minx slipped between the folds of the cloak and curled into a ball against his bare chest. Her purr was audible over the crackle of the campfire, and Tabitha remembered how blissfully she had slept in that exact spot the previous night.

"Traitor," she whispered, fervently hoping that she was jealous of the man and not the cat.

Colin squatted beside the fire to drape the cloak over the woman's sleeping form. She'd curled in on herself and, despite her uncommon height, looked small and disturbingly vulnerable. Exhaustion had stripped her of her curious bravado. With her lips turned downward in a sad little bow and violet smudging the pale skin beneath her eyes, she looked lost in some fundamental way—like a child wandering alone in a strange and dangerous wood.

A wayward lock of hair had fallen across her eyes. He brushed it away, sifting its feathery softness through his fingertips. She nestled into the cloak and turned her face toward his touch, inadvertently grazing his wrist with her lips. Colin jerked his hand back, pricked by the reminder that she was no child, but a woman grown, ripe with all the perils and delights of her fickle sex.

It seemed a lifetime since he'd allowed himself to stroke a lass's hair or draw her into his arms when she shivered. An eternity since he'd felt the alluring softness of a woman's body against him.

Or beneath him.

He scowled, betrayed by the swift and devastating surge of lust in his groin. He'd never encountered a woman quite like this one. Regan had been sketched in ethereal shades of primrose and silver, easy to capture, yet impossible to hold. She'd flowed like summer rain through his hands until she was no more.

But this woman was no wraith to vanish before his eyes. She was warm and vibrant and solid to the touch.

He'd grown accustomed to looming over ladies who kept their heads meekly bowed and their hands cupped over their mouths to hide their shy smiles and crooked teeth.

But throughout the grueling day, he had only to turn his head and Tabitha was there, her pearly teeth flashing, her parted lips a breath away from his own.

Was it any wonder he hadn't been able to resist kissing her in the cavern? That he'd yearned to discover if she tasted as intoxicating as she smelled—like sunshine and honeyed mead on a hot summer day? But that brief sip had only betrayed him by whetting his thirst.

He muttered an oath, then shot a silent prayer skyward, begging his Lord's pardon for blaspheming.

In the brothels of Egypt, he'd encountered a multitude of women schooled in the arts of pleasure. Their pouting ruby lips and khol-lined eyes had promised erotic delights beyond any mere mortal's imaginings. He'd seen stalwart knights break marriage oaths and risk eternal damnation for the fleeting privilege of being tangled in their jasmine-scented hair for one night of ecstasy.

Yet this odd woman with her bold speech and hacked-off hair stirred him as those exotic beauties never had.

He reached for a corner of the cloak, surprised to find his hand unsteady. He had no further reason to resist temptation. His crusade was done, his vow fulfilled, his penance paid. She would make no protest if he drew back the cloak and covered her body with his own. He would not be the first stranger to seek release between her milky thighs, nor would he be the last. Mummers were known for passing their women around like flagons of wine, sampling their sweetness until each had drunk their fill.

But Colin hesitated, his reluctance even more inexplicable than his lust. Her innocent slumber might be naught but another cunning illusion like the forgiveness she'd offered him, yet he was loath to disturb it. He surprised himself by gently tucking the cloak around her and retreating to his own side of the fire. Perhaps its flames would serve to remind him that a passion that burned too hot could bring destruction as well as pleasure.

CHAPTER 10

When Tabitha awoke the next morning, the fire had died to ash and the knight was gone.

She scrambled to her feet in a blind panic, throwing aside the cloak that enveloped her. A gauzy mist enshrouded the clearing, giving it all the welcoming charm of a graveyard at midnight on Halloween. The pearly light drifting through the interwoven branches made it impossible to tell if it was dawn or noon.

A sleek head loomed out of the mist.

Tabitha clapped a hand over her mouth to muffle a scream before collapsing to her knees in relief. Sir Colin might abandon her, but she knew from the gentle way he handled the animal that he would never forsake his horse.

The stallion surveyed her with limpid brown eyes before lowering his head to a clump of moss. While Tabitha was fingering the woolen folds of the cloak, wondering how it had come to be wrapped around her with such care, Lucy toddled over to butt her in the thigh.

She scratched beneath the kitten's chin, mocking Colin's burr. "Did Prince Surly abandon ye? Or has he gone on a quest fer a saucer o' cream and a box o' Tender Vittles fer his wee lassie?''

With the morning hush came a startling realization. For the first time since arriving in this wretched century, she was alone. Her heartbeat quickened. If she squandered this opportunity, there was no telling when or *if* the wary Scot would grant her another moment of privacy with the amulet.

She drew the emerald from her shirt. It made her nervous just to look at it, she'd grown so accustomed to bungling her every wish. She took one last look around the clearing, wondering what Colin would think when he returned to find her gone.

"Good riddance, most likely," she whispered, ignoring a pang of regret. Perhaps for the first time in their lives, her parents needed her. A man like Colin never would.

Before she could lose her nerve, she snatched Lucy to her chest, gripped the amulet, and closed her eyes. "I wish . . ." She drew in a deep breath before blurting out, "I wish I were home."

A whisper of a breeze tickled her cheek. She opened one eye. The mist, the clearing, the grazing stallion all remained. She stole a quick glance around to make sure Colin hadn't returned to watch her make an idiot of herself. But her only audience, aside from the horse and kitten, was the gnarled trees that looked suspiciously like the ones that had hurled the apples at Dorothy in *The Wizard of Oz.*

Thankful her mother couldn't see her at that moment, Tabitha rose to her feet, clicked the heels of her chipmunk slippers together three times in quick succession, and mumbled, "There's no place like home. There's no place like home."

"I'll not argue the sentiment, lass. 'Tis a noble one indeed."

Tabitha's eyes flew open. Colin was leaning against a nearby tree, his amber-flecked eyes glittering with amusement. Drops of water beaded in the midnight-black of his chest hair, glistening like diamonds. With his damp hair slicked back from his face and the stubble shading his jaw darkening to a true beard, he looked more like a rapacious pirate than a noble knight.

Tabitha blushed and stammered, "I was p-p-practicing a dance." To reinforce her fib, she shuffled her way through a clumsy soft shoe routine, ignoring Lucy's violent squirming. "If I'm to find work with another troupe of mummers, I need to develop a new act."

Colin pushed himself away from the tree and closed the distance between them. "I wouldn't take up story-telling if I were you because you're nearly as wretched a liar as you are a mummer."

Oh, God, he knew, Tabitha thought. He knew she was just some pathetic no-talent enchantress from the twenty-first century. Lucy wiggled out of her grip and darted for freedom, but Tabitha stood her ground, even when Colin gently pried open her fingers to reveal the amulet.

"You stole it, did you not?"

"What?"

He nodded toward the emerald. "The necklace. You stole it. 'Tis why the mummers cast you out. They're too dependent on the goodwill of the nobles to tolerate petty thievery among their ranks. Did they punish you by chopping off your hair in that atrocious manner?"

Frowning, Tabitha touched a hand to her hair. The blunt bob had cost her over two hundred dollars at Henri Bendel's on Fifth Avenue.

He surprised her by sifting a sandy lock through his fingers, his gaze compassionate, almost tender. "You're fortunate 'twas only your hair and not your hand, lass. Your hair will grow back."

Thankful to him for providing her with such a rich, if felonious, history, Tabitha lowered her lashes, struggling to look suitably contrite. "I never meant to take the necklace, sir. I'd just never seen anything quite so pretty." She cringed, deciding the faux British accent was a bad idea. It made her sound like the illegitimate child of Eliza Doolittle and Dr. Doolittle.

Colin tugged gently on the amulet. "These woods are crawling with outlaws and thieves. Perhaps 'twould be best if you gave it to me for safekeeping."

"No!" she nearly shouted, backing away until the chain was pulled taut between them. "It's mine. I've already paid the price for stealing it so I should be allowed to keep it."

He chose to ignore her absurd logic. "I'm not robbing you. I'll return your treasure to you when I deem it fitting."

Panic gripped Tabitha. She might not get home *with* the amulet, but she'd certainly never get home *without* it. But she didn't want her protests to heighten his suspicions. "Oh, yeah? What if you decide to give it to some buxom serving wench instead? Or pawn it so you can buy yourself a new sword." Against her will, her gaze darted to his naked chest, her throat going dry. "Or a new shirt."

He narrowed his eyes, warning her that she had finally succeeded in exasperating him. Wrapping the delicate chain around his fist, he reeled her in until her face was an unsteady breath away from his own. The muscles corded in his sun-bronzed forearm reminded her what a powerful man he was. He could take the amulet if he wished. He could take whatever he wanted from her without her consent and there was nothing she could do to stop him. The realization made her breathless.

"I'll return the bauble to you, lass. I said I would and I meant it."

"Swear it," she whispered, hoping she wasn't pressing her luck.

"Very well," he growled. "You have my oath on it."

Tabitha hesitated, searching his eyes. Given his obsession with honor, she could believe he would honor his vow.

Still holding her gaze, he freed the chain and held out his hand.

Drawing the necklace over her head, she dropped it into his hand. She felt a twinge of despair as his fingers closed around it. He'd just gained more leverage over her than she'd ever allowed any man.

He pointed a chiding finger at her, adding insult to injury. "I won't have you stealing from my people. They've suffered enough at Brisbane's hands. If you accept my hospitality, you'll abide by my laws or you'll answer to me." His stern gaze warned her that there was far more at stake than just a few paltry inches of hair.

"Yes, sir," she bit off. Tabitha Lennox wasn't accustomed to taking orders from anyone, especially not some down-on-his-luck Lancelot wannabe.

Satisfied with her promise, he tucked the amulet into the waistband of his breeches and sauntered over to the horse.

Tabitha glared at his back. "You needn't act so morally superior, you know. You did steal the Scot-Killer's dagger."

He flashed her a roguish grin as he draped the narrow

saddle over the stallion's back. "Aye, lass, but not before making sure he'd have no further need of it."

By noon of that day, Tabitha was entertaining gleeful fantasies of burying Sir Orrick's dagger between a certain Scotsman's shoulder blades. Especially after he insisted they walk for long, tedious stretches to keep from tiring the poor horse.

"Poor horse couldn't be any more tired than me," Tabitha mumbled, trudging through a streambed. The rubber soles of her slippers sucked at the muck, darkening the chipmunks' rubbery grins to thunderous scowls.

She supposed she had no one to blame for her misery but herself. They'd come to a standoff that morning when Colin had tried to slip off the horse, leaving her astride. Tabitha had dismounted so quickly she'd nearly ended up straddling his broad shoulders.

"Oh, no, you don't," she protested as he lowered her to the ground. "I'm not riding Pegasus here all by myself. You can ride and I'll walk."

"I can't ride while a woman walks. 'Twouldn't be chivalrous."

Neither relented, so it seemed they were both going to walk all the way to Colin's castle with the stallion prancing merrily along behind them, an indolent Lucy his only passenger. Each time they crested a hill, Tabitha would crane her neck, hoping desperately to find a replica of Sleeping Beauty's castle silhouetted against the horizon.

She had paused for the dozenth time to poke her head through a break in the foliage when Colin wrapped the elastic at the waistband of her pajama bottoms around his fist and hauled her back. "What ails you, woman? If you insist on dawdling, we won't make Ravenshaw lands until midnight."

"Midnight?" Tabitha echoed faintly.

"Aye. 'Tis another half day's journey before we reach Castle Raven."

Swallowing a mournful sigh, Tabitha plodded along behind him, regretting that she hadn't made more use of the electronic treadmill tucked away in a corner of her walk-in closet. The sun bore down on her face, baking her tender skin and blinding her with its glare. She'd spent so much of her life squinting at a blinking cursor in a darkened office that she felt like a mole emerging from its tunnel.

She should have never let Colin believe she was a felon. He kept stealing wary glances over his shoulder, as if he expected her to ambush him and wrest the amulet from his pants. She hoped he would relax his vigilance once they arrived at his castle. Without the amulet to control her magic, she feared it would only be a matter of time before she muttered some absentminded wish that would destroy them both.

When Colin half turned, those forbidding brows nearly meeting over his eyes, her frayed nerves finally snapped. "Oh, for heaven's sake, would you stop glowering at me! I'm a petty thief, not a serial killer. I've no intention of—"

He touched a finger to his lips. "Hush, lass," he whispered urgently.

That was when she realized he wasn't gazing at her at all, but at something just over her left shoulder. Her nape began to prickle. She'd been so preoccupied with her own misery that she'd nearly forgotten they were being pursued by a homicidal maniac with an army of thugs at his disposal. Perhaps one of Brisbane's men had been more cunning than Colin had anticipated and was even now crouched in the bushes with an arrow pointed at her back. A feeble squeak escaped her.

Colin crooked a finger at her and stretched out his other hand. She eased toward him, shaken to realize how quickly she'd come to rely on his muscular frame to shield her from disaster. Just as her fingertips brushed his, the rustling she'd dreaded erupted from behind her.

She froze, waiting for the arrow to tear through her spine.

"Unhand that fair maiden, you lusty rogue, or I'll lop off your head and feed it to my hounds!"

Tabitha whirled around. At first she thought they were being accosted by the Tin Man from *The Wizard of Oz*. Then she realized the man who'd emerged from the bushes was garbed from jaw to toe in glistening chain mail. A flat-topped helm obscured his face and made his voice sound as if it was echoing out of the bottom of a tuna fish can.

Feminism be damned, she took an instinctive step behind Colin. He did not disappoint. Emitting another of those bone-chilling roars, he hurled himself across the clearing at the interloper. The two men crashed to the ground with a clamor that set her ears to ringing. Arms and legs locked, they rolled away from her, then back again until they were engaged in mortal combat practically at her feet. Her heart lodged in her throat when she realized the stranger was squeezing Colin's naked back between his mail gauntlets.

Terrified the thug would snap Colin's spine, she jerked off his fancy helm and began to tug hard at his ginger curls.

The stranger howled, his voice no longer muffled by the helm. "Sweet Christ, Colin, get your wench off me before she snatches me bald!"

As his words sank in, Tabitha realized that the grunts

she had mistaken for curses were actually laughter, the blows nothing more lethal than mock wrestling accompanied by welcoming thumps on the back.

She backed away, dusting hair from her hands, while the two men roared with laughter like drunken frat boys at a keg party.

"I fail to see the humor in the situation," she said stiffly, trying not to notice how attractive Colin looked with his eyes crinkled by amusement instead of gloom. "I've been trained to defend myself, you know. I might have gouged out your friend's eyes or kneed him in the groin."

"That would have been a tragedy indeed," Colin said, "Arjon prizes his groin even more than his hair."

" 'Tis because my groin shows no sign of receding," the other man retorted, ruefully fingering his high forehead as he climbed to his feet. "Sir Arjon Flenoy, my lady." He retrieved his helm and swept her a bow that made Brisbane's flamboyance seem almost restrained. "At your humble and eternal service."

"For a price," Colin muttered, rising to brush himself off.

Arjon jerked a thumb at his friend. "Pay the Scot no heed, my lady. He quibbles because I choose to sell my sword while he barters his for mere salvation. My masters always pay while his . . . ?" He lifted his shoulders in a Gallic shrug that made Tabitha homesick for her mother.

"Pleased to make your acquaintance, sir." Unsure whether to curtsy or offer her hand, Tabitha did both.

Arjon brought her hand to his lips. "Where did a clod like Colin find such a beauteous Amazon?"

Before Tabitha could reply, Colin said, "I found her in Roger's dungeon. Imprisoned without cause just as I was."

Tabitha shot him a glance, wondering why he didn't warn his friend that he believed her to be a common criminal. His amber eyes were unreadable.

"Has anyone ever told you what delectable teeth you have?" Arjon asked, showering moist kisses from her knuckles to her wrist.

"All the better to bite you with," she retorted, retrieving her hand and wiping it on her pajama bottoms.

He arched a devilish eyebrow. "An intriguing possibility. Later perhaps?"

The seductive sparkle in the Norman knight's sherry-brown eyes might have been more persuasive if he didn't sound like Pepe Le Pew. Tabitha laughed, charmed despite his incorrigible flirting.

Colin's scowl had returned in full force. "If you're done drooling on the lady, Arjon, I had hoped to make Castle Raven by nightfall."

The sparkle fled his friend's eyes. "I was on my way there to prey upon your hospitality when Cuthbert sent word that you'd been taken. I went charging to your rescue, but deduced you'd escaped when I found the forest crawling with Brisbane's men." His brow crumpled in a puzzled frown. "I feared I was done for, but at dawn, a herald blew a signal and the rats went scurrying back to their master, every last one of them."

Colin gazed in what Tabitha assumed was the general direction of England, squinting against the wind. "Roger probably just crawled back into his castle to lick his wounds. He always had a tendency to sulk when he'd been trounced. He'll rally in a sennight or two." Despite his confident words, Colin appeared troubled by Brisbane's inexplicable retreat. He shook off his apprehension and clapped Arjon on the shoulder. "So you were rushing to rescue me, eh? You should guard your reputation with more care. 'Twould bode ill for your purse if word got around that you were risking your neck for free."

Arjon responded with a somber smile. "For you, my friend, I would risk all." His smile brightened as he turned it on Tabitha. "I owe my life to this man. He dove sword first into a horde of slavering infidels to liberate me from their clutches. You should have seen him—roaring like a lion, his sword flashing in the sun like a Berserker's blade. 'Twas a sight to drive the pagans to their knees."

Colin rolled his eyes skyward. "Pay him no heed, my lady. Arjon tends to exaggerate my battle conquests almost as much as he exaggerates his romantic ones."

Tabitha was torn between being impressed by Colin's valor and shaken by yet another reminder of how casually he risked his life. "Perhaps Sir Colin is simply suffering from a martyr complex," she said coolly.

Arjon frowned. "A martyr's what?"

"A martyr complex. Some people who are plagued by feelings of guilt or unworthiness feel compelled to thrust themselves into life-threatening situations. They believe they can only prove their worth and redeem themselves by offering up the ultimate self-sacrifice—their life."

Colin's thunderous expression warned her that she had struck a raw nerve.

Arjon grinned. "Beauty *and* wit in a woman. 'Tis a dangerous combination, my friend."

"Aye," Colin said softly, his gaze lingering ever so briefly on her lips. "More dangerous than you know."

The remainder of their journey passed surprisingly smoothly, accompanied by the music of Arjon's chattering. Colin readily traded banter with his friend, but all Tabitha got from him was a few terse grunts. She suspected he regretted confiding in her and was now trying to put distance between them.

It was easy enough since Arjon insisted she ride with him. His dappled gelding didn't have the unpredictable temperament of Colin's stallion. When Tabitha worried aloud that their combined weights might fatigue the horse, Flenoy scoffed that her dainty weight could surely be borne by a dragonfly. His observation earned them both a look of withering scorn from Colin.

Arjon's gallantry, however, did not extend to Lucy. He broke into a fit of violent sneezing each time he looked at the little cat. Tabitha suspected allergies were not the cause. Her Uncle Sven also suffered from a fear of felines. To Colin's chagrin, Lucy seemed perfectly content to bob along on his lap.

As the afternoon waned, the sunlight melted to gloom and mist began to creep out from the fern-shrouded hollows, dampening even Arjon's merry spirits. Colin paused beneath the sheltering boughs of an elm to peel off the cloak and pass it to Arjon.

"How gallant of you," Arjon exclaimed. "I was in dire fear of taking a chill."

Colin glowered at him. " 'Tis not for you, but for the woman."

Lips pursed in a mock pout, Arjon handed Tabitha the cloak. Before she could thank Colin, he drove his horse up a stony crag, seemingly impervious to the tendrils of mist caressing his naked back.

Tabitha drew the cloak up over her hair. The masculine tang of leather and woodsmoke clung to the wool, warming her more than its sturdy weave. But as the spectral twilight deepened, even hugging the cloak tight around her couldn't keep out the damp fog.

By the time they reached the peak of the hill, her teeth were chattering. Colin had dismounted and stood gazing across a sweeping valley. Arjon drew the gelding alongside him, the last of his exuberance seeping out of him on a low whistle.

Needing to stretch her aching legs, Tabitha slid off the horse and squinted through the mist, picking out the shape of a blackened ruin on the opposite cliff. Perhaps Colin had given up all hope of reaching his castle by nightfall and decided they should seek shelter, however dubious, in that charred crypt.

When neither man showed any sign of breaking the pensive silence, she touched Colin's shoulder. "Where are we?"

"Home," he whispered hoarsely.

astle Raven had been aptly named. The towering fortress perched on top of the jagged bluff like the nest of some mythical bird. Although it was twice as imposing in size, it looked nothing like the Disney palace Tabitha had envisioned. But then again, Sleeping Beauty's dainty abode had never suffered Brisbane's vengeful wrath. Its crenellated ramparts had never been shattered by massive rocks hurled from a catapult. Its delicate walls had never been licked by flame, nor had its iron-banded door ever splintered beneath the relentless blows of a battering ram.

As they rode through the gates of the meandering wall that encompassed both village and castle, Colin's eyes mirrored the desolation surrounding them. Tabitha wondered how many times he must have dreamed of returning to this place in the past six years. He had probably expected to be welcomed by a flourish of trumpets and the delighted cries of his family, not the wind wailing a lament through the broken stone. She shivered at the melancholy sound, reminded of how very far she was from her own home and family.

Perversely enough, the mist had disappeared while they crossed the valley, blown on its journey by stubborn gusts that scattered the clouds and tinted the sky with a mocking hint of sunset. The ruins of several wattle and daub huts huddled in the shadow of the wall that had failed to protect them. Their thatched roofs had been scorched bald by flaming arrows, their timbers cracked and battered. Nothing stirred in their wreckage.

"They've gone," Colin said bluntly. "Nor can I blame them. There was naught left for them here. No shelter. No food. No laird. Only death." His gaze swept the barren courtyard, lingering on the fresh graves that scarred the trampled grass. Tabitha wondered if one of them belonged to his father. His jaw hardened. "Roger didn't even value the castle enough to seize it for his own. He simply wanted to destroy it because it was mine."

"How could your God let such a thing happen?" Tabitha asked softly.

" 'Twas the Church that was pledged to protect my property. Why should I blame God for the greed of a handful of priests who would prefer to grow fat on Roger's bribes than fulfill their vows?"

"Let's take our leave of this accursed place," Arjon suggested, his nervous gaze darting over the carnage. "I know many a nobleman who would be willing to pay handsomely for a sword as bold as yours. We'll have great adventures and bed scores of comely wenches—" He grunted in pain as Tabitha involuntarily dug her fingernails into his shoulder.

"Sorry," she mumbled. "I thought I was falling."

Leaving Lucy perched on his saddle, Colin slipped off the stallion and picked his way over the rubble. Arjon withdrew their horse to a respectful distance, allowing his friend to make peace with his past.

When Colin hesitated, frozen in a posture of waiting stillness that was almost painful to watch, Tabitha wondered if he was seeing the castle as it must have been before he went crusading—a bustling, thriving community, ringing with laughter and song.

From the corner of her eye, she caught a flicker of movement. If Arjon hadn't tensed, she might have thought she'd imagined it. But the flicker materialized into a tall, gaunt woman emerging from beneath a collapsed timber. A hollow-eyed child clung to her skirts.

The woman's boldness seemed to act as a catalyst. Tabitha held her breath as other shadowy figures came creeping out from the ruins. Two. Three. Five. Ten. Sixteen. Thirty. A small army of women, children, and old men, dressed in rags, yet armored in pride, bowed but not beaten. At first Tabitha thought all the children were girls, but squinting revealed that many of them were boys. Hard-eyed, long-haired boys teetering on the brink of manhood, young enough to have been spared death, but not the devastation of its aftermath.

They were all so riveted by Colin's abrupt appearance that they didn't even seem to see Arjon's horse standing in the shadow of the wall.

Colin stood deathly still as they drew near to him, as if he feared any sudden movement might send them scurrying back to their burrows.

The first woman stopped directly in front of him. Her little girl hung back, eyeing Colin with disturbing apathy.

"Is he a ghost?" a plump woman whispered.

"Don't be a dunce, Iselda," the tall woman replied, her tart voice warning that she had little tolerance for nonsense. "Of course, he's a ghost."

An elderly woman puffing on a crude pipe nodded sagely, her chin whiskers bobbing. "Magwyn's right. Chauncey saw Lord Colin taken with his own eyes.

Brisbane wouldn't have been fool enough to let him live."

A rabbit-eyed young woman with white-blond hair wrung her pale hands. "But why has he returned? Perhaps he is an angel sent to warn us of some dire misfortune about to befall us."

Magwyn's laughter was bitter enough to make Tabitha flinch. "If so, his warnin' comes a wee bit late. You would think one of God's own would be more vigilant in his duties."

"Cease your blasphemin', child," chided the elderly woman. "We should pray and seek God's counsel in determinin' the purpose o' this heavenly visitation."

As the old woman knelt, her companions dropped obediently to their knees. The woman they called Magwyn finally followed suit, although her shoulders remained rigid and her head was the last to bow.

But it was Magwyn Colin reached toward, Magwyn's chin he cupped gently in his hand, urging her to lift her head and meet his eyes. She gazed up at him in stunned bewilderment, covering his hand with her own as if to assure herself it was real.

"You're no ghost," she blurted out.

Magwyn's exclamation caused her companions to jerk up their own heads and gape at their laird.

"No, I'm not," he assured them. "Despite Brisbane's earnest strivings to make one of me."

Tears tumbled down the woman's cheeks as she bowed her head and brought Colin's hand to her lips. "He's alive! Praise God, our laird is alive!"

"Arise, Magwyn." He drew her to her feet with the hand she continued to clutch. His voice was gentle, but his face was as hard as Tabitha had ever seen it. "You may kneel to God whenever you like, but as long as I'm laird of Ravenshaw, you'll never again bend your knee to any man."

The women, children, and old men enveloped him in a flurry of embraces, their excited chatter punctuated by cries of "Lord Colin is alive!" and "He's no angel!"

"*I* could have told you that," Arjon called out, sending his gelding prancing into their midst.

"Sir Arjon! Why, look, 'tis Sir Arjon!" they exclaimed to one another, welcoming him into their celebration with eager hands and open arms.

"Hide your hearts," Magwyn warned, tossing him a laughing kiss. "Or this Norman rascal will make off with them."

The rabbit-eyed blonde shot Tabitha a sullen glance. "Looks like he's already made off with hers."

Tabitha was brimming with joy on their behalf, but as every villager in the courtyard craned their necks to gape at her, she could feel her features stiffening into an expressionless mask. She felt like she was back in high school, where her painful shyness had so frequently been mistaken for disdain.

"Who's your woman, Sir Arjon?" Magwyn asked, her smile curious, but not unkind.

"I'm n-not—" Tabitha began, blushing furiously.

Before she could stammer to a finish, Colin seized her hand, dragging her off the horse and into his arms.

He slanted her a glance, his eyes sparkling with an enigmatic blend of amusement and warning. "She's not Sir Arjon's woman. She's mine."

Tabitha was still fuming over Colin's claim that night as she feasted beneath a Tiffany showcase of glittering stars. The glare of city lights had blinded her for so long that she'd forgotten how dazzling a summer night could be. The stars dangled above the valley like plump teardrop diamonds, inviting the most daring of dreamers to pluck one from its black velvet cradle. But Tabitha knew that if she was foolish enough to stretch out her hand, they would twinkle their way right out of her reach.

"Partridge, my lady?"

Before Tabitha could decline, the server plopped a roasted bird on the hunk of brown bread that rested in front of her. She gave the thing a tentative poke. She was starving, but prior to tonight, her only acquaintance with partridges had been watching *The Partridge Family* on Nick at Nite.

She glanced around, looking for her fork. The withered gnome of a man to her left had picked up his entire bird and was tearing off gouts of juicy flesh with his rotting teeth. Grease trickled down his chin.

Tabitha shuddered and leaned over to peer beneath the table, thinking her fork might have fallen in all the confusion. Lucy, however, had no patience for such niceties. While her attention was diverted, the kitten pounced on the partridge and dragged it into the grass. Tabitha's stomach growled in protest as she watched the cat devour her supper.

Sighing, she tore off a chunk of the stale bread and popped it into her mouth. It seemed she wasn't the only one fascinated by Lucy's insatiable appetite. What Tabitha had mistaken for a bundle of rags turned out to be a child huddled beneath a nearby table, her wary eyes nearly eclipsed by strands of lank blond hair. Eager for company, Tabitha offered the little girl an encouraging smile. She ducked back into the shadows as if Tabitha had snarled at her.

A chipped mug appeared at her elbow. "Mead, my lady?"

Tabitha turned to say "Thank you" but her invisible benefactor was already gone.

Colin's arrogant boast seemed to have conferred upon her a status no less than royalty. She'd been seated at the head table and was now being offered the choicest morsels of wild game with a deference that both amused and alarmed her. The acerbic Magwyn had even provided her with a gown and a ribbon to bind back her shaggy hair.

Although Tabitha had been happy to shed her ragged pajamas, she'd always preferred trousers to dresses. She ran a hand over her naked calf, regretting that she hadn't had the foresight to wish for a disposable razor before surrendering the amulet to Colin. The gown's flowing skirts made her feel almost absurdly feminine. And vulnerable. Especially since she'd discarded her cotton panties before realizing she wouldn't be offered a fresh pair.

She had at least remembered to slip her glasses out of her pajamas before Magwyn had made off with them. She patted her skirt pocket, comforted by their familiar contours. Until she could coax Colin into returning the amulet, they were all she had left of home.

She took a sip of the mead, grimacing at its cloying sweetness. The exalted Laird of Ravenshaw had yet to make an appearance.

A freckled boy thin enough to be an understudy from the cast of *Oliver!* loomed over her. "Hotchpotch, my lady?"

"Yes, please, thank you very much." Tabitha feared it might be unwise to turn down any offer of food, however ridiculous. Besides, the meaty aroma wafting from the iron pot tucked beneath his arm made her mouth water.

The boy hesitated, steaming ladle in hand, and stared

at the table in dismay. "Why have you eaten your trencher?"

She glanced down to discover a pile of crumbs where her bread had been. "Because I was hungry."

"But where am I to put your stew?"

She blushed, realizing she had just committed the unpardonable faux pas of eating her plate. "Never mind. I'm not hungry anymore."

The boy went off, shaking his head and muttering under his breath. Tabitha rested her chin on her hand, thinking this wasn't much different from those intolerable banquets her father hosted for his board of directors every Christmas. She always managed to say the wrong thing, offend the wealthiest stockholder, or use the incorrect fork. At least she didn't have to worry about *that* here.

Two strapping boys armed with sticks raced around the table. Their mock swordplay earned them approving cheers from the other boys and laughter from their mothers. A herd of toddlers tumbled and cavorted around a crackling bonfire. Earthenware pitchers of ale and mead flowed freely along the lengths of all seven tables, passed from hand to hand with affectionate nudges and ribald jokes. The food was plain, but plentiful, and shared by all.

Their unrestrained merriment baffled Tabitha. She'd been known to brood for weeks because a computer virus wiped out a day's worth of programming. These women had lost everything—their homes, their husbands, their daughters' innocence, yet they celebrated their laird's return without a hint of self-pity.

A boy with a thatch of dark hair began to pluck out a melody on a delicate handheld harp. Urged on by her beaming mother, a little girl pressed a carved pipe to her rosebud lips. The mingled voices of string and reed rose into the night with piercing sweetness. In the twenty-first century, the song would have been classified as New Age, but its melody was as timeless as the stars themselves. To Tabitha, it echoed like a druid's hymn or the seductive whisper of a fairy king coaxing a mortal woman into his bed.

Shaking off the whimsical thought, she pushed aside the mead. The honeyed brew must be going to her head.

A small boy knelt to drum on a calfskin stretched taut across an iron cauldron. But as a stranger garbed all in black came sauntering down the hill from the village, Tabitha could no longer distinguish the primitive drum beat from the pounding of her heart.

CHAPTER 12

T abitha understood for the first time just how betrayed poor Beauty must have felt when her rumpled Beast turned into a prince.

Colin still looked nothing like Prince Charming, but with a pair of dark hose clinging to his muscular calves and his broad shoulders draped in an ebony tunic emblazoned with a silver raven, he could have easily passed as a distant cousin of the Prince of Darkness. He'd even shaved his scruffy beard.

The Scot-Killer's dagger was tucked in his belt like a badge of honor. He'd braided the hair around his face into two plaits, then drawn the plaits back in a leather thong, using them to harness the rest of the unruly mass. Tabitha felt a ridiculous urge to rush over and tug loose a few strands. To rumple his tunic and dab a smudge of dirt on his nose.

As she watched him weave among his people to greet old friends and settle petty disputes, offering a clap on the shoulder here and an encouraging smile there, she drained the mug of mead without realizing it. She was beginning to understand why he exuded such raw confidence, even in the face of Brisbane's treachery. In this isolated kingdom of Castle Raven, he was both lord and law. Although it had taken his father's untimely death to bring him to the throne, he sat it with the assurance of a man who'd been born to the privilege. Would she possess half as much grace, she wondered, if forced to step into her father's shoes at Lennox Enterprises?

He paused to bestow a kiss on the gnarled hand of a blushing crone. As he straightened, their eyes met over the old woman's fuzzy head. A mocking hint of a dimple touched one cheek. She sensed that he presented far more danger to her in this place, especially if he decided to make good his claim on her.

Her own words came back to haunt her—*Or you'll what? Carry me off to your castle and ravish me?* The taunt didn't seem quite as witty as it had when she'd mistaken him for George Ruggles from Accounting. Or when she was still wearing underwear.

Colin's path veered in her direction. If he hadn't taken the amulet from her, she would have wished herself invisible.

"My lady," he murmured, sliding onto the bench opposite her.

"Mr. Ravenshaw," she replied stiffly, refusing to give him the satisfaction of addressing him as "My lord."

"Have you been enjoying the festivities?"

She couldn't have said why his bemused smile put her on the defensive. "I haven't been stealing the silver, if that's what you're asking. Especially since there doesn't seem to be any to steal."

"Is that why you're in such a prickly temper?"

"I am not . . . !" Her indignant protest sputtered to a halt as she realized that in fact she was. "Well, you'd be in a prickly temper, too, if the cat gobbled up your partridge, you ate your own plate, and you had to wear this ridiculous dress."

His gaze dropped briefly to the embroidered bodice.

"Magwyn was married in that gown. Iselda told me she risked her life to drag it from the flames when Roger's men torched her cottage."

Colin spoke without a hint of reproach, but Tabitha felt shame coil deep within her. She had a walk-in closet full of designer clothes at home, but none stitched with such care or offered with such generosity of spirit.

Before she could apologize for being an ungrateful brat, Arjon and his blond admirer stumbled over to join them, reeking of ale and breathless with laughter. The woman had sheathed her claws since deciding Tabitha was no rival for Arjon's fickle affections. She draped herself over the knight's lap and twined one possessive arm around his neck to toy with the curls at his nape.

"Have you been reviewing the troops?" Arjon asked, bypassing a mug to gulp directly from a pitcher of mead.

Colin nodded ruefully. "It seems the lads of Ravenshaw have organized themselves into a fighting force to be reckoned with. If I hadn't returned, they planned to march on Brisbane's castle and avenge their laird's honor."

Arjon hefted the flagon. "To the lads! The future of Ravenshaw!"

As one of the long-haired, wild-eyed boys hurtled himself over a table to tackle another, Colin made a sound that was half laugh, half groan. "I'd as soon arm the women with pitchforks and rocks than lead that band of ruffians into battle. I've little choice but to appeal to the MacDuff for men and supplies."

A weighted look passed between the two men.

"Who's the MacDuff?" Tabitha asked.

When Colin busied himself with pouring a mug of mead instead of answering, Arjon said, "MacDuff is the laird who fostered Colin when he was but a lowly page. His lands border Ravenshaw to the north."

"Will he help you?" she asked, addressing Colin directly.

"Aye," he said shortly. "He's been like a second father to me."

He didn't seem inclined to elaborate and before she could press, a flock of merrymakers led by Magwyn descended on them. Ignoring Arjon's reproachful sneeze, Tabitha plopped Lucy into her lap to keep the cat from being trampled. A ring of curious children soon surrounded her.

"Will the wee kitty bite?" asked one earnest little fellow.

"Not if you're very gentle with her."

"Does she eat mouses?" a freckled girl asked, her green eyes shining with delight as Tabitha allowed her to stroke the kitten's soft fur.

"I don't know. She's never seen a real mouse."

As the children clucked and cooed over the preening cat, Tabitha became aware of another child lurking on the fringes of the torchlight. The same ragged little girl who had huddled beneath the table. Her enormous eyes didn't seem quite so hollow when touched by yearning.

Tabitha cupped the kitten in her hands and held it out. "Would you like to pet her, sweetheart?"

The little girl jumped guiltily, then darted away, melting into the shadows like a wraith.

As Tabitha entrusted the kitten to the little boy and his delighted cohorts, Magwyn shook her head sadly. "Me Jenny ain't spoke a word since Brisbane's men took after her. She won't bathe or let me comb her hair. She's turned skittish like a wild creature, always runnin' away before I can lay hands on her." A wistful smile touched the woman's lips, giving her gaunt face a raw-boned beauty. "You should have seen her before—always chatterin', beggin' me to tuck some flowers in her bonny curls or stitch her a new dress."

Tabitha gazed into the darkness where the child had disappeared. She couldn't have been any more than eight or nine years old. "How do you bear it?"

Jenny's mother shrugged, the gesture more weary than bitter. "Women have always been the spoils of battle."

"But Jenny isn't a woman. She's a child."

Magwyn rose from the bench, slanting Tabitha a pitying glance. "Not no more, she ain't."

Tabitha's throat tightened with rage at the terrible injustice that had been done to the little girl. She shifted her burning gaze to Colin, realizing that despite his casual posture, he had been eavesdropping on the entire exchange.

"Is that what you believe?" she snapped, relieved to have found a masculine target for her wrath. "That women are nothing more than the spoils of battle? You just returned from six years of war, didn't you? Did you consider raping your enemies' wives and daughters a regrettable, if agreeable, duty?"

"No. But I did find it my regrettable, if agreeable, duty to execute any man who did."

The tension seeped out of her. She should have known Colin would appoint himself the avenging angel of the Holy Crusade. Before she could make amends, he turned his face away in a cool rebuff. She could almost believe she'd insulted him.

A cheer went up from the opposite table. "To Auld Nana!"

"Auld Nana!" the others shouted, lifting their mugs in tribute.

"Nana," Colin echoed softly, following suit.

"Who's Nana?" Tabitha whispered to Arjon.

"Auld Nana was Colin's nurse and his father's nurse before him."

She nearly giggled aloud at the thought of a fierce warrior like Colin having a "Nana."

"You would've been proud of her, master," said Iselda, the plump matron who had first thought Colin a ghost. "Nana fought like a Valkyrie to protect your stepmother's babe after our dear lady perished. She knew what that child meant to her, comin' so late in life after so many years of strugglin' to give your father a bairn. When it appeared the battle was lost, Nana carried the child up to the chapel and barricaded the door against those murderin' English." Her righteous zeal faded on a sigh. "She had no way of knowin' the siege would go on for more than a fortnight after that. No one saw either of them alive again."

"I trust you gave her dear old bones a proper burial," Colin said.

The revelry lapsed into an uncomfortable silence, broken only by the distant squeal of a frolicking child. Arjon arched an inquisitive eyebrow at the amorous blonde, but she avoided his gaze by burying her face in the crook of his neck.

"Iselda?" Colin prodded. "You did lay my sister's bones in the family crypt, did you not?"

The woman's broad face flushed. She twisted her skirt between her florid hands. "Well, me laird, not exactly . . ."

It was Magwyn who came charging to her rescue. "We ain't been back. When Brisbane called off his dogs, we dragged out all the food stores from the cellars and all the valuables we could carry from the solar—trunks filled with clothes like those you're wearin', silver plate, salt, spices—but not one of us has set foot in the castle since."

Colin rose to his feet. "Why in God's name not? Your cottages aren't fit for habitation. Did you fear I would punish you for seeking shelter in the castle?"

" 'Tweren't you we was afraid of." She signed a cross on her breast as her gaze drifted to the ruin brooding against the night sky. " 'Twas whatever dwells within those walls."

"Restless spirits, me laird," Iselda blurted out. "Flickering lights in the black o' night. A murdered babe wailin' for vengeance. We've all heard it, we have, every last one of us."

Iselda's confession was greeted by frightened murmurs and timid nods. As Tabitha followed Colin's haunted gaze to the tower at the peak of the castle, she shivered despite herself.

She half expected the fearless warrior to mock their alarm, but instead he nodded gravely. " 'Tis pleasant enough to camp beneath the stars in summer, but it won't do for winter. I'll fetch a priest from MacDuff to sprinkle holy water around the tower and pray for the unshriven souls of the dead."

The women nodded to one another, looking pleased if not precisely comforted by his promise. Their murmurs were interrupted by a bearded old man who came trotting up to bob an awkward bow in Colin's direction.

"Sir . . . ?" The man scratched his bald pate, as if suddenly remembering his master's recent promotion. "Um, me laird, if you and your lady are ready to retire, your pavilion is prepared."

"Well done, Ewan. My lady?" Colin extended his hand, his eyes glittering with unmistakable challenge.

Tabitha wondered what would happen if she refused

his invitation. But then she became aware of the shy, sidelong glances directed their way. Arjon winked at her before bestowing a wet, openmouthed kiss on his clinging companion. Tabitha's cheeks heated, but she discovered she couldn't stand to embarrass Colin in front of his people.

"My laird," she murmured, deliberately mocking his burr as she trusted her hand to his. "'Twould be an honor."

Tabitha had always considered herself as big boned as an ox, but Colin's broad palm swallowed her hand. She'd meant to pull her hand away as soon as they were out of sight of the others, but as they climbed the steep hill, he laced his fingers through hers, making her his reluctant captive.

"Do you believe in ghosts?" he asked as the shadow of the castle darkened their path.

She edged nearer to him. "No. Do you?"

"I once did. But I fear 'twas naught but wishful thinking. My stepmother always said that the dead punish us with their absence, not their presence."

"You loved her, didn't you?"

Affection warmed his gruff voice. "Aye. My own mother died young. Blythe was the only mother I ever knew."

"And your father?"

"He loved her, too."

Tabitha wondered if Colin had deliberately misunderstood her question, but as a shaft of moonlight struck his shuttered face, she didn't dare ask. A welcoming oasis of light loomed out of the darkness. Her steps faltered.

Colin tugged her gently, but inexorably, toward the

round pavilion perched at the edge of the wood. As Tabitha ducked into the tent's interior, her uneasiness bloomed into full-blown apprehension.

Ewan had made every effort to see to his laird's comfort. The torchlight's lambent glow bathed a nest of colorful pillows and a small table occupied by a narrow pitcher and two silver chalices. Thanks to Colin's earlier boast, his man must have assumed they would be sharing the narrow cot draped with furs. The sandalwood perfume of incense wafted from a tiny brass burner, making Tabitha nervously wonder what other exotic tastes Colin might have acquired in the Holy Land.

The knight seemed infuriatingly at ease in this den of sensual iniquity. After sealing the tent's flap behind them, he poured himself a chalice of something burgundy and reclined on the pillows like a smug sultan. Tabitha stood stiffly by the table, biting her bottom lip to keep from wishing for an iron chastity belt. Without a key.

"What ails you, lass? Lucy got your tongue?" When that dig failed to provoke a response, he sighed. "Are you still sulking because I took your precious bauble into my care?" Setting aside the chalice, he canted his arms behind his head like a *Playgirl* centerfold and cocked an eyebrow at her. "Did it never occur to you that there might be a way for you to earn it back?"

Tabitha gasped. He was actually trying to coerce her into sex.

Unable to bear the sight of his mischievous grin, she spun around and gripped the edge of the table.

"You drive a steep bargain, *sir*," she said softly, her voice laced with bitterness.

" 'Tis your own fault for enticing me, my lady. What you bestowed upon me in the cavern must surely be only a sample of your talents."

Tabitha swung around to face him. She didn't know what outraged her more—that he blamed her for inciting his crude lust as men had been doing to innocent women for centuries or that he'd spoiled her memory of the tender kiss they'd shared.

She dug her fingernails into her palms. "I hate to disappoint you, but my 'talents' don't extend much beyond what you've already 'sampled.'"

He took a sip of the wine. "Oh, come now. You must have learned something while you were traveling with the mummers. Another trick like the one you showed me or a song perhaps?" His expression was almost boyishly hopeful.

"A song?"

"Aye. A *chanson de geste* or a ballad of courtly love."

"Courtney Love?" she echoed, even more baffled by his mention of the infamous alternative rock singer who'd dominated the pages of the *Global Inquirer* at the end of the twentieth century.

"*Courtly* love. The tragic tale of a noble knight pining for the unrequited affection of his lady."

Tabitha sank down on the edge of the cot. Colin didn't want her. He wanted a lullaby. He'd been more impressed by her poorly executed magic trick than her kiss. Well, that was a relief . . . wasn't it?

She hummed a few experimental notes of the song welling up from her subconscious.

Colin sat up straight, his eagerness betraying what it must be like to live in a time without video or audio discs, a time when even books were a rare and costly luxury. "What melody is that? I've not heard it before."

She hummed another bar. "'Camelot,'" she admitted, almost as startled by the realization as he was.

Although Tabitha had always hated the maudlin musical, her mother had forced her to sit through endless revivals. Against her will, her methodical mind had memorized the entire score, every sentimental note. With all this talk of knights and castles and holy quests, it was hardly surprising Lerner and Loewe's winsome melody was the first to come to mind.

"Sing some more," Colin commanded, settling back on the pillows and waving a regal hand at her.

Amused by his exalted manner, Tabitha complied, her airy soprano pleasant, if not spectacular. Each time she stopped, Colin would order or cajole her to continue, relenting only long enough to press a chalice into her hand so she could moisten her throat with wine.

She was secretly flattered by the attention. Although he'd been stripped of his chain mail at Brisbane's castle, she couldn't shake the feeling that this was the first time she'd actually seen the knight without his armor.

He nodded sagely at Lancelot's boastful declarations in "C'est Moi" and chuckled at the naughty puns in "The Lusty Month of May." His expression became strangely pensive during the wistful strains of "If Ever I Would Leave You" and he visibly tensed when Guenevere faced death at the stake as punishment for her adulterous affair.

By the time Tabitha sang the final reprise, her voice was hoarse with strain. The last tremulous note seemed to hang in the air long after it was done. She glanced over to find Colin sprawled on the pillows, his dark lashes flush against his cheeks, his breathing hushed and even. Lucy had slipped into the tent while Tabitha sang and curled up at his side. His hand was cupped protectively around the little cat.

"Ever the lady's champion," Tabitha murmured, caught off guard by a surge of wry tenderness.

She knelt at his side, planning to throw one of the furs over him. But instead her hand crept toward his face, freeing a few rebellious tendrils from his plaits. He didn't stir at her touch.

Hearing the ancient legend through Colin's ears had been like hearing it for the first time. Although she pitied Lancelot and Guenevere, torn between their devotion to their king and their passion for each other, it was Arthur who stirred her heart. Arthur with his eternal innocence, his unwavering commitment to an impossible dream, his rare ability to cherish the moment, even knowing it could never last.

As she threaded her fingers through the midnight silk of Colin's hair, she couldn't help but wonder how he had lost his innocence and what dreams he'd been forced to sacrifice along the way.

A baby's plaintive wail froze Tabitha's hand. Gooseflesh broke out on her arms. Holding her breath, she tilted her head in the direction of the castle. But the unearthly cry had been hushed as abruptly as it had sounded. It did not come again.

After several minutes of eyeing the narrow cot and waiting in vain for her heart to slow to its normal rhythm, Tabitha dragged the furs onto the floor and curled up at Colin's side with Lucy nestled between them.

CHAPTER 13

Colin awoke the next morning to find the woman gone and the sheath on his belt empty. He sprang to his feet, his outraged gaze sweeping the deserted tent. "That miserable little thief!"

He examined the hem of his tunic to find the emerald necklace still nestled within its secret pocket. Apparently, Tabitha's devotion to the stolen trinket hadn't been sufficient to keep her by his side. She had sung for him as sweetly as any troubadour, luring him into a deep and dreamless sleep, then fled.

The sight of the pelts lying in a rumpled nest on the floor did little to improve his temper. He snatched them up in his fist, bringing them to his nose. The fur was warm, her scent still fresh.

He hurled them to the floor, determined to hunt her down before she reached the sanctuary of some shepherd's croft or kirk. He wasn't sure what he'd do with her once he caught her, but several diabolical possibilities were already circling through his mind.

He ducked out of the tent, trusting that Ewan would have tethered his stallion within easy reach. The beast laid his ears back and pranced in place, sensing his master's agitation. He should be thankful the wench hadn't stolen his horse as well. He felt naked without a blade, but he would have felt doubly so deprived of his mount.

He had the horse untethered and one foot in the stirrups when he heard it. He cocked his head to the side, frowning in bewilderment. At first he thought it only a haunting echo from the previous night, but then it came again—a faint ribbon of melody unfurling on the morning breeze. Leaving the horse with a reassuring pat, he stole through the underbrush, drawn by that elusive thread as if it were a siren's song and he a spellbound sailor rushing willingly to his doom.

Brushing aside a pine bough, he emerged from the shadowy copse, seeking the source of that beguiling melody.

A shaft of morning sunlight struck him between the eyes like a mace. He blinked to restore his vision, then wished he hadn't as the sight before him wrung a bellow of mingled rage and horror from his throat.

Tabitha had never dreamed that warbling a mocking rendition of "Someday My Prince Will Come" would bring an enraged Scotsman charging to her side. Her first instinct was to cover her breasts with her hands. But that was before she remembered she was fully clothed. She'd simply looped the gown's cumbersome skirts through her legs to reveal a pale calf lathered with the coarse brown soap she'd borrowed from Magwyn that morning. A thin trickle of blood was inching through the soapy froth toward her ankle.

She might have run from Colin's furious approach if she hadn't been standing in the middle of a pool, the hilt of Colin's dagger in her hand, one foot braced on the flat rock where Lucy sat grooming her furry little tummy.

He charged right into the pool, sending a cascade of waves splashing over the rock. Lucy jumped up and shook herself, shooting him a chiding glance.

He spread his arms in a desperate appeal. "Good God, woman, have you pudding for brains? What in the holy name of St. Andrew do you think you're doing?"

Tabitha glanced down at her exposed calf, then at the dagger in her hand. "I'm shaving my legs."

"Och!" Colin's wail couldn't have been any more heartrending had she plunged the dagger into his heart. He shook his head, looking even more reproachful than the bedraggled kitten. "Have you no respect for a man's blade, lass? I suppose I'll wake tomorrow to find you pruning your toenails with it or chopping onions for haggis. 'Tis a pity Brisbane took my best sword. You could have used it to plow a field or dig for grubworms."

Realization was beginning to dawn. Although she'd never been exposed to the consequences of such intimacy, Tabitha had read on-line articles in *Cosmo* about husbands throwing tantrums when their wives borrowed their face razors to shave their legs. It was rather reassuring to learn that men had evolved so little in seven centuries. She might have laughed had Colin's expression not been so appalled.

She decided to test her theory. "Didn't you use this very dagger to shave your face yesterday?"

He stroked the morning stubble on his jaw indignantly. "Aye, but I'll not use it again. You've ruined the blade. 'Twould probably slip and cut my throat."

Tabitha rolled her eyes. "Just as I thought." She swished the dagger in the water before handing it to him, hilt first. "I'm sorry. I should have asked before I borrowed it."

He tested the blade against his thumb, glowering at her when it failed to prick his skin.

She wagged a finger at him. "Don't glare at me like that. Your dagger did more damage to me than I did to it."

He looked concerned. "Are you wounded, lass?"

She splashed away the soap, wincing at the sting of the icy water. "The way you came charging out of the woods at me, I'm lucky I didn't amputate my foot. I thought you were a bear."

She'd barely taken one limping step toward shore before he tucked the dagger into his belt and swept her up in his arms. Tabitha gasped, afraid he was going to drop her. But he easily handled her gangly form, reminding her that there were far more differences between men and women than simply height. Such as the well-defined slabs of muscle in Colin's shoulders, back, and arms.

As he lowered her to a weathered tree stump, she untangled her arms from his neck, annoyed at the feeling she was clinging to him like a child. "There's no need to call 911. I just nicked myself shaving. If I only had a pinch of toilet paper to stick on it . . ."

He dropped to one knee and dabbed at the shallow cut with a clump of moss. Even after the bleeding was stanched, his warm palm lingered against her calf.

"Why would you do such a thing?" he asked softly as he studied the results of her handiwork.

Tabitha felt nearly as bewildered as he sounded. "I told you I was sorry. I shouldn't have borrowed your dagger without consulting—"

" 'Tis not the dagger that troubles me." His hand began a slow ascent, his inquisitive touch raising goose-flesh on her freshly denuded skin. " 'Tis your legs. Why would you wish to shear the down from them?"

She was reluctant to admit that she'd always been

somewhat vain about her legs. Even though she kept them sheathed in Dockers or tweed most of the time, they were still her best feature—long, supple, and slender. They'd never seemed longer than they did at that moment, with Colin stroking his way toward her thigh with mesmerizing thoroughness. She almost came off the rock when his callused fingertips grazed the sensitive skin behind her knee.

"It's a custom where I'm from," she blurted out. "All the women do it."

His fingers tarried at her knee, but his gaze rose to her face, making her wonder if he had felt the violent throb of her pulse.

"There were women in Egypt," he said, his voice disarmingly husky, "who honored such customs. Most of them had migrated to the brothels from the Sultan's harem. Some had been slaves, others cherished wives. They scented the hair on their heads with jasmine, but kept every other inch of their flesh as smooth as silk and oiled with sandalwood so a man would know no hindrance to his touch and a woman no hindrance to her pleasure."

His golden gaze mesmerized her. She tried to draw in a breath, but it stalled in her throat, stymied by the glimpse of sensual decadence his hoarse revelation afforded her. A sensual decadence he couldn't have learned from an X-rated web site or the dog-eared pages of some men's magazine.

She had a vivid vision of Colin sweeping across the desert on his stallion, his white robes billowing behind him, the sun caressing his swarthy skin. He swung down off the horse and ducked into a perfumed bower where a bevy of sultry-eyed *Playboy* centerfolds awaited him on a bed of silk pillows, their flawless skin glistening with oil, their gold bracelets jingling a melodic welcome as they drew him into their embrace.

Disgruntled, she brushed his hand away and jerked down her skirt. "I can assure you, sir, that I didn't use your precious dagger on anything but my legs. I'm sorry if you don't approve."

She launched herself off the stump only to have him seize her by the hand and bring her up short.

He rose to his full height, drawing their lips into dangerous proximity. "I don't approve." He hesitated just long enough for her to bristle anew. "But I like it."

If he'd tempered his confession with a grin or a leer, Tabitha might have been able to come up with a retort. But his somber expression unnerved her. Her Uncle Sven had taught her how to fend off a mugger, not how to deny a battered knight who was gazing at her as if he were a lonely sultan and she were the most beautiful harem girl in all the world.

Her eyes drifted shut, inviting him to take what she was too much of a coward to offer. His lips had barely grazed hers when she remembered she no longer wore the amulet to shield her from catastrophe.

She sprang away from him, horrified to realize she might have been only a kiss away from turning him into a three-toed sloth. Frustration made her lash out. "Telling your people that I'm your woman doesn't make it true. Women aren't possessions to be claimed and bartered."

He raised an eyebrow, reminding her that in this century, women were exactly that. "I meant you no dishonor by offering you my protection."

"You also offered me my necklace for a song. Or has the price risen? What is it now? Your kingdom for a kiss?"

He took a step toward her. "Would you pay, my lady?"

She took an instinctive step backward, terrified that she would.

His lips quirked in a rueful smile. "I thought not. I suppose you'll just have to earn back your treasure by proving yourself worthy of my trust."

"And just how do I do that?" she asked.

"Not by sneaking out of my pavilion at dawn and scaring the bloody hell out of—"

He averted his eyes and blew out a massive sigh, revealing more than he'd intended to. Tabitha suddenly understood his desperate charge through the brush. He had yelled at her the way a parent might yell at a lost child they'd found licking an ice cream cone down at the police station instead of lying on a slab at the city morgue.

He dragged a hand through his sleep-tousled hair. "I didn't mean to bellow at you, lass. If you'll fetch the kitten, I'll make amends by having Ewan draw you a proper bath." He started to turn away, then drew the dagger from his belt and pressed its hilt into her palm. " 'Twould be best if you didn't prowl the woods unarmed. Not with Roger somewhere out there just waiting to pounce."

As he ducked back through the bushes, she shook her head in amazement. No one in New York had probably even noticed her disappearance yet, but Colin had missed her immediately. She started to smile, but her pleasure rapidly dwindled as she imagined him searching just as frantically for her after she had disappeared into the future.

How long would he search before realizing she was gone forever?

• • •

As Tabitha sank chin-deep into the steaming bathwater, she would have forgiven Colin almost anything.

Anything except being so adept at stealing past the defenses she'd spent twenty-three years erecting.

She ducked beneath the water, then rubbed soap into her hair as if to scrub away the disturbing thought. The round wooden tub was much humbler than the sunken marble whirlpool she was used to, but after two days with no bath, it was sheer bliss. Lucy perched on its edge, batting the stray soap bubbles into submission with her tiny paws.

Sunlight dappled the tent walls, dispelling Tabitha's ridiculous fears from the previous night. She'd probably just heard some village woman's infant stirring fretfully in its sleep. Even now, she could hear distant shouts and laughter, but she was confident no one would dare disturb the laird's lady in her bath. The thought made her giggle.

She might have lingered in the bath all morning if the water hadn't begun to cool. She climbed out of the tub, wincing as she finger-combed the tangles from her thick hair. If she could have coaxed Colin out of the amulet at that moment, she wouldn't have wished for anything more dramatic than some cream rinse and a blow dryer.

Her nape began to tingle with unease. It seemed her privacy had been only an illusion. Someone was watching her.

Snatching up one of the rough linen towels Ewan had left, Tabitha whirled around. She was alone. Alone except for the suspicious hump lying beneath the furs on the cot—a hump Tabitha would have sworn wasn't there when she climbed into the tub.

Resisting her first instinct to bash it with something

heavy, Tabitha crept over, lifted a corner of one pelt, and peeped underneath.

An elf peeped back at her.

She dropped the pelt. "Why shouldn't there be an elf?" she muttered. "I've met knights in shining armor and evil barons, even heard baby ghosts. Why should an elf be so inconceivable?"

But after several seconds of pensive thought, her natural skepticism prevailed. She swept back the pelts to find a child huddled on the cot. The upturned nose, green eyes, and tangled snarl of hair didn't belong to any woodland sprite after all, but to Magwyn's daughter Jenny.

Still clutching the towel around her, Tabitha stumbled backward, giving the child ample room to flee. She'd never been particularly comfortable around children, having spent so little time in their company. Even as a little girl, she'd much preferred communicating with her laptop computer.

But Jenny climbed off the cot and crept toward Tabitha, her gaze fastened on something behind her head. Tabitha looked around for something to distract the child, and spotted Lucy still sitting on the rim of the tub.

She scooped up the kitten and held it out. "Did you come to pet the pretty kitty?"

When Jenny hung shyly back, Tabitha rubbed Lucy's downy fur against her own cheek. "There's nothing to be afraid of. Lucy likes little girls."

Jenny stretched out one grubby hand, the gesture tentative, yet trusting. To Tabitha's surprise Jenny reached past the kitten to capture a strand of her damp hair.

Tabitha sank to her knees as Jenny tugged on her hair. It hadn't been Lucy the child had been drawn to but Tabitha's hair! Jenny stroked and patted the thick tendrils, a wistful smile hovering around her lips.

Even when Lucy wiggled out of her grasp and bounded to the floor, Tabitha held herself absolutely still, as afraid the child would flee as she'd been afraid she wouldn't only seconds before. Then Jenny ran to the table and grabbed the dagger Tabitha had left lying so carelessly on its surface.

Tabitha sprang to her feet. "Jenny, no! Put the knife down. It's very sharp."

Jenny nodded with grim satisfaction. She pointed at Tabitha's head, then grabbed a handful of her own waist-length hair and made a mock sawing motion.

Tabitha sank back down to the child's eye level. She might very well be witnessing her first attempt at communication since Brisbane's men had attacked her. But when she realized what the little girl wanted her to do, she said, "Oh, Jenny, you can't want me to cut your hair like mine? What would your mother say?" She captured a stray tendril of the girl's hair, finding a glint of gold buried within the filthy dun. "Your hair is so pretty."

Jenny backed away, giving her head a savage shake. In her eyes, Tabitha caught a glimpse of hatred, not just for the men who had raped her, but for herself.

A tear slipped down Tabitha's cheek. "Oh, God," she whispered. "They told you your hair was pretty, didn't they? The men who hurt you."

Jenny nodded, then fisted her hands in the snarls on each side of her head, tugging until her eyes began to water with pain.

"They held you by your hair while they . . . ?" Tabitha closed her eyes, the image too horrible to bear.

A small hand brushed her wet cheek, coaxing her to open them. Jenny blinked at her with her solemn green eyes, as if to comfort her.

If Tabitha had been wearing the amulet at that moment, she would have wished to restore this child's faith in her own worth. She would have given Jenny her voice back and somehow made her believe that she wasn't at fault for the terrible thing that had happened to her.

But Tabitha had only one gift to give. She climbed to her feet and briskly dashed her tears away. "You can't expect me to cut such a dirty mop of hair, little miss. If you want your way, you'll have to let me wash it first."

Jenny eyed the tub with sullen suspicion, but did no more than drag her feet in protest when Tabitha placed a firm hand on her shoulder and steered her toward it.

When Magwyn saw what Tabitha had done to her daughter, she fainted dead away.

Bleating like frightened sheep, the other women gathered around their fallen comrade. Iselda dropped to her well-cushioned knees and began fanning her friend with a card of wool.

A tall, scrawny old woman whose wispy top knot made her look like a brittle cotton swab shifted her pipe to the corner of her mouth. "Shorn her like a lamb, haven't ye? Wee lass looks more like a lad."

Magwyn sat up, hearing just enough of that dour pronouncement to set up a keening wail. Tabitha would have clapped her hands over her ears if Jenny hadn't been clinging to one of them, wide-eyed with fascination at the chaos her appearance had provoked.

"Now, Magwyn," Tabitha began in what she hoped was a soothing tone. "You don't understand. Jenny begged me to—"

She hopped backward as Magwyn sprang to her feet, her freckled hands curled into claws. The woman's eyes seemed to spit sparks of green fire. "How dare you take a knife to my daughter's crowning glory? Hasn't she suffered enough shame at the hands of the English?"

Like the most trite of tourists, Tabitha wanted to whine that she was American, for God's sake, not English. But since America hadn't been discovered yet, she doubted it would matter. The women were milling around as if hoping to witness a full-fledged brawl.

"I was simply trying to help. When Jenny came to me—"

Magwyn's face crumpled, a glimpse of pain coming through her rage. "Came to you, my arse! If she was goin' to come to anyone, don't you think she'd have come to her own mother?"

Ever the peacemaker, Iselda stepped between them. She wisely chose to address Tabitha, the more rational of the two women at the moment. "Surely you can understand Magwyn's dismay, lass. 'Tis only for the most vile of sins that a woman might have her hair chopped off." She ticked them off on her plump fingers. "Thievery, adultery, immodesty, sodomy, whoring, fornica—" She blushed to the roots of her hair as her gaze strayed to Tabitha's blunt bob.

Tabitha stiffened. They probably believed she had committed most of those lewd sins and a few unspeakable others not only with their laird, but with several men before him. The irony almost made her laugh. Almost.

"Council's in session, Magwyn," said the old woman, puffing serenely on her pipe. "You should take yer complaint to the laird."

"Aye, the laird!" echoed one woman.

"Granny Cora's right. He'll know what to do with her," murmured another.

After a moment of tense silence, Magwyn finally nodded. She snatched her daughter's hand out of Tabitha's grip as the women formed an impenetrable cordon, herding the accused before them. Tabitha's confident stride didn't falter until it occurred to her that she had no way of knowing if Colin would take her side or what the consequences would be if he didn't.

CHAPTER 14

Whenthe mob of women came marching down the hill, Colin was on the verge of banging either his head or someone else's against the council table. He welcomed the interruption. Even the shrill cacophony of irate female voices seemed preferable to spending another moment arguing with lads who fancied themselves men and men behaving as if they were lads.

His relief lasted only until he saw Tabitha marching at the head of the mob.

As she approached, Colin rose to his feet, preparing himself to meet some unspoken challenge. Ever since their encounter at the pool, he'd been plagued by images of her silky smooth legs wrapped around his waist.

Despite the proud tilt of her head, or perhaps because of it, he feared Tabitha wasn't the leader of the mob, but the victim of it. As they reached the table, Magwyn gave her a hard shove, confirming his suspicions.

He caught her before she could stumble. "What is the meaning of this?" He addressed the soft-spoken question not to the woman in his arms, but to Magwyn, who was glaring at him with stony disapproval.

She answered him by drawing a child out from behind her skirts and thrusting her forward. "Look! Just look what the wench did to my babe!"

Colin frowned and blinked rapidly, hardly recognizing the feral creature he'd so briefly glimpsed the night before. A shining cap of curls crowned the moppet's head and she was scrubbed so clean and pink she practically glowed.

" 'Tis a vast improvement. I should think you'd be pleased."

"Her hair!" Magwyn wailed. "Look how she butchered my Jenny's beautiful hair!"

Colin sighed and turned Tabitha around to face him, resting his hands lightly on her shoulders. "Did you cut the child's hair?"

She met his gaze boldly. "Yes."

"Why?"

"Because she asked me to."

Magwyn snorted. "I suppose next you'll be claimin' she spoke to you when she's spoken nary a whisper to her very own mother for over a month." Several of the women scoffed in agreement.

"I never claimed she spoke to me. She simply indicated that she wanted her hair cut like mine. Once I started trimming, she decided she wanted it even shorter and I didn't have the heart to deny her."

"Why did she seek such a strange favor?" Colin asked.

Tabitha pressed her lips together, going as mute as Jenny. Despite his frustration, Colin had to admire a woman who could be trusted with secrets. Especially a child's secrets.

Since it seemed he'd glean no more information from Tabitha, he freed her and crooked a finger at Jenny. "Come here, lass."

He did not beg or cajole. He simply commanded. And to everyone's astonishment, the child obeyed.

He squatted down to her eye level, keenly aware that Tabitha was watching him with an unfathomable expression in her gray eyes. "Did you want this lady to cut your hair?"

Jenny tucked her head shyly, then nodded.

"And do you fancy it?"

She nodded again, more violently this time.

"So do I," he confessed, rumpling the soft curls. The matter-of-fact gesture coaxed a shy, gap-toothed smile from the child.

Magwyn gasped. "Why, 'tis the first time I've seen her smile since . . ." As she lifted her eyes from Jenny to Tabitha, her expression shifted from awe to dismay. "It seems I've misjudged you, my lady," she said stiffly. "Can you find it in your heart to forgive me?"

"Consider it done," Tabitha replied. "I really should have asked your permission first."

"A common refrain," Colin murmured in her ear. "Considering you'd still have done exactly as you pleased."

He savored the openly hostile glare she shot him. Before she could fashion a tart retort, the women gathered around her, acting on Magwyn's cue to welcome her back into their fold.

Iselda took her by the arm. "Now that the wee misunderstandin' has been cleared up, you can join us in our weavin', dearie."

"Weaving?" Tabitha echoed.

"Aye," said Granny Cora, tugging on her other arm. "And after the weavin', we'll butcher a nice fat sow for supper and let you pickle the entrails."

"Pickles?" she repeated even more faintly. "I never cared for pickles."

As the women urged Tabitha up the hill, she was no less a captive than she'd been marching down it. She cast Colin a helpless glance over her shoulder. He grinned. What did she expect him to do? Charge after her, roaring a battle cry, and rescue her from an afternoon of domestic drudgery?

When she dragged her feet, even Magwyn smiled. "Come along, lass. We should leave the menfolk to their council."

Tabitha stopped dead in her tracks. No amount of gentle tugging could prod her back into motion.

Colin felt a surge of apprehension as she pivoted to face him. A predatory gleam lit her eyes as her gaze swept the long table and the ring of surly faces surrounding it. "A council? Would that be anything like a board meeting?"

Chauncey, the late tanner's overgrown son, surged to his feet, sweeping his waist-length tangle of hair out of his eyes. "We'll not have our laird beholden to a blustering braggart like MacDuff. I say we march on Brisbane's castle by night just as we planned before Laird Colin returned."

This proposal roused a chorus of enthusiastic "Ayes!" from the boys flanking Chauncey and a round of contemptuous "Pshaws" from the old men on the opposite side of the table.

Tabitha pounded on the table with her makeshift gavel, making Colin wince. "You're out of order, young man. Another outburst like that and I'll be forced to fine you."

Chauncey sank down on the bench, pouting like a chastened toddler.

One of the old men stood, his snowy beard bobbing

against his sunken chest. "Don't heed the foolhardy lad, me laird. Why I was—"

Tabitha cleared her throat pointedly.

The old man spat on the grass. "Permission to speak, lass?" he drawled with acid sarcasm.

"Permission granted," she purred, waving the gavel as if it were a royal scepter.

The old man shuffled back around to face Colin. "I was advisin' yer da on matters of war when ye were still suckin' Nana's teat."

A dull flush crawled up Colin's throat. Tabitha bit her lip to keep from giggling, but Arjon made no effort to hide his amused smirk.

The old man shook his fist in the air. "And I say we petition the MacDuff for men and weapons. We'll take our stand here at Castle Raven, just as we always have."

"Look what that got us last time," the sullen Chauncey muttered. "Our das killed and our mothers and sisters raped."

The table erupted in ominous grumbles that rapidly escalated to shouted insults regarding the participants' questionable parentage and unnatural affection for sheep. Tabitha slammed down the gavel before they could come to outright blows, but it was Colin rising to his feet that finally silenced them.

"I weary of this infernal bickering," he said, his soft voice mesmerizing them. "If you cannot—"

"Sir?" Tabitha interrupted with a long-suffering sigh. "Do I have to remind you of proper protocol?"

Colin swung toward her and thundered, "Do I have to remind you that I am laird of this castle?"

Several of the men flinched at the earth-trembling volume of his voice, but Tabitha simply gave him one of her most infuriating smiles. "And I'm Chairman of the Board, which, according to Robert's Rules of Order, grants me the authority to govern this meeting as I see fit."

He glared at her in stony silence.

She pointed the gavel at him. "You may speak."

His powerful hands clenched and unclenched as if fixed around her throat. "As most of you know, this council is naught but a formality. I value your wisdom, but 'tis I, as Laird of Ravenshaw, who will make the final decision." He nodded toward the old men. "I'll seek out the MacDuff as you advise." Before they could so much as nod their satisfaction, he turned toward the boys. "But I've no intention of waiting for Roger to return and pick our bones clean. Once we've made our alliance with the MacDuff, we'll take the battle to Brisbane."

Led by the exuberant Chauncey, the boys erupted in hoarse cheers. Tabitha raised her voice in a vain attempt to be heard above the din. "A motion has been made. All in favor say 'Aye.' Those opposed—"

"Bring me the map of Brisbane's lands," Colin commanded, neatly cutting her off.

"Aye, my lord." Ewan hastened to spread a parchment on the table before his master. Colin leaned forward until his nose practically touched the map.

Wisely deciding her role as self-appointed Chairman of the Board of Ravenshaw Enterprises had just been usurped by its president and CEO, Tabitha came around the table to peer over Colin's shoulder. The map was covered with incomprehensible scrawls and calligraphy so cramped it appeared to have been inked by nearsighted elves. She absently drew her glasses from her skirt pocket and slipped them on.

Her brow furrowed as she studied the map. She assumed the strange hush that had fallen over the men was the result of a similar concentration.

But when the silence stretched to near snapping point, she glanced up to find them staring at her nose. She reached up, thinking to rub away a smudge of dirt, only to encounter the wire bridge of her glasses. As Colin turned to see what had captured his men's fickle attention, apprehension blossomed in Tabitha's belly.

He straightened, cocking his head first one way, then the other, as if studying her from all angles might explain the inexplicable. His fingers brushed her temples as he drew the glasses off of her. She couldn't have felt any more vulnerable had he stripped her naked in front of his men.

She held her breath, anticipating questions she didn't dare answer. But he simply held the glasses up to the sunlight, smudging the lenses with his broad thumbs, then slipped them over his own eyes, holding them in place as if not trusting the strength of the earpieces.

As he blinked in wonder at his surroundings, Tabitha's breath caught in a strange little hiccup. Oddly enough, the glasses enhanced his rugged masculine appeal instead of detracting from it. She couldn't decide if he looked more like a gorgeous accountant or a brainy GQ model. His men watched warily as he leaned over the map.

"Arjon," he said, stabbing a finger toward an incomprehensible squiggle, "what river is this?"

Arjon leaned closer. "That would be the Tweed."

Colin broke into a dazzling grin. "Just as I thought. And this patch of hills?"

"The Combies." Arjon went on naming landmark after landmark until Colin was nearly shouting them in unison with him.

Suddenly Tabitha understood why he was always glowering at her or slaying her with that daunting Clint

Eastwood squint. He was probably more nearsighted than she was!

"Miraculous," he breathed, shaking his head. "I never dreamed such marvels existed. Not even the Sultan of Egypt possessed such a treasure." He shifted his gaze to his friend's face, recoiling in mock horror. "Why, Arjon, you're much uglier than I realized!"

The men, including Arjon, burst out laughing. Tabitha might have laughed, too, but as Colin turned the full force of those magnificent golden eyes on her, she realized too late that the joke was on her.

"And you, my lady," he said softly, tracing her perfectly ordinary features with his bemused gaze, "are even more beautiful." Almost as if his confession disturbed him as deeply as it had her, he drew off the glasses and held them out to her. "However wondrous, I mustn't grow too attached to these. I believe they belong to you."

Tabitha backed away from him, nearly stumbling over her own feet. "You keep them. Really. I don't need them anymore."

She could see far too clearly without them. She could see the sunlight glinting off Colin's glossy, dark hair, the beguiling crinkles around his eyes, the rueful smile curling the very corner of his mouth that she ached to kiss.

"Please keep them. They're just two pieces of warped glass I use in my magic act. Nothing but a petty trick." A trick indeed, Tabitha thought. A cruel trick of both time and fate. Colin's smile faded as she continued to retreat. "Consider them a gift. A token of my appreciation for your many kindnesses."

Before she could blurt out anything even more damning, she turned and fled up the hill, her vision distorted by tears.

•   •   •

Tabitha tossed and turned on the narrow cot, envying Colin both his nest of pillows and his serene sleep. Even with the furs arranged beneath her, she might as well have been resting on a bed of rocks. Desperation poked and prodded her, making even the pretense of sleep impossible.

The night was as restless as she was. The wind prowled around the tent like a fretful dragon, whipping branches against its billowing walls and moaning a doleful refrain.

After fleeing the council meeting, she'd spent the afternoon combing the tent for the amulet. It was more imperative than ever that she return to the century where she belonged. Not just for her parents' sake, but for her own. This century was far too untidy for her tastes—both in its dangers and its passions. She had to return to her family, to her career, to an apartment that even now seemed more sterile than cozy, while she still had the will to do so.

But her frantic hunt had yielded nothing. Colin had apparently secured the necklace on his person. And that was one area she wasn't about to search.

She threw herself to her side, stealing a guilty glance at him. He reclined on his back with Lucy curled in the crook of his elbow. They both appeared blissfully untroubled by the rising wind or her mounting misery. Colin's lips were slightly parted. She wondered if he would wake up if she gently pressed her mouth against them. Stifling a groan, she rolled to her back.

How humiliating to discover that despite her lofty IQ, she was no more immune to a buff set of biceps and a sooty pair of lashes than any other woman!

It's just a crush, she assured herself firmly, no different from the one she'd had on Steve Kaufman in the tenth grade. Time had eventually eased even her wistful pining for him.

Once she returned to the twenty-first century, she'd have plenty of time to get over Colin. A lifetime to be precise, a lifetime of knowing she'd been attracted to a man who'd been dead for over seven hundred years, yet made every man she'd ever met seem like nothing more than an insipid phantom.

Tabitha dragged one of the furs over her head, preferring the stifling heat to the temptation of gazing in calf-like adoration at Colin's sleeping face.

She might have happily smothered herself if an eerie wail hadn't pierced the droning of the wind. Throwing back the furs, Tabitha sat straight up, struggling to hear over the erratic throb of her heart in her ears.

Then it came again—an infant's unmistakable cry, borne on the wind like a banshee's lament.

Her first instinct was to leap off the cot into Colin's arms. But she was a card-carrying member of Mensa, not some quivering damsel in distress. She did not believe in knights in shining armor capable of protecting her from all harm, nor did she believe in ghosts. Colin was just a man like any other and there had to be some mundane scientific explanation for the unearthly sound.

She slipped off the cot, determined to get to the bottom of this before Colin was awakened by what he believed to be the ghostly echo of his sister's cry.

The castle loomed over Tabitha like some ancient tomb shadowed by mystery and menace.

She picked her way over the shattered stones that littered the courtyard, cursing herself with each painful step for not wearing her slippers. The wind sent clouds scudding across the moon in tattered shreds, veiling the fitful moonlight. Tabitha looked longingly over her shoulder toward the tent where Colin lay sleeping.

But another haunting cry beckoned her forward. Groaning with effort, she wrestled open the tower's heavy wooden door and slipped inside.

The instant the door drifted shut behind her, the crying stopped. Tabitha stood frozen in the inky blackness, the sudden silence more threatening than any spectral shriek.

"What did you expect?" she muttered through her chattering teeth. "That Colin's sister was going to jump out at you wearing a white bedsheet and yell 'Boo!'"

The wind obliged her expectations by seizing a shutter set high in the stone wall and slamming it open with a deafening crash. Tabitha jumped. Moonlight now came streaming through the narrow window, revealing a set of stone steps that seemed to wind into infinity.

She peered upward into the gathering shadows. "Can't be any worse than the Haunted House at Disney World." Her voice faded to a dubious whisper. "Can it?"

She began to climb, trying not to notice the grim blots that stained many of the steps. Apprehension had her huffing and puffing by the time she reached the first landing. She paused and cocked her head to listen, praying she had only imagined the furtive whisper of a footfall behind her. The rasp of her breathing echoed in the narrow stairwell until she would have almost sworn some unseen thing was panting in time with her, mocking her growing panic.

She climbed faster, feeling more like the pursued than the pursuer. She no longer knew if she was rushing toward whatever lay in wait at the top of the stairs or fleeing from some terrible threat that lurked behind her. Her uncertainty mirrored her emotional predicament.

She was living in the present, yet trapped somewhere between the future and the past.

She ran toward the second landing, hoping to take shelter in its shadows. But when she looked over her shoulder, she crashed into something warm and solid. A scream tore from her throat. She might have gone on screaming forever if it weren't for the powerful hand that clamped itself firmly over her mouth.

CHAPTER ✳ 15

Tabitha's assailant was no ethereal wisp or shadowy phantom. He was not spirit, but flesh—an ingenious melding of muscle and sinew strong enough to pin her against the wall without causing her even a twinge of pain. The rasp of his breathing mingled with her own. She smelled woodsmoke in his hair, tasted sweat and leather on the palm pressed against her lips. As the fear melted from her bones, she sagged against him, exulting in the very mortality that made them both vulnerable.

"Stop shrieking, lass." Colin's harsh voice came out of the darkness, coupled with the feral gleam of his eyes. "Before you wake both the living and the dead."

She managed a shaky nod. He slowly withdrew his hand, his fingertips lingering against her bottom lip for an immeasurable second. Instead of stepping away from her, he braced his palms against the wall on each side of her shoulders, managing to loom over her despite their similar heights. He kept one knee cocked between her own, which would put her in a very awkward position indeed if she attempted a step in any direction.

"How . . . ?" she croaked, then paused to clear her

throat. "I left you sleeping in the tent. How did you get into the castle . . . up the stairs?"

"I took the secret passageway from the garden."

"Then you must have heard it," she said, excited to learn she wasn't the only one going mad. "The crying!"

"I heard naught. Naught but the wailing of the wind and the sound of you creeping out of the tent and breaking the oath you made to me."

Tabitha would have almost sworn she heard a note of hurt in that fierce, proud voice. She wanted to see his expression, but the moonlight pooled on the stairs below them, refusing to brave the shadows. "I slipped out of the tent because I heard a baby crying."

"You should be ashamed, lass!" The raw bitterness in his voice stunned her. "Defiling my poor dead sister's memory to shield your own greed! Do you think I'm as gullible and superstitious as those women in the village? I suppose next you'll be trying to convince me the shade of my father is rising from his grave and the sky is teeming with witches."

The word sent a faint tremor through her. A tremor she knew he must have felt, given their proximity. If they got any closer, her teeth were going to start chattering again. "If you don't believe I heard crying, then why do you think I was wandering around this godforsaken ruin in the dead of night? For my aerobic benefit?"

"To rob me blind, of course. 'Twas a temptation you could not resist, I suppose. Knowing all the wealth of Ravenshaw sat moldering behind these castle walls, ripe for the picking. I knew you were the sort of woman to prey upon a man's weakness the first time I laid eyes on you."

Tabitha's outrage obscured her common sense.

"That's an unfair accusation, isn't it, coming from a man with no discernible weaknesses?"

He put his hands on her then and they both knew it was a mistake. She should have swayed away from the possessive grip of his hands on her shoulders, but instead she swayed nearer, mesmerized by the glint in his eyes as a cobra is mesmerized by the undulating rhythm of its master's dance.

"Why I ought to—" he bit off through his clenched teeth.

"What?" she demanded, tingling with the awareness that she was taunting him at her own risk. "Have me dragged before your precious council? Chop off the rest of my hair? Kiss me?" Her lips parted, inviting him . . . no, begging him, to do just that.

She knew the instant their lips met that she had ignited a sweet and perilous magic. Only this time it wasn't Colin at risk of turning into a frog, but she who was being transformed from cool-headed girl to hot-blooded woman.

If he had given her a barbarian's crude caress, it might have quenched her impossible longing for him. Instead, he took her mouth with a tender sweep of his tongue that only whet her desire. His lips slanted across hers again and again—tasting, teasing, nipping, claiming— until she was limp with need. She clung to his muscled forearms, savoring the thrill of his tongue thrusting deep into her mouth. He groaned his approval as her own tongue responded to the suggestive rhythm, shyly at first, then with helpless abandon.

It was every good-night kiss Tabitha had never gotten, every backseat prom night pass she'd never intercepted, every erotic dream she'd never confessed. Colin had accused her of being a thief, but he was the one stealing her breath, her will, her very heart. If this delicious communion was his idea of punishment, then she wanted to die in his arms, unrepentant, a victim of all the wicked sins she'd never had the courage to indulge in.

A soft, broken sound escaped her as he dragged his mouth from hers and pressed it to the pulse throbbing in her throat. He murmured her name, inhaling the fragrance of her hair as if it were scented with the most precious of perfumes.

Even as she tipped her head to the side, urging him to taste the sensitive skin behind her ear, Tabitha was compelled to try to break the spell his kiss had cast. She barely recognized her breathy voice. "There's a perfectly s-s-sound scientific explanation for the physical attraction between us. It's simply a result of"—she whimpered with pleasure as he caught her earlobe between his teeth and gently tugged—"r-r-rioting pheromones. Pheromones are chemical substances that can serve as sexual stimuli between two otherwise wildly"—the word deepened to a moan as he probed the virgin shell of her ear with the tip of his tongue—"incompatible individuals."

"Tabitha?" he whispered hoarsely in her ear.

"Yes, Colin."

"Hush."

Just in case she had any intention of disobeying him, he wrapped his arms around her, crushing her breasts to his chest, and seized her mouth with his own, his kiss even darker and more demanding than before. He kissed her as if he would die from want of her and Tabitha found his need irresistible. No one had ever really needed her before. Even her parents had always had each other.

She might have melted down the wall into a puddle of

pure delight had his knee not been there to brace her. She gasped at the sweet friction of his muscular thigh riding between her legs. She was only too aware that the coarse fabric of Magwyn's gown was all that separated him from flesh throbbing in anticipation of his touch.

If he hadn't stiffened in her arms, she might have thought the sharp cry was her own.

An infant's wail came echoing down the enclosed staircase with eerie clarity. They peered upward into the shadows, struggling to steady their ragged breathing, Colin wide-eyed with shock. She clutched his arms.

He touched a finger to her tingling lips, then gestured for her to follow him up the winding stairs.

"No," she whispered.

"I'll not leave you here alone, lass."

"And I'm not going anywhere until you apologize."

"For kissing you?" he hissed, putting his face close to hers as if he just might do it again.

"For accusing me of breaking into your castle to rob you." Tabitha knew she was being childish, but for some reason it was very important to her that Colin clear her name.

It took him a tense moment to accept that his thunderous scowl alone wasn't going to budge her. "Very well," he growled through clenched teeth. "I humbly beg your pardon, my lady."

As he wheeled around and started up the stairs, Tabitha hurried after him, more afraid of being left behind than forging ahead. "I'm not *your* lady."

"Yet," he said evenly, infuriating her anew with his boundless arrogance.

"Ever," she muttered at his back, but even to her, the denial sounded hollow and unconvincing.

•　　•　　•

As they crept up the stairs, Tabitha clutched the back of Colin's tunic the way a toddler would clutch a security blanket. He might very well need both of his arms to defend them against the unseen horror that awaited them in the chapel tower. Although he wore no dagger or sword, she had already learned that a man like Colin was never truly unarmed.

Just as they reached the iron-banded door at the top of the stairs, the crying ceased. The ominous silence echoed like a dirge. Tabitha shuddered.

Colin reached around and squeezed her trembling hands. "Don't be afraid, lass. 'Tis probably naught but the wind whistling through a crack in the stone."

She offered him a tremulous smile, trying not to cower. Easing her even more firmly behind him, he splayed his hand against the door and thrust it open in one decisive motion.

An array of bewildering impressions bombarded Tabitha's fear-numbed senses: a gold crucifix hanging askew on a plastered wall; the muffled coo of a dove; slender candles flickering on a carved altar. Disengaging himself from her grip, Colin drifted forward, drawn inexorably toward that row of flickering beacons in a place where he had expected to find only darkness.

A tranquil hush hung over the chapel. Which only made the shock more keen when something large and squat came charging at Colin out of a shadowy corner, bawling like an enraged heifer.

Caught off guard by the flying tackle, he went sailing backward, striking his head against the wall with a resounding thud. Plaster dust clouded the air. Choking back a scream, Tabitha raced toward the altar. She snatched up a candlestick, determined to bash Colin's assailant over the head with it.

A woman's plaintive wail of dismay froze her fingers around the polished brass.

"Colin! Master Colin, is that you?"

Tabitha slowly turned to find Colin being cradled across the lap of a woman large enough to be a defensive end for the New York Giants. The candlestick slid from her hand to clatter on the plank floor.

"Och, Colin, me puir wee laddie!" the woman crooned. "I've gone and killed you, I have!" Flesh jiggled on her arms as she pressed Colin's face to the spongy mountains of her breasts, rocking him as if he were an infant.

As he struggled his way free to keep from smothering, Tabitha fought a hysterical desire to giggle.

"Auld Nana?" he whispered, blinking up at the woman through dazed eyes. "Is that you, Nana? I thought you were dead."

"And I, you, m' sweet lad," she murmured, stroking his dark curls. " 'Twould seem we were both wrong."

Colin shook his head as if to clear it, then scrambled to his feet. He jerked his tunic straight, his stormy glower warning Tabitha not to laugh. But she was too busy scanning the shadows for the source of that peculiar cooing. Perhaps a dove had flown in through the shattered stained-glass window over the nave.

As Colin helped Nana to her feet, groaning beneath his breath with effort, Tabitha murmured, "Colin?"

"Aye?"

"If Nana's no ghost"—she pointed toward the basket in the corner, her finger trembling—"then neither is she."

Colin gazed at Tabitha for a long moment as if afraid to look at the basket, hope chasing doubt across his face. Nana clasped her beefy hands and stood silently as he took one step toward the corner, then another, his confident gait robbed of its swagger. As he lowered his powerful body to kneel beside the makeshift cradle, an inexpressible tenderness softened his rugged features.

He reached into the basket and lifted the baby girl nestled within as if she were fashioned of spun glass, a treasure beyond price. Dark curls, nearly identical to his own, furred her tiny pink head. She cooed down at him in delight, then burped as if she'd just downed an entire pint of Molson's.

It was in that moment when Colin turned to her with tears of wonder and thanksgiving misting his eyes that Tabitha knew she was lost.

More lost than she'd been when she tumbled into this alien century. More lost than when his lips had tenderly grazed hers for the very first time.

She wanted him to look at her that way as she marched down a flower-strewn aisle to stand at his side. She wanted him to hold *her* children with the fierce strength in his warrior's hands gentled by love.

She managed to smile at him through her own unshed tears, thrown off balance by the most damning truth of all. She wanted him.

Sir Colin of Ravenshaw, the seventh laird of Castle Raven, marched down the moonlit hill, a conquering hero at last.

Tabitha trailed shyly at his heels with a beaming Nana lumbering behind. The child in his arms had set up a lusty wail, but he simply pressed a kiss to the tip of her adorable little nose, making no attempt to quiet her. The baby puckered her pliant features into a miniature of her brother's habitual scowl. The poor thing probably had gas, Tabitha thought. God only knew what Nana had been feeding her.

As her churlish bellow rolled through their camp, Colin's people came spilling out of their tents and bedrolls, obviously fearing they had been set upon by an entire horde of murderous apparitions. They swarmed around their laird, seeking comfort in his unexpected presence.

Arjon and the blonde emerged from the same rumpled bedroll while Granny Cora limped out with her unlit pipe still clenched between her yellowed teeth. Jenny clung to her mama's shift, her freshly cropped curls tousled by sleep.

"Dear God in heaven! What terrible noise is that?" Magwyn cried, clapping her hands over her ears.

Colin grinned down at his squalling charge. "Is that any way to address your lady? I find her tones to be rather dulcet. I suspect she'll be a fine singer someday." Almost as if responding to her besotted brother's praise, the baby waved her fat little arms and lapsed into a happy chortle.

Tabitha had never been one to "ooh" and "ah" over drooling infants, but even to her skeptical eye, there was something alluring about the child's rebellious curls and petulant rosebud of a mouth.

Iselda pointed a trembling finger at Colin's burden before swooning in Magwyn's arms. Magwyn staggered beneath her bulk.

" 'Tis the ghost!" called out Chauncey, tripping over his overgrown feet. "The ghost from the tower!"

Nana boxed his ears and shoved her way through the mob like a running back plowing through the defensive line. A symphony of grunts and groans marked her progress as she smashed toes and elbowed spleens.

"She's no ghost, you buffoon, and neither am I."

"Auld Nana!" breathed Magwyn. "You're alive."

"No thanks to the likes of you," Nana retorted. "I

suppose it never occurred to any of you to trot your lazy arses up the stairs and tell puir Auld Nana the siege was done."

"Now, Nana," Colin said, "if they had, you would have ambushed them just as you did me." He addressed the gaping crowd. "You should have seen her. She came charging out of the darkness, howling like a blood-maddened Valkyrie, determined to defend her precious lady to the death. She was magnificent!"

Her pride mollified, Nana tucked her chins and gave his cheek a sound pinch. "Go on with you, sugar-tongued lad."

Tabitha took a step backward, hoping to melt into the crowd and seek the shelter of Colin's pavilion. Her feelings for him were still too new and tender to withstand public scrutiny.

Arjon yawned and ruffled his hair into feathery tufts. "Just how did you come to be prowling around the castle in the dead of night? We've been abed for hours." His companion giggled, her swollen lips suggesting they'd been indulging in more pleasurable pursuits than sleep. Tabitha touched a finger to her own lips, wondering if they looked as thoroughly kissed as they felt.

Depositing the baby in Nana's arms, Colin replied, "It seems there was only one among us bold enough to beard the dreaded Ravenshaw ghost in its lair." Before Tabitha could duck out of his reach, he drew her into the heart of their circle and turned her to face the villagers. " 'Twas Tabitha who dared to mock superstition and enter the castle. Tabitha who braved all manner of fearsome trials"—this with an audible smirk in his voice—"to free your lady and Auld Nana from their tower prison."

"It was nothing," she mumbled.

Colin continued as if she hadn't spoken, fumbling

with the hem of his tunic. "In honor of her bravery, I would like to present her with a token of my own heart-felt gratitude."

Tabitha's breath caught on a wheeze, but it was too late to stop him. He was already lowering the amulet over her head. Even in the hazy moonlight, the emerald shimmered against her breast like the eye of a dragon.

She gazed down at the stone with a mixture of awe and dread. She'd never dreamed Colin's trust would be such a terrible burden. It both bound her to him and gave her the means to abandon him forever. The decision was hers.

Logically, she knew it would be safe to turn in his arms, safe to kiss him without risking some manner of magical calamity. Yet somehow it was more dangerous than ever before. So she stood stiffly—without turning, without touching, without acknowledging the gift of his trust.

"To Tabitha!" shouted Chauncey.

"Aye! To the Lady Tabitha!"

They all took up the joyous cry, startling the baby into a fresh wail. Her voice was nearly drowned out by Colin's rich laughter as he wrapped his arms around Tabitha from behind and hugged her to his heart. She squeezed her eyes shut. She had traveled over seven hundred years from home only to find the place where she had always belonged.

CHAPTER 16

C astle Raven was open for business. Daybreak found its denizens scurrying in and out of the castle like a colony of industrious ants. With the ghost banished and their tiny lady freed from her tower prison, Colin's people were eager to reclaim both their home and their lives.

When Tabitha had finally drifted into a troubled sleep the night before, Colin had been huddled over the baby's basket, counting each of her even breaths. Tabitha had awakened at dawn to find him sprawled on his stomach on the floor of the tent, sound asleep. After covering him with one of the furs, she'd crept over to take his place, standing guard against the fleeing darkness.

Despite several eager offers, he still refused to relinquish the baby he'd christened Wee Blythe to any of the village women. He insisted on directing most of the repair efforts while carrying the baby in the crook of his arm like a squirming football. He wore Tabitha's wireframed glasses perched low on his nose and it was the very incongruity that made him so irresistible.

The village women had to settle for fussing over Nana. Accepting that her precious charge was safe at last had done wonders for the old woman's paranoia. The near madness she'd suffered in the tower seemed to be subsiding with encouraging haste, allowing her to accept Granny Cora's offer to share a pipe beneath the refreshing shade of a willow.

Tabitha would have found their joy infectious if her own mood hadn't kept veering between exhilaration and despair. Every time her gaze accidentally brushed Colin's, she feared they would change the course of history by discovering electricity five centuries before Benjamin Franklin. The unspoken promise in his eyes sent heat sizzling through her, melting the core of ice around her heart and sending the runoff to pool in more pro vocative places.

But when he turned away to shout a fresh order at Ewan or Chauncey, despair gripped her. She knew she owed him the truth. Even if it meant risking the fragile bond that had grown between them. She had to tell him that she didn't belong in his arms, in his life, even in his century. But she no longer knew if she could find the courage to leave him.

And what about her parents? If their plane had gone down over the Bermuda Triangle, her return to the twenty-first century wouldn't bring them back. But if they were alive, her unexplained disappearance would break their hearts. They might live out their lives believing she'd been prey to a kidnapper or serial killer. She squeezed the amulet, almost wishing Colin had tossed the hateful thing down some bottomless well.

"Lady Tabby!" A fair-haired, baby-faced little boy with an irrepressible cowlick poked his head through an arrow loop set high in the castle wall. "Do come, Lady Tabby! 'Tis wee Lucy who needs rescuin' now."

"I'll be right there, Thomas." Tabitha rushed up the stairs and enhanced her reputation for daring heroics by saving Lucy from a rather fierce-looking mouse who had cornered the baffled kitten on a window ledge.

As she emerged from the castle, crooning to the cat in her arms, Arjon dropped his bundle of singed tapestries to pinch back a sneeze. "Should have left the little monster for rat bait."

"Shame on you, Sir Arjon," she retorted, kissing Lucy's fuzzy head. "It's not very chivalrous to insult a lady."

"I've seen him bed women with longer whiskers," Colin called out from atop a pile of salvaged wood.

The worldly Arjon blushed and the women beating the soot from the heather-stuffed mattresses tittered. Colin winked at Tabitha over the top of her glasses, tilting her world on edge once more.

She absently deposited Lucy in an empty cooking cauldron, oblivious to the wicked arch of Arjon's eyebrows.

"Jenny, you take care up there," Magwyn shouted, distracted from scraping tarnish from a silver candlestick by the sight of her daughter scampering over the tower ramparts like a lithe little monkey.

Jenny just giggled and waved before lurching after the other children. Magwyn shook her head and went back to her chore. "I ought to give the child a sound thrashing, but I can't resist her laughter after all this time. 'Tis music to my ears."

Tabitha smiled, remembering the first time she had heard Colin laugh aloud.

But then Magwyn glanced back up at the ramparts, and her face went stark white. Tabitha followed her gaze skyward, shading her eyes against the morning sun. Fear plunged through her heart.

Jenny wasn't laughing anymore. She was dangling from an outcropping of stone by her frail fingertips, poised above a sheer drop of seventy feet to the cobble-stones below.

Magwyn's scream was the voice of every mother's nightmare. The icy aria seemed to go on and on, freezing everyone in the courtyard with horror.

Everyone but Colin.

Handing the baby off to Nana, he raced for the tower. Tabitha knew he wasn't going to make it. He was a hero, not a superhero. And when he failed, he would blame himself, just as he blamed himself for Regan's suicide.

She could almost hear Jenny's grunt of effort, feel the rough stone scraping the tender skin off her fingers, suffer her burning shame as the little girl wet herself for the first time in years.

As Jenny's left hand lost its grip and clutched desperately at the air, Magwyn's own fists clenched and unclenched as if she didn't know whether to hide her face in her hands or shake her fist at the unforgiving sky.

Colin was just dragging open the outer door to the tower when Jenny fell. Oddly enough, it was Magwyn who went dead silent as Jenny's shrill scream lacerated their ears. Colin turned to watch, his face awash in helplessness and horror, as the child plunged toward the ground, her arms and legs cartwheeling madly.

Tabitha did not remember grabbing the amulet. Could not have pinpointed at what precise second she abandoned her insecurities, overcame her repressions, and wished, harder than she'd ever wished in her entire life.

Jenny's scream dwindled to a delighted, "Aa-a-a-a-h . . . !" as her fall slowed to a float. She drifted toward the earth, her skirt billowing outward like Mary Poppins's parasol, and landed with feathery grace in Tabitha's outstretched arms. Tabitha buried her face in the child's sweaty throat, cherishing the feel of her solid little body.

The child wiggled out of Tabitha's fierce grip, drawing back to gaze raptly at her face. Her voice, husky from disuse, seemed to echo through the courtyard. " 'Twas a bonny catch, Lady Tabby. Are you a witch?"

Tabitha swept her gaze around the ring of astounded faces. Colin slowly drew off the glasses, staring at her with the same baffled astonishment as the rest of them. She briefly closed her eyes to blot out his face, praying he would understand.

She could not lie to the hopeful child in her arms, nor could she go on lying to Colin. The past had become her present and he had become the only future she could envision. What better time than here and now to embrace the heritage she'd always denied? Here in this enchanted kingdom where knights in shining armor fought to slay the dragons of evil and the most powerful spell of all was true love. Tabitha almost wished her mother was there to witness her proud declaration.

She smiled tenderly at Jenny, but her gaze drifted over the child's head, coming to rest lovingly on Colin's bewildered face. "Yes, darling. I'm a witch."

Silence greeted her words. A silence so profound Tabitha could hear the papery rustle of swallow wings in the chapel nave high above, the scrape of a dislodged stone as someone took an involuntary step backward.

Her glasses slipped from Colin's limp fingers. His face went utterly expressionless. The tan bled from his swarthy skin, bleaching it white. It was almost as if her abrupt confession had turned him to a pillar of salt.

Tabitha's second clue that something was wrong came when Magwyn tore Jenny out of her arms. "But, Mama," the little girl wailed. "Falling was fun! Might I do it again?"

"Hush, child," Magwyn said harshly. She backed away from Tabitha, wearing a mask of mingled horror and betrayal.

It didn't take her long to realize Magwyn's reaction mirrored that of the crowd surrounding them. Some were backing away; others were muttering beneath their breaths and tracing crosses on their breasts. She watched in helpless dismay as, one by one, faces that had been beaming at her only minutes before closed in on themselves, becoming the forbidding visages of strangers. Only Arjon's eyes betrayed a flicker of sympathy, which was somehow more damning than the open condemnation of the others.

"Oops," she whispered.

She'd made some colossal social blunders before, but this might even be worse than the time she'd stepped on the First Lady's train at a presidential dinner given in her father's honor. Or the time she'd called the wife of a potential multimillion-dollar client by his mistress's name.

"Burn her!" shouted an old man, waving his palsied fist in the air.

"Aye, she's a confessed witch. We must burn her," Granny Cora echoed sadly.

"I thought you only burned heretics," Tabitha said weakly.

Chauncey, ever helpful, chimed in. "We strangle witches. *Then* we burn 'em."

The accusing mutters rose to shouts. Tabitha touched a hand to her throat, backing toward Colin without even realizing it. Jenny began to cry, her heartfelt wails only adding to the chaos.

"Enough!"

Colin's shout silenced them all, even a startled Jenny. As he rested his hands on Tabitha's shoulders, she sagged against him in relief. She should have known he would never allow his people to harm her. He was her hero, her champion, her destiny—the man she'd crossed over seven centuries to love.

He caressed her fluted collarbones with a tenderness that made her want to melt into a puddle at his boots.

"I'm the one who brought this witch into our midst." His soft, despairing voice rasped like steel on velvet in the tense silence. " 'Tis my duty to burn her."

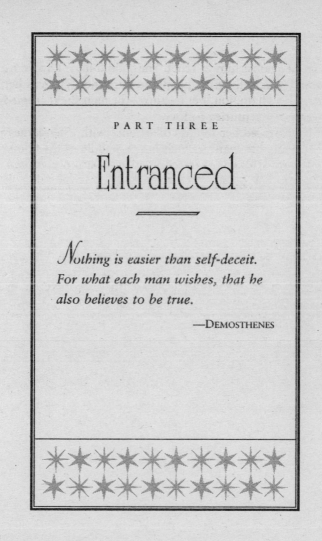

PART THREE

Entranced

*Nothing is easier than self-deceit.
For what each man wishes, that he
also believes to be true.*

—DEMOSTHENES

"This is probably going to hurt you much more than it will me." Tabitha swiped her sweat-dampened bangs out of her eyes with her bound wrists as she trudged up the steep slope behind Colin. "I told my daddy that once when he was planning to punish me for hacking into his bank account and making electronic transfers to Greenpeace, and he laughed so hard, he forgot to spank me."

Colin's face betrayed no sign of amusement. It was as still and resolute as it had been since that terrible moment when she'd confessed her secret.

She sighed, not knowing how much longer she could keep up her nervous stream of chatter. They'd been climbing the mountainside for most of the afternoon, yet he hadn't uttered a single word. She'd been a victim of his brooding silences before, but this one was different somehow, like a deep, dark stream winding through an underground cavern. She might have thought she was marching heavenward alone if it wasn't for the stout length of rope wrapped around her wrists and Colin's fist.

Despite the cord that bound them, he hadn't touched her once since passing his stern judgment. It had been

Ewan who wrapped the rope around her wrists at his master's command, Chauncey who had given the other end of it into his hands. Tabitha had simply fallen into step behind him, keenly aware of the amulet bouncing between her breasts. Surely Colin must suspect the charm possessed magical powers. Yet he'd bound her wrists in front of her, leaving her fingers free to grasp it if she dared.

The summer afternoon mocked her with its beauty. Wildflowers sprouted from every rocky crevice, spilling down the hillside in a dazzling waterfall of color. A stand of firs loomed overhead, promising shade and respite for the weary traveler. A buoyant breeze caressed her face. The Scottish terrain painted an idyllic backdrop for one of her mother's fairy tales—*The Princess and the Pyre* perhaps. Or *Little Roasted Riding Hood*. Eyeing the sharp glint of the axe dangling from Colin's belt, Tabitha shuddered, fearing such a grim fairy tale could never have a happy ending.

"You should have given me back my pajamas," she informed Colin's unyielding back. "Federal law requires them to be flame retardant."

They'd nearly reached the top of the hill. Colin remained as stoic and immovable as Abraham preparing to slay his beloved son at his Lord's command. The analogy failed to comfort her.

"I hope you remembered to bring the weenies. Because I forgot the marshmallows." When he continued to ignore her ferocious cheer, she added, "It's terribly clever of you to pretend you're going to torch me. Once your people see the smoke, they'll assume you've done your duty and I can just be on my way with no one the wiser."

Colin lifted a fir bough, motioning for her to pass. She should have had to brush against him, but he shrank away from her, sending a fresh bolt of despair deep into her heart. If she could just get him to speak to her . . . look at her . . . touch her . . .

A ramshackle cottage squatted in the center of the clearing, looking less than enchanted. Its thatched roof resembled a moth-eaten toupee.

"What charming accommodations!" Tabitha said as he marched her through the weeds flourishing around the stone stoop and thrust open the door. "Not quite up to the elegant standards of Brisbane's dungeon, but far more—" Before her eyes could adjust to the gloom, he neatly reversed their positions and slammed the door in her face. A bolt thudded into its mooring.

Her voice trailed to a whisper. ". . . habitable."

She sagged against the door, overwhelmed by loneliness. There was a vast deal of difference in being imprisoned with Colin and being imprisoned by him. She would have gladly returned to that tiny cell in Brisbane's dungeon and faced the threat of decapitation all over again for the privilege of sleeping in Colin's arms one more night.

Battling the inertia of hopelessness, she pushed away from the door and slowly toured her cottage prison. Narrow shutters covered the windows, filtering out all but the most tenacious of sunbeams. Dust motes peppered the hazy air, drifting past a stone hearth whose ashes had long grown cold, a mattress gowned in a threadbare quilt, a pair of half-melted candles. Cobwebs draped the rough-hewn rafters, fluttering in the musty draft like tattered wedding veils. A length of rope dangled from the center beam.

Tabitha reached up with her bound hands and absently touched it. The end was frayed as if it had been cut or severed by a violent tug. Without warning, Colin's words spilled through her mind.

When I finally went to the cottage where we trysted to tell Regan I would make her my wife, I found her hanging from the rafters, my unborn child dead in her womb.

Tabitha jerked her hands back as if the rope carried live electrical current. The jolt shot straight to her heart. She spun around, her pulse racing. She no longer needed magic to travel to the past, only imagination.

A fire crackled on the hearth, casting its merry glow over the lover's bower Colin had painstakingly prepared for his lady. Perfumed candles scented the air. A clean quilt draped the mattress he'd stuffed with dried heather that very morning. He was warming his chapped palms over the fire when the door burst open and Regan came running in, her cloak frosted with snowflakes, her pale cheeks rosy from the cold.

Colin eased her hood from her silvery blond hair, his hands shaking with want, yet unspeakably gentle. His lips claimed hers and they fell upon the mattress together, shedding their clothes with all the guilty abandon of any two teenagers eager to explore all the pleasures they'd just discovered their nubile bodies were capable of.

Tabitha felt nothing but tenderness for the boy Colin had been—slender and newly muscled, a shadow of the man he would become etched in his unlined face, his smooth jaw, his bright, trusting eyes.

But Regan's image tasted bitter, like ashes in her mouth. Pity for the girl's fate mingled with jealousy. If Colin did what his thirteenth-century conscience demanded of him, Tabitha would never lay in his arms, her heartbeat unsteady and her skin flushed from his lovemaking. He would never stroke her hair or steal a kiss or touch her breasts as if he'd waited his entire life to do so. For one brief shining moment, Regan had had everything Tabitha had ever wanted.

And been foolish enough to squander it at the end of that rope.

A darker image replaced the first—*Colin and Regan quarreling—hurtling cruel, foolish words at one another as only those very young or very much in love will do. Regan, her wan face blotchy with tearstains, paced the cottage, wringing her hands until one of them darted out like a nervous bird to slap Colin full across the face. Colin stood paralyzed by the blow from his beloved, finally turning on his heel and leaving the cottage without a word.*

Tabitha sank to her knees and pressed the heels of her hands to her eyes in a vain attempt to blot out the image she knew would follow.

A slender figure stood in the doorway of the cottage, framed by the pale winter sunshine. He was no longer a man, but simply a boy on the brink of manhood clutching a fistful of dried heather in one hand and his heart in the other. A shadow crossed his face, once, twice, as the thing dangling from the rafters swung slowly to and fro, as if nudged by an invisible hand.

Colin drifted toward the unspeakable thing, deafened to everything but the lazy creak of the rope. He blinked up at it, his golden eyes blank with shock. Comprehension slowly dawned, more brutal and merciless than the numbness that had preceded it. Roaring in agony, he rushed toward Regan, seizing her around the waist and lifting her as if it were not a lifetime too late to coax a breath into her mottled throat.

He clawed at the rope, wrenching it in two with the sheer force of his desperation. Regan fell into his arms, cold and stiff where once she had been warm and pliant.

*Cradling her to his breast, he sank to his knees and
tipped back his head in a soundless howl of grief.*

When Tabitha lowered her hands from her eyes, they
were wet with tears. She rose to her feet, scrubbing
roughly at her cheeks with her forearm. She was no
Regan to manipulate a man with tears and accusations.

She stumbled to the window and pried away a rotted
slat of shutter with her fingernails. Colin was nowhere
in sight, but she could hear the rhythmic *thunk* of his
axe biting into wood.

A stray sunbeam caressed the amulet, making it glis-
ten in the murky light. Tabitha brushed the stone with
her fingertips, understanding now why Colin had ordered Ewan to bind her wrists so loosely and leave her
fingers free. If he returned to find the cottage empty and
her returned to whatever mysterious place she had come
from, he'd be spared the terrible burden of fulfilling his
pledge to his people and his God. He'd be alone once
more with only his regrets for company.

Consoled by an almost supernatural calm, Tabitha
curled up in the windowsill, determined to do what Regan hadn't had the courage to do.

Be there when Colin came for her.

The moon floated over the clearing, chasing the shadows of twilight back to their mossy hollows. It was the
first silvery flush of nightfall when the curtain between
the seen and unseen worlds evaporated to nothing more
than a gauzy veil, easily disturbed by a reckless mortal
hand. Tabitha wouldn't have been surprised to see a
band of fairy folk emerge from beneath their leafy stalks
to caper around the stake in the middle of the clearing.

It was a fine and sturdy stake, set deep in the ground,
jutting boldly into the night. Its thick length had been

hewn from the smooth trunk of an alder so as not to abrade the tender flesh of its victim. Moonlight laced the web of brush piled with painstaking care around its base. Tabitha had no doubt the brittle kindling had also been chosen with efficiency and comfort in mind. It would burn hot and fast, obliterating all trace of the woman condemned to writhe in its hellish embrace.

Her executioner had been on his knees for a dark eternity. But instead of humbly bowing his head, he appeared to be locked in mortal combat with his creator. He'd thrown back his broad shoulders and tipped his face heavenward to search the black void of the sky. His tortured profile was both beautiful and terrible to behold, like a Renaissance fresco of a fallen angel battling to reclaim his rightful place in God's court.

When he finally bowed his head and climbed to his feet, Tabitha knew exactly who had lost the battle.

She stood in the center of the cottage, wanting to be on her feet when he came for her. She stood straight and tall, refusing to slump. Colin's God might be required to grant him mercy, but she wasn't.

He fumbled with the bolt, his hands robbed of their usual grace. His clumsiness betrayed just how much it would cost him to open that door.

When it finally swung open, Tabitha half expected to find a slender, dark-haired boy silhouetted against the moonlight. But it was a man's rugged shadow that fell across her, a man who held the power of life and death in his loosely coiled hands.

His resolute expression shielded the dismay he must have felt at discovering she hadn't accepted his invitation to vanish into thin air. He looped the trailing end of the rope around his fist, and gently led her across the dew-spangled grass to the stake that was to be her funeral pyre.

He refused to meet her eyes as he inclined his head and unknotted the ropes at her wrists.

"I have to admire you for sticking to your principles," she said lightly. "Where I come from, most men don't have any."

That earned her a smoldering scowl, the first he'd given her in that endless day. She didn't even struggle as he waltzed her backward to the stake, then went around to bind her hands behind her. His hot breath fanned her hair. It took him one, two, three tries to tighten the bonds to his satisfaction. By the time he was through, his hands were shaking harder than hers.

By not using the amulet to save herself, Tabitha knew she was taking a terrible chance. But for the first time in her life, she was compelled to put her faith in someone other than herself. If it turned out that she'd misjudged Colin, it would just be the ultimate screwup in a life devoted to screwing up.

He came to stand in front of her, each of his movements labored, as if he'd aged a decade in the time it had taken to bind her to the stake.

"You *are* going to strangle me first, aren't you? I'd be very disappointed if you didn't. You've always impressed me as a stickler for protocol." Tabitha nursed an absurd flicker of hope. To strangle her he would have to touch her.

"You've left me no choice," he said hoarsely. " 'Thou shalt not suffer a witch to live.' "

" 'Thou shalt not kill,' " she shot back at him, thankful she'd memorized at least that one commandment.

He paced a few steps away, as if refusing to look at her was becoming more and more of a challenge. "Have you any words to offer in your defense?"

It put a strain on her shoulders, but Tabitha still managed to shrug. "I always paid off my credit cards before the interest came due."

"Stop mocking me," he roared, spinning around to glare at her.

Her hope flared into triumph. "Or you'll what? Choke me to death, then burn my corpse to ashes?"

When Colin strode forward and seized her by the throat, she thought he was going to do exactly that. But his desperate grip was tempered by gentleness, his voice low and pleading. "Deny it, my lady! Deny the charge of witchcraft and I'll free you. Even if it should cost me my eternal soul. Deny it and I'll send you on your way. You will never lay eyes on my face again."

Her helpless gaze traced his stubborn chin, that deliciously soft lower lip. How could she tell him that was the one threat she feared more than death?

She longed to do as he said, if only for his sake, but she'd spent her entire life living a lie. If Arian were there at that moment, Tabitha hoped her mother would appreciate the fact that she was willing to die for something she'd always resented. She'd finally come to realize that her supernatural powers were as much a part of her as her size ten feet and the bland color of her hair.

"I can't deny it," she said softly. "Not even for you."

Despair darkened his eyes. His hands drifted upward, freeing the feathery strands of her hair from Magwyn's ribbon until they fell in a soft cloud around her face. Tabitha tipped her head back, unable to resist his tender seduction. He cupped her throat in his palms, pressing his powerful thumbs to the pulse that beat in its fragile hollow.

"Close your eyes," he rasped.

Tabitha couldn't have said why she obeyed—to spare him the agony of watching the spark of life fade from her eyes or to blot out the sight of his beautiful, merciless face. His grip tightened. Her lashes fluttered downward as she waited to die at the hands of the man she loved.

It wasn't death that came out of the darkness, but Colin's kiss. His lips seized hers with a fierceness that made her gasp. He took advantage of her shock by driving his tongue even deeper into her mouth, kindling a fire of another kind—dark, erotic, and all-consuming. She writhed in its flames, feeling as wild and wanton as the godless creature he thought her to be.

Wondering dreamily if he intended to kiss her to death, she surged against the bonds, her breasts straining against his chest, her nipples abraded to exquisite sensitivity by the rough linen of Magwyn's gown. He pressed her backward until she was pinioned between the stake and the unyielding length of male flesh throbbing beneath his hose. As the flames licked lower, Tabitha moaned in mingled terror and delight.

She had not forgotten that she was in the thirteenth century and wearing no underwear. A less honorable man in this century or any other would have shoved up her gown and dragged her astride him then and there. There were no witnesses and he had only to burn the evidence of his hypocrisy.

But Colin was, above all else, an honorable man.

Tabitha sagged against the stake as he stumbled away from her, his golden eyes reflecting the fierce war being waged within him. "Truly, my lady, you have bewitched me! Damn you!"

Tabitha might have laughed if his expression hadn't been so desperate. He hadn't even looked at the Big Macs with such unabashed yearning. "According to you, I'm already damned, aren't I? But that doesn't stop you from wanting me, does it?"

"And why should it? You've used your dark arts to enchant me from the first moment I laid eyes on you."

She had to laugh at this absurd accusation. "Which of my charms couldn't you resist, Colin? Was it the way my flannel pajamas bunched between my thighs when I walked or the fact that my breath smelled like spearmint toothpaste?"

" 'Twas the way the sunlight shimmered in your hair, the way you smelled so fresh and clean—like soap and woman mingled into some intoxicating perfume no mortal man could resist."

Tabitha thought the blush she felt crawling up her body might ignite the kindling and incinerate her. Colin stood like a sorcerer in the moonlight, weaving his own incantation. She was mesmerized nearly as much by the movement of his lips as his husky words.

" 'Twas the way you smiled so boldly to hide your fear of me, the grace with which you shoved my sword away from your heart, though your hand trembled with terror. 'Twas your foolhardy courage when you defied Brisbane on my behalf without a care for your own life."

"I thought you hated me for that," she whispered.

"I did. Nearly as much as I wanted you."

Tabitha Lennox, who had always thought of herself as plain and clumsy and cowardly, was horrified to feel a tear tumble from her lashes. Colin's blunt confession had robbed her of her sarcasm—the only weapon she had left in her pitiful arsenal. She began to struggle against the ropes in earnest, desperate to swipe away the tear before he saw it. But another followed it, then another, until they were trickling down her cheeks in a steady stream. She hung her head and sniffled in shame.

Colin tipped her chin up and peered into her face.

"What manner of trickery is this? 'Tis common knowledge witches cannot weep."

Tabitha gave him a watery glare, but her voice still broke on a strangled sob. "They can if you're breaking their heart."

Both bewildered and beguiled, he touched her cheek with shattering gentleness, smearing a salty teardrop with his thumb before bringing it to his lips. As he tasted her tears, an expression of helpless wonder surged across his face.

"Oh, Tabitha," he whispered. "My brave, sweet, beautiful witch . . ."

His kiss was different from any that had come before it. Losing none of its eloquence, his tongue swirled over her lips, begging her pardon, coaxing her to part them and let him taste the balm of her forgiveness. When she did, he deepened his kiss, drawing her lower lip into his mouth and tenderly suckling.

All the while he was kissing her, his hands were working at the knots of her bonds until all she had to do when they fell away was melt into his arms.

CHAPTER 18

C olin scooped her up as if she weighed no more than Jenny and carried her toward the cottage. Tabitha buried her tear-streaked face against his throat, inhaling the leathery spice of his skin. He kicked the cottage door open and laid her down on the threadbare mattress as if it were a bed of roses. She supposed it should have bothered her that Colin and Regan had once shared that same mattress, but the present was too precious to allow it to be overshadowed by the past or the future.

As he stood over her, unbuckling his belt of braided silver, his eyes smoldered with a hunger that took her breath away. "There's no help for it, my lady. If you're to burn, then we shall burn together."

He drew his tunic over his head, rumpling his dark hair. The sight of his bare chest made Tabitha's mouth go dry with want. He'd been a stranger to her less than a week ago, but now she ached to know his body the same way she knew her own. Every crisp, curling hair, every pale scar, every delectable inch of it.

Embracing the role of wanton enchantress, she seized his hand and pulled him down on top of her. He succumbed to her bidding without a struggle, sinking into a wet, openmouthed kiss that should have qualified as a sex act all by itself. Then, as if to atone for that bit of naughtiness, he tenderly sipped the last traces of tears from her cheeks. As his lips nuzzled her cheeks, her eyelids, the sensitive cleft above her upper lip, Tabitha sighed, adrift on a sea of bliss.

When her eyes fluttered open, Colin was gazing down at her, his face somber in the moonlight streaming through the open door. "Would you lay with me, my lady?"

She had expected a mandate, not an invitation. The humble entreaty of this powerful man touched a chord deep in her soul. Threading her fingers through his hair, she whispered, "I would be honored, sir."

She expected him to kiss her again, but he surprised her by drawing her up and gently wrestling Magwyn's gown over her head. Before Tabitha could prepare herself for the shock, she was in his arms wearing nothing but the amulet. Her palms darted from her breasts to the toffee-colored curls at the juncture of her thighs, then back again. Knowing she must look utterly ridiculous, she finally contented herself with fluffing up her hair.

Colin studied her with blatant fascination before offering her a crooked grin that made her heart thud dully in her ears. "I've never seen a woman blush all over. 'Tis a most enchanting trait."

"Why, thank you," she replied breathlessly.

He drew her close for a kiss, but she pushed at his muscled shoulders. "Not so fast. I'm afraid my advanced state of nudity puts me at a distinct disadvantage."

He arched one eyebrow at her. "And what would you suggest we do about that?"

She gave his hose a nervous nod, utterly captivated by

this wickedly playful Colin. "You might dispose of those."

"Very well, my lady. Your wish is my com—"

Tabitha clapped a hand over his mouth, shaking her head in warning. He simply kissed her palm and nodded, reassuring her that the time to discuss that particular quandary would come later. Much later.

As Colin drew off his boots, then untied the points of his hose and peeled them off, Tabitha's facade of sophistication shattered. Her first instinct was to recoil and protest that he was crazy if he thought he was going to put that thing anywhere in her. But her bout of maidenly horror was overwhelmed by a compulsion to touch him, to run her trembling fingertips along the velvety shaft springing so boldly from its nest of dark curls. So she did. And although she would have sworn it was impossible, she felt him lengthen and thicken even more beneath her touch.

With a heartrending groan, he tore himself away from her. He sat on the edge of the mattress and buried his head in his hands, breathing as if he'd been wrestling a dragon.

Tabitha gazed helplessly at the moon-gilded curve of his back, fighting the urge to weep with frustration. Had she, in her ignorance, done something unacceptable? Had she feinted left when she should have dodged right?

Practically forgetting that she was naked, she crept up beside him and gently touched his shoulder. "Was it something I said?"

He lifted his head, his expression haunted enough to frighten her anew. " 'Tis not you, Tabitha. 'Tis me."

Without even thinking about it, Tabitha blurted out the worst fear of any single woman living alone in New York City. "Oh, God, you're not gay, are you?"

He slanted her a strange look. "No, I'm rather morose at the moment."

Tabitha might have laughed with relief if his expression hadn't been so glum. She waited for him to elaborate.

"If I had been able to resist Regan when she offered herself to me, she might not have died. 'Twas my own voracious carnal appetites that cost an innocent girl her life."

A shiver of mingled apprehension and delight danced down Tabitha's spine. Would she be woman enough to satisfy those appetites?

"Despite those appetites"—he shook his head as if to clear it—"no, *because* of them, I swore an oath of celibacy before I took up the cross. I vowed to keep myself chaste as long as I was marching beneath the banner of the Lord. So while others sought out whores to relieve their baser needs, I was on my knees. Praying for fortitude," he added wryly.

She frowned, touched and confused by his confession. "I don't understand. If you've been celibate for the last six years, what were you doing in all those Egyptian brothels?"

He rolled his eyes heavenward. "Waiting for Arjon."

Tabitha didn't know whether to laugh or cry. She couldn't help but appreciate the irony of a virgin trying to seduce a celibate.

She patted his shoulder. "Don't be afraid. It's probably just like riding a"—she rejected "bicycle" and "camel," then fumbled for a more appropriate reference—"horse. It'll all come back to you once you begin."

His eyes sparkled with amusement as he cupped her cheek in his hand. "I haven't forgotten what to do, my lady. 'Tis simply that I want you so desperately I fear 'twill be over before it's begun."

Tabitha sighed, her heart melting along with various other nether regions of her body. "Oh, Colin. I don't mind a little urgency. There'll be plenty of time for the rest later."

But would there be? She tried to ignore a pang of doubt. If the amulet had taught her anything, it was just how capricious time could be.

Determined to set both her mind and his own at ease, she smiled brightly. "Let's just get on with it, shall we?"

She lay back on the mattress and squeezed her eyes shut, bracing herself for the medieval version of "wham-bam-thank-you-wench."

"What in the holy name of St. Andrew are you doing?"

She opened one eye to find Colin scowling down at her. "Waiting for you to make love to me."

"You look more like you're waiting for the blacksmith to pull a tooth."

Sighing, she opened both eyes. Shouldn't he look more pleased that she'd decided to suffer his lusty mauling with such good grace? "I haven't forgotten that you're a semibarbarian, you know. You've never had the chance to read *Cosmo* so it wouldn't be fair of me to expect you to label all my erogenous zones or know precisely which button to push to drive me wild with desire."

She'd never seen that one expressive eyebrow of his shoot quite so high. "No, I don't suppose it would." He leaned over her, the thoughtful gleam in his eyes making her quiver with alarm. "Perhaps you're right. Perhaps you should just close your eyes and suffer my brutish attentions without complaint."

Tabitha obeyed, if somewhat suspiciously.

"And don't open them," he whispered, brushing his warm lips down the side of her throat. "No matter what I do to you."

His husky voice ignited a dark shiver of anticipation. As he nuzzled the sensitive hollow at the base of her throat, a dreamy languor melted through her limbs.

"The women at the brothel always considered my celibacy something of a challenge," he murmured between slow, luscious tastes of her skin. "While Arjon was upstairs taking his pleasure, they would wager among themselves who would be the first to coax me into breaking my vow. They amused each other by gathering around me and describing in delicious detail all the sinfully wicked things they yearned to do to me and those they wanted me to do to them."

"Oh," Tabitha breathed as his mouth wandered lower, grazing the swell of each breast with exquisite tenderness.

"I've never seen this *Cosmo* of yours, but they did show me ancient illustrated manuscripts that depicted acts of love certain to test both the agility and the imagination of the lovers. I found them to be very instructive."

"Oh!" This time her voice came out somewhere between a squeak and a sob. The sob deepened to a moan as he lapped at one distended nipple, his tongue rough as a cat's, yet smooth as silk. Her illusions that foreplay had been invented in the twenty-first century crumbled like sugar candy beneath his erotic kiss.

As he drew her nipple into his mouth and suckled her, stirring a kindred tug deep within her womb, she tangled her hands in his hair. "Oh, Colin, I thought you couldn't wait."

He dipped his tongue into her navel, eliciting an even more primal shiver. "Ah, but those cunning women also taught me 'twas possible for a man to delay his own pleasure in order to prolong his lady's."

"But you've already delayed yours for six years and if you prolong mine anymore, I think I'm going to die," she wailed.

"Then you shall suffer the sweetest death a woman can know."

Her eyes flew open, but he warned, "No peeking. Barbarians haven't any patience for peeking."

Even with her eyes closed, Tabitha could feel his gaze burn her naked skin, more tangible than a touch. Or at least she thought so until his fingers grazed the soft curls between her legs. Whimpering in latent shyness, she turned her face toward the mattress while Colin petted and stroked her. When she was nearly purring with pleasure, his fingers delved deeper, breaching her damp curls.

"If I weren't such an untutored barbarian and I wanted to drive you wild with desire, I might just touch you here." The flick of his fingertip against that sensitive nubbin of flesh made her gasp with delight. "Or here." His clever fingers dipped lower still, gently probing as if he were parting the petals of some delicate flower to seek the teardrops of nectar within.

Tabitha's whimper deepened to a moan. Through a haze of bliss, she felt Colin's hands stroking her thighs, easing them apart. She tensed, bracing herself for a foreign invasion, only to realize with a shock that it wasn't his sex pressed against her, but—oh, wonder of wonders—his mouth. She arched off the mattress, utterly beguiled by the hot, moist sweetness of his lips, the swirling magic of his tongue.

Colin might not have succumbed to the wiles of those decadent women, but he must have memorized their whispered enticements. He proved himself a master of devilish invention, holding her in bondage to the darkness and her need until molten pleasure was dripping from the very core of her. When she was poised on the brink of madness, he filled that aching hollow with his thickest finger. She cried out his name as waves of rapture racked her entire body.

Then he was on top of her as he'd been in that meadow the first day they met, kissing her sweat-dampened throat and whispering in her ear. "That, my lady, is what I would do were I a learned enough man to drive you wild with desire."

No longer content to be passive, Tabitha fisted her hands in his hair and dragged his lips to hers. It was his turn to moan with delight as their tongues entwined in sweet communion. Her trepidation had been replaced by a primitive compulsion to drive *him* wild with desire, to make him cry out *her* name as if it were a magical incantation. Her sex was throbbing for his attention and she knew from the feel of him, hot and heavy against her belly, that he was more than willing and able to provide it.

She opened her thighs in invitation, but there was no need to guide him into her. He found the heart of her with unerring instinct, grunting into her mouth as he thrust deep and hard, filling her to the brim.

Tabitha had braced herself for a twinge of discomfort; she had not expected this searing pain as her body struggled valiantly to welcome him. She bit her lip, but not before a sharp cry could escape.

Colin froze. He was so still she could feel her sheath pulsing around him with each of her shuddering heartbeats. She opened her eyes to find him gazing down at her with a perplexing mix of awe and shock. If she hadn't known better, she would have thought she'd betrayed him for a second time.

Longing only to erase that inexplicable expression, she wrapped her legs around his waist and gave her hips an amateur wiggle.

Colin threw back his head with a guttural groan, then shook it as if to ward off a spell. He cupped her face in his hands and kissed her again, something both fierce and reverent in his touch. As his body began to move within her in a tender, deliberate cadence, her pain slowly melted to a different kind of ache—an ache that craved the sweet friction of the man she loved riding deep inside of her, an ache that demanded to be satisfied. Satisfy her he did, stroking her mouth with his tongue and her body with his sex until she was meeting his every thrust with one of her own.

Only then did he liberate himself from six years of brutal self-denial. Only then did he roar her name and allow his ecstasy to come spilling out of him in a white-hot torrent. Tabitha cried out her own delight as he buried himself as deep within her as he could go, shuddering to miraculous completion.

They lay entwined in each other's arms, their breath mingled, their sated bodies slick with sweat, their hearts beating in perfect accord, as if they were still one flesh.

Until Colin lifted his head to glower at her. "You didn't . . . ?"

Tabitha nodded smugly. "Oh, yes, I did. Before."

"But not when I . . ."

"Of course not. Women aren't designed for that. Mutual orgasms are nothing but a myth like Bigfoot and unicorns and knights"—her voice trailed to a whisper as she blinked up at him—"in shining armor."

A slow, dangerous grin curved his lips. "Is that so, my lady?"

Tabitha squeaked in surprise as Colin gently guided her over on her stomach. "It gives you great pleasure to prove me wrong, doesn't it?" she asked breathlessly.

He brushed his lips across her nape, making her shiver with anticipation. "Not nearly as much pleasure as it will give you."

CHAPTER 19

Sunshine draped Tabitha's naked body like a warm, fuzzy blanket. She stretched without opening her eyes, exulting in the delicious languor melting through her muscles. For the first time, she truly understood why Scarlett O'Hara had awakened with such a feline smile on her lips the morning after Rhett had carried her up those curving stairs. Summoning barely enough energy to lift her hand, she gave the mattress beside her a seeking pat. It was empty and cold.

Her eyes flew open.

A shirtless Colin sat on the edge of the hearth, dragging on his second boot. His brooding glower had returned, darker than ever before.

"Good morning," she murmured, hoping he would find the husky edge of sleep in her voice irresistibly sexy.

"Good day, my lady."

His clipped words snapped her fully awake. She fumbled for the threadbare quilt, drawing it up to her chin. He probably found her shyness ridiculous, given the nature and shameless variety of the intimacies they'd shared during the night. But this surly stranger seemed like an evil twin of the man who had given her pleasure so intense it had made her sob aloud, then dried her tears with his kisses.

Oh, God, she thought, what if he was the kind of man who lost interest in a woman after he'd slept with her? Not that they'd done much sleeping.

Colin donned his tunic, his motions as curt as his expression. Leaning over a tarnished basin, he splashed his face and hair with water he must have fetched from a nearby stream while she was sleeping. He was without a doubt the cleanest barbarian she'd ever met.

With his unruly mop of hair slicked back from his unshaven face, he looked younger and more vulnerable, giving Tabitha the courage to confront him.

She sat up and forced herself to relinquish her death grip on the quilt, letting it catch on the swell of her breasts. "If I didn't know better, I'd think you had a wife waiting at home."

His hands froze in the motion of securing his silver belt around his lean hips. He slowly lifted his head, his stricken stare betraying the last emotion she'd expected to see on his face.

Guilt.

She was suddenly afraid.

Then his expression was masked, and she wondered if she'd imagined it. "I should be getting back to the castle. I've tarried here long enough."

Tabitha sniffed. "That's odd. You didn't seem to be in any hurry last night."

He strode toward the door without answering. For one heartbreaking moment, she thought he was actually going to leave her there—naked and alone, the provocative musk of their lovemaking still clinging to her skin.

But then he wheeled around and paced the length of the cottage. His hand shot through his hair, ruffling the damp tendrils until they were once again as wild as his eyes.

Coming to an abrupt halt, he pointed at the mattress. "I might have taken even less haste with you had you warned me about *that*."

Tabitha studied the brownish stains on the faded fabric, then coolly met Colin's accusing gaze. She refused to cringe in Victorian horror. "You didn't strike me as the sort of man who would faint at the sight of blood."

"But 'tis *your* blood, lass." His voice faded to an anguished whisper. "Why didn't you tell me you'd never before lain with a man?"

She shrugged. "What was I supposed to do? Sing a couple of choruses of 'The Simple Joys of Maidenhood'? Swoon into your arms and whimper, 'Be gentle with me, kind sirrah'?" Overcome by shyness, she said softly, "You were already being gentle with me." She reached for his hand, but he drew out of her reach, making her frown. "That's odd. Your conscience didn't seem to be bothering you the second time we made love. Or the third. Or the—"

"Enough!" He cast her a sheepish look from beneath his lashes. " 'Twas too late then. The damage had been done."

Tabitha sighed, growing more exasperated by the second. "So if I'd have told you I was a virgin, you wouldn't have spent the night making mad, passionate love to me?"

"Yes!" he snapped, then just as vehemently, "No!" His shoulders slumped. "I do not know." His helpless gaze searched her face. "How was I to guess you were a maiden? You made no protest when I took you to my bed. You spoke frankly about carnal matters. You traveled with a troupe of mummers. And you're a witch," he added, throwing out his arms as if that explained everything.

For several seconds after he spoke, Tabitha could hear nothing but the low-pitched roaring in her ears.

When she finally replied, her voice was deceptively soft. "Ah, and witches are notoriously easy, aren't they?"

He stabbed a finger at her. "Oh, no, my lady, you are most certainly not easy. You are one of the most difficult women I have ever encountered." He rubbed the shadow of beard on his jaw, realizing he wasn't making much headway in his attempt to reason with her. " 'Tis a well-known fact that witches delight in enslaving mortal men with their carnal wiles." His gaze was almost pitying. "You cannot help it, lass. 'Tis your nature."

Tossing a corner of the quilt over her shoulder so it enveloped her like a queen's mantle, Tabitha rose to her full height. She remained standing on the mattress purely for the pleasure of sneering down her nose at him. "You're absolutely right, Colin. I'm just another one of Satan's sluts. Now that you've introduced me to the delights of fornication, I'm looking forward to spending most of my dateless evenings dancing naked around a bonfire, copulating with demons who have cloven hooves and enormous forked—"

"Tabitha!"

"—tails," she finished, stepping off the mattress. She began to back him toward the hearth, her voice rising with each word. "Or maybe I'll just skip the demons and tumble into bed with the next holier-than-thou, self-righteous prig of a knight who tries to burn me at the stake!"

Colin tilted his head to the side and blinked at her. "Have I offended you?"

Her shriek was one of pure frustration. Flattening her

palm on his chest, she gave him a hard shove. He sat down abruptly on the hearth behind him.

Tabitha whirled around, no longer able to bear the sight of his smug face. The sweeping maneuver might have been more impressive if she hadn't stumbled over the hem of the quilt and had to clutch the window shutter to keep from falling flat on her face.

She tried, but it was impossible to hide the bitterness in her voice. "If I had known you were going to be so disappointed in my lack of experience, I'd have taken dozens of lovers. I'd have purchased a charter membership in a harem and lost my virginity to an entire tribe of sweaty, grunting infidels." Unshed tears clogged her throat as she leaned her cheek against the shutter and whispered, "I'm sorry you were the first."

"I'm not." The words were spoken so softly they might have been conjured out of thin air. Colin's hands came to rest gently on her shoulders, squeezing them through the quilt. "Oh, I wanted to be. A virgin witch was the last thing I needed in my life at the moment. But all I could feel in that moment you surrendered your innocence to me was joy and a ridiculous pride, as if someone had given me a gift I would never deserve."

Tabitha turned in his arms, torn between disbelief and wonder. Colin cupped her cheek in his hand, a wry half smile curving his lips, his golden eyes unguarded. "My lady," he murmured, and for the first time, Tabitha sensed the words came from his heart.

She threw her arms around his neck and pressed her lips to his. Without its anchor, the quilt slid down to pool at their feet, but Tabitha was too lost in Colin's tender kiss to notice.

Nor did she notice the man leaning against the doorjamb with arms crossed until his honeyed Gallic voice poured over them. "My, my, this certainly gives new meaning to being burned at the stake."

Colin sprang in front of her and snatched up the quilt, tossing it over her head in his haste to shield her. Disoriented by shock, it took Tabitha several muffled curses to battle her way out. Clutching the blanket around her like an oversized bath towel, she peeped over Colin's shoulder to find Arjon smirking at her. He softened his leer with a mischievous wink.

"You might have knocked," Colin said, his scowl returning.

"You might have closed the door," Arjon retorted. " 'Tis fortunate I left Chauncey outside to mind the horses. His mother begged me to accept him as my squire, but I don't think this was quite the education the dear woman had in mind."

Colin snorted. "If the lad's to travel more than a league with you as his master, he'll lose his blush soon enough."

"Ah, but I can see the *bewitching* Lady Tabitha hasn't lost hers." Arjon cast the mattress a knowing glance. "Her blush, that is."

Tabitha's cheeks flamed even hotter. Oh, why couldn't she be one of those sophisticated women who languished in bed blowing smoke rings at her lover after a torrid night of passion? Instead, she was forced to blow a disheveled strand of hair out of her eyes before it blinded her.

Arjon only worsened her discomfort by circling them like a sleek hound, his aristocratic nostrils flaring as he sniffed at the air. "Most curious, is it not? Not a hint of smoke nor a speck of ash do I detect on the lady's milky skin."

"You knew!" Tabitha accused, jabbing him in the chest. Since he was wearing his mail breastplate, she only succeeded in jamming her finger. "You knew Colin wasn't going to burn me at the stake, didn't you?"

He gave her another of those infuriating Gallic shrugs. "One can never predict what a Scotsman will do. They're all quite mad, you know. Especially when afflicted with *mal d'amour*."

"Seasickness?" she ventured, sucking on her injured knuckle.

He favored her with a patronizing smile. "Lovesickness, my dear."

Colin shoved his way between the two of them and marched to the hearth, the back of his neck darkened to an endearing shade of fuchsia. "The only affliction I'm suffering from is having such a braying jackass for a friend. And to what, pray tell, do we owe the honor of this unexpected visit?"

The amusement fled Arjon's face, leaving it uncharacteristically somber. " 'Tis the MacDuff."

An odd flicker of emotion darted between the two men, jarring Tabitha. She'd never imagined that Colin could look furtive. It definitely didn't suit him.

Arjon cast her an enigmatic glance. "One of my men sent word that Brisbane has dispatched an envoy bearing gifts to MacDuff's castle. If he convinces the old rogue to break faith with you and forge an alliance with him, Ravenshaw will be surrounded by enemies on all borders and you'll have no chance of survival."

Colin fisted one hand against the mantel and gazed into the cold, dead ashes in the grate. "How much time do we have?"

"If we leave now, we can arrive at MacDuff's castle several hours before Brisbane's messenger."

No longer caring if she tripped over the quilt, Tabitha dove for her discarded gown. "I can be ready in five minutes. Just let me get dressed and wash my—"

"No!" Colin's command startled them all.

Tabitha straightened, gripping the rumpled gown.

He seemed to be having difficulty meeting her eyes. " 'Twould not be safe. The MacDuff is nearly as unpredictable as Roger when he chooses to be. I'll not risk your comely neck again."

She smiled sweetly at him. "How chivalrous of you! Then while you're gone, I'll just march back down the mountain to Castle Raven where I can bask in the adoration of your people. That is, until they decide to roast me with an apple in my mouth."

Arjon nodded thoughtfully. "She is no lackwit, I fear. I warned you about that."

Colin shot him a savage glare, then sighed. " 'Tis God's truth you speak, lass. You'll not be safe at Ravenshaw either until I can return with you. Once I've commanded them not to harm you, my people will obey. My word is their law."

She brightened. "Then you'll just have to take me with you."

His eyes narrowed speculatively. Without a word of explanation, he marched across the cottage, took her hand, and pulled her toward the door. She was about to protest that she couldn't ride all the way to MacDuff's wearing nothing but a quilt when they emerged into the blinding sunshine. She found herself blinking into Chauncey's shocked eyes.

The boy dropped the reins of Colin's stallion and snatched off his cap, plainly torn between bowing and fleeing down the hillside in horror.

"Chauncey," Colin said, "I want you to remain here at the cottage and guard the lady until we return from the MacDuff's."

His master's faith in him seemed to restore his swagger. "Aye, me laird, I'll see to it the vixen don't escape."

Colin rolled his eyes. "I'm not appointing you Lady Tabitha's jailer. I want you to guard her against all harm." He slanted Tabitha a look that warmed her heart and almost made her forget he was leaving her. "She is a most precious charge."

"Oh." The hulking boy looked vaguely disappointed. "Very well, sir. I'll look after the witch." He cut her a wary look. "If she'll promise not to cast any spells on me."

Tabitha gave the amulet a mocking stroke, but Colin shook his head at her in warning.

Before she could come up with any more compelling arguments for taking her along, he had swung himself astride the stallion.

While Arjon was mounting his own horse, Colin unhooked one of the bulging knapsacks from his saddle and tossed it to Chauncey. "No witch burning, lad."

The boy cast the handsome stake with its thicket of crisp brush a crestfallen look. "Aye, sir."

Colin shifted his scowl to Tabitha. "And you? *No witchcraft!*"

"Yes, Darrin," she muttered.

He squinted at her. "What was that?"

She bobbed a mocking curtsy. "Yes, darling."

He nodded his approval and wheeled the horse around. Tabitha's spirits plummeted. He was just going to ride out of her life without giving her so much as an affectionate pat on the head.

But as he and Arjon reached the edge of the clearing, he drew back on the reins and clucked a command at the stallion. The horse pranced around to face her in an equine minuet of breathtaking grace. The morning wind rippled through Colin's hair, making him look as if he could have ridden straight from the gilt-edged pages of one of her mama's books. Tabitha's breath caught with poignant yearning. Until that very moment, she'd never realized how much it had cost her to stop believing in those fairy tales.

He nudged the horse into motion with his well-muscled thighs. As the beast came trotting toward her, Tabitha stood her ground, trusting that Colin would not trample her fragile heart underfoot. Drawing the horse to a rearing halt, he leaned down, wrapped one powerful arm around her back, and lifted her to his kiss.

As his tongue swept through her mouth like sweet wildfire, Arjon and Chauncey seemed to vanish as if she'd wished them gone. She and Colin were alone just as they'd been during the night, free to pour all their passion into each other.

As he lowered her to the ground, she clutched both the quilt and his knee, surprised her trembling legs would support her.

He reached down and stroked her tousled hair, the fierce light in his eyes softened by tenderness. "All will be well, my lady. I swear it."

Tabitha gazed after him long after he was gone, bittersweet longing tightening her throat. If his vow was true, then why had she tasted such desperation in his kiss?

Tabitha and Chauncey perched on the stoop of the cottage like a pair of sulking gargoyles. They relaxed their bored vigil only long enough to exchange a sullen glance or pinch another hunk of bread off the loaf they'd shared for lunch. The moments crawled past, ticked off by some giant invisible clock.

Tabitha yawned. Chauncey scratched at his waist-length mop of auburn hair. She eased a few inches away, wondering if he had head lice and if so, just how far they could jump.

She squinted up at the pale disk of the sun. The men had been gone for less than two hours and already her patience was waning.

She brushed a bread crumb from the wrinkled skirt of Magwyn's gown. "They could be gone for days, couldn't they?"

"Weeks," he replied glumly.

She looked at Chauncey. Chauncey looked at the sprightly sorrel tethered to a nearby cedar.

"You didn't want to be stuck here with me, did you?"

"No, my lady."

"You wanted to go with Sir Arjon, didn't you? To serve as his squire."

"Aye, my lady." His expression was growing more wretched by the second.

"But Colin told you to stay here and you always do what Colin tells you, don't you?"

He nodded. "With the old master gone, Sir Colin is my laird."

"Well, he's not mine." Tabitha rose and started for the horse, the skirt whipping around her ankles with each of her determined strides. "And if he thinks I'm going to spend my life hanging out of castle windows tearfully waving a kerchief while he gallops off to fight pagans or Brisbane or whatever dragons he believes he's been divinely appointed to slay on any given Friday, then he's got a few things to learn about modern relationships. And Tabitha Lennox is just the woman to teach him." She threw a searching glance over her shoulder. "Aren't you coming?"

Chauncey sprang to his feet, slack-jawed with shock. "We dare not disobey Laird Colin. His word is—"

"—the law," Tabitha finished with a weary sigh.

"Well, this is one law I have every intention of breaking. Do you know the way to MacDuff's castle?"

Chauncey nodded. Apprehension had bleached his face, making his freckles stand out.

"Then I'll have to insist that you accompany me."

He stole another longing look at the horse, a thread of excitement creeping into his voice. "If I do, Laird Colin will surely punish me."

She narrowed her eyes and lowered her voice to a menacing purr. "And if you don't, you'll be stuck here with one very unhappy witch."

Tabitha had never before used the threat of magic to intimidate anyone. She nursed a brief spark of guilt, but as the boy started eagerly for the horse, it was smothered by a flood of wicked exhilaration. After all, she was only making him do what he really wanted to do anyway. What harm could there be in that?

Chauncey mounted and she swung herself behind him, biting back a wince of pain. But the tenderness lingering between her legs only strengthened her resolve. She belonged at Colin's side and she had every intention of proving it to him. Even if it killed her.

Now that Chauncey had decided to commit himself to the low road, he did so with enthusiasm, pointing out a barely discernible path that wound its way through the dense underbrush. "I know a shorter way. I didn't tell Laird Colin because I didn't want him to tell Mum I'd been sneakin' over to MacDuff lands to court one of the auld tyrant's milkmaids."

Which is how a beaming Tabitha and a cringing Chauncey came to arrive at the perimeter of MacDuff's moat approximately three minutes before Colin and Arjon came cantering across the meadow. Before Colin could rein his horse to a complete halt, Chauncey had flung himself off the sorrel, landing on his knees in the grass.

He clutched at his laird's leg, his voice cracking from the strain of being a boy trapped in a man's body. "Oh, please, sir, don't have me flogged. The witch made me bring her. I begged her not to, but she fixed me with a devilish glare and enslaved me with a wiggle of her fingertips." He shot Tabitha a triumphant glance from beneath his stringy bangs before smothering Colin's leg with kisses.

She rolled her eyes and sniffed. "I did no such thing. The boy was just as eager to come as I was."

Colin struggled to disengage his ankle from Chauncey's grip. "Cease slobbering on my boots, lad! I've no intention of flogging you."

That promise only succeeded in earning him a fresh spate of kisses. "Bless you, my laird. You are the most kind, generous master Ravenshaw has ever known. I tried to resist the witch, truly I did, but her charms beguiled me." He shuddered. " 'Twas most distressing."

Colin turned his narrow gaze on Tabitha. "Believe me, I know just how persuasive the lady can be."

Her sunny smile failed to warm his stormy glower. She had expected him to be furious with her for disobeying him. She had not expected to find such a wild glint in his eye. He looked almost . . . trapped. Although he'd faced the monstrous Scot-Killer in armed combat without betraying even a trace of fear, her unexpected arrival seemed to have thrown him into a panic.

Arjon clapped him on the back. "Come, my friend. Your lady has proven her devotion and risked much to join you. Is that any way to welcome her?"

His manic joy only intensified the apprehension prickling down Tabitha's spine. If the impish Norman knight was *that* happy, it couldn't bode well for any of them, especially Colin.

Tabitha blinked up at the imposing edifice looming over them. "So what do we do now? Ring the doorbell?"

It seemed that wouldn't be necessary. With a deafening clanking of chains, the massive drawbridge began to lower. Tabitha could not quite suppress a wistful sigh. Here at last was a castle worthy of her mother's fantasies. Soaring towers and flying turrets crowned walls of white stone. Wrought-iron bars shielded the lower windows, but high above them, ruby and emerald panes of stained glass basked in the glow of the sun. A graceful standard rippled from the highest tower, boldly proclaiming the might and splendor of the lord who dwelled within. As the drawbridge crept downward, Tabitha would have almost sworn she could hear the distant strains of "Camelot" wafting on the wind.

She stole a glance at Colin. His expression was so grim she might have thought the gates of hell were creaking open to swallow him up. Kneeing Chauncey out of the way, he slid off his horse, plainly wanting to face whatever terror would emerge from that yawning abyss on his own two feet.

Utterly baffled, she looked at Arjon. His expectant smirk revealed nothing. The drawbridge thudded to a halt at their feet. But the creature who appeared at its peak was hardly the horned demon Tabitha had expected.

What enchanted castle, after all, would be complete without a fairy princess?

The lithe sprite came scampering down the ramp, a cloud of ebony ringlets rippling behind her. Her tiny feet barely seemed to skim the planks and her every movement was a study in artless grace. Tabitha sat up straighter in the saddle, making a conscious effort not to slump.

"Colin!" The girl sang his name as if it were an angel's hymn before throwing her arms around his neck and smothering his flushed face with kisses. Her feet dangled nearly a foot off the grass.

Tabitha frowned. That was odd. Colin had never mentioned a sister. And he certainly wasn't old enough to have a daughter so . . . so . . . voluptuous.

"Oh, Colin," the petite pixie chirped. "I thought you were never coming back! Papa vowed you were a man of honor, but six years is a very, very long time to wait. It seemed like an eternity."

Colin pried her arms from his neck and gently set her on her feet. She beamed up at him, her lovely face so radiant Tabitha almost wished for a pair of sunglasses.

His answering smile was wan. "My goodness, Lyssandra, how you've"—his despairing gaze seemed to drop of its own volition to a bosom that was even now threatening to burst from its silk confines—"grown."

Arjon reached down and nudged Chauncey's jaw shut before he could drool.

"As have you, my lord. When you left, you were little more than a lad." The girl trailed one coral-tipped finger down his chest, stopping only when she reached the silver links of the belt slung low on his hips. She fluttered her fringe of sooty eyelashes, managing to look both shy and seductive. "Now you're a man full grown."

"That's it," Tabitha muttered beneath her breath. She slung one leg over the horse, fully prepared to jump down and snatch the little minx bald.

The appearance of a second figure on the drawbridge stopped her. "Ravenshaw, is that you?"

The demand boomed like a cannon blast, rattling glass and teeth for miles around.

The flush drained from Colin's face, leaving it drawn and pale. This must be the demon he had feared!

"Aye, sir. 'Tis me." He squared off with the newcomer with all the enthusiasm of a condemned man facing a firing squad.

The squat stranger rested his hands on his hips. Although his legs were spindly, his girth was ample. He possessed what, in less polite twenty-first-century terms, could only be called a beer belly. "Rumor has it that you've been home for nearly a sennight, yet haven't troubled yourself to ride over and greet the lord who fostered you. Have you forgotten the manners I taught you?"

"No, sir. I've simply been otherwise occupied."

Tabitha could sense Colin struggling, for some inexplicable reason, not to look at her.

"And I suppose you expect me to overlook your churlish lack of courtesy?"

"If it pleases you, my lord."

The man rocked back on his heels, startling them all with a boisterous laugh. "Always could charm the devil himself, couldn't you? Very well then, lad. All is forgiven now that you've finally come home to claim your bride."

Tabitha swayed and would have fallen off the horse if Arjon's hand hadn't steadied her shoulder. Lyssandra, still beaming, slipped her slender arms around Colin's waist and snuggled her cheek against his chest as if that was where it had always belonged. Colin slowly turned his head to meet Tabitha's stricken gaze, his eyes darkened in appeal.

CHAPTER 20

Tabitha Lennox was a loser.

She'd been born a loser and she would die a loser and no amount of money or magic could change that one fundamental truth. She'd been born to both power and privilege, but had spent every waking moment since that snowy Connecticut night bumbling her way from catastrophe to disaster with all the hapless ineptitude of a gate crasher at the party of life.

And now she'd traveled over seven hundred years into the past to find the man of her dreams only to discover he belonged to another woman.

Not just any woman, either, but a fairy princess who slept in a tower and possessed the gamine flair of Audrey Hepburn and the petite grace of a Ukrainian gymnast. As Tabitha watched Lyssandra flit about the bedroom, filling the awkward silence with her musical chatter, she was tempted to peek over the girl's shoulder and check for wings. She fingered the amulet, battling a spiteful urge to wish for a giant fly swatter.

She would never know how she'd survived those first dark moments outside the castle. It had taken every ounce of spinal starch she possessed to slide off the sorrel without doubling over.

But she had.

She'd even managed to paste on a brilliant smile and slip her hand into Lyssandra's, assuring the blushing bride-to-be that she and Colin would surely be very happy together. If her bloodless fingers felt like ice, Lyssandra had been too polite to comment.

Rubbing the back of his neck in abject misery, Colin had fumbled for an introduction. Tabitha would have let him twist in the wind if she hadn't been afraid he was going to introduce her as his spinster aunt. So she'd cranked up her smile another hundred watts and blithely announced that she was Colin's cousin visiting from the distant village of Gotham.

Unfortunately, that had led to the discovery that Lyssandra's ethereal beauty was surpassed only by her generosity of spirit. The girl's velvety brown eyes had sympathetically taken in Tabitha's travel-stained gown and disheveled hair. She'd chided Colin and Arjon for their thoughtlessness, then gathered Tabitha under her gossamer wings and hustled her up the winding stairs for a medieval makeover.

She wasn't even to be allowed the satisfaction of hating Colin's fiancée. After only an afternoon in her company, it was apparent that everyone loved Lyssandra—from the lowliest servant who hastened to do her bidding to the pug-nosed terrier who crouched at his mistress's dainty feet, following her every move with his moist, adoring eyes. If *everyone* loved Lyssandra, how could Colin not? Tabitha thought despairingly.

There was even something naggingly familiar about the girl. Her aimless chatter and tinkling laughter was oddly comforting. Perhaps she was just one of those rare people you meet once and feel like you've known forever. Or at least for seven hundred years.

As Lyssandra fluttered from the four-poster bed to an

ornate chest, Tabitha slumped on her stool, feeling more like Quasimodo with each passing moment. Although she was fresh from a jasmine-scented bath, she could already feel herself wilting—a homely dandelion smothered by the shadow of a rose.

Lyssandra threw open the chest and dove in, tossing veils left and girdles right in her frenzied search for something Tabitha could wear to the banquet the MacDuff was hosting in honor of his prodigal son-in-law-to-be.

Even muffled, Lyssandra's voice retained its enchanting lilt. "I had no inkling that Colin had a cousin. 'Tis odd he never mentioned you."

"I could say the same," Tabitha muttered, wondering if she could live with herself if she tiptoed over and slammed the lid of the chest.

Lyssandra bounced up, gripping a bouquet of hair ribbons. "Are the two of you very close?"

We were last night, she mentally replied, blinded by a vision of their moonlit bodies entwined in a lover's kiss. Blinking back the threat of tears, she inflicted an airy smile on her stiff lips. "Where I come from, you might call us kissing cousins."

Lyssandra clutched the ribbons to her heart with all the drama of a lovesick teenager, which, as Tabitha noted, she probably was. "I do believe I should swoon if Colin kissed me." She demonstrated her faint by tumbling back into the chest. "Ah-ha!" she trilled, popping back up like a manic-depressive jack-in-the-box. "Here's one that might fit you. Let's try it, shall we?"

Whipping several yards of brocaded damask from the chest, the woman-child skipped across the chamber, even doing a flawless pirouette around Tabitha's stool. Before Tabitha could protest, she was tugged to her feet and the sleeveless slip she'd been forced to don after her bath was covered by her hostess's find.

The gorgeous smock, too tight in the shoulders, too loose in the bodice, fell to just below her knees.

"I do believe my slip is showing."

"Oh, that won't do at all." Lyssandra's dismayed pout was the only mirror Tabitha needed to know she must look like a giraffe wearing a tutu. The girl's expression was so crestfallen, Tabitha almost apologized for disappointing her.

Then a sparkle of inspiration lit those almond-shaped eyes. "Don't give up hope. All is not lost. I know just the thing."

As Colin's fiancée dashed from the room, Tabitha sank down on the stool, more dejected than before. Longing for Lucy's purring company, she reached to pet the terrier. He bared his crooked teeth and growled at her.

Tabitha and the ill-tempered little beast were still glaring at each other when Lyssandra swept back into the tower, a shimmering length of silk the rich blue of morning glories cradled in her arms.

She stroked the exquisite fabric as if it were woven of moonbeams and spiderwebs. " 'Twas my mother's. She died when I was five, but I still remember how willowy and graceful she was." Lyssandra smiled tenderly at Tabitha. "Just like you."

Tabitha jumped to her feet, nearly stumbling over the stool, and backed away. "Oh, no, I really couldn't. I'm a terrible klutz. I'd probably get my heel caught in the hem or dribble grape juice down the front of it." She lifted her hands in an imploring motion only to feel the shoulder seams of the gown she was wearing give with a woeful groan. "See! That's exactly what I mean."

"Oh, pooh," Lyssandra said. "That old rag means naught to me." As if to prove it, she literally ripped the gown from Tabitha's body, then dropped the cloud of silk over her head.

As Lyssandra gave her mother's gown a tug here and a tuck there, Tabitha sighed in resignation. How could one oppose someone who actually said things like "Oh, pooh"? And she had to admit, as she stole a tentative glance downward, that the gown fit as if it had been personally tailored for her by Christian Dior.

Lyssandra draped a wide gold belt around her hips before shooing her back toward the stool. Tabitha obediently plopped down, robbed of her will to resist the little tyrant.

As Lyssandra began to do mysterious things with her hair, wielding an ivory comb as if it were a scythe, Tabitha asked, "Isn't six years a long time to be engaged?"

"So it would seem." The girl's wistful sigh bubbled into a giggle. "But Colin and I have been betrothed for almost thirteen years, since I was five and he eleven."

Tabitha didn't know whether to be heartened or horrified. "It must have been love at first sight," she said weakly.

Curling an uncooperative strand of Tabitha's hair around her finger, Lyssandra nodded. "I shall never forget the first time I saw him. He came to be a page at Papa's court when I was four and he was ten. He was the most handsome lad you could imagine with those flashing eyes and dark curls."

Tabitha squirmed on the stool. The girl's naked adoration was all too familiar.

"Even as a boy, Colin was always so gentle and patient with me." Lyssandra wrinkled her pert nose, only succeeding in making herself look even more adorable. "Unlike that nasty Norman."

Tabitha was surprised into a laugh. "Sir Arjon?"

"Aye, Arjon. I begged Papa to send him back to Normandy, but he'd promised Arjon's father he'd try to instill the fear of God into him. He was a most horrid boy. Always yanking my hair and dropping beetles down my back." Her dulcet voice oozed contempt. "I loathed him." Lyssandra sighed. "But my beloved Colin was always there to champion me. He challenged Arjon to a duel once on my behalf. Papa would only allow them to use sticks, of course, but Colin buffeted Arjon so hard, he knocked him right into the horse trough. I laughed until my sides ached."

Tabitha put a hand to her own stomach. She was beginning to feel distinctly nauseous and she suspected it wasn't from lack of food. She didn't think she could stand to hear any more gushing tales about Colin and his lady fair.

Lyssandra spared her that torture by giving each of her cheeks a maternal tweak and tugging her to her feet. Then Tabitha was ushered over to a candlelit alcove where an enormous mirror hung in a gilded frame composed entirely of entwined hands. Tabitha shook off an absurd impulse to ask it who was the fairest of them all. She had no desire to hear its answer.

But as Lyssandra urged her closer to her shimmering reflection, she realized the mirror must be enchanted after all. For the woman peering shyly back at her was a stranger.

This woman was not gawky, but statuesque. The silk smock draped her in regal elegance, its pleated train rippling around her ankles like a waterfall. The fabric's rich hue darkened her eyes until she could almost pretend they were a subtle blue instead of ordinary gray.

Being deprived of the Big Macs and pints of Häagen-Dazs she gobbled more out of boredom than hunger had carved intriguing hollows beneath her cheeks. If she squinted, she could almost catch a glimpse of the legendary Lennox bone structure that had always made her father look like a Nordic prince.

The sun had washed away her city pallor, burnishing her skin and ripening her hair to honey-gold. The gleaming tendrils curled lightly against her shoulders, framing a face that had traded its pinched expression for the becoming vulnerability of a woman in love. Even her lips seemed softer and fuller, as if still savoring the memory of a lover's kisses. With a mixture of wonder and despair, Tabitha touched her fingertips to those lips, just as Colin had done so tenderly the night before.

"You are a rare beauty, are you not, my lady?" Lyssandra said softly before indulging in a melodramatic moan. "Why, oh, why couldn't I have been tall like my mother instead of stunted like Papa?" She stamped her slippered foot. "If I stand too close to you tonight, someone may very well mistake me for one of Papa's dwarves."

Tabitha burst into helpless laughter. It seemed she had made a terrible mistake. Colin's fiancée was not a fairy princess after all, but a fairy godmother, generous enough to bestow glass slippers on even the most skeptical of Cinderellas. It was precisely at that moment that she realized why Lyssandra seemed so achingly familiar to her.

She reminded her of her own mother.

Even with her eyes shining with unshed tears, Tabitha could not resist drawing the girl into a laughing hug.

Colin tossed back his third mug of ale, his gaze straying with increasing frequency to the vaulted ceiling of the MacDuff's great hall.

Although MacDuff's feast was being given in his honor, he felt more like a fool than a guest. He wouldn't even have flinched had one of the jesters trotted over and smacked him upside the head with a pig's bladder on a stick. 'Twould be no more than he deserved for breaking both the gentle hearts entrusted into his unworthy hands.

A trio of pipers bleated out a winsome melody. The beaming audience of ladies and knights broke into delighted applause as a dwarf acrobat somersaulted over a ferret prancing across the tiled floor on his hind legs. Colin had long suspected MacDuff of keeping dwarves so there would always be someone in the hall shorter than he was.

Almost as if his canny host had sensed the unkind thought, MacDuff caught his eye and lifted his jeweled goblet in an enigmatic toast. Brisbane's envoy had arrived shortly before the banquet began and Colin could only too well imagine the poison the pockmarked, mustachioed knight was pouring into the MacDuff's attentive ear.

He supposed he would find out soon enough. When he was joined by his betrothed and they made their way through the adoring crowd to the seat of honor on the dais.

He'd returned to gazing dourly at the ceiling when Arjon slid onto the bench next to him. "Expecting it to collapse on your head at any moment?"

"I should be so lucky." Colin reached for the flagon of ale only to find it empty.

His friend swiped a fresh one from a passing page and thrust it into his hand. " 'Tis fortunate you gave up women instead of strong drink."

Colin groaned. "I should have stayed celibate and become a monk." He started to pour himself another mug of ale, then shrugged and began to drink directly from the flagon. "Or a eunuch."

Arjon winced and crossed his hose-clad legs. "Ah, but then you'd have been forever denied those tender pleasures of the flesh. Most especially, the Lady Tabitha's delectable flesh."

His friend had known him too long and too well. Colin could do nothing to hide the naked longing in his eyes. So he simply shifted them back to the ceiling and muttered, "What in the name of St. Andrew could they be doing up there? Snatching each other bald?"

"From the murderous glint in your lady's eyes when she discovered your perfidy, I'd wager she'd rather snatch you bald. Or turn you into the randy goat she believes you to be."

Borne on a wave of panic, Colin surged to his feet. "Oh, dear God, I almost forgot about Tabitha's powers. What if she turns Lyssa into a moat rat?"

Arjon grabbed his elbow and tugged him back down. " 'Twould well suit the brat's shrewish temperament."

Colin jerked his arm free, relieved to have found a target for his frustration. "Lyssa was always a very sweet girl. You only dislike her because she's the only female you never could charm."

The Norman snorted into his goblet. "I'd sooner charm a cobra."

They drank in disagreeable silence for several minutes before Arjon jabbed Colin with his elbow. Shuddering, he nodded toward the stairs. "Now there's a sight to chill a man's blood."

Colin followed his friend's gaze to find his lover and his betrothed descending the stairs arm in arm, their bright and dark heads inclined toward one another as if sharing secrets hoarded for a lifetime. If that weren't enough to make him break out in an icy sweat, he would have almost sworn he heard one of them whisper his name and the other reply with a merry peal of laughter.

CHAPTER 21

Tabitha had never seen a man look quite so miserable and never enjoyed it quite so much.

Colin sat at the head table on the dais, trapped between his jovial host and his radiant bride-to-be. A roguish hint of beard had darkened his jaw, deepening the furrows around his mouth. His eyes still had the dangerous gleam of a stallion on the verge of bolting. Even with his hair bound neatly at his nape, Tabitha had never seen him look more like a barbarian.

His misery couldn't quite take the sting out of her own suffering. It still hurt too much to see those striking dark heads together. Even she had to admit they made the perfect couple. Lyssandra was just the right height to look up to him.

The knuckles wrapped around the stem of the golden goblet he shared with his fiancée whitened with strain as he was forced to endure toast after toast to his impending nuptials.

A shriveled old man hefted his mug. "I wish the lad potent vigor in the marriage bed."

"And out of it," croaked one of the anonymous squires lounging against the back wall, sounding suspiciously like Chauncey. The jest incited several hearty guffaws and a blush from Lyssandra.

Colin shot Tabitha an anguished look, but she ignored him, making a major production out of picking the almonds out of her pudding.

A jug-eared lord lurched to his feet, sloshing ale over the rim of his goblet. "May God bless you with a passel of brats to kiss your cheeks and tug your ears."

"*His* brats apparently didn't know when to let go," Arjon murmured, spooning in another mouthful of pudding.

Tabitha gave her dinner companion a rueful glance. After the guests of honor had taken their seats, she and Arjon had been ushered to an adjoining table on the dais, near enough to bask in Colin's and Lyssandra's glow without casting a shadow over it. The man Arjon had identified as Brisbane's messenger flanked MacDuff's other side, watching the proceedings with a sour smile.

An elderly knight rose from his bench, his drooping mustache adding a note of gravity to the occasion. "To Sir Colin, a knight dedicated to the service of God and king. His conduct both on the battlefield and off of it epitomizes bravery, nobility, justice, and—"

"Fidelity!" Before Tabitha was even aware she was going to stand, she was on her feet. Keenly aware of the sudden silence and the amused quirk of Arjon's eyebrow, she lifted her goblet and smiled sweetly at Colin, who looked close to strangling on a mouthful of ale. "To Sir Colin, a paragon of Christian virtue."

Her mocking tribute sent a chorus of "Huzzahs!" thundering to the rafters. She sank back into her seat. She would have been far too shy to initiate a toast at a Lennox Enterprises banquet, but having nothing left to lose was making her reckless.

The MacDuff nodded. "Well spoken, my lady. Your eloquence does both you and your cousin honor."

Colin's eyes narrowed, but it was that hint of a scowl that gave Tabitha a thrill of hope. Before she could savor her triumph, a battalion of pages bearing bacon-wrapped hens dressed with real feathers swept into the hall.

Lyssandra picked at the steaming skin of her bird with a delicate ivory-handled knife, but her father used his bulbous fingers to tear apart the succulent flesh. Colin seemed to have embraced a liquid diet. Each time he took a sip, an eager page rushed forward to splash more ale in his cup.

As his guests followed their host's cue and dug into their meals with relish, the MacDuff gestured, sending bits of chicken flying. "If you'd give me leave to summon the priest to read the banns, lad, we could have the ceremony on the morrow."

Tabitha had never been so glad to see the stubborn jut of Colin's jaw. "I've told you before," he said. "I'll not wed Lyssa till she's turned eighteen."

"Now, Papa. Don't nag poor Colin." The girl's weary sigh warned that this was a quarrel of long standing. "After all, I'll be eighteen in less than two months."

Ignoring his daughter's pleas, the MacDuff pointed his knife at Colin. "Your mother was naught but thirteen when she bore you."

"Aye. And fifteen when she died two stillborn babes later." Colin's eyes were beginning to smolder.

Tabitha brushed a hand over her own belly, remembering for the first time what their unprotected sex might lead to. In the twenty-first century, any knight worth his salt would carry a crisp packet of condoms. Her distress was softened by a wondrous vision of a dark-haired, golden-eyed little boy stretching out his arms to her.

She might have remained in her dreamy trance for the rest of the meal if Arjon hadn't popped a sugared rose petal into her gaping mouth.

The MacDuff was still needling Colin. "Your father informed me that the two of you quarreled bitterly the night you went galloping off on your ridiculous"—he cleared his throat, remembering his audience of eavesdroppers—"*noble* quest. He begged you to wed Lyssandra before you departed. If you'd have heeded his wishes, he might not have died estranged from his only son."

Colin slammed his goblet down on the table. "Lyssandra was eleven years old at the time."

"Soon to be twelve. Old enough for you to put your babe in her belly and cement my alliance with your father before you committed your sword to the Lord."

Colin rose to his feet. Planting both palms on the table, he leaned over into the MacDuff's face. Tabitha had to strain to hear the lethal softness of his voice. "And if I had, would my father be alive today? Would you have sent men to his aid when Brisbane attacked or simply ignored his desperate pleas for help?"

MacDuff licked each finger in turn, the arch of his snowy eyebrows painstakingly bland. "Didn't Lyssandra tell you? I'd packed my entire household off to Castle Arran for the spring. We knew nothing of the siege until we returned. And by then, as you know, 'twas too late."

The tension in Colin's stance showed no sign of abating. Lyssandra tugged at his sleeve, her lovely face reflecting her distress. "Papa speaks the truth, Colin. Your stepmother was a dear friend to me. I cried for days when we learned of her death."

Colin straightened, gently shaking off her hand. "Is that why your father is entertaining her murderer's minion at his table?"

Brisbane's sallow knight had been watching the entire exchange, all but drooling with anticipation.

The MacDuff's ruddy cheeks puffed up with self-righteous indignation. "The quarrel between you and Lord Brisbane is an old one, in which I claim no part." His acid tone indicated that he knew *exactly* what had precipitated that quarrel. "Once you've wed my daughter, son, you'll have every right to tell me who I should entertain. And who I should wage war against. But until that time, I shall dine with, *and kill,* whomever I please." He rose and clapped his pudgy hands, coolly dismissing Colin. "Let's have some music, minstrels. 'Tis dull as a tomb in here."

As the pipers resumed their melody, Colin dropped back into his chair. The calculating glint in his eyes warned it was less a retreat than a reprieve. Several of the diners rose to join the dance, including the MacDuff and Brisbane's man, leaving them in awkward silence.

All innocence, Arjon blinked at Tabitha and asked in a voice strident enough to carry all the way back to her penthouse on Fifth Avenue, "Haven't you some skill as a troubadour, Lady Tabitha?"

"No!" Colin said firmly even as delight brightened Lyssandra's face.

"Oh, do sing for us, Tabby! I grow so weary of Papa's minstrels. Perhaps you could teach me a new tune."

"Heaven forbid," Arjon said dryly. "The brat never could do more than squall like a dying cat."

Lyssandra's smile puckered into a pout. "And have you forgotten, Sir Arjon, that I can also scratch like one?"

He fingered his chin. "How could I when my face still bears the scars from your claws?"

"I should have scratched out your eyes. 'Twould have been no more than you deserved for setting my braid afire."

"Children!" Colin snapped. "Can't the two of you declare a truce? People are beginning to stare."

"He started it," Lyssandra mumbled, scowling into her pudding with uncharacteristic petulance. "Forgive me, Lady Tabitha. I shouldn't have presumed upon your generosity. You're a guest here at MacDuff, not one of Papa's trained dwarves."

Tabitha surprised herself by gliding smoothly to her feet. "Why, I'd be honored to sing for you."

Colin leaned forward in his chair. "I'd rather you didn't strain your delicate throat, *cousin*."

She fingered the amulet. "Perhaps you'd prefer I show Lyssandra a few of my magic tricks. As you know, I haven't quite perfected making things disappear."

Lyssandra clapped her graceful hands. "Oh, I do love magic even more than music."

"Sing," Colin said flatly. "By all means, sing for us."

He watched warily as his fiancée led her to a stool at the side of the dais. If he was expecting a few wistful verses of "If Ever I Would Leave You," he would be disappointed.

Intrigued by the prospect of a new diversion, the acrobats collapsed in mid-tumble and the dancers drifted back to their benches. Hoping their standards of entertainment weren't any higher than Colin's, Tabitha cleared her throat, then threw back her head and launched into a soulful rendition of "Your Cheatin' Heart." She knew she was a success when the minstrels exchanged a baffled glance, shrugged, then began to strum along on their lutes in a flawless country twang.

She followed an enthusiastic round of cheers and applause with a mocking "Torn Between Two Lovers," then belted out a rafter-shaking chorus of "Who's Sorry Now?" When she dared to glance over at Colin, his hands were clenched around the goblet as if he longed to clamp them over his ears or her mouth. From his murderous expression, she suspected the latter.

She might have stopped there if Lyssandra hadn't chosen that moment to brush his taut jaw with a tender kiss. Tabitha felt a stab of pain beyond jealousy. So she leaned back on the stool as if it were the top of a piano in a smoke-filled bar and began to softly sing Nina Simone's stirring blues classic "The Other Woman." The minstrels lowered their lutes, reluctant to disturb the sultry intimacy of the melody.

Yearning robbed Tabitha's voice of its sarcasm. She could only gaze at Colin as if he were the only man in the hall, her heart laid bare by the simple lyrics. Taking another sip of ale, he met her gaze squarely. The Mac-Duff's shrewd eyes missed little, but the sentimental Lyssandra was occupied with dabbing crystalline teardrops from her cheeks. Snorting in disgust, Arjon tossed a kerchief at her. She blew her dainty nose on it and handed it back to him, ignoring his grimace.

As the last note warbled from Tabitha's throat, Colin stood. She hoped in that moment that he would come to her. That he woyld march across that dais, draw her into his arms, and proudly proclaim that she was the only woman he adored.

Snatching up a full flagon of ale, he shoved back his chair and pushed his way through the crowd, passing through the outer door without once looking back.

•   •   •

Tabitha tossed and turned on the feather mattress, feeling as if she were drowning in its smothering softness, unable to find a comfortable position. Finally she sat up and hugged her knees.

Moonlight streamed through the stained-glass window, painting the tiled floor an ethereal shade of rose. Too restless to sit and brood, Tabitha clambered down from the tall four-poster and padded across the room, the sleeveless slip she wore brushing the floor. Lyssandra had been shocked when she'd asked to sleep in the garment, informing her primly that it was customary to slumber in the nude.

The chamber Colin's fiancée had provided for her was every little girl's fantasy. As she unlatched the window and gazed into the deserted night, she wouldn't have been surprised to see Rapunzel Barbie and Prince Charming Ken come cruising up the drawbridge in their pink convertible.

Every little girl's fantasy had turned into her nightmare. She yearned to escape the colorful tapestries that draped the walls and the murals painted on the ceiling. They only mocked her with their images of fair ladies, bold knights, and golden-horned unicorns resting their heads shyly in the laps of virginal princesses.

The cool night breeze ruffled her tousled bangs. She was no longer a virgin and she'd never been a princess. She had simply been deluding herself. She was Tabitha Lennox—girl genius, M.I.T. graduate, and department head of the Lennox Enterprises Virtual Reality Division. She didn't belong in this enchanted kingdom any more than she'd ever belonged anywhere but her tidy penthouse. She should be there now, sipping espresso, listening to jazz, and watching rain course down the smog-tinted windows.

She lifted her amulet to the moonlight, marveling at its unearthly beauty. There was nothing left for her to do but bow out gracefully and leave Colin and Lyssandra to their own happy ending. She could only hope her parents would forgive her once she returned to her own time. She had left their fates hanging in the balance while she chased a dream. A dream that had turned out to be as ridiculous as it was elusive.

She wondered if Colin would feel regret or relief when he discovered she was gone. At least he'd be spared the unpleasant task of sharpening his feathered quill and writing her a Dear Jane letter. Maybe someday he would even be able to look back upon the night they'd shared as a magical interlude, unspoiled by bitterness or remorse.

She clutched the amulet and closed her eyes. Her lips moved, but a wish would not come. She was as mute as she'd been all those years before when she'd suppressed her every dream and desire.

Trembling with frustration, she opened her eyes. Maybe her wish was not sincere enough. Or maybe she was just left-brained enough to demand a sense of closure. Maybe the right words would continue to elude her until she could coolly shake Colin's hand and thank him for looking after her during her brief visit to his century.

Tomorrow, she decided firmly. Tomorrow she would bid Sir Colin of Ravenshaw a dignified farewell and begin methodically searching for the wish that would carry her home.

Home.

As Tabitha climbed back into the big, empty bed, she wondered why the word tasted so dry in her mouth.

•　•　•

She was having the most magical dream.

Even a twinge of wistful sadness wasn't enough to spoil its dark enchantment. Colin was on top of her again. His breath fanned her throat, intoxicating her with the musky sweet aroma of hops. His warm, moist lips devoured the curve of her cheek before finding their way to her mouth where he drank thoroughly and deeply of her kiss. She moaned, exulting in his unabashed masculinity. He was rough where she was smooth, hard where she was soft, salty where she was sweet.

She stroked his muscular forearms, beguiled by his urgency. Even as he tenderly ravished her mouth with his tongue, he was easing up her nightgown, filling his callused palms with her breasts and gently squeezing. It was as if the touch of her skin was something he craved to feed some shameless hunger he would never be able to satisfy.

She barely had time to savor that new delight before he reached between her legs and cupped her there. His questing fingers created an exquisite friction that coaxed a hot surge of nectar from her throbbing core.

A sweet dream indeed.

If only . . .

Tabitha turned her head to the side of the feather pillow, the refrain a wordless sigh. If only this weren't a dream. If only Colin were really in her arms. If only she had one more night to prove to him that no woman, in this century or any other, could ever love him like she could.

If only she wouldn't wake up before this delectable fantasy came to fruition.

Freed from the inhibitions of consciousness, her knees fell apart without shyness or shame. If Colin were really in her bed, she would draw him down and nibble that sulky lower lip of his as she guided him gently into the very heart of her. But her arms remained empty, the ache deep within her unfulfilled.

"Damn it to bloody hell!"

It was that muffled blasphemy uttered in a thick Scottish burr that broke the spell.

Tabitha's eyes flew open to find Colin crouched at the bottom of the bed in a puddle of moonlight, fumbling with the ties of his hose.

He slowly lifted his head to meet her shocked gaze, then flashed her a lopsided grin and touched a finger to his lips. "Shhhhh. Mustn't wake my sweet lady before I've had my way with her."

If only . . .

All of her tender resolutions forgotten, Tabitha planted her foot in the middle of his chest and shoved, sending him sailing off the bed.

CHAPTER 22

Tabitha jerked down her nightgown and sat up, growing slowly aware of the ominous silence. Not a sound came from the floor at the foot of the bed—not a grunt or a groan or even a drunken snore.

"Oh, God," she whispered. "What if he hit his head on the hearth? What if I've killed him?"

Terrified she was going to find Colin sprawled in a pool of his own blood, she scrambled to the foot of the bed. Just as she was peeping over the footboard, Colin sat up, and she clapped a hand over her mouth to muffle a shriek of fright.

Gingerly rubbing the back of his head, he shot her a rueful glance. "Can't say I didn't deserve that."

He looked so boyishly sheepish that it was all Tabitha could do not to bound off the bed, cradle his head against her breasts, and croon, "Och, Colin, me puir wee laddie!" just as Nana had done after she'd clobbered him in the chapel at Castle Raven.

Instead, she summoned all of her indignation and climbed down out of the bed to stand over him, hands on hips. "You're drunk!"

"Aye." He flashed her another of those roguish grins. "Drunk with desire for you, my lady."

She refused to be charmed. "I've heard better pickup lines at the water cooler at work. Just how did you get in here? Did you scale the wall and crawl through the window? Sneak through a secret passageway?"

He pointed. "The door."

"Oh." Tabitha was vaguely disappointed by the lack of drama. "Well, you ought to be ashamed of yourself. Creeping into a woman's bed in the dead of night to seduce her with your fiancée only a few doors away. And after all your pious talk about honor and chivalry! Why, you're nothing but a knight in shining tin!"

Colin blinked up at her, but she couldn't tell if he was dazed from drink or his tumble off the bed. His voice softened to an awed whisper. "You look more like an angel than a witch with the light of heaven shining through your gown that way."

Tabitha hadn't realized she was standing in front of the window. She glanced down to discover the moonlight had rendered the slip virtually sheer. She reached for the blanket, then paused and straightened, meeting Colin's gaze boldly.

His simmering eyes lingered on the curves outlined beneath the clinging fabric, even as his mouth took on a wry twist. "An avenging angel, it seems. I've kept myself pure for so long that I forgot how merciless such creatures could be to a fallen sinner."

She folded her arms over her chest, blocking part of his view. "The same way you forgot to tell me you were engaged?"

He managed to look even more wounded than he had when she'd kicked him out of her bed. "I did so tell you. I told you I'd been betrothed since I was a boy."

Tabitha was startled to realize he'd told her exactly

that. In the forest after they'd escaped Brisbane's clutches. She frowned. "But you implied that you broke off your engagement so you could marry Regan."

" 'Twas my intention. But as you know, Regan never learned of my plan. And after she was dead, it mattered naught to me who I wed." The moonlight unearthed a glint of sobriety in his eyes. "Truth be told, I never thought I would return from the Holy Land."

"No doubt you were hoping to martyr yourself." She sniffed. "A pity you failed."

Gripping one of the bedposts, he dragged himself to his feet, making a visible effort not to stagger. Tabitha had to curl her hands into fists to keep from touching him.

He was wise enough not to touch her. "When I left here, Lyssa was naught but a child in ribbons and braids."

"Well, in case you haven't noticed, she's all grown up now."

He chuckled, the throaty rumble reflecting more despair than amusement. "Oh, I've noticed."

"Do you love her?" Tabitha blurted out the question without considering the consequences.

She swung away from him and closed her eyes, as if the absence of light would somehow blot out the echo of his answer. This was the moment, she knew, the moment when she should wish him happiness with his new bride and say good-bye. But her throat ached so hard she couldn't speak at all.

"I love her as if she were my little sister. In truth, I've never been able to imagine taking her to my bed."

Tabitha's knees folded, but Colin was there to catch her. There to slip his arms around her waist and draw her against the muscled warmth of his body. There to nuzzle his lips against her nape, making her shiver with desire, and gently steer her toward the bed.

But before she could go, she had one more question for him. A question that had been nagging at her since she'd first learned of Lyssandra's existence. "Did your people at Castle Raven know you were engaged to the MacDuff's daughter?"

"Aye," he whispered against her jasmine-scented skin, his heated breath making her tingle all over. " 'Twas never a secret."

"Then why did they treat me with such respect? If Lyssandra was going to be your wife, then who did they think I was?"

He pressed his hips against her rump, proving that drink had not hampered his desire for her. "My paramour, of course."

Wrenching herself from his grasp, Tabitha whirled around to face him.

He took a step toward her. "Why are you looking at me like that, lass? 'Tis well within a man's rights to have both."

She narrowed her eyes, wanting to make sure she understood him. "A wife *and* a paramour?"

"Aye." He reached for her, but she took another step backward, rounding the corner of the bed.

"And what about your wife's rights? What would she gain from such an arrangement?"

"She would have my name. My protection. My fond regard."

"Your children?" she prodded.

He nodded, but seemed to be having difficulty meeting her eyes again. " 'Twould be my duty to provide her with a son."

"And if you accidentally provided her with a daughter? I guess you'd just have to keep trying, eh?" Colin reached for her again, but she danced just out of his grasp. "What about love, Colin? Is that the one right you'd deny your wife?"

Scowling, he rubbed the back of his neck. "Christ, lass, you're making my head ache with all these riddles. 'Tis unheard of for a man to be in love with his own wife. Just ask Arjon. He's spent his entire life being in love with other men's wives and they with him."

Tabitha noticed that he was beginning to speak with more bluster than conviction. "So in two months when Lyssandra turns eighteen, you still intend to marry her, however repugnant the thought of sleeping with her."

"I haven't any choice. I gave my word."

"You were just a child, Colin. You didn't make the pledge. Your father did."

"But 'tis my sacred duty to honor it. 'Twould be unfair if I did not."

"Honor! You're talking about spending your entire life living a lie. What does that have to do with honor? With fairness?"

He turned on his heel and paced away from her, his voice rising to a shout. "You are the most vexing woman! You just drop into my life out of nowhere—"

"Oh, you don't know the half of it."

"—and expect me to have no obligations, no pledges to fulfill. Is that fair?"

"Probably not," she admitted softly.

He sank down on a wooden chest and dragged a hand through his hair, letting her see the full extent of his desperation for the first time. "You heard MacDuff's thinly veiled threats tonight. If I break my vow to him, he'll ally himself with Roger." His gaze was both fierce and imploring. "I cannot fight them both. My people will perish."

Their familiar faces drifted before Tabitha's eyes in a

vivid tableau: Magwyn with her gaunt beauty and stern pride; courageous Auld Nana; Granny Cora puffing serenely on her pipe; the irrepressible Chauncey; sweet little Jenny, who'd just rediscovered her voice and her smile. And Wee Blythe, the innocent baby Colin had cradled in his arms as if she were a treasure beyond price.

How could she ask him to choose between her and those he was sworn to protect?

Suddenly inspired, she dropped to her knees and clasped his thigh. "I can help you. I can do more for you than the MacDuff can. I can rid your life of Brisbane forever."

He frowned at her. "How?"

She held up the amulet. "With this."

Tabitha could almost see his hand tremble with the urge to trace a cross on his breast. "I cannot, lass. 'Tis a devil's trinket."

His words stung her to the heart. She rose and backed away from him. "Then I must be the devil's hand-maiden."

He eyed her with hopeless longing before hoarsely confessing, "No matter what the Church says, I cannot believe that of you."

Tabitha remembered something her mother had told her long ago, when she'd been a sullen thirteen-year-old sobbing over a ruined birthday. Tabitha said to Colin, "Didn't it ever occur to you that this God of yours might have given me my powers? And if he did, wouldn't he want me to use them for good? To rid the world of a monster like Brisbane before he can destroy any more innocent people?"

Colin shook his head, his face implacable. "I cannot fight evil with evil. If I do, then I've gained naught for all my striving."

Tabitha bowed her head, knowing there was no moving him.

He stood, his voice hoarse with hope. "Even if I marry, we can still be together. I have a small holding in the Highlands. 'Tis isolated, but lovely beyond imagining. I'll come to you as often as I dare and you'll lack for naught. I cannot offer you my name, Tabitha, but you will have my heart."

She turned her face away so he wouldn't see the tears beginning to trickle down her cheeks. She didn't cry prettily like Lyssandra.

He stretched out a hand, inviting her to join him in the silvery pool of moonlight. "Come to bed with me, lass. Please."

Even desperate and half-drunk, he was temptation itself, more irresistible now that she'd seen the dents in his armor. A naive girl can be infatuated with a knight, but only a woman can love the man inside the armor. How easy it would be to tumble into that rumpled bed with him! To let him do to her all the naughty, delicious things he longed to do. To hold him in her arms until the inescapable light of dawn forced him to sneak out of her bed like a thief.

She'd always known they came from different times, different cultures, different worlds. She'd just never guessed it was a gap that couldn't be breached, not even by love.

She gazed at him through a veil of tears. "I can't be your wife, Colin. And I won't be your paramour."

His hand fell to his side and he grew very pale and still, as if she'd dealt him a death blow.

She struggled to smile through her tears. "Wasn't it you who told me courtly love was 'the tragic tale of a noble knight pining for the unrequited affection of his lady'? Maybe they'll write a ballad about us someday."

"You are more canny than I realized, my lady. And more pitiless."

It was a tribute to his rigid self-control that he managed to turn on his heel and make it as far as the door without staggering. But when he reached the door, he hesitated. A spark of hope flickered to life in Tabitha's heart.

When Colin turned, his resolute expression doused it. "Give me your charm, lass. I'll not have you rushing off on some daft quest to confront Brisbane. I've no need to hide behind a woman's skirts."

Tabitha was shaken that he'd read her half-formed intentions so accurately. "If you marry Lyssandra so her father will fight on your side, that's exactly what you'll be doing."

Colin refused to be diverted. He advanced on her, holding out his hand. "I'll not let you put yourself in peril again. Brisbane is a dangerous man."

Tabitha held up the amulet. "And with this, I'm a dangerous woman."

"More dangerous to yourself than anyone else. Whether you choose to spend your life with me," he faltered and had to swallow hard before continuing, "or with some other man, I want it to be a long and prosperous one. Which is why I intend to keep your charm until your temper has had time to cool."

His fist closed around the chain, warning her that this time he wouldn't tolerate her refusal.

Her whisper was choked by the threat of tears. "I trusted you enough to give you the amulet once before. Can't you trust me enough to let me keep it?"

Although regret clouded his eyes, his only reply was to snap the fragile gold chain, catching the emerald in his hand.

Then the door slammed and he was gone, leaving

Tabitha to sink to her knees and bury her face in the bedclothes.

Tabitha hurried across the deserted courtyard, checking over her shoulder for signs of pursuit. Other than the yellow hound who dogged her heels for a few steps before growing bored and loping away, no one at Castle MacDuff seemed to care that she was leaving. The eastern horizon was slowly melting from black to gray and the rising wind smelled of rain, a scent as timeless and unmistakable as the fragrance of Colin's skin.

She once again wore Magwyn's battered gown, but she still felt strangely naked. She touched the hollow of her breastbone, missing the weight of her mother's amulet. But she refused to let Colin's stubbornness stop her from giving him a wedding gift that would guarantee years of peace for both him and his unborn children.

She, Tabitha Lennox, who had once called a security guard to come kill a spider in her bathroom, was off to confront a homicidal maniac on behalf of the man she loved. She might not have the amulet to focus her magic, but she had plenty of twenty-first-century know-how and her own powerful, if somewhat erratic, talents to fall back on.

Lifting her skirt, she stepped over a heap of squires snoring off the effects of last night's merriment. She had hoped to find Chauncey among them, but feared he was off wooing that milkmaid of his. She glanced over her shoulder again, but the shadow she thought she saw flitting across the courtyard must have only been a swallow or a bat.

As she slipped into the stables, the horses welcomed her with sleepy whickers. The musty smell of hay tickled her nose, making her pinch back a sneeze. She moved from stall to stall, searching for a familiar face. But the face that emerged as a caped figure glided out of the shadows and pushed back its hood was not the one she would have chosen.

Lyssandra was no less lovely with her cheeks streaked with tears and violet smudges beneath her eyes. She didn't say a word, simply hugged herself and gazed at Tabitha in sullen accusation.

To Tabitha's relief, she spotted Chauncey's even-tempered sorrel in the very next stall. "Good morning, Lyssandra," she said brightly, throwing open the stall and dragging a saddle down from its wooden peg. "I really must be getting back to Gotham. If you'll just tell my cousin—"

"He is not your cousin."

Lowering the saddle, Tabitha slowly turned to face Lyssandra. She owed her at least that much. "How did you know?"

"Because I heard him yelling at you last night." A scornful smile curved her lips. "He never yells at me. He always treats me with the most unfailing courtesy."

"I know what you think you heard. But nothing happened between the two of us last night."

"Only because you sent him away."

Tabitha wanted to deny it, but she had nothing left to offer this kind and generous girl but the truth. "He's still going to marry you, you know. As soon as you turn eighteen." She nearly choked on the words, but managed to get them out. "He'll be a good husband."

"Aye." Bitterness darkened Lyssandra's eyes, making her look less like a girl than a woman. "He'll kiss me on the cheek and bring me sweetmeats for supper. He'll rock my children in his arms and praise my handling of the castle accounts. But when he gazes out the window on a moonlit night, 'twill be you he's thinking of."

Tabitha shook her head, blinking back tears. "He'll forget me."

"I pray to God so." Then as if ashamed of her fierce declaration, she whispered, "Where will you go?"

Tabitha wasn't sure how to answer that question. By abandoning the amulet, she might very well be risking her only way back to the twenty-first century. But if she returned to this place and saw Colin's face again, she might lose her will to leave him. She might end up living in that Highland castle, forced to love him only in shadow instead of sunshine. She might grow old and bitter while she waited for him to leave this woman's side and come to hers.

Knowing that could never be enough for any of them, she said softly, "I'll go far away from here. So far he'll never find me."

Satisfied with her answer, Lyssandra pointed to a sleek gray horse in a nearby stall. "You can take my steed if you want. Colin gave him to me on my tenth birthday. He's gentle, but as fast as the wind."

Tabitha nervously eyed the elegant beast. "No, thank you. I'd rather take Chauncey's horse. At least he's familiar with me." She hoisted the saddle on the sorrel's back, determined to go before her courage faltered.

After watching her fumble with the leather straps for several seconds, Lyssandra stepped in and tightened the girth with a few expert jerks.

As Tabitha led the horse through the stable doors, the girl trailed behind her. Squinting against the brisk wind, Tabitha searched the horizon, realizing she didn't have the faintest idea how to get where she needed to go. She would have wished herself to Brisbane's castle, but given the unpredictable outcome of her wishes without the amulet to temper them, she feared landing in his dungeon or on one of those deadly spikes capping his castle walls.

She shuddered. "I have some unfinished business to take care of. I don't suppose you could point me toward England?"

Lyssandra's brow puckered in a frown. She pointed left, then right, then left again. Before Tabitha could mount, the girl pulled off her cloak and thrust it at her. "The sky bodes ill for your journey."

Tabitha wrapped the warm woolen cloak around her, and clambered into the saddle. The only thing she knew for sure was that she was facing the horse's head instead of his swishing tail. As she drew the hood up over her hair, the first raindrops began to fall.

Lyssandra gripped her ankle. "Take care, my lady." From the girl's troubled expression, Tabitha sensed she was sincere.

She wanted to smile, but all she could manage was a fierce nod. "And you take care of him."

She didn't wait to hear Lyssandra's response. As Chauncey's sorrel cantered across the drawbridge, she glanced back only once to find the girl still standing by the stables, growing smaller with every hoofbeat. Then she turned her face toward the future, thankful for a wind strong enough to snatch her tears before they could fall.

CHAPTER 23

"It appears the wages of sin is the sleep of the dead."

At that dour pronouncement, Colin pried open one eye to find Arjon standing over his bed, grinning impishly down at him.

He groaned and burrowed his head beneath the feather pillow. "'Tis punishment enough that God would send a fiend such as you to torment me."

"Ah, but friend or fiend remains to be seen."

Tossing the pillow at Arjon, Colin sat up. The sudden motion nearly undid him. He squeezed his skull between his palms in a vain attempt to make it stop throbbing. "Would you please go tell MacDuff's priest to stop ringing those damnable bells?"

The Norman cocked his head to the side, listening intently. "'Tis naught but the tolling of your conscience, I fear." Each chiding cluck of his tongue sounded like the clash of a cymbal to Colin's ears. "Oh, how the mighty are fallen!"

Colin swung his legs over the side of the bed, wincing as a lance of pain shot through his head. "You may gloat all you like, but please refrain from quoting scripture at me. 'Tis most unsettling coming from those lascivious lips of yours."

"And there you go insulting me when I've come to take pity on your tarnished soul." Arjon pressed a mug into his hands.

Colin scowled down into the foul-smelling concoction. "What manner of poison is this?"

"No poison, but an antidote to that venom you quaffed last night."

Shooting him a skeptical glare, Colin downed the murky contents of the mug, then shuddered. The stuff cleared some of the fog from his head, but did nothing to relieve the bitter taste in his mouth. A bitterness caused less by too much strong drink than by the caustic words he and Tabitha had exchanged.

"Tabitha . . ." he murmured, overcome by a wave of heartsickness.

Prodded by a hazy memory, he reached beneath his pillow to find a tangled chain. He unfurled its tarnished length until an emerald twirled before his eyes, mocking their bleariness with its undaunted sparkle.

By taking the charm, he had thought only to protect Tabitha from herself. But he could still see the unshed tears glistening in her eyes when she had all but begged him to trust her. He feared he had broken her heart as carelessly as he had broken the delicate chain.

He vaguely remembered stumbling back to his chamber after their quarrel, thinking to drown his misery in a fresh flagon of ale. But the words they'd spoken still haunted him, echoing with the ring of finality.

"Have you seen her?" he asked Arjon.

Arjon sighed. "You have more pressing problems than your lady fair. At this very moment, the MacDuff is in council with that viper of Brisbane's. They've been locked away for nearly an hour and after that touching little performance you and Tabitha gave in the hall last night, I'd wager 'tis not the price of hay nor the crown's exorbitant taxes they're discussing."

Colin blinked up at him. "Were we so obvious?"

"You'd have had to have been as blinded by love as MacDuff's witless daughter not to notice."

"Lyssa," Colin whispered, passing a hand over his eyes. "Christ, I never wanted to hurt her."

"So don't."

Colin had never seen the even-tempered Norman angry before, but he would have almost sworn it was fury simmering in his friend's eyes.

"Go to the MacDuff now and cast yourself upon his mercy. Despite all his boasting and bullying, he was always fond of you. Tell him Tabitha was naught more than a casual indiscretion, both regretted and repented. Then make Lyssa your wife. Today. Before you break her silly heart."

Colin had passed out in his hose so there was nothing for him to do but grab a clean tunic from his knapsack and draw on his boots and spurs. He tied a knot in the chain of Tabitha's charm before dropping it over his head.

"Now there's a good lad. We'll make a husband of you yet." Arjon leaned against the doorjamb. His smile had returned, although its edge was sharper than usual.

It faded altogether when he saw Colin's determined expression. "I must speak with Tabitha first. I fear I wounded her sorely last night." Buckling on his sword, he started for the door.

"She's gone," Arjon said flatly.

Colin slowly lifted his head, praying the clamor in it had affected his hearing.

Arjon nodded. "She rode out at dawn. I saw her from my window."

Colin measured out each word as if it would be his last. "And you didn't awaken me?"

His friend's face crumpled into a plea, although for understanding or forgiveness Colin could not have said. "Let her go," he whispered fiercely. "Please."

"I can't," Colin bit off through clenched teeth before shoving past his friend as if he weren't even there.

Colin took the winding stairs three at a time, bursting out of the castle only to be buffeted back by a gust of wind and rain. The storm raged in earnest now, rumbling its displeasure and hurtling angry bolts of lightning through the boiling clouds. It made him half mad to think of Tabitha out there somewhere, lost and alone without even her charm to protect her.

He started for the stables, praying Chauncey or some other squire had recovered from last night's revelry enough to have noted the direction she had taken. Rain sheeted across the cobblestones, blinding him. He didn't see the small figure huddled beneath the stable's dripping eaves until he was almost upon her. She was soaked to the skin and her teeth were chattering.

He squatted beside her and gently peeled a sodden strand of hair from her cheek. "Lyssa, what in God's name are you doing out here?"

Her dark eyes were haunted, her lashes damp with tears. "I let her go. I knew it was going to storm, but I let her go anyway. I was glad she was going. I prayed she would never come back."

Colin slowly withdrew his hand, intensifying her shivers. "Which way?"

"South, I think. She asked me to point her toward England."

"England?" He frowned.

"She said she had some unfinished business to take care of. And then she was going far away. So far you'd never find her."

"Dear God," Colin breathed, realization dawning.

He had rejected Tabitha's offer of help and robbed her of her precious charm, yet she'd still gone off to confront Brisbane on her own. He cursed himself for not anticipating this. After all, he'd seen her reckless courage firsthand, seen her stand off Roger's men and snarling dogs with a sword she could barely lift.

"I offered her my steed . . ."

"*Your* steed!" Colin snatched Lyssandra up by the shoulders, giving her a harsh shake. "Sweet Christ, the lass is the clumsiest rider I've ever seen. If the horse makes one misstep, she'll fall off and break her fool neck."

Before Lyssandra could stutter an explanation, he was gone, plunging into the stables and reappearing with one muscular leg already thrown over his stallion's back. Horse and rider raced across the courtyard and down the drawbridge, the rumble of their hoofbeats drowned out by a sharp clap of thunder.

"Oh, dear God, what have I done?" Lyssandra stood in the pouring rain, feeling as wretched as she'd ever felt in her sheltered life. "Papa," she finally whispered, cheered by a faint surge of hope. "Papa will know what to do."

Lyssandra crept through the marble-pillared corridor outside her papa's solar, only too aware that she was leaving muddy puddles on his imported tiles with every step. Although there were many grand rooms in the castle, the solar was the grandest of all. Behind that gilded door lay the most precious of her father's treasures—his illuminated manuscripts, jeweled chalices, and chests full of gold and silver plate. She'd spent countless hours as a child playing at his feet while he tallied the coins gathered by his tax collectors or polished some new trinket to a brilliant shine.

She splayed her hand against the door, but hesitated when it was only partly ajar, trying to make her teeth stop chattering. Her papa had never approved of any display of weakness.

Before she could paste on a brave smile, someone within the room said, "There goes the damn fool now."

Lyssandra frowned. She could almost hear the sneer in the unfamiliar voice.

"What did I tell you? He's like a hound after a bitch in heat. He was all but sniffing under her skirts last night in the hall."

She recognized her papa's voice, yet its smug cadences sounded more foreign than the stranger's. A chill that had nothing to do with her wet clothes prickled down her spine.

Suddenly she wanted to back away, to flee to the haven of her bedchamber. To burrow beneath her blankets and pretend she was still the little girl who was going to grow up and marry Sir Colin of Ravenshaw someday. But when she heard her father speak again, she knew the time for pretending was done.

"I can't believe the fool thought I'd let my only daughter wed a penniless laird living in a burned-out ruin. Since God in his infinite idiocy provided me no sons, Lyssandra is all I have to barter. She's not much, I'll admit, but she can at least turn up her heels to earn me a powerful ally in my old age."

Lyssandra cupped a hand over her mouth, praying she would not be ill.

She heard the sharp scratch of a nib on parchment.

"There," her father said. "Once the ink is dry on this betrothal contract, you may take her away with my blessing. I'm sure she'll make your master a charming and biddable wife."

"And very grateful he will be," replied the fawning stranger. "Not just for accepting his humble suit, but for taking care of the other unpleasantness. As you learned when you agreed to remove your household to Castle Arran for the spring, Lord Brisbane can be very generous to his allies."

"Generous indeed. Once Ravenshaw is dead, your master and I plan to split his holdings between us. The castle might be in ruins, but the land is fertile and ripe for the plucking." Her papa chuckled. "At least the bastard spared me the untidiness of murdering him in his bed. Bloodstains can be the very devil to remove."

"How will you finish him then?"

"Consider the task done. As soon as his whore fled the castle this morning, I anticipated his reaction and dispatched archers to every border. Neither of them will pass alive."

"B-b-but that was not our agreement." The man's voice trembled with rising hysteria. "The woman was not to be harmed. She was to be delivered to my master along with your daughter."

"I'll not have my daughter transported to her new household with a common whore. 'Twould reflect poorly on me. After he's planted his brat in Lyssandra's womb, your master can find himself another doxy."

"But you swore . . . !"

Lyssandra knew she had no more time to listen to the men quarrel. She had to go. Had to take her steed and warn Tabitha and Colin that they were riding into a trap. Before it was too late.

She began to back away from the door one step at a

time, terrified the sodden squelch of her slippers would alert the men to her presence. She had nearly reached the last pillar, where she might dare to turn and flee, when a ruthless hand shot out and clamped itself over her mouth, muffling her startled scream.

Colin drew his mount to a halt at the crest of the hill and squinted through the pouring rain. Although he was soaked to the bone, he'd grown numb to the rain's chill and deaf to the sullen growls of thunder many leagues ago. All of his senses were focused on finding Tabitha's trail.

A trail that seemed to wander in befuddled circles until a gully swollen with rain would wash it away, leaving him as helpless as he'd been before. While picking his way through a grove of trees, he had found traces of crushed leaves and bent branches, indicating that she might have already taken a tumble. But to his keen relief, her broken body had been nowhere in sight. A pair of muddy hoofprints too deep to belong to a riderless horse had reassured him that she'd simply dragged herself back up on the horse and kept going.

"Probably cursing my name all the while," he murmured, feeling a wistful smile tug at his lips.

He was at least heartened to learn she hadn't yet made it to the southern border of MacDuff's land. That lay just ahead and he hoped if he waited at the top of this hill, he might be able to cut her off before she did. The hill gave him a clean sweep of the valley below, with nothing to mar his view but the rain dripping from his lashes and a dense stand of birches.

The storm seemed to be worsening instead of abating. Thunder cracked like a whip and the wind set up a banshee's howl. Colin shook off a shiver and crossed himself. There were some who believed the banshee's wail warned of death to come, but he had always preferred to entrust his fate into the hands of God.

That faith was rewarded when a cloaked and hooded figure came cantering into view, riding straight for MacDuff's border. He squinted against the rain, but even from that distance, he would have almost sworn the sleek beast was Lyssandra's steed. Colin's heart soared. Once he had Tabitha in his arms again, he would never let her go.

He could not have said what drew his eye to the stand of birches in that moment. It could have been the ghost of a hunch or simply a calculated movement where there should have been nothing but silvery leaves trembling in the wind. A bony finger of dread tickled his nape.

A lone man crouched among the bracken at the foot of the tallest tree, his dark green tunic and hose making him nearly indistinguishable from the glossy leaves.

He reached behind him with methodical precision and drew a feathered arrow from the quiver strapped to his back.

Colin drew his sword, reflexes honed in six years of battle making it possible for him to move when he should have been paralyzed with horror.

When he drove his spurs into the stallion's flanks, the figure cantering through the meadow below was halfway across the valley floor, a vulnerable target to any assassin. Sword in hand, Colin went flying down the hill, racing the storm, racing death, racing time itself. With eerie clarity, a flash of lightning illuminated the bowman, forcing Colin to watch him nock his arrow and draw back the bowstring until it trembled with tension. The man waited, patient enough to choose the precise moment when he could best drive the feathered shaft through his victim's heart.

Dear God in heaven, he wasn't going to make it. Colin acknowledged his failure with a mighty roar, but a deafening crack of thunder drowned out his warning.

He drew back his sword just as the bowman let fly his arrow.

His aim was true. The rider lurched, then went spinning off the horse, arms flung outward in supplication.

With a cry of inhuman anguish, Colin plunged his blade through the assassin's chest, pinning him to the trunk of the birch meant to serve as his shield. The force of the blow dragged Colin off the stallion's back. He crashed to the ground, doubling over in agony as if it had been his own heart that had stopped beating in that moment.

CHAPTER 24

When Colin staggered from the birch copse to find Tabitha sitting in the rain, cradling the fallen rider across her lap, he dropped to his knees, no longer able to stand. He might have remained thus forever, frozen in shock and wonder, if she hadn't lifted her head and cast him a beseeching look. Tears trickled down her cheeks, mingling with the rain.

He crept closer. His brain was slowly beginning to thaw and as he reached to draw the hood from the motionless figure, he feared a river of dark curls might spill from its confines.

But it was Chauncey who lay across Tabitha's lap, the squire's ruddy face pale now in death. She brushed a lock of hair from his sightless eyes with a bloodstained hand.

"I was just over that rise when I heard him coming. I think he was coming to warn me." Her voice was soft and halting and after too many nights spent on blood-drenched battlefields, Colin recognized the stress of shock. He ached to touch her, but knew the best thing he could do was to just let her talk. "I got tired of going in circles and falling off the horse, you see, so I decided to walk him for a while. It really wasn't his fault. He's a very nice horse, just not too fond of thunder."

Colin glanced up to find the sorrel standing patiently a few feet away, ignoring the snorting attempts of Lyssandra's steed to win his attention.

Although the arrow protruding from Chauncey's back forced Tabitha to hold him awkwardly, she still managed to rock him in her arms. "I made him bring me to MacDuff's castle, you know. He begged me to stay at the cottage and obey you, but I thought it would all just be a grand adventure. A game. I didn't realize we were playing for keeps. If I had, he might be alive. Now he'll never argue with his mother again or have mock sword fights with his friends or kiss a pretty milkmaid or—"

"Tabitha . . ." Colin longed to take her burden of guilt and anguish upon his own broad shoulders, but knew it was one she would insist on bearing all alone.

As her gaze locked on his chest, Colin could hardly stand to see the pathetic spark of hope that lit her eyes. "The amulet, Colin! Give me the amulet!"

He drew the chain over his head and dropped the emerald into her outstretched hand. He could have told her that some magic could only be performed by the deft hand of God, but feared she must discover that for herself.

She screwed her eyes shut, her lips moving in a fierce litany. When she finally opened them several moments later, fresh tears clung to her lashes and Chauncey's body still lay limp across her lap. "I wished. I wished with all my heart that he would breathe again. What good is magic if it won't make your wishes come true?"

Bitterness darkened her eyes as she drew back her arm and flung the amulet as far as it would go.

When Colin gently took Chauncey's limp body from

her arms, she did not protest, but simply sat with her mouth pressed to her knee, rocking in the rain.

When Tabitha finally climbed to her feet an eternity later, she felt as if she were waking from a daze. The rain had softened to a misty shower, gentle enough to heal the ugly gashes left by the storm. Colin was nowhere in sight, but she could hear the rhythmic clack of rock against rock somewhere in the nearby woods.

She followed the sound, pushing aside a cedar bough to find him placing stones on top of a shallow grave. She could tell by his mud-streaked arms and dirt-encrusted fingernails that even without tools, he'd managed to dig some kind of hollow in the saturated soil.

He wept without shame or apology, without sobs or even a change in expression, just an endless river of tears coursing down his cheeks. Realizing how selfish she had been to wallow in her own grief without once thinking of his, Tabitha began to gather stones in her skirt. They worked side by side until the homely grave was covered, then sank to the ground, muddy and exhausted.

Colin scrubbed at his eyes, leaving streaks of dirt. " 'Twas as if I were burying them all. My father. Blythe. Regan. Even my very own mother, who's been dead since I was naught more than a wee lad."

Tabitha leaned her head against his shoulder. "Most men would crumble under the weight of so much loss."

He cupped her throat and turned her face toward him, a fierce light in his eyes. "Never have I known a grief so keen as when I thought it was you who had gone down beneath that arrow. Even when, for an instant, I believed it to be Lyssa lying dead in your arms, all I could feel was relief because it was not you."

If his confession hadn't taken her breath away, she might have scolded him for daring to voice such a terrible thing. As it was, she could only gaze helplessly up at him until he closed her eyes by kissing each eyelid in turn.

As his seeking lips melted against her own, he swept her up in his arms. He carried her through the forest and laid her down on a bed of ferns, the sky their only canopy. Tabitha knew she should be scandalized by the clumsy haste with which they tugged at each other's clothes, but she was as eager as he was to feel the misty rain against her skin. To let it wash away the dirt and blood and taint of death.

She understood now why Colin's people had been so quick to seize the joy of the moment. In a world without prenatal care or vaccinations or policemen or antibiotics, any moment might very well be their last. Although it felt as if the imprints Colin made on her flesh would be branded into her skin forever, she knew they, like the moments they shared, would be only too fleeting.

They mourned Chauncey's death, yet celebrated life in its most fundamental essence. They didn't just offer each other comfort, but an affirmation, unspeakably tender, unspeakably primal. Casting her inhibitions to the wind, Tabitha lowered her head and worshiped him with her mouth, delighting in the dark power and passion of the mysterious union. He tangled his hands in her hair and groaned her name as if it were his most fervent prayer.

When his body trembled on the brink of explosion, he drew her lips to his and thrust his tongue in her mouth, kissing her as if he could go on forever. She rubbed her breasts against his chest with kittenish abandon, marveling because this magnificent man with his stubborn chin and golden tiger eyes was hers for the taking.

Take him she did, slipping astride him with more grace than she'd ever exhibited in ballet class. Her entire body quivered with delight as his big hands framed her hips, driving her down until she contained the rigid length and breadth of him deep inside of her.

This time there was no pain, only pleasure. A pleasure so poignant and intense it brought fresh tears to her eyes. But these tears were cleansing, and even as Colin kissed them away, she was beginning to move until everything melted to insignificance except the sinuous friction of their flesh.

But Colin still remembered to reach between them, to stroke that tender bud above where their bodies were joined until shudder after shudder of exquisite rapture racked her.

As his own roar of ecstasy echoed through the forest, she threw back her head in exultation. She, Tabitha Lennox, who had kept her training wheels on her bike until she was twelve, had dared to ride a dragon.

When Tabitha awoke, she was lying stark naked on a bed of ferns. She shaded her eyes against the sun, trying to gauge how long she'd slept. Beads of rain still sparkled like diamonds on every leaf and blade of grass. She sat up and fumbled around for her discarded gown, feeling like some sort of wanton fairy enchanted by a mortal. She wryly shook her head, thinking the opposite must be true. No man with Colin's stamina could be completely mortal.

She found her damp gown hanging on a nearby branch. She dragged it on, but it wasn't until her fingers brushed her breastbone that she remembered flinging the amulet into the mist. A pang of regret stabbed her.

Worthless or not, the amulet might very well be the only heirloom she would ever receive from her mother.

"I trust you enjoyed your nap?"

She whirled around to find Colin emerging from the sun-dappled shadows of the forest. The suggestive quirk of his lips might not have made her heart beat faster if the memory of all the delicious things those lips had done to her hadn't been so fresh. With his tousled hair and bearded jaw, he looked extremely sexy. And dangerous. Especially since he was wiping blood from the blade of the sword in his hand with what used to be her slip.

She knew she ought to be disturbed by the evidence of bloodshed, but instead felt a rush of savage satisfaction. "By any chance, did that blood once belong to Brisbane's man?"

He sheathed the weapon, his expression grim. "Not Brisbane's man. MacDuff's."

Frowning, Tabitha hugged back a shiver. "I don't understand. Why would MacDuff try to kill me?"

Colin shrugged. "Perhaps because he suspected 'twas you I loved instead of his daughter."

The hush within Tabitha was so quiet, even the birds seemed to stop singing. "What did you say?"

Colin's lips curved in that tender half smile she could never resist. "I love you."

Horrified, she clapped a hand over his mouth. "Don't say that. Please don't say that." She freed his mouth and backed away from him, wringing her hands. "Oh, dear Lord, what have I done now?"

He eyed her askance, thoroughly bemused by her odd behavior. "Why are you so distressed, lass? You've done naught but win my heart."

"Steal it, more likely!" She paced around him in a frantic circle. "Don't you realize what I've done? I must have been talking in my sleep. I've wished you would love me almost from the first moment I saw you, but I never spoke the words out loud, I swear it." She paused long enough to check his brow for fever. "Oh, you poor thing. I'm so sorry."

Colin laughed aloud. "Contrary to what you may believe, my lady, you've cast no spell upon me. At least not the kind you think."

"Why, of course I have. Oh, no," she muttered. "What if you start acting like Brent Vondervan did in the fourth grade when my mother cast a love spell on him? I guess you can't offer me peanut butter sandwiches from your lunch box, but you might stop bossing me around and being grumpy and growling at me." She shuddered. "I won't be able to stand it if you're polite."

He caught her by the wrist, stilling her aimless flight, and forced her to look at him. "Is it truly so inconceivable that I would love you?"

She nodded. "I'm shy and clumsy and always blurt out the wrong thing in social situations. I babble when I'm nervous. I hog the blankets because I've always slept alone. I eat too much ice cream when I'm depressed. And when I'm PMS, I'm a real witch." She grimaced. "Well, really cranky anyway. I hate to exercise and I never remember to screw the lid back on the toothpaste tube after I brush." He still didn't look convinced so she added, "And I'm entirely too tall." She swallowed, finding it more and more difficult to squeeze words past the lump in her throat. "How could you love me?"

He framed her face between his hands, searching her features as if to etch them upon his memory. His soft chuckle was belied by the somber glow in his eyes. "How could I not?"

"Oh . . ." The sigh escaped her on a breath of pure

happiness, but Colin was there to capture it with his lips.

"Tabitha?" he murmured between kisses.

"Yes," she whispered, clinging to his brawny shoulders to keep from melting all over him.

"Who is this Brent fellow? And what is a peanut sand witch? And a psychodontist and an orthotherapist? Why would one want to service a room and who in God's name taught you that atrocious song you sang last night—the one that made you sound like you were braying through your nose?"

Tabitha drew back to look at him, realizing the time of reckoning had come. "You've been much more attentive than I realized."

He nodded. "I don't understand much of what you say, but I do remember it."

She reluctantly extracted herself from his arms and gestured to a fallen log. "Maybe you should sit down."

He obliged her, eyeing her somewhat warily. Tabitha paced the clearing, trying to find the best way to begin. Her mother had always taught her that if she ever got lost, she should go back to the place where she had last seen herself.

So she did.

She took Colin back to that snowy New York night when she'd accidentally wandered so far from home. Although too nervous to meet his gaze directly, she would steal a glance at him every now and then to find him listening intently to her rambling tale, his face carefully blank. She suspected she'd had that precise look on her own face when she'd viewed her mother's video and first learned of the amulet's existence. He even managed a polite nod at pivotal points in her story.

"So you see," she finished, smiling brightly at him, "my so-called 'supernatural' powers are probably nothing more than the result of a hyperdeveloped sense or a mutated gene. The amulet was nothing more than a positronic conduit designed to enhance them. Doesn't that make you feel better?"

He sat in silence for so long that Tabitha started to fidget. Then he dragged a hand through his hair, rumpling it beyond repair. "Indeed, my lady, you've truly set my heart at ease. I'm not in love with a witch. I'm in love with a lunatic."

She blinked hopefully at him. "Is one more socially acceptable than the other?"

He rose and began to pace in the opposite direction. " 'Tis not a matter of acceptance, but of convenience. Witches must be burned at the stake. I can just lock you away in a convent with all the other madwomen."

She shook her head in dismay. "I was afraid you'd take this badly. That's why I didn't tell you sooner."

He spun around on his heel to gape at her. "Badly?" His voice rose to a roar. "Badly? You tell me you've journeyed to this place from seven hundred years in the future—"

"Seven hundred and sixty-six," she gently corrected.

His glare could have scorched grass. "—*seven hundred and sixty-six years* in the future and just expect me to believe such an absurd tale."

"Brent Vondervan was a boy I had a crush on in the fourth grade. A sandwich is a hunk of meat positioned between two pieces of sliced bread. A psychotherapist offers counseling services for mental or emotional disturbances. An orthodontist uses a variety of plastic and metal appliances to straighten crooked teeth. Room service is how you order food in an expensive hotel. The atrocious song was 'Your Cheatin' Heart,' written and recorded by Mr. Hank Williams, Sr., in Nashville, Tennessee, in 1953 and you're supposed to sing it through your nose or it wouldn't sound like authentic country music."

Colin sat down on the log again, so hard he almost tumbled off the other side. " 'Tis true, is it not?" he said hoarsely. "You're not of this time, but of another. You do not belong here."

Tabitha had never expected him to look so stricken. She knelt between his knees, resting her hands on his thighs, and gazed tenderly up at him. "I belong wherever you are."

"But your parents . . . ? If they're still alive, they must feel you belong with them."

She lowered her eyes, disquieted by his concern. "My mother's a hopeless romantic. If she were here at this moment, I'm sure she would tell me to follow my heart, even if it led me away from her."

"And your father?"

She laughed. "He'd probably punch you in the nose. He still tends to think of me as Daddy's little girl."

"He sounds like a fine man." Colin tipped her chin up, forcing her to meet his gaze. "Will you be able to live with the uncertainty? With never knowing if they're somewhere in the future missing you, mourning you as you might have mourned them if they had never been found?"

The answer didn't come as readily to her lips as she had hoped, but fortunately Colin was distracted by the thunder of approaching hoofbeats. As the horse slowed to a walk, passing dangerously close to their hiding place, they scrambled behind a gnarled oak, fearing they were being stalked by another of MacDuff's assassins. Colin gripped the hilt of his sword, but the tension in his arm relaxed when a melodious feminine voice was followed by a sardonic Gallic growl.

"If you had taken the right fork as I suggested instead of the left one, we could have been here an hour ago."

"You're a worse nag than this wretched horse. Curb your saucy tongue, wench, or I'll curb it for you."

"I'd like to see you try."

Silence greeted this ominous challenge. Colin drew Tabitha toward a break in the bushes. "We'd best make sure they're not killing each other. As you well know, Arjon and Lyssandra have never borne any great fondness toward one another."

Colin's jaw dropped as they emerged from the tunnel of bracken to find his best friend and his fiancée locked in a passionate embrace. A bored-looking horse stood a few feet away, lazily swishing his tail.

Tabitha nudged Colin. "Just think what they might be doing if they were fond of each other."

At the sound of her voice, Arjon and Lyssandra broke away from their kiss with a guilty start. Lyssandra's creamy cheeks were flushed with rose, her eyes luminous. Tabitha knew the look only too well. Her own face had probably mirrored it only minutes before. She bit back a smile as she noted the way Lyssandra squared her delicate chin and boldly met their gazes, the way Arjon's arm moved to shield his lady fair.

"Ah, here's your betrothed now," he said. "You may challenge me to a joust if you wish, Ravenshaw, but I must have her."

Edging even closer to Arjon, Lyssandra blinked prettily at Colin, who still hadn't recovered from his daze. " 'Twas never my intention to break your heart, sir. But now that I've finally found my true love, I can only pray that you'll find the courage to press on."

Arjon narrowed his eyes at his friend, struggling to send a frantic message, but Colin was not receiving. He might have stood frozen there forever with his mouth hanging open if Tabitha hadn't jabbed him in the side.

He coughed, then cleared his throat as if to strangle back a disbelieving laugh. Only Tabitha was near enough to see the sparkle of amusement in his eyes. " 'Twill be a lonely struggle, lass, but I suppose my shattered heart will mend. In time. *Lots* of time," he added gruffly. He strode across the clearing and pumped Arjon's hand.

"Congratulations, my friend. You've won one of the fairest hearts in all of Scotland." Arjon grimaced as he gave the bones an extra squeeze. "If you ever break it, you'll answer to me."

The Norman snatched his hand back and clapped it over his own heart. "Have no fear! My heartbreaking days are over. I never realized it until I held her squirming in my arms while she tried to bite me and I had to kiss her to muffle her shrieks, but I was only biding my time until the brat grew into a woman."

Lyssandra fluttered her eyelashes at him. "All the woman you'll ever need."

"My precise sentiments," replied Arjon, all but cooing.

Tabitha rolled her eyes. "I thought the two of you despised each other."

"What choice did I have?" Arjon asked. "I might have yearned for Lyssa in my most secret heart, but I knew she belonged to Colin and could never be mine."

"So he labored diligently to make me hate him—putting spiders in my bed, using my dolls for archery practice, calling me dreadful names."

Arjon pressed a fervent kiss to her knuckles. "Consider them endearments, my adorable little shrew."

It was Colin's turn to roll his eyes. "What are the two of you doing out here?"

"Looking for you," Arjon replied. He exchanged a glance with Lyssandra. "It seems Brisbane and the Mac-Duff are in league. They have been for quite some time."

Colin's face went deathly still. "How long?"

There was no way for Arjon to soften the blow. "Since before the siege. Lyssa overheard her father and Brisbane's man discussing their plans to be rid of you and divide your holdings among themselves. The Mac-Duff had already signed a betrothal contract, giving Lyssa into Roger's hands."

Lyssandra placed her hand on Colin's arm. "I knew naught of his treachery, Colin, I swear it. I pray you'll believe me."

Tabitha had never loved him more than she did at that moment when he gently covered Lyssandra's hand with his own, even managing a strained smile. "Of course, I believe you. 'Tis you who were wronged even more than I. Your father's betrayal must have cut you to the heart."

She nodded, brushing a tear from her cheek. "He said the most vile things."

Arjon gathered her into his arms, the tenderness in his touch assuring Tabitha that his conversion to monogamy was sincere. "If I hadn't intercepted her in the corridor outside her father's solar, the foolhardy lass would have ridden out all by herself to warn you about the MacDuff's assassins."

Tabitha glanced nervously around, every shadow suddenly a menace. "How many are there?"

Arjon rested his hand on the hilt of his sword, his grin cold. "Three less than there were before."

"Make it four," Colin said.

Arjon frowned. "We sent Chauncey this way on Lyssandra's steed. Have you seen him?"

Colin nodded grimly. "Seen him and buried him. He took an arrow meant for Tabitha."

They shared a moment of somber silence mourning the courageous boy before Lyssandra turned her puzzled gaze on Tabitha. "Brisbane's man said his master wanted you alive. He seemed very distressed when my father informed him that you were also to die. 'Twas almost as if he feared for his own life if he failed to bring you back."

Tabitha exchanged a troubled look with Colin. Brisbane's personal attention was certainly not something she cared to attract. "Do you think he might suspect . . . ?"

Colin nodded. " 'Tis a possibility. Roger always was a canny wretch."

He strode to the edge of the clearing and stood with his back to them, hands on hips. Tabitha ached to go to him, but knew he needed some room to absorb all that he'd learned in so short a time.

Arjon was not as comfortable with Colin's brooding silence as she was. "If you're resolved to go after Brisbane, I think it's safe to venture we can no longer rely on the MacDuff for reinforcements."

Colin swung around to face him. "You should take Lyssa and go before the MacDuff realizes you're gone. As far away from here as you dare. This is not your fight."

Arjon grinned. "You know I never could resist a lost cause. How do you think I ended up on Crusade?" He sobered. "If it's your fight, my friend, 'tis mine as well."

"And mine," Lyssandra added, stepping forward.

Colin surveyed them for a long moment before nodding. "This cause may not be as lost as you think. I have one weapon Brisbane can never match."

Tabitha stood rooted to the forest floor as Colin approached. He reached into his tunic and unfurled a delicate chain he'd obviously made a painstaking effort to find and repair while she was napping. She was less mesmerized by the emerald's gleam than by the tender glow in his eyes as he lowered the chain over her head until the amulet came to rest against her heart.

Arjon arched a skeptical eyebrow. "And what would that weapon be?"

Colin grazed her cheek with a kiss as he turned her to face them. "The most beautiful witch in all of Christendom."

CHAPTER ✳ 25

When Colin and Tabitha came riding into the courtyard at Castle Raven, they were greeted by stunned silence and disbelieving stares. As if the shock of their laird having his arm firmly around the waist of a confessed witch he'd vowed to burn wasn't enough, Colin's betrothed rode on the horse behind them, practically perched in Sir Arjon's lap.

His people stood frozen in dumb astonishment until Jenny squirmed out of her mother's grip and came pelting across the cobblestones. "Lady Tabby! Lady Tabby!" Tabitha slid off the horse just as the little girl flung herself into her arms. "See, Mama," she said, beaming as she pressed her cheek to Tabitha's, "I told you the nice witch would come back!"

Magwyn swaggered forward, hands on hips. "Aye, and a bonny sight she is. For a ghost."

Tabitha's first instinct was to recoil from the woman's withering sarcasm, but she and Colin had agreed that if she was ever to be truly accepted by his people, it would have to be by choice, not decree. She could almost feel the warmth of his love like a hand at her back, gently propelling her forward.

Gripping Jenny's small hand for courage, she faced

Magwyn. She could tell from the way the others hung back that this one woman's rejection or acceptance would decide her fate.

"I'm sorry to disappoint you, but I'm not a ghost because your laird decided not to burn me."

"But you are a witch."

"I am." Her bold confession stirred a nervous refrain of murmurs. "But I don't worship Satan and I've never, to my knowledge, used my powers for evil. Nor do I plan to."

Magwyn's eyes narrowed thoughtfully. Tabitha would have almost sworn the woman wanted to believe her. But she knew she was battling a lifetime of superstition and fear. If she'd grown up in a world as dangerous and capricious as theirs, she might have preferred to blame her own bad luck on black cats or evil spirits.

As Magwyn pondered her words, help came from an unexpected quarter. In full princess mode, Lyssandra wiggled out of Arjon's arms and flung herself from the horse.

She seized Tabitha's other hand and stamped her dainty foot. "Whatever her temperament might be, Lady Tabitha is my friend. And if any one of you dares to speak ill of her, they'll answer to me!"

Arjon applauded. "Huzzah, my sweet!"

Colin's people shuffled their feet and avoided each other's eyes as if shamed by the girl's passionate defense. All except for Arjon's blond doxy, who'd been glaring daggers at Lyssandra while the rest of them gaped at Tabitha.

"That one must be a witch, too," she said in a stage whisper loud enough to be heard back on Broadway. "I think we should burn the both of them."

"Hush, Nessa," Magwyn said sharply. "You've no right to sharpen your claws on Sir Arjon's lady when you've already lured one of Iselda's sons into your bed since he's been gone."

The girl subsided with a sulky pout while Iselda rolled her eyes and one of the more strapping boys blushed to the roots of his hair.

Despite her defense of Lyssandra, Magwyn's expression remained so unrelenting that Tabitha feared the worst. "Come here, Jenny." Shooting Tabitha an uncertain glance, the little girl obeyed her mother. Although Magwyn's jaw was rigid, she stroked the little girl's cropped curls with a gentleness that bordered on reverence. "Whatever you may be, you gave my daughter back her smile, her voice, even her life. Perhaps what you speak is the truth. Perhaps it matters naught what power a woman possesses, but only how she chooses to wield it."

"Well spoken, Magwyn," Colin said, slipping off the horse to rest his hands on Tabitha's shoulders. "I couldn't have said it better myself."

Tabitha's heart swelled with happiness as they gathered around to shyly welcome her back into their fold, assuring her that Lucy had been well tended in her absence and giving Wee Blythe into Colin's eager hands.

But her happiness faltered when she saw a woman with a careworn face craning her neck to see over the heads of the others. "Where's my lad? Has anyone seen my lad?"

This was the moment Tabitha knew Colin had been dreading. Sobering, he handed the baby to Auld Nana before taking the woman's chapped hands in his own.

He gazed down into her face, his expression indescribably tender. "I'm sorry, Gunna, but Chauncey's dead, another victim of Brisbane's treachery. He died a hero, sacrificing his life to save an innocent woman."

The woman collapsed in Colin's arms, muffling her

broken wail against his shoulder. It was only then that Tabitha became aware of the ring of sullen young faces lurking at the fringes of the crowd. She would have sworn they'd only been boys when she and Colin left, but now their narrowed eyes held the determined glint of men.

The one with the longest hair and meanest eyes stepped forward. "How many more, my laird?" he demanded. "How many more of our own will die before we strike back?"

Colin's hands were gentle against the woman's heaving shoulders, but his eyes glittered like the sharpest of diamonds as he uttered the one word they'd all been waiting to hear.

"None."

Lord Brisbane woke up smiling.

He'd done so with increasing frequency since dispatching Iago to the MacDuff's castle. His sleep had been warmed by visions of a certain self-righteous knight being roasted on one of Satan's spits. Last night's dream, in which a swarm of little red imps had scampered around Colin, poking him with their tiny pitchforks until he screamed like a woman, had been particularly entertaining.

Roger was still chuckling when he swept aside the hangings of his luxuriant four-poster and climbed down from the bed. His cheerful demeanor earned him an apprehensive look from the flock of servants who huddled in the corner, just waiting to do their master's bidding.

A stooped old fellow rushed over with a brass pot, and Roger relieved himself with a hearty sigh of satisfaction, caring little that he splashed piss on the poor man's feet.

While the wretch was emptying the pot down the privy hole, Roger stretched out his arms, allowing his servants to drape him in one of the elegant robes he preferred. Although the floor-length garment was customarily worn over a linen shirt, Roger preferred the rich caress of velvet directly against his skin. He stood like a marble statue while they shaved him, coiffed his sleek blond hair, and perfumed his throat with lemon cologne imported from Sicily.

He wanted to look his very best. For this was the day all of his dreams would come true.

He'd already had his garrison throw open the bailey gates in welcome. At any time now his emissary would come riding through those gates at the head of the processional the MacDuff would have provided to escort his spoiled daughter to the arms of her eager bridegroom.

The MacDuff would never suspect it was not his mewling brat Roger awaited with such gleeful anticipation, but the woman who would travel with her. The woman who had realized the one ambition that had always eluded him—corrupting Colin's soul.

His only regret was that he was to be denied the pleasure of gloating over his friend's fall from grace. He'd decided it would be best to arrange Colin's death before the pious fool had the opportunity to drop to his knees and beg his Lord's pardon for slaking his carnal desires with a witch. Roger rolled his eyes. It would be just like God in his sniveling mercy and compassion to forgive him. If *he* were God, he would never forgive anyone anything. It was too much fun holding a grudge.

When his servants were done grooming him, they staggered over with an enormous mirror and held it up in front of him so he could admire his reflection from all angles. Ignoring their grunts of exertion, he stroked his smooth chin, thinking how delightful it was going to be to have his very own witch. Once he'd planted an heir in the belly of the MacDuff's daughter, he'd have the witch cast some deadly spell on his blustering father-in-law. Then, murmuring his sympathy all the while, he would step in and claim the MacDuff's land as well as Colin's, crowning himself ruler of a vast empire that would stretch from northern England to southern Scotland.

He fluffed up his bangs. 'Twas a pity Regan was dead. She would have made a most regal queen.

He was still preening when the old fellow who had emptied the chamber pot tapped him on the shoulder. "My lord?"

"Mmmmm?" he murmured.

The man cast the balcony window a shaken glance. "There's someone comin'."

Roger bared his teeth in a smile, admiring their ivory gleam. "Of course, there's someone coming. 'Twould be Iago, coming to grant all of my fondest desires."

The fellow cleared his throat. "I don't think this would be Master Iago, my lord."

Roger frowned, then smoothed the tiny crinkles at the corners of his eyes with his thumbs. "You're not paid to think."

"I'm not paid at all, sir, but I still don't think this would be Master Iago."

Roger whirled around, planning to box the insolent wretch's ears, but a distant sound stilled his hand in midmotion.

He cocked his head to the side, trying to identify the elusive strains. "What the hell . . . ?"

They were slowly swelling in volume, drawing Roger toward the balcony. When he saw what was marching through the gates of his bailey wall, he had to brace his hands against the stone railing to keep from tumbling off the balcony.

Pouring into his courtyard was the most motley, rag-tag band of invaders he had ever seen. Some were horsed, but most marched on foot, tattered rags their only armor. Stooped, white-haired old men marched next to fresh-faced lads, and most astonishing of all, there were women! Wild-eyed harpies and withered crones armed just like their male comrades with long-handled scythes, rusty knives, and blunt clubs.

A massive woman hugged an iron cauldron in the crook of her arm, banging on its hollow bottom to keep time with the stirring melody of their song. It was one of those rousing Crusade anthems, deliberately composed to incite some devout warrior with visions of sainthood into offering up his life for a hopeless cause.

Roger dug his fingernails into the casement, seized by outrage.

How dare these wretched peasants march through his open gates and spoil his fine mood? How dare they make his courtyard ring with music?

But when he saw the man riding to the head of their pathetic processional, he knew exactly how they dared.

The magnificent ebony stallion pranced forward, the man seated on his back looking as if he were lord not only of the horse, but of all he would ever survey. Clenched in his gauntleted fist was a staff bearing the Ravenshaw standard. He reached the front of their ranks just as the song soared to its majestic climax, the silver raven on its bed of black silk rippling proudly in the wind.

Silence reigned until Brisbane spat out, "Christ, Colin, you've more lives than a cat."

"I should hope so, Roger, given your disturbing fondness for trying to murder me."

Roger scanned the mob. "And what have you done with Iago?"

Colin shrugged. "The last we heard, your henchman was on his way to London. As I'm sure you've already guessed, his mission failed. Which means the MacDuff won't be sending any reinforcements your way. 'Tis rumored that he's nursing his grief over his daughter's sudden elopement by withdrawing his entire household to Castle Arran. Permanently."

Roger barked with laughter. "And why would I need reinforcements against this motley band of outlaws?"

Instead of replying, Ravenshaw reached into his saddlebag and drew forth a parchment scroll. He unrolled it with a flourish, his voice booming through the courtyard. "I hereby proclaim that from this moment forward this castle is under siege and demand the immediate surrender of its lord—Roger Basil Henry Joseph Maximillian, Baron Brisbane."

Roger glanced wildly at his bailey walls where his guards had taken up an offensive position, swords drawn and crossbows slotted with lethal bolts. The captain of his garrison was helping his men roll a mangonel into place. Roger knew at his command, the miniature catapult would hurl a shower of rocks down upon the vulnerable heads of the intruders.

"Have you lost your wits, man? I can almost understand your ridiculous need to martyr yourself, but must you make saints of your people as well?"

Colin continued to read as if he hadn't spoken. "Upon surrender, you'll be taken to the court of Alexander the Third where you'll be judged for the murders of the sixth Lord of Ravenshaw, his noble wife, Blythe, and four score and ten of the King's loyal Scottish subjects."

Roger drew himself up to his full height, quivering with rage. "Henry is *my* king. I'll not answer to you or that barbarian Scot for my crimes."

As Colin let the scroll snap shut, his mocking smile chilled Roger to the marrow. "Oh, but I think you will."

His army parted to reveal a lone woman.

A woman who did not slump, but stood straight and tall. A woman wearing a shimmering purple gown and stroking the tiny black cat cradled in her arms without the slightest hint of clumsiness. A woman who glided forward to stand beside Ravenshaw's horse with all the arrogant grace of a guardian angel.

A woman who terrified him.

The sun glinted off her golden hair, the belt draped around her slender hips, the plump emerald nestled between her breasts.

Roger did the only thing he could think of. He looked the captain of his archers straight in the eye and bellowed, "Fire!"

CHAPTER 26

As Tabitha awaited Colin's prearranged signal, she prayed the knocking of her knees wouldn't drown out his people's singing. It had taken her nearly three days to teach them all the words to "Do You Hear the People Sing?" from *Les Misérables,* but she had finally succeeded. Their rendition had given her chills. She doubted even the finest Broadway cast could imbue the song, with its stirring melody and hope for a brighter tomorrow, with so much heartfelt emotion. She'd felt a genuine flare of triumph when she saw Arjon's former doxy reach over and squeeze Lyssandra's hand during the chorus.

She was terrified she would trip over her hem when Colin summoned her forward. Granny Cora had been forced to stitch nearly five extra inches of silk to one of Lady Blythe's most beautiful gowns before it would fit her. Lucy nuzzled Tabitha's hair as if to whisper words of comfort. Brisbane would never suspect the cat was nothing but a harmless prop.

"Oh, but I think you will."

Colin's rich voice cut through her reverie. His people parted like the Red Sea, clearing a path for her. If she hadn't known Colin was waiting for her at the end of that path, she would never have had the confidence to put one foot in front of the other until she stood beside his horse. She would never have had the pleasure of watching Brisbane's sneer fade . . .

. . . a second before he looked at someone on the wall behind them and yelled, "Fire!"

As she grabbed the amulet, Tabitha knew an instant of pure panic. What if Colin had been a fool to put his faith in her? What if she failed as she'd failed so many times in the past? What if her incompetence left the courtyard littered with their bodies?

The crossbows loosed their missiles with a mighty *thrum.*

It was the image of an arrow piercing Colin's bold and noble heart that gave her the courage to spin around and make a wish.

The feathered shafts shooting toward them melted to nothing but feathers, drifting harmlessly to the ground. As she turned back toward the castle, Colin gave her a bone-melting smile and his people cheered. Having been previously deprived of the opportunity by her ballet instructor and chorus director, she could not resist making a pleased little bow.

"You might perform your heroics with a little more haste," Arjon hissed, looking a little green around the gills.

It seemed she would soon get another chance, for at Brisbane's frantic command, the catapult perched on the wall high above them sent an avalanche of deadly rocks hurtling toward their heads.

Tabitha whispered a wish and the rocks turned to rose petals, raining down around them in a fragrant shower.

She blew a petal off her nose, a surge of naughty

exultation making her giggle. She'd never dreamed being a witch could be so much fun.

"Engage them, you fools!" Brisbane shouted, hysteria rising in his voice. "Cut them down where they stand!"

His men hung back for an infinitesimal second, plainly cowed by the strange goings-on. But their fear of their sadistic lord still surpassed their fear of Tabitha. So it was with false bravado and savage snarls, they came plunging down the gatehouse stairs, blades at the ready. But when they reached the courtyard, their weapons had turned into Nerf swords.

One man drove his blade toward Magwyn's chest, only to discover the spongy toy went limp at its first contact with human flesh. He was still staring at it in dumb amazement when Magwyn whacked him over the head with a stick. He went down like a stone.

Auld Nana dispatched another of the guards by cramming the iron cauldron over his head. He staggered away, bleating piteously until he slammed into a wall. Nana ducked her head and made an offensive run at the enemy, sending guards flying in every direction.

One of the guards charged straight for Lyssandra only to falter at finding such a rose among the thorns. She smiled sweetly at him. Before ramming her dainty fist into his nose.

"Oh, Arjon," she wailed, "I think I broke a fingernail."

Her beloved stopped pummeling a guard long enough to press a passionate kiss on the wounded appendage.

The wild young boys who had yearned for a fight for so long threw themselves into the melee with such blood-chilling howls the guards feared Tabitha had summoned a horde of demons to defeat them. Rose petals and feathers soon choked the air.

"Get it off me!" screamed one of the guards as a toothless old man gummed his leg.

Tabitha stood gently stroking Lucy while chaos reigned around her. Colin dispatched more than his share of attackers, wheeling the stallion from cluster to cluster of fighting and subduing all challengers with the flat blade of his sword.

Soon the courtyard was littered with unconscious bodies, none of them their own. The guards who could still walk, limp, or crawl scrambled away like rats scurrying for their holes, leaving Brisbane standing alone on the balcony.

Colin wheeled the stallion back around, shooting him a triumphant look. "Do you surrender, sir?"

Roger's shoulders slumped. He nodded sadly. "Aye, my friend. I surrender."

As he disappeared from the balcony, Colin and Tabitha exchanged a baffled glance, having prepared for every eventuality except this one.

When Brisbane emerged from the castle, arms raised and hands dangling limply above his head, his demeanor was so pathetic even Tabitha might have felt sorry for him if she hadn't known what a monster he was. After much frantic searching, they discovered they hadn't a scrap of rope among them, so it fell to Tabitha to conjure up a shiny pair of handcuffs.

Brisbane didn't even protest when Colin slipped them on his wrists and snapped them shut. He couldn't seem to summon up any resistance more potent than a labored sigh. After Colin had lifted Tabitha up on the stallion to ride sidesaddle in front of him, their captive fell obediently into step behind the horse's twitching tail.

As they passed through the bailey gates, they encountered no further opposition from Brisbane's garrison. When they'd traveled a brief distance, Tabitha would have even sworn she heard a faint cheer go up from the castle walls behind them.

Colin's people were equally jubilant. They clapped each other on the back and congratulated each other on their valor. They sang snatches of song both on-key and off—in Lyssandra's case, as Arjon had warned, mostly off. The boys mock-wrestled and relived every glorious moment of their first real skirmish while the old men swapped tales of battles fought in the full vigor of manhood, but never forgotten.

As they started across the idyllic meadow where she had first met Colin, Tabitha cradled Lucy in her arms and turned her face to the sun, basking in its warmth. If someone had told her that someday she would be riding through this very meadow in the arms of a prince among men, her hair sprinkled with rose petals, and her heart brimming with love, she would have told them they were either crazy or hopelessly misguided.

Until she'd gazed into Colin's golden eyes, she had believed that princes were for other women and love was for fools.

Brisbane's voice cut through her pleasure like the whine of a pesky mosquito. " 'Tis a pity we've come to such a pass, my lady. Did Colin never tell you that the two of us were once like brothers? At least until he decided to avail himself of my sister."

Colin's arm tightened around her waist. " 'Tis an old quarrel, Roger, and a tired one. As you well know, 'twas Regan who first crept into my bed one moonless night when I was still half asleep. Had I my wits about me, I might have found the strength to resist her."

Their handcuffed captive was walking beside them

now, nearly trotting to match the pace of Colin's stallion. "You would have broken her heart either way. She loved you, you know."

Colin's sigh ruffled Tabitha's hair. "Regan's love is the cross I've borne since her death."

"She loved you," he repeated, as if Colin had not even spoken. "But she loved me first."

Colin reined in the horse. Brisbane stumbled to a halt, his subservient mask slipping to reveal a sneer of triumph. The chattering crowd streamed around the two men, unaware of the brewing conflict. Despite the warmth of the sun, Tabitha felt a chill of foreboding.

"Don't listen to him, Colin," she said, longing only to free him from the chains of the past. "He'd say anything to hurt you."

"That's right, witch," Brisbane snarled. "Anything at all. Even the truth."

"The word is a mockery on your lips," Colin said.

Brisbane's grin was icy cold. "Regan and I had been lovers since we were naught but thirteen years old. Did you truly believe it was your child she carried? 'Twas her idea to trick you into bedding and wedding her so no one would ever know the babe was mine. When I threatened to tell you the truth, she hanged herself. She was too spineless to live without your love."

Tabitha gasped. For the first time, she understood Brisbane's bitter jealousy and unrelenting hatred. He honestly believed that Colin had usurped him as his sister's lover.

"Why you wretched son of a—!" Colin launched himself off the stallion, slamming his fist into Brisbane's face.

Tabitha screamed. Slipping Lucy into a saddlebag, she tumbled off the horse in Colin's wake and grabbed the back of his tunic. Brisbane lay cringing on the ground, his cuffed hands rendering him helpless to defend himself against Colin's savage blows.

"Stop him!" she shouted at the gaping onlookers. "Before he kills Brisbane!"

It wasn't that she didn't think Brisbane deserved to die. She just didn't want Colin to have to live with both the twins' deaths on his conscience.

She nearly sobbed with relief when Arjon shouldered his way through the crowd.

Surrendering her frantic grip on Colin's tunic, she grabbed Arjon by the arm. "You've got to stop him!"

Arjon cast the grappling men a casual look. Colin had his powerful hands around Brisbane's throat and was slowly squeezing the life from him. Roger's face was already beginning to turn a becoming shade of purple. "Why?"

"Because Colin will never be able to live with himself if he murders a defenseless man."

Arjon sighed and rolled his eyes heavenward. "Very well. If you insist."

He beckoned toward the others. In the end, only one of them was strong enough to get Colin in a headlock and drag him off Brisbane.

Colin rolled to his back, gasping for breath, and shot his assailant a wounded glare. "Christ, Nana, you almost strangled me."

The old woman planted her hands on her meaty hips. "If I've told you once, lad, I've told you a hundred times—never make me ask you to do somethin' more than once."

Since it seemed Colin would survive, Tabitha dropped to her knees at Brisbane's side. "Oh," she breathed, studying his limp limbs and waxy pallor. "I think we're too late."

She leaned over to check his mottled throat for a

pulse and that was how, when Brisbane opened his eyes, her amulet happened to be dangling in front of them like a fat, juicy fig. His cuffed hands shot out and since Tabitha thought he was dead, his earsplitting screech sent her tumbling back on her bottom. He snapped the amulet's chain with a single vicious wrench, bounded to his feet, and went running across the field like the White Rabbit in *Alice in Wonderland*. Several of the boys loped after him.

"Tabitha!" Colin bellowed, struggling to a sitting position.

She scrambled to his side. "Don't worry, love. Brisbane's not a witch. In his hands the amulet's nothing but a harmless piece of jewelry. He can't even—"

A jagged bolt of lightning shot out of the clear blue sky, striking the ground directly behind them. They looked at the charred crater, then at each other, then at Brisbane, who was gleefully hopping up and down at the edge of the forest.

"Scatter!" Colin bellowed.

He didn't have to ask twice. As a supernatural current charged the air, his people fled in all directions, some of the more agile boys making it as far as the forest, others taking cover in the sparse stands of oak that dotted the meadow. Even his riderless stallion flew past them as if winged, making for the nearest shelter.

Colin grabbed Tabitha's hand and they went flying across the meadow, rolling down an incline and into a shallow ditch just as another bolt of lightning seared the grass where they had been sitting only seconds before.

As they lay nose to nose in the grass, struggling to catch their breaths, Colin arched one eyebrow and growled, "You were saying, lass?"

CHAPTER 27

"Mama always said I didn't pay enough attention when she talked. But she talked *all* the time. And she was my mother, for heaven's sake! How was I to know she was ever going to say anything important? Oh, no. The video! Now I understand why Daddy wanted the amulet destroyed and why Mama let him believe she flushed it down the commode all those years ago. They both knew that if it fell into the wrong hands . . ." Tabitha groaned and banged her head against the soft turf.

"Sweeting?" Colin said from somewhere above her.

"Hmm?"

"Are you quite done having hysterics?"

She sat up, spitting out a clump of grass. "I think so."

Colin was peering over the rim of the ditch, his hand on the hilt of his sword. "He's got the manacles off and he's waving them at us in a most insolent manner. You do realize, of course, that he planned this entire escapade. I should have known he was too arrogant to surrender without a fight to the death."

"Why couldn't I have just let you strangle him? Remind me not to stop you next time."

He massaged his throat. "Next time I'll let Auld Nana strangle him."

Tabitha scooted to the top of the ditch on her elbows and gently touched his arm. "I'm sorry about Regan. She must have felt trapped in an intolerable situation. I'm sure she never really wanted to deceive you."

Colin shook his head. "If she had only trusted me enough to confide in me . . . I wouldn't have hated her. I would have tried to help her."

"I know," Tabitha replied, smiling wryly. "You never could resist a damsel in distress."

If they hadn't exchanged a loving glance, they might not have become aware of the ominous silence.

"What's Brisbane doing now?" Tabitha peeped over the edge of the ditch, unable to bear the suspense.

"He's disappeared into the forest."

"Maybe he's headed back to his castle to establish his evil empire. After all, he can rule the world from there just as well as anywhere else." Groaning with despair, she tugged on Colin's sleeve. "We can't leave the amulet in his hands, you know. If we can't get it back, then we'll have to find some way to destroy it."

"But if we destroy it . . . ?"

She finished the thought before he could. "I'll never get home." She gazed helplessly at him, tracing the rugged features she'd come to know as well as her own. A future with him would mean bitter-cold winters with no central heat or electric blankets. But a future without him would mean bitter-cold springs, falls, and summers for the rest of her life. She flashed him a tremulous smile. "It's a risk I'm willing to take."

His tender scowl meant more to her than all the smiles in the world. He reached for her, and even though she was lying in a ditch with grass stuck in the most unlikely places, his touch still made desire burn thick and hot in her veins.

He pressed a fierce kiss to her lips, then plucked a rose petal from her hair. "You may not have your charm, lass, but you're still a bonny witch. You can defeat him with your magic. I have faith in you."

His solemn regard only worsened the sick feeling in the pit of her stomach. "Colin, there's something you should know . . ."

But before she could finish, a sound both terrible and familiar reached their ears, throbbing like a jungle full of natives beating a single massive drum. The ground beneath them began to tremble, then quake—a thousand times worse than it had on the day Brisbane's men had come thundering out of the forest.

"I have a very bad feeling about this," Colin murmured.

They both peeked over the rim of the ditch. The meadow was still deserted, but deep in the forest, the tops of the trees were beginning to sway.

Colin drew his sword and started to rise, but Tabitha latched on to his ankle with both hands, dragging him back down.

"Colin, you can't! Brisbane will destroy you. You heard him. He blames you for stealing his sister's heart away from him."

He struggled out of her grip. "I can't just lay here on my belly, lass, and let him slaughter us. If I can lure him out, then you can use your magic to defeat him."

"That might not be such a good—" She grabbed for his ankle again, but he had already vaulted over the rim of the ditch and was striding boldly toward the center of the meadow. She scrambled up to stand at the edge of the ditch, refusing to cower while he marched so bravely to his doom.

The rumble swelled until she couldn't tell its rhythmic *boom-boom* from the shuddering of her heart. In that very moment when she thought she would scream if something didn't happen, Brisbane's creation came crashing out of the forest, paralyzing her scream into a squeak.

From its spiny tail to its majestic head, the dragon was armored in shimmering emerald scales. Tabitha recoiled, squinting at the curious creature. It wasn't a particularly graceful dragon. It came galumphing across the meadow, huffing and puffing like one of Puff's asthmatic cousins from the land of Honah Lee. If one of its clawed feet hadn't been large enough around to squash Colin into the grass, leaving nothing but a smear, it might have been comical instead of intimidating.

As its clumsy charge gathered speed, its fat legs pumping like pistons, Tabitha whispered, "Please, God." Suddenly it wasn't enough to invoke some watered-down concept of a Higher Power. This time, she was placing a person-to-person call to Colin's God, in all of His might, majesty, and mercy.

Colin had taken his stand in the middle of the meadow. He stood with legs splayed and sword outstretched, refusing to betray even a trace of fear. He'd probably been dreaming of this moment since boyhood. Just waiting for the opportunity to engage an enemy who wasn't chosen by his king or his church, but was instead a monster of pure malevolence, deserving of its fate.

As the dragon raced toward him, it threw back its serpentine head and loosed a bone-rattling roar that made Tabitha long to clap her hands over her ears.

Instead, she covered her eyes with her hand, unable to watch Colin fling himself into the jaws of death as he had so many times in the past. But when she stole a peek through her fingers, he was glancing over his shoulder at her. And that one panicked glance proved once and for all that Sir Colin of Ravenshaw had finally found something to live for.

He looked at the charging dragon; he looked at her. Then he began to frantically backpedal his way across the meadow.

"Tabitha!" he yelled. "Do something!"

Laughing through her tears, she reached for the amulet before remembering it wasn't there. She would just have to rely on her own God-given talents this time. Her magic might not be strong enough to defeat Brisbane's enchanted dragon, but she could certainly put something in its path to distract it.

She just hadn't planned on that something being a brigade of shuffling mummies. One minute she was wishing she knew what her mother would do in a situation like this and the next, the meadow was full of moaning zombies. How her brain had made the connection between "mommy" and "mummy" she would never know. The creatures shambled blindly about, arms outstretched, tattered wrappings trailing through the grass behind them. Oh, well, she thought ruefully, at least they weren't mummers.

The dragon stormed right through them, his massive tail cracking like a whip. He stomped on some and hurled others high in the air like crash test dummies, snapping off heads and limbs with equal glee.

Tabitha grimaced, shooting God a silent prayer of thanksgiving that Colin hadn't met a similar fate. At least the mummies were already dead. She frowned. Or were they undead?

Having made short work of her first line of defense, the dragon whirled around, searching for fresher prey. Colin had made it to the shelter of a lone oak, but between the dragon and the tree lay a squirming saddle-bag.

Tabitha gasped. Lucy! The saddlebag must have fallen off when Colin's stallion had dashed for the forest.

Her frantic wish had the opposite effect she'd intended, for suddenly the meadow was teeming with kittens of every hue. They milled around the dragon, rubbing their furry little heads against his squat legs and mewing plaintively.

She cast Colin's tree a desperate glance, wondering if he was beginning to suspect her magic had gone haywire without the amulet to direct it.

The dragon might have begun making hors d'oeuvres of the bewhiskered darlings if Arjon hadn't come staggering out from a nearby stand of oaks, sneezing with every breath. It was fortunate his eyes were watering so badly he couldn't see. Tabitha feared the sight of that many felines might send him into a panic.

She must have done something right, for with her next breath, the kittens vanished, leaving Lyssandra free to dart out and drag Arjon back to their shelter. But the squirming saddlebag remained, a vulnerable target for the dragon's wrath. Tabitha held her breath as he waddled over to it, each thud of his clawed feet shuddering the ground. There was something disturbingly familiar in the way his aristocratic nostrils flared as he lowered his massive head and sniffed at the leather pouch.

Tabitha dared not trust any more of her desires to wishes. It was almost as if Colin knew what she was going to do before she did. He started out from behind his tree at the precise moment she went running across the meadow, holding her skirt high and yearning for a sturdy pair of Dockers.

Terrified the dragon was going to devour the helpless

kitten in one chomp, she dove for the saddlebag, planning to scoop it up and race for the woods before the dragon even saw her. She might have succeeded if not for the extra inches of silk Granny Cora had sewn to her hem. Just as she snagged the pouch and hooked it over her shoulder, the clinging fabric tangled around her legs, sending her sprawling to her knees at the dragon's feet.

"Don't move, Tabitha," Colin barked from directly behind her. "Don't even breathe."

Having never been particularly good at following orders, Tabitha slowly lifted her head to find the dragon's jagged, glistening teeth an inch from her nose. His breath reeked of carrion and brimstone and she began to tremble in primitive horror.

But nothing was more horrible than the sound that rumbled from his throat when he threw his head back to the sky and began to laugh. It was in that moment that both she and Colin realized that Brisbane hadn't just summoned a demon from the bowels of hell. He'd turned himself into one.

And hanging around his scaly neck on a golden chain as thick as a man's forearm was Tabitha's amulet.

CHAPTER 28

"This incarnation suits you, Roger. I always knew you were a monster at heart."

Tabitha ached to see Colin's face as he spoke, but didn't dare move a muscle. Brisbane the Dragon chuckled, sending an icy chill down her spine. A spine soon to be crushed by a foot the size of a California redwood.

"Better a monster than a saint. At least we monsters are allowed to indulge our appetites with delectable morsels such as your lady. Perhaps just a taste . . ." Before either of them could react, the dragon's tongue darted out, licking her from chin to forehead.

Shrieking in disgust, Tabitha came up swinging. She would have nailed Brisbane on his bulbous snout if Colin hadn't grabbed her around the waist and dragged her backward. Her joy at being in his arms again was eclipsed by terror as Brisbane stalked them across the grass. Miraculously, the saddlebag was still hooked over her shoulder. Lucy was beginning to wiggle in earnest.

Colin kept his left arm anchored firmly around her waist. His right was occupied with his outstretched sword, the gleaming blade all that stood between them and disaster.

Brisbane sighed, making them both recoil from the foul stench of his breath. " 'Twill be the fulfillment of a life's dream to pick my teeth with your bones."

"I'd rather pick your teeth with my sword," Colin retorted.

The dragon's lumbering steps picked up speed, forcing them to waltz backward in double time. Smoke was beginning to roil from those gaping nostrils.

"Now might be a nice time for one of your spells," Colin muttered out of the corner of his mouth.

Given her current run of luck, Tabitha was afraid she'd wish them inside the dragon's stomach and spare him the inconvenience of swallowing them. "I think you'd better take care of this one. After all, you are my hero," she whispered back.

"Do you mean . . . ?"

She nodded. "It's the only way."

But still he hesitated. "Are you sure, lass?"

"I've never been more sure of anything in my life."

He gave her a squeeze that warmed her all the way to her bones.

"Bidding your whore a tender farewell?" Brisbane growled. "How touching! I'd weep if I weren't so happy."

Tabitha suspected his good cheer didn't bode well for either of them. Her suspicions were confirmed when his tail lashed out, knocking them both off their feet. Colin bore the brunt of their fall, but before he could recover, that pesky tail of Brisbane's snaked around her ankle and began to tug.

Colin grabbed for her, but Tabitha fought her way free from his desperate grip, knowing he would need both hands for what he must do. She tried not to panic as she went sliding across the grass toward Brisbane's yawning maw. Her fingernails dug into the dirt, but found nothing of substance to cling to.

"You'll be sorry if you eat me," Tabitha shouted, casting Colin a frantic glance. "I'll give you the worst case of heartburn you've ever had."

The dragon loomed over her, baring his teeth in a ghastly smile. "What's a little indigestion among friends?"

Tabitha could almost hear the cold smile in Colin's voice. "We're not your friends."

Without warning, he leaped over her and charged. A battle cry tore from his throat as he shifted his grip on the sword's hilt, using both hands and every ounce of his might to ram the blade through the amulet and into Brisbane's black heart.

The dragon flung back his head, unleashing a deafening roar of rage and pain. Tabitha went sailing as the beast's mighty tail thrashed from side to side, uprooting trees and tearing great gouts of earth from the meadow. Colin let go of the sword, tumbling back to the grass just in time to roll to safety.

Tabitha landed fifty feet away in a clump of soft grass. She clapped her hands over her ears, screaming without even realizing it as the sky darkened and a web of supernatural lightning enveloped the dragon. His roar went on and on until it became a high-pitched keening—half beast and half human. Tabitha closed her eyes and when she opened them again, the meadow was drenched in sunshine and Lord Brisbane lay on his back in the grass, Colin's sword protruding from his chest and blood trickling from the corner of his pale mouth.

She drew Lucy from the knapsack and buried her mouth in the kitten's soft fur. It was done. Colin was free from his past and she from her future. They were free to build a life together in the present, free to savor every precious moment as if it were to be their last.

She rose with Lucy in her arms, wanting her loving smile to be the first thing Colin saw when he staggered to his feet.

He was already standing. His people were swarming out from their hiding places to clap him on the back, but Tabitha could barely hear their shouts and cheers. Maybe the dragon's unearthly howl had temporarily deafened her. Frowning, she held Lucy to her ear. The kitten's purr seemed as boisterous as ever.

Colin cast a frantic glance in her direction. "Where's Tabitha?"

She cocked her head to the side. Oddly enough, she could read his lips, but she couldn't hear him.

"I'm right here," she shouted.

Then with an icy chill, she realized she wasn't.

For the sun no longer warmed her and the whisper of the wind stirring the tall grasses was nothing but a memory. There were no chirping birds or whirring grasshoppers. The meadow had no more substance than a watercolor painting, glimpsed briefly on a museum wall and seen afterward only in dreams.

She clutched Lucy, who with her downy fur and stout little body, had become the only thing of substance in her universe.

That was when she realized they had made a horrible miscalculation. They had assumed that destroying the amulet would forever close the door to the future, not send it crashing open.

Colin was gazing at the place where she should have been in helpless horror. Arjon and Lyssandra had joined him, their own faces reflecting their bewildered dismay. Oh, God, what did they see? she wondered. A ghostly outline of a woman clutching a cat, tears streaming down her face?

Tabitha began to run toward Colin, longing only to reach him before she faded away altogether, longing to breathe the leather and woodsmoke scent of his skin one last time so she would never forget it. But the grass no longer crunched beneath her feet and every step she took seemed to carry her farther away from him.

She was still running when she saw Brisbane sit up, wrench the sword from his chest with inhuman strength, and draw back his arm to hurl it at Colin's back.

A scream tore from her throat, but she was the only one who heard it. Then everything went black and the meadow and Colin were gone forever.

CHAPTER 29

Tabitha woke up crying, her sense of loss so keen she wished she were dead.

But as they always had before, wishes failed her, leaving her no choice but to uncurl herself from her fetal position, shake the glass out of her hair, and slowly sit up.

She was sitting in the middle of her living-room floor, still wearing a wrinkled, grass-stained medieval gown. Every time she moved, bits of safety glass that had once been the screen of her computer monitor tinkled to the carpet. The monitor sat on the workstation above her, its guts visible through a gaping hole in its belly.

Her heart almost stopped when she caught a whiff of dragon breath. Then she realized it was just the stench of melted plastic and scorched wiring. Smoke was wafting up in wispy little curlicues from the analysis pad where her amulet had once rested.

Everything was exactly as she'd left it. Her abandoned ice cream bowl sat on the floor near the window. The manila envelope that had contained her mother's video disc rested on the coffee table. Even the snow continued to drift past the window, its tranquil beauty a mocking reminder that winter still held the city in its relentless grip.

How could the world seem so much the same when everything had changed forever?

No one had missed her. No one had even realized she was gone. Because the amulet had returned her to the precise moment when she had left. If it wasn't for the emptiness of her arms and the desolate ache in her heart, it might have been as if none of it had ever happened. As if Sir Colin of Ravenshaw had never existed except in her repressed imagination.

Lucy clambered into her lap, demanding attention. Tabitha snatched up the little cat and buried her nose in its fur. The kitten smelled of rich earth and fresh grass and wildflowers. Tabitha rocked back and forth, inhaling those summer fragrances as if she could bottle them up in her lungs and savor them forever.

When something mechanical *dinged,* it took her a confused moment to recognize it as the bell heralding the arrival of the elevator. The sofa blocked her view, but whoever was disembarking began to talk even before the doors glided shut.

"—so terribly sorry, *ma chérie.* I had no idea your Uncle Cop was going to give you such a fright. I hope you don't mind Sven giving us the key to the elevator. As soon as we got off the plane and Cop told us what he'd done, we rushed right over. If we had known making an unscheduled fuel stop in the Bermuda Triangle was going to cause such a stir, we wouldn't have done it. I hope you didn't think—"

"Mama?" Utterly dazed, Tabitha blinked up at the petite brunette who rounded the corner of the sofa. She was wearing sandals, a floral sarong, and sunglasses.

The man accompanying her was wearing a wool Burberry coat with its collar turned up. His broad shoulders were dusted with snow and the wings of silver at his temples only made him look more striking than she remembered. He looked solid, vital, and very much alive.

He blinked down at her with smoky eyes identical to her own. "Good God, baby, what happened to you?"

Tabitha's face crumpled as she whispered, "Daddy?"

Then she did something she hadn't done in a very long time. She cried in her mother's arms while her father stroked her hair.

In the end she told them everything.

Given their own experiences with the amulet, they had no choice but to believe her. Her mother earned a dark glower and a stern "I told you so" from Tristan for keeping the amulet squirreled away in the showerhead all those years, but as Tabitha had long suspected, he couldn't stay mad at Arian for more than a few minutes.

They sat huddled on the sofa until the snow stopped and dawn tinted the sky a pearlescent pink. Her father wrapped a blanket around her, but she couldn't seem to stop shivering until he awkwardly draped an arm over her shoulders and hugged her close. Her mother sat on her other side, pressing mug after mug of warm milk into her hands until drowsiness began to take the edge off her anguish.

And all the while she talked. Tabitha doubted she'd spoken that many words to her parents in her entire lifetime, but it all came pouring out—her first disastrous meeting with Colin; his delighted grin when he tasted the Big Mac; the mercy he'd shown when he defied both superstition and law and freed her from the stake.

She painted word pictures for them until they could see and hear the people she spoke of as clearly as she could—Auld Nana, her broad face wreathed in a smile; sweet Jenny with her elfin nose and cropped curls; Arjon with his dry wit and fondness for a pretty face; the lovely Lyssandra, who'd finally won his fickle heart. She told them about everything except the shattering pleasure she and Colin had discovered in each other's arms and that last awful moment she couldn't bear to relive. Maybe if she never said the words aloud, they wouldn't be true.

When she was done, they sat in silence for a long time before Tabitha turned to her mother. "Please, Mama, you have to help me get back. I know he'll wait for me. If I can just find a way back . . ."

Arian shook her head sadly. "I'm sorry, darling, but traveling through time without the amulet is completely beyond my capabilities. And yours," she added gently.

Tabitha shifted her frantic gaze to her father. "You can make it work, can't you, Daddy? You're the one who designed the amulet all those years ago. All you have to do is make another one. I know you have a photographic mind. Even if you've destroyed the specs, you must remember how to re-create it."

Tristan shot Arian a helpless look before covering Tabitha's hands with his own. "And risk it falling into the hands of another monster like this Brisbane? Is that what your Colin would want?"

Tabitha bowed her head. "No," she finally said softly. "He wouldn't want that at all."

She withdrew her hands from her father's and stood. "Thank you for coming by," she said, her voice so lifeless her parents exchanged another anguished glance. "I think I'll take the day off if you don't mind."

As Tabitha shuffled off to the bedroom, the blanket dragging the floor behind her, Arian cast her husband a beseeching look, tears sparkling in her eyes. "Oh, honey, what are we going to do? She was always such a self-sufficient little thing. I never thought she needed us."

Tristan drew her close, brushing her hair with a kiss so she wouldn't see the calculating glint in his eyes. "Well, she needs us now. And I have every intention of being there for her."

Tabitha called in sick for five weeks.

She spent most of her time lying on the sofa in her pajamas, watching soap operas and game shows, barely moving, barely thinking, and never crying. She also spent hours sitting cross-legged at the window with Lucy in her lap, gazing dry-eyed at a world full of strangers. The days and nights began to blend into one formless mist, broken only by the daily visits from her parents, who came bearing crock pots of chicken soup and gourmet meals from her favorite restaurants. Soon her refrigerator was crammed with their untouched offerings.

After four and a half weeks, they could no longer hide their concern behind brave smiles and false cheer. Fearing that she'd picked up smallpox or the plague or some other obscure disease from her trip to the Middle Ages, her father insisted that she see a doctor.

Tabitha informed him that she didn't need a doctor.

She wasn't sick.

She was dying.

Although her body had been transported neatly back to where the amulet must have figured it belonged, it was nothing but an empty shell. She'd left her heart in that sunlit meadow with Colin.

Her father had finally gotten angry and shouted that it was time for her to stop mooning over a man she could never have, but she'd seen the fear in his eyes and was sorry to have caused it. But not sorry enough to eat the Big Mac in the crumpled sack he carried.

Later that afternoon she was lying on the couch staring sightlessly at the television when her mother stormed off the elevator, snatched up the remote, and thumbed off the power.

Before Tabitha could murmur a protest, Arian stamped her small foot, reminding her eerily of Lyssandra, and shouted, "Your father went to McDonald's for you! Do you understand how hard that was for him? He's never set foot in any restaurant that boasts less than a four-star rating." Her mother paced the length of the coffee table, then whirled around to point a finger at her. "He could have sent your Uncle Sven or one of his other security men, but no! He had to go himself. He had to make sure his baby girl got the freshest sesame seed bun and the crispest pickles in the entire franchise. Why, he practically made the poor manager cry!"

Tabitha couldn't have explained why, but her own eyes were beginning to fill with tears. When Arian hurled a crumpled sack at her, she was so surprised she caught it.

"I told Daddy I wasn't hungry," she whispered weakly.

"Open it," Arian commanded.

Tabitha obeyed, staring with shock at the contents. It was a home pregnancy test, the kind you could purchase over the counter at any drugstore. She'd never even suspected her sheltered mother of knowing about such things. After all, Arian had been born in 1669 when such things didn't exist.

"You may have given your father the PG version of your little adventures, but I know that look in your eyes.

I've seen it often enough in my own." Arian nodded toward the bathroom. "Go."

Refusing to even let herself hope, Tabitha obeyed. As she passed the bathroom mirror, her reflection caught her eye for the first time since returning from the past. She could not help but stare. The woman gazing back at her was a painfully thin stranger with gaunt hollows beneath her cheekbones and dark circles around her eyes. Tabitha felt a bleak flare of shame. The woman in the mirror didn't look like someone Colin would have fallen in love with.

When Tabitha emerged from the bathroom, Arian was sitting on the sofa, stroking the kitten in her lap. She watched her daughter warily, but neither said a word.

Tabitha simply went to the refrigerator, fished out the crumpled McDonald's sack, and began to cram bites of Big Mac into her mouth as fast as she could. She ate as if she were starving, as if she hadn't eaten for years and would never get the chance to eat again. When she finished the sandwich, even licking her fingers clean of dripping sauce, Arian handed her a banana cream pie and a tablespoon, grinning through her tears.

Tabitha went to the doctor the very next day.

To her father's pretended chagrin, twenty-first century medical technology determined that she hadn't picked up the plague or the pox, but a baby boy. Although Tristan blustered and fussed because some Scottish ne'er-do-well had gotten his little girl pregnant, he went to F.A.O. Schwarz that very afternoon and bought a stuffed giraffe so big they had to fold it to get it on the elevator.

Tabitha still wasn't sleeping well, but now at night

when she lay in the darkness aching with emptiness, she would fold her hands over her stomach and whisper to the baby. She told him stories about his father—a bold and true knight who always fought on the side of right and had once slain a dragon to win the heart of his lady fair.

She returned to her job the following week. She was surprised by how easy it was to throw herself back into her daily routine, to let the soothing rhythms of work dull the loneliness gnawing at her soul. She only had one bad moment on her first day back, when she was delivering a late report to the Accounting Department.

A dark-haired man was sauntering down the carpeted corridor ahead of her, his rolling gait betraying just a hint of a swagger. As she teetered after him on her high heels, Tabitha's heart began to skip more beats than it hit.

"Sir," she cried, unable to keep the pleading note from her voice. "Wait, please wait."

But when he turned around, his eyes weren't the color of sunlight, but a dull muddy brown. He looked blankly at her. "Yes? Can I help you?"

She recoiled a few steps, swallowing a bitter lump of disappointment. "I thought you were someone else. I'm sorry, Mr. . . . ?"

He extended his hand. "Ruggles. George Ruggles."

At one time Tabitha might have thought his bland face, neatly trimmed hair, and friendly smile were handsome, but now she preferred men with at least a day's growth of razor stubble and hair that looked as if it hadn't been combed in a week, even if it had.

Weekends were the hardest for her and one Saturday morning in early spring she found herself standing on the steps of the New York Public Library without knowing how she'd gotten there. The stone lions flanking the entrance were rumored to be the guardians of the truth, but she was afraid their noble and uncompromising visages might reveal more than she could bear.

But as she touched a hand to her belly, she knew she owed the child she carried more than fairy tales.

She could have probably found the information she was looking for on-line, but she'd always loved the vast Main Reading Room with its diffuse sunlight and bronze reading lamps. After she'd made her request, she sat at one of the tables and patiently waited, hoping the staff wouldn't be as efficient as she remembered. But a smiling blond woman quickly appeared with her selection.

As Tabitha thumbed through the thick sheaf of photocopies, her hands began to shake. She didn't even know why it should matter if Colin died that sunny morning in the meadow. After all, whether he lived or died in that moment, he'd still been dead for over seven hundred years. Even his bones would be nothing but dust by now.

But she pored over the genealogical charts anyway, learning that the name Ravenshaw had eventually become Renshaw, slowly tracing its evolution backward through the centuries until she found the notation she was looking for.

A tear splashed on the page as she traced his name with her finger. It seemed that Laird Colin of Ravenshaw, the seventh son to bear the family title, had lived to the ripe old age of eighty-seven. Despite the exceptional length of his life, he had married only once. His wife was not named, but she had borne him three sons and two daughters, all remarkably healthy and long-lived for children of their era. Their love had spawned a family dynasty that continued over several pages, stretching all the way to the present day.

Tabitha's tears were flowing freely now. She cupped a trembling hand over her mouth, the joy she felt at learning Colin had survived Brisbane's attack marred by bittersweet envy of the nameless, faceless woman who had shared his life, his love, and his bed for over fifty years.

The blond attendant who had brought her the photocopies appeared at her shoulder. "Miss, are you all right?"

"I don't think so," she whispered before snatching up her purse and fleeing the woman's puzzled gaze.

CHAPTER 30

Michael Copperfield pushed open the swinging door to Lennox Labs and poked his head inside. The lab was deserted. Most of the employees had taken off early, eager to rush home and prepare for the cocktail party their boss was hosting later that evening. A cocktail party where the new Vice President of Operations of Lennox Enterprises was to be named and honored by a fawning throng of New York luminaries and the media.

"Tristan?" he called out.

There was no reply. Feeling a little like a thief, he stole past the glowing banks of monitors, seeking Tristan's inner sanctum. Despite all the success Tristan had achieved in the financial world, he always seemed to be most at home in his state-of-the-art laboratory where science and computer technology so frequently fused to create magic.

It was a measure of his friend's concentration that he hadn't even bothered to key in the sequence of numbers that would close the secret panel and hide his private lab from prying eyes.

Tristan was hunched over a sterile white counter, frantically scribbling figures on a yellow pad. He wore a rumpled lab coat and his immaculately moussed hair looked as if he'd been running a weed-eater through it. The ruthless fluorescents highlighted the shadows beneath his eyes.

Crossing his arms, Copperfield leaned against the door frame. "How many days has it been since you've slept?"

Tristan started, then turned, eyeing him over the gold rims of the antique reading glasses he so stubbornly clung to. "I caught a little nap . . ." His lips moved as he silently counted. "Saturday, I think."

Cop sighed. "You're not nineteen years old anymore, you know. Does Arian know what you're up to?"

His friend's shrug was sheepish. "I think she suspects."

"What about Tabitha?"

Tristan shook his head. "I don't want her to know. There's no point in getting her hopes up. I don't think she could survive having them crushed again."

Copperfield frowned. "I thought she was doing better. I saw her on the elevator yesterday and she looked damn good. She even seemed excited about her new position."

"Oh, she's putting on a brave face. She's determined to make a life for herself and the baby, which is why I offered her the Vice Presidency of Operations. But her smile still doesn't quite reach her eyes." He dragged off his glasses and pinched the bridge of his nose, revealing his weariness. "There were so many years when I could have given my little girl anything her heart desired and she never asked. Now the one time she asks, I can't help her." He slid his glasses back on, giving his friend a bleak smile. "It's killing me, Cop."

Copperfield propped himself up on one of the stools that flanked the counter. "I thought there was more at stake than just what Tabitha wanted. Didn't you swear you'd never risk the amulet's technology falling into the hands of another sadistic son of a bitch like Arthur Linnet?" He shuddered, remembering their own near fatal trip to the past all those years ago. "From what you told me about this Brisbane, he sounds like Arthur's even more evil twin."

"Ah, but that's the beauty of my new design." Tristan marched over to the nearest keyboard, a hint of the old excitement in his eyes. An impenetrable tangle of wires rested on an analysis pad next to the computer. "I'm not trying to create a tool for wish fulfillment. I'm trying to deliberately duplicate what Tabitha achieved by accident that night in her apartment. By locating and isolating the one component within the amulet that allowed both Tabitha and Arian to breach the time continuum, I hope to create a stable conduit that could be used to travel back and forth across time."

Copperfield was thankful he was already sitting down. Tristan had attempted to defy both the forces of science and nature before, but this time he was afraid his friend's desperate desire to help his only child had finally pushed him over the edge. Cop cleared his throat, but could not quite dislodge the lump of skepticism that had lodged in it. "You're trying to build a tunnel between the centuries?"

"Precisely! A tunnel that could only be accessed and operated from this very location."

Cop forced a strained smile. "My, my, wouldn't that be convenient come Christmas, Thanksgiving, and the baby's first birthday!"

Tristan slanted him a glance that was a curious mixture of guilt and defiance. "I want my daughter to be happy, but I'm not sure I'm willing to give her up forever." He slid the mouse across its pad, highlighting a complex chain of numbers on the glowing screen. "I had a breakthrough today. I think I just might be on to something here."

His fingers flew across the keyboard, inputting the final sequence of his formula with a flourish. Something popped and sparks flew. Copperfield ducked behind the counter, having been the victim of Tristan's flying test tubes and exploding Bunsen burners too many times in the past.

He didn't dare peek over the counter until he heard Tristan bite off a less than paternal oath. His friend was staring down at the mass of singed wire on the analysis pad, his hair charged with static electricity, his face blackened with soot, and his shoulders slumped in defeat.

Cop gently took him by the elbow and led him toward the door. "Come on, Pops, we've got to get you scrubbed and in your tuxedo. Your daughter's party is less than an hour away and Arian would never forgive you if you missed it."

As Cop dimmed the lights, neither of them noticed that they'd left the panel to the private laboratory ajar.

Sven Nordgard had been Chief of Security of Lennox Enterprises for nearly twenty-four years.

Although he'd never fulfilled his dream of starring in a successful string of action-adventure films and his TriBeCa loft was still papered with blowups of the romance novel covers he had so proudly posed for in his youth, the towering Norwegian took great pride in his current job.

Which is how he happened to be patrolling the hall outside Lennox Labs a half hour before the party on the eighty-fifth floor was scheduled to begin. He knew the job could have been entrusted to one of his underlings, but it was his policy to do a final walk-through of the Tower from top to bottom before any major event. In all of his countless patrols, he'd yet to find any potential assassins, kidnappers, or terrorists. But he never stopped hoping.

As he passed the lab, he heard a whisper of movement behind him. He whirled around, drawing his gun from his shoulder holster. His heart thudded with anticipation as he slunk back to the lab doors and keyed in the sequence of numbers that would release their computerized lock.

At the telltale click, Sven burst through the swinging doors and dropped to one knee. He swept the perimeter of the room with his outstretched gun, bellowing, "Freeze!"

The laboratory was empty, its gleaming tile floor reflecting nothing but the dim reddish glow of the security lights overhead.

Disappointed, Sven sighed and holstered the gun. As he exited the swinging doors, he would have almost sworn he felt something brush against his leg. His nose began to twitch. The twitching worsened until he sneezed—once, twice, and, after a brief respite, a third time. He hastened his steps down the corridor and glanced nervously over his shoulder, wondering if Tabitha's kitten had escaped the penthouse again. He'd never cared for cats, especially black ones. He'd much rather confront an Uzi-toting terrorist.

He thought he saw a murky shadow slink through the swinging doors of the lab, but rather than return to investigate, he managed to convince himself it was just a trick of his watering eyes.

•   •   •

Lucy was a very unhappy little cat.

She missed the warm summer wind stirring her whiskers and the fat, juicy grasshoppers she loved to crunch between her teeth. She missed the children who rubbed her furry tummy and crooned what a bonny wee cat she was. And she missed the man with the gentle hands and rumbling voice that perfectly complemented her purr.

But most of all, she missed her mistress's laughter.

So it was in a fit of boredom and defiance that she'd stowed away on the elevator when a maid had arrived to turn down her mistress's bed for the night. Not even anticipation of the dish of leftover caviar her mistress was sure to bring her when she returned from her party could coax her to remain in that lonely apartment with its recycled air and sealed windows.

She slinked past the blond giant, silently chuckling at his fear of her, and butted open the swinging door to the lab with her head, hoping to find some mischief to get into. Her pupils expanded, her extraordinary eyes automatically adjusting to the dim light. She reached into a trash can with her paw, overturning it, but scowled to find it empty. Overzealous janitors and exterminators were the bane of her existence.

She trotted into the next room, mewing in triumph when she spotted a juicy mouse cord dangling from an overhead counter. She gripped it between her teeth, giving it a fierce little shake. The hard-shelled mouse came tumbling off the counter. Lucy settled into a tense crouch, waiting for it to make a dash for freedom so she could pounce on it and subdue it with her mighty claws.

But the disagreeable thing just laid there on its back, refusing to join the game. Wrinkling her nose at its cowardice, she bounded to the countertop, landing on a computer keyboard.

A jumble of numbers appeared on the glowing monitor. Lucy spent several minutes batting at them before realizing they were out of her reach.

Bored with that game, she pranced merrily over the numerical keyboard, enjoying the satisfying *click-click* of her paws striking the numbers.

Until a sizzling jolt of electricity charged the air.

Lucy jumped a foot, her fur bristling to twice its normal size. She'd felt that peculiar sensation once before, and if her mistress had been in the lab at that moment, the kitten would have run up her sleeve or her dress or whatever shelter was most readily available.

But this time, Lucy was on her own. As a shimmering ribbon of mist appeared in the air, she pranced sideways down the countertop, hissing to hide her terror.

The mist slowly coalesced into a tear in the fabric of the room. Lucy blinked in astonishment as a rush of warm wind poured through the circular tunnel, perfuming the stale air with a breath of summer. She crept nearer, curiosity overcoming her fear.

She was perched at the very edge of the hole when a bright yellow butterfly fluttered through the tear and perched on her nose. She shook her head and when the butterfly took off, disappearing into the rift, she bounded after it.

Colin lay on his back in the meadow, gazing up at the crisp blue sky. The air was hot and hazy, but he could feel deep in his bones that it was summer's last gasp. Autumn was coming, and after autumn, winter, when a mantle of snow would bury the meadow, freezing every bloom, every branch, and every blade of grass.

He'd already worn the grass bald on this small hillock. But he would have sworn it was where he had last seen Tabitha. She had been nothing more than a glimmer in the air, but sometimes when the breeze blew soft and sweet, he swore he could still catch a whiff of her scent and his entire body would ache with need.

He knew his time for languishing in the meadow must soon come to an end. His people already thought him half-mad for pitching his pavilion so far from home and even Arjon had begun to cast him pitying glances when he visited with news and fresh supplies. But Arjon had no right to pity him, not when he had the woman he loved in his arms and in his bed. Not when she had become his wife and would bear his child during those very months when winter was laying its bitter blanket over the meadow.

Sighing, Colin sat up. There were times when he wished Brisbane had killed him in that moment when Tabitha had vanished. But Auld Nana never would stand for anyone bullying her babes. So she'd snapped Roger's neck like a twig, forcing Colin to keep living, even without a reason.

Colin shook his head to clear it. This was not what Tabitha would have wished for him and he knew it. She wouldn't have wanted him to waste his life pining for something that could never be. She would want him to rise from this place and march boldly toward the future, to seek some manner of happiness, even if it was only a shadow of the joy they might have shared together.

He'd never lacked for courage, but rising from that hillock was the hardest thing Sir Colin of Ravenshaw had ever done. He knew he was bidding farewell to his fondest dream. He would never taste Tabitha's sweet lips again. He would never hold her gray-eyed babes with their sunny hair and shy smiles. He would never watch a mist of silver creep over her own golden hair as they grew old in each other's arms.

As he stood, the wind ruffled his hair and a fat yellow butterfly floated past his nose. Which wouldn't have been so jarring if the cat chasing it hadn't jumped on his calf, claws extended, and started climbing up his leg.

Grimacing in pain, he detached the creature from his hose and held it up to his face. "Sweet *Jesu,* are you trying to kill me . . . ?" His question died on a hoarse croak of wonder. "Lucy?"

The cat greeted him with a joyful meow.

Colin stroked the kitten between its pointy little ears, wondering if grief had finally made him mad. " 'Tis impossible," he breathed. "You can't be here. You disappeared with Tabitha."

As if to mock his stunned disbelief, the little cat slipped from his numb grip and scampered across the meadow. After a moment of hesitation, Colin hurried after her, unwilling to let her out of his sight.

But he had no choice when she disappeared into the yawning mouth of a tunnel that hadn't been there only seconds before.

Sven Nordgard had a guilty conscience.

He had gotten only as far as the twenty-fifth floor on his methodical patrol of the Tower before making an abrupt about-face and marching to the nearest elevator that would carry him to the thirteenth floor where the lab was located. He was almost sure he'd failed to secure the laboratory door when he'd fled the corridor, driven by visions of yowling cats as big as panthers leaping at him out of the darkness, razor-sharp claws extended to slash his throat.

As the elevator glided to a halt, he took a deep breath, inflating his barrel-shaped chest to its most intimidating size. He vowed to himself that he would never again let his cowardly terror of felines deter him from his duty.

The elevator doors slid open. Before Sven could draw his gun, the man standing just outside of them pressed the tip of a sword to his heart and growled, "What in the name of God have you done with my woman?"

CHAPTER 31

As Tabitha entered Lennox Tower's most sumptuous ballroom with its black marble floor and walls of solid glass overlooking the lights of the city, cameras clicked and flashed from one end of the room to the other.

One of the female reporters thrust a microphone into her face. "So where has your father been hiding you all these years, Miss Lennox? In the attic?"

Tabitha smiled. "My father has always encouraged me to take an active role in the company. It was my choice to keep a low profile."

She felt a surge of relief when Tristan appeared at her side, slipping a protective arm around her waist. Her father had had far more experience dealing with the press than she had, although not all of it positive. He looked both regal and composed in his custom-tailored tuxedo. Arian and Uncle Cop hovered just behind the reporters, prepared to devise a hasty exit if required. Her mother stood on tiptoe to give Tabitha an encouraging wink before taking a sip of her wine.

"Mr. Lennox, do you think your daughter possesses the necessary qualifications to succeed at such a high-profile job?"

Tristan's smile was almost lethally pleasant. "My daughter is qualified to succeed at any job she chooses, David. Including yours."

That earned him a laugh from all the reporters, even the one he'd needled.

"You were seen going into an obstetrician's office yesterday afternoon, Miss Lennox. Rumor has it that you're pregnant. If so, will motherhood interfere with your new duties?"

Giving Tabitha time to recover her shaken composure, Tristan cocked an eyebrow at the reporter. "You're the father of two active boys, Ben. Does that interfere with your job?"

"Would you care to reveal the identity of the baby's father, Tabitha? Will he be taking an active role in the child's life?"

Tabitha felt Tristan tense. Knowing he couldn't run interference for her forever, she put a restraining hand on his chest. "It's all right, Daddy."

As she stepped away from her father's sheltering arm, Tabitha caught a glimpse of her reflection in the window. She looked trim and elegant in her simple black sheath, her freshly cut hair a shining cap that framed her face and brushed her shoulders. She no longer slumped to hide her height and her skin was infused with the wondrous glow of carrying Colin's child.

She touched a hand to her belly. She wouldn't be trim much longer, but she would eagerly welcome the visible proof that she had once been loved by a man like Colin.

A few months ago she would have stammered and squirmed in such a situation, but as she faced the pack of reporters sniffing for any whiff of scandal, she held her head high and smiled through a sheen of tears. "I can only tell you that the father of my baby was . . ." she faltered, ". . . *is* one of the finest men I will ever have the honor to know—a true hero in every sense of the word. It's one of the keenest regrets of my life that it will be impossible for him to take an active role in the raising of our child."

Her cryptic answer only sent them into a feeding frenzy.

"By his choice or yours, Miss Lennox?"

"Is he married?"

"Is he gay?"

Tristan was about to step back into the fray when a cellular telephone chirped. Nearly growling with impatience, he withdrew from everyone's earshot and drew a flip phone from his tuxedo jacket.

"Lennox," he barked into the mouthpiece. "What the hell are you babbling about, Sven? You know I don't speak Norwegian." He paused. "An intruder? Are you sure? Well, get some backup and call the police. Disarm him if you can. That's what I pay you eighty thousand a year for." A longer pause. "He disarmed *you*?" Tristan's voice rose to a shout, provoking several curious stares, including his wife's. "With *what*? A sword!" As the blood drained from his head, Tristan almost dropped the phone, but caught it before it could hit the floor. "For God's sake, don't shoot him! What do you mean he's already coming . . . ?"

Tristan didn't have time to ask for clarification, for the elevator door at the far end of the ballroom was already gliding open to reveal its only occupant.

Tristan dropped the phone at the precise moment Arian's wineglass slipped from her hand to shatter on the marble floor. As their guests pivoted and craned their necks to catch a glimpse of the new arrival, a wave of stunned murmurs surged through the ballroom.

Relieved to be rescued from the press's hounding, Tabitha turned to see what all the fuss was about.

And found herself gazing into the golden eyes of a knight in shining armor. He marched off the elevator and across the ballroom, his scowl fierce enough to send even the most intrepid gawkers scrambling backward. He looked more than capable of using the massive sword sheathed at his hip to lop off the head of anyone foolish enough to stand in his way. His dark hair haloed his face in a frightful tangle.

Tabitha stood utterly still, terrified that if she so much as breathed she would wake herself up and this dream would end like all the others, leaving her to cry herself back to sleep.

An elderly woman who had been on the board of Lennox Enterprises since long before Tabitha was born said, "Look at that outrageous costume! He must be a male stripper." She turned up her patrician nose and sniffed in disdain. "I always thought Lennox had better taste in entertainment."

"Oh, I hope not," her blue-haired companion replied, eyeing the intruder's well-muscled shoulders with the appreciation of a connoisseur.

The knight's relentless approach scattered the lingering reporters and photographers, although several of them retained enough of their wits to fumble in their camera bags for fresh film and batteries.

Although Tabitha still hadn't breathed, she could do nothing about the tears trickling steadily down her cheeks. As Colin knelt on one knee at her feet and brought her hand to his lips, they fell on his head like a gentle spring rain sent by God to thaw the frozen earth.

"My lady," he whispered, tasting her skin as if he would have liked to devour her where she stood.

Her breath escaped in a joyous sob. Then she was on her knees and in the arms of the man she loved, kissing his brow, his cheeks, his nose, and finally his soft, remarkable mouth. They were both oblivious to the cameras flashing and the reporters frantically scribbling notes. Time ceased to exist except for that one moment that seemed as if it would surely go on forever.

Until Tristan reached down and tapped Colin on the shoulder.

Tabitha moaned a protest as Colin reluctantly disengaged his lips from hers and turned his head to find himself gazing into a stern masculine visage. He glanced back at Tabitha, then at Tristan. The resemblance was unmistakable.

As Colin rose, the two men sized each other up like rival bulldogs vying for the same bone. Tristan was taller, but Colin was the more muscular of the two.

Colin cleared his throat as if that bone had become lodged in it. "You must be Tabitha's father. 'Tis an honor to meet you, sir. I should like to pledge my troth to your daughter and pray you'll grant me your leave to make her my wife."

A thrill of pride and happiness shot through Tabitha's veins.

But that was before her father slammed his fist into Colin's jaw, sending him sprawling back to the floor.

"Daddy!" she wailed, crawling to Colin's side.

"Tristan, really!" Arian rolled her eyes.

Colin rubbed his jaw, shooting Tabitha a rueful glance. "*You* claimed he'd punch me in the nose."

Tristan stood over him, massaging his knuckles. "That was for breaking my little girl's heart and getting her pregnant without marrying her first." He extended his hand, a radiant smile breaking over his face. "Welcome to the family, son."

As her father tugged Colin to his feet, clapping him on the back as if he were a long-lost fraternity brother, Tabitha sprang to her own feet. "Hey, wait just a minute! This is the twenty-first century, you know. Don't I get a say in who I'm going to marry?"

Colin drew her into his arms, cupping one of his powerful hands gently over her stomach. His misty eyes reflected her own wonder. "I fear you've no choice, lass. If 'tis my bairn tucked away in there, Auld Nana will insist I make you my wife. Wee Blythe won't be wee forever and Nana won't be happy until she has another Ravenshaw babe in her nursery."

Tabitha wrapped her arms around his neck. Colin didn't know it yet, but Auld Nana would soon have a nursery full of their babies—three boys and two girls to be exact. "Then I think she's going to be very happy indeed."

"Not as happy as I'm going to make you, lass," he vowed, kissing her softly on the lips.

"I don't understand," she murmured. "How did you get here?"

Uncle Cop cleared his throat and pointed at Tristan.

Tabitha noted the shadows of exhaustion beneath her father's eyes for the first time. "Daddy?"

He nodded. "I can't explain exactly *how* I did it. I thought my last experiment ended in disaster, but I must have stumbled on something without realizing it."

Tabitha reached out and patted his freshly shaven cheek. "Oh, Daddy, you were always my hero."

He kissed her fingers before placing her hand on Colin's shoulder and backing into Arian's waiting arms. "That's one job title I'm ready to relinquish to someone more qualified."

Colin nodded. "Thank you, sir. You won't regret it."

The reporters were beginning to crowd around them in earnest. Tristan retrieved his flip phone from the floor before it could be trampled, nodding toward the elevator. "You two go on. I'll have Sven waiting to escort you back to the laboratory."

Tabitha squealed with surprise as Colin scooped her up in his brawny arms and started for the elevator. The reporters trailed after them, giving him a wide berth, but still daring to snap photos and shout questions at his broad back.

"How long have the two of you known each other?"

"Seven hundred and sixty-six years," Colin replied without missing a step.

"Are you the father of Miss Lennox's baby, sir?"

"I'm going to be the father of all her babes."

"Do the two of you plan to make your home in New York or somewhere else?"

Tabitha and Colin exchanged a startled glance before bursting into laughter and saying in unison, "Somewhere else."

As they boarded the elevator and turned around, Tristan and Arian were elbowing their way to the front of the crowd. Tristan reached around and punched the button for the thirteenth floor while Arian blew them a frantic kiss.

Her mother was forced to yell over the clamor of the crowd. "Your father says we can come visit you when the baby's born. And at Christmas and Thanksgiving."

"And Candlemas," Colin added sternly.

"Bring diapers," Tabitha shouted back. "And cream rinse and antibiotics and toilet paper and aspirin and chocolate and soap." The elevator door began to glide shut. "And tampons!"

Then they were alone at last with no shouting reporters, no flashing cameras, and no well-meaning parents. She gazed shyly into Colin's dark-lashed eyes, finally understanding why all of her earlier attempts to wish herself home had failed.

Because no matter how far she traveled through time, this man's arms would always be her home.

As the elevator started downward, Colin arched one eyebrow at her. Tabitha suspected she was going to see that same naughty expression on her firstborn son's face only too soon. "Do you ever wish time could stop for just a wee bit, lass?"

Tabitha grinned. "That's one wish I can grant."

As her lips melted against his, she reached out and pushed the Emergency button, bringing time to a grinding halt.

Epilogue

From the front page of the *Global Inquirer*, New York City, May 18, 2020:

BILLIONAIRE INDUSTRIALIST ANNOUNCES MARRIAGE OF ONLY DAUGHTER

Mr. and Mrs. Tristan and Arian Lennox announced the marriage of their only daughter Tabitha at a press conference held at Lennox Enterprises this morning. The groom created quite a stir last week when he marched into an exclusive cocktail party dressed as a knight in shining armor, dropped to his knees at Miss Lennox's feet, and proposed. Although the romantic gesture had many of the guests swooning in envy, Mrs. Flora Biddlesworth informed this reporter that she was sure she'd seen the mystery man moonlighting at a strip club on the east side of town. When Mrs. Biddlesworth was asked if it was her habit to frequent such establishments, she declined further comment.

About the Author

USA Today bestseller Teresa Medeiros has well over two million copies of her books in print. She was recently chosen one of the Top Ten Favorite Romance Authors by *Affaire de Coeur* magazine and won the *Romantic Times* Reviewers Choice Award for Best Historical Love and Laughter. A former Army brat and registered nurse, Teresa wrote her first novel at the age of twenty-one and has since gone on to win the hearts of critics and readers alike. Teresa currently lives in Kentucky with her husband, Michael, four cats, and one floppy-eared Doberman. Writing romance allows her to express her own heartfelt beliefs in faith, hope, and the enduring power of love to bring about a happy ending.

Watch for the next romance
from the nationally bestselling

Teresa Medeiros

On sale in early summer 1998

*R*ead on for a sneak preview of her work in
progress, the spectacular tale of a fiery beauty
with a passion for revenge . . . and a dark-
lashed, gray-green-eyed bounty hunter with a
passion for justice.

He was there. Now that she knew he was there, she could almost feel him. Coiled. Deadly. Waiting for her.

She swallowed in a vain attempt to stifle the flutter of raw excitement in her throat. She had never dreamed her quest for justice would be fulfilled with such ease. Shock made her voice sound distant and quavery, even to her own ears. "You must fetch the sheriff immediately, sir. I shall insist he march over and take the renegade into custody."

The cowpoke scratched his balding head, his expression oddly reticent. "Uh, miss, the sheriff is already at the saloon. Been there since this mornin'."

Esmerelda blinked in confusion. "And what, pray tell, is he doing there?"

"Playin' poker, most likely. He and Billy've had a runnin' game for almost three years now."

Her eyes widened in disbelief. Nearly choking on her outrage, she glanced around frantically, earning nothing but a tip of a passing banker's hat for her trouble. "What manner of place is this Calamity? Surely the townsfolk aren't content to stand idly by while their sheriff consorts with outlaws!"

"Aw, don't be so hard on Sheriff McGuire. He'd arrest Billy if he thought it'd do any good. But our jail cain't hold him. Before the marshal could come to take him to Santa Fe for trial, his brothers would just bring a bunch o' dynamite and bust him out. You see, miss, Billy's brothers is outlaws to the last man. And you don't want to mess with them Darlin' boys. They set a high store by Billy, him bein' the baby o' the family and all."

Esmerelda clenched her teeth against a frisson of rage, finding it hard to imagine a cold-blooded killer like Billy Darling being anyone's baby. Her brother's face drifted through her memory as it had so many times in the past few months—his smooth cheeks pale and bloated, his sable hair dulled by blood, the spark of mischief in his eyes doused by the icy black waters of death.

Beset by a strange and dangerous calm, Esme dipped a hand into her reticule to caress its sleek contents.

As she stepped off the sidewalk into the dusty street, the cowhand called after her. "Miss! Oh, miss, you forgot your trunk."

"Mind it for me, will you?" she replied, studying the beckoning doors of the saloon through narrowed eyes. "I won't be long."

Esmerelda Fine's arrival in Calamity had garnered more attention than she realized. While the townsfolk had grown accustomed to the stagecoach passing through once a month on a lazy Friday afternoon, they were not accustomed to seeing anyone actually disembark from it. Especially not a slender wren of a lady garbed in a bustle and bonnet the provincial folk of Calamity assumed were the very pinnacle of city fashion.

When Esmerelda plunged into the dusty street without a visible care for her high-heeled kid leather boots, curtains twitched and children came creeping out of alleyways. When it appeared her destination was none other than the Deadwood Saloon, shopkeepers emerged from their deserted stores to sweep the sidewalks, trading curious and wary looks.

They breathed a collective sigh of relief when Esmerelda paused just outside the saloon, obviously realizing her error. No true lady would ever darken the doorstep of such an establishment. The townsfolk nodded and smiled at one another, their faith in the innate nobility of womankind restored.

Until the young lady squared her slender shoulders, thrust open the swinging doors, and disappeared inside.

The sudden shift from sunlight to gloom nearly

blinded Esmerelda. Long shadows cut a swath through the interior of the saloon, painting it in grimy shades of dun and gray. The isinglass windowpanes admitted only enough light to gild the dust motes drifting through the air. As Esmerelda's eyes slowly adjusted, she was bombarded by a host of scattered impressions.

A garishly painted woman straddled a chair in front of the piano, banging out a rollicking dance-hall tune with her crimson fingernails. A bartender hunched behind a long counter, polishing glasses in front of a row of amber-tinted bottles. A handful of stragglers slumped at the bar, but most of the chatter and merriment in the room seemed to be coming from a table situated just below the balcony.

Two bleary-eyed cowboys flanked a broad-shouldered man whose mouth was dwarfed by a drooping mustache. His blond hair flowed to his shoulders like lustrous waves of corn silk. A tin star was pinned to his satin waistcoat.

The esteemed Sheriff McGuire, Esmerelda deduced, fortified by a fresh surge of contempt.

The trail of bills and silver scattered across the table's pitted surface led directly to a fourth man. A man who sat with his face shadowed by his hat brim, a thin cigar clamped between his lips, a dimpled whore perched on one knee.

He was watching her, Esmerelda realized, repressing a shiver. His regard might be nothing more than a wary gleam penetrating the shadows, but it was powerful enough to draw every other eye in the saloon to her frozen form. It was almost as if she hadn't existed until the moment he had chosen to take notice of her.

The piano fell mute. The bartender's cloth ceased its circular motions. Curious faces appeared in the saloon windows, struggling to peer through the gloom. Avid eyes peeped over the top of the saloon door, abandoning all pretense of discretion.

Chin up and one foot in front of the other, Esmerelda heard a voice in her head say. *If you keep putting one foot in front of the other, girl, then you'll eventually get where you're going.* Although she had never actually heard her grandfather speak, Esmerelda knew exactly who that voice belonged to. She might loathe the man for turning his back on her mother, but it was his pitiless scolding that had prodded her to get off the bed and stop feeling sorry for herself, even when her parents' cold and still bodies had been laid out in the next room in their Sunday best. Had given her the strength to dry little Bartholomew's tears when she was still blinded by her own.

Despite her hatred of her grandfather, or perhaps because of it, his gruff, no-nonsense tones had never failed to calm her fears.

Until now.

She marched to the table, stopping directly across from the man she had come to find. The woman on his lap wrapped a possessive hand around his nape, surveying her with sloe-eyed amusement.

"Mr. William Darling?" Esmerelda queried, wincing when her voice cracked in the unnatural silence.

For a long moment, his only acknowledgment of her presence was the faint twitch of a muscle in his jaw. Smoke wafted from his cigar, curling toward her like tendrils of brimstone.

"I am," he finally drawled, stubbing out the cigar and tipping back his hat with one finger.

Esmerelda had braced herself to confront a bewhiskered fiend. Which explained why she nearly dropped her reticule when the shadows retreated to reveal lean cheeks shaded by the barest hint of stubble and a pair of dark-lashed, gray-green eyes that failed to betray even a glimmer of shiftiness. Those eyes assessed her, taking her measure with disturbing bluntness.

Casting a desperate prayer heavenward that she had practiced in front of the mirror often enough to do it without trembling, Esmerelda fished the derringer from the satin-lined depths of her reticule and leveled it at his heart.

"You're under arrest, Mr. Darling. I'm taking you in."

Billy Darling was a jovial drunk.

Which explained the dangerous edge to his temper as he surveyed the haughty young miss who had presumed to interrupt his poker game. His first whiskey of the day sat untouched on the table just inches from his finger-tips. The way his day was going, he doubted it would be his last.

The woman disagreed. Noting the direction of his glance, she gave the brimming glass an imperious nod. "You'd best finish your whiskey, sir. It may be the last you taste for a very long while."

Billy barely resisted the urge to burst out laughing. Instead, he curled his fingers around the glass and lifted it in a genuine salute to her audacity. She really ought to be flattered by the stir her announcement had caused. Noreen had gone tumbling off his lap in a flurry of scarlet petticoats, while Dauber and Seal went diving under a nearby table, scattering bills and coins in their wake.

Only Drew had remained upright, but even he had scooted his chair back a good two feet and thrown his hands into the air. The waxed tips of his mustache quivered with alarm. Billy suspected he would have joined the cowboys under the table if he hadn't feared rumpling the new paisley waistcoat he'd had shipped all the way from Philadelphia. You could almost always count on Drew's vanity overruling his cowardice.

It wasn't the first time Billy had faced a woman across the barrel of a gun, and it probably wouldn't be the last. Hell, he'd even been shot once by a jealous whore in Abilene. But she'd cried so prettily and tended the wound and the rest of him with such gratifying remorse, he'd forgiven her before the bleeding stopped.

It wasn't even that he particularly minded being shot by a woman. He just wanted to do something to deserve it first.

He sipped the whiskey, narrowing his eyes to study the woman over the rim of the glass. Her hands might be steady, but the flush heightening her color betrayed her agitation. Any woman with a gun was dangerous, but he suspected this one was more dangerous than most. Her delicate nostrils flared like a high-strung mare's each time she drew in a breath.

He searched his memory for any transgression he might have committed against her. She didn't look the sort to thrust some squalling brat into his face, claiming it was his. He was forced to swallow a shudder of distaste along with a mouthful of whiskey at the thought of inflicting another Darling on the hapless world.

He allowed his gaze to roam briefly over her trim form. She was as slender as a reed—downright underfed by his standards. She most definitely didn't favor the busty whores who bore the brunt of his romantic attentions.

Billy frowned. In the past few years, he'd woken up on more than one occasion with women whose faces and names he could barely remember, but it troubled him to think such an encounter could have escaped him completely. He studied the pristine curve of the woman's cheek, wishing he could see the hue of the hair hidden by that ridiculous bird's nest of a bonnet. But as his gaze lingered on her mouth, he decided he had never known her, biblically or otherwise. If he'd ever persuaded those prim lips to part for him or made those snowy cheeks flush with pleasure instead of indignation, he damn well would have remembered it.

He drained the remainder of the whiskey in a single searing swallow and returned the glass to the table with a thump that made her flinch. "Why don't you put the gun down? You really don't want to get powder burns on your lovely gloves, do you, Miss . . . ?"

"Fine," she offered tersely. "Miss Esmerelda Fine."

She flung her name at him like a challenge, but it failed to trigger even a whisper of recognition. "Esmerelda? Now, that's a rather lofty name for such a little bit of a lady. Suppose I just call you Esme?"

He would have thought it impossible, but her mouth grew even more pinched. "I'd rather you didn't. My brother was the only one who called me Esme." Then those same lips surprised him by curving in a sweetly mocking smile. "Unless, of course, you would prefer I call you *Darling*?"

Billy scowled at her. "The last man who cast aspersions on my family name, *Miss Fine,* got a bellyful of lead." Actually, he'd only gotten a bloody nose, but since Billy didn't intend to give either to this persistent young lady, he didn't see any harm in embellishing.

"It wouldn't have been my brother, by any chance, would it? Is that why you gunned down a defenseless man? For hurting your poor, delicate feelings?"

"Ah," Billy said, his good humor returning as he folded his arms over his chest and tilted his chair back on two legs. "Now we're getting somewhere. Do refresh my memory, Miss Fine. You can't expect me to remember every man I'm supposed to have killed."

He noted with a surprising flicker of remorse that his jibe had drawn blood. The hand wrapped around the derringer wavered ever so slightly. Dauber and Seal cowered deeper under their table, all but hugging each other.

"I should have expected such callous disregard from an animal like you, Mr. Darling. A cold-blooded assassin masquerading as a legitimate bounty hunter." Her contemptuous gaze flicked to Drew. "Sheriff, I demand that you arrest this man immediately for the murder of Bartholomew Fine III."

"What happened to the first two Bartholomews?" Dauber whispered. "Billy kill them, too?" He grunted as Seal elbowed him in the ribs.

Drew twirled one tip of his mustache, a habit he indulged only in moments of great duress. "Now, miss, there's no reason to get your pretty little feathers all in a ruffle. I'm sure that whatever private quarrel you and Mr. Darling might have, it can be settled in a civilized manner without the discharge of firearms in this respectable establishment."

"Private quarrel?" The woman's voice rose to a near shriek. "According to that wanted poster out there, this man is a public menace with a price on his head. I insist that you take him in!"

Drew sputtered an ineffectual retort, but Billy's melted-butter-and-molasses drawl cut right through it. "And just where do you propose he take me?"

Miss Fine blinked, her face going blank for a gratifying moment. "Why, the jail, I suppose."

Billy slanted Drew a woeful look. Avoiding Miss Fine's eyes, Drew polished his badge with his ruffled shirtsleeve before mumbling, "Sorry, miss, but the jail's full. Dangerous outlaws, you know. Can't have them running amok through the town."

Righting his chair, Billy favored her with a rueful grin, briefly entertaining the notion that she and her sad little bonnet just might admit defeat and creep away to let him finish his poker game in peace.

His hopes were dashed when she swayed forward, her voice husky with menace. "If this miserable excuse for a lawman—"

"Now, wait just one minute there!" Drew cried. "There's no need to insult my . . ." His defense subsided to a sulky pout as she briefly turned the gun on him before aiming it square at Billy's heart.

"If this miserable excuse for a lawman won't take you in," she repeated firmly, "then I will. I'll take you to Santa Fe and turn you over to the federal marshal myself. Why, I'll hog-tie you to the back of a stagecoach and drag you all the way to Boston if I have to, Mr. Darling."

Rubbing the back of his neck, Billy sighed wearily. She'd left him with no choice but to call her bluff. As the smile faded from his eyes, the bartender vanished behind the bar, Drew inched his chair backward, and Dauber plugged his ears with his fingertips.

Billy rested his hands palms-down on the table, flexing his fingers with deceptive indolence. "Oh, yeah?" he drawled. "Who says?"

Little Miss Fine-and-Mighty cocked the derringer, her delicate knuckles white with strain. "I've got one shot in this chamber that says you're coming with me."

The Colt .45 appeared in Billy's hand as if by magic, accompanied by a personable grin. "And I've got six shots in this here Colt that say I'm not."

Esmerelda stared dumbly at the gun in Darling's hand. His movements hadn't betrayed even a hint of a blur. One second his hand had been empty. The next it had been cradling an enormous black pistol. The imposing barrel dwarfed the stunted mouth of her derringer, robbing it of its menace and making it look like nothing more than an ineffectual toy. Darling's smile was unflinching, but all traces of green had disappeared from his eyes, leaving them ruthless chips of flint.

Esmerelda sucked in a steadying breath, cringing when it caught in a squeak. She'd spent many sleepless nights in the past few months dreaming of the moment when she would confront her brother's murderer. But none of the possible scenarios had included engaging him in a standoff. Billy Darling was rumored to be a crack shot, lethally accurate at thirty yards, much less four feet. What was the proper etiquette in these situations? she wondered. Should she suggest they choose seconds? Step outside and draw at twenty paces? She flexed her numb fingers, choking back a hysterical giggle.

Almost as if he'd read her mind, he said, "It has occurred to me, Miss Fine, that this may very well be your first gunfight. We have both drawn our weapons, so all that remains is to determine which one of us has the guts to pull the trigger. If you'd rather not find out, then I suggest you lay your gun on the table and back out of here. Nice and slow."

"Now, Billy," the sheriff whined. "You know you've never shot a woman before."

Darling's affable smile did not waver. "Nor has one ever given me cause to."

"Drop your weapon, sir," Esmerelda commanded, praying the derringer wouldn't slip out of her sweat-dampened glove. She waited a respectable interval before adding a timid "P-p-please."

"I asked you first."

Her hands were starting to shake in earnest and there seemed to be little she could do to still their violent trembling. The sight infused her with frustration and a bone-deep weariness. She had sold everything she'd worked for since she was twelve years old—her beloved school, her tidy little house with its red shutters and geranium-filled window boxes, the precious books she'd bought with pennies hoarded from her own food money. She'd forfeited all she held dear just to come to this godforsaken town and bring her brother's killer to justice. And there he sat, smirking at her with cool aplomb, all the while knowing that he had crushed her brother's life beneath his bootheel like a discarded cigar butt.

He had robbed her of everything that made life worth living, and now he dared to threaten that life itself.

Esmerelda suddenly realized that she didn't want justice. She wanted vengeance. Her finger tightened on the trigger. A scalding tear trickled down her cheek, then another. She dashed them away with one hand, but fresh ones sprang into their place to blur her vision.

She did not see the sheriff rock back in his chair, grinning with relief. Billy Darling might be able to stand down the meanest desperado in five territories or gun down a fleeing outlaw without blinking an eye, but he never could abide a woman's tears.

"Aw, hell, honey, don't cry. I didn't mean to scare you. . . ."

Billy was out of his seat and halfway around the table, hand outstretched, when Esmerelda Fine, who had never so much as swatted a fly without a pang of regret, closed her eyes and squeezed the trigger.

Enter to win in Bantam Books'

Romance Readers Never Go to Bed Alone!

SWEEPSTAKES

You could win ...

Grand Prize Dream Getaway for Two to
BRACO VILLAGE RESORT, JAMAICA,
courtesy of Empress Travel with round-trip coach air
travel on American Airlines!

or one of 3 sensational First Prizes ...

A Touch of Enchantment "Year of Flowers"
delivered to your home or office!

∎

The Silver Rose custom-designed sterling silver charm!

∎

The Mermaid Weekend Getaway for Two!

or one of 10 terrific Second Prizes ...
A trio of romance novels and a custom-created
**"ROMANCE READERS NEVER GO TO BED
ALONE!"** nightshirt!

NAME: _____ AGE: _____

ADDRESS: _____

CITY: _____ STATE: _____ ZIP: _____

PHONE:(DAY) _____ (NIGHT) _____

**ENTRIES MUST BE RECEIVED BY NO LATER
THAN SEPTEMBER 1, 1997**

Bantam

Grand Prize Dream Getaway courtesy of

EMPRESS TRAVEL **Braco** village resort **American Airlines**

BANTAM BOOKS ROMANCE READERS NEVER GO TO BED ALONE! Official Entry Rules

HOW TO ENTER

1. No purchase is necessary. Enter by completing the ROMANCE READERS NEVER GO TO BED ALONE! SWEEPSTAKES entry coupon or by printing your name, address, age and phone number on a 3 x 5 card and sending the coupon or card to: BANTAM BOOKS ROMANCE READERS NEVER GO TO BED ALONE! SWEEPSTAKES, BANTAM BOOKS, DEPT. RR-1, 1540 Broadway, NY, NY 10036

PRIZES

2. One (1) Grand Prize:

A 7-night Dream Getaway for two to BRACO VILLAGE RESORT, Jamaica, the luxurious all-inclusive resort and round-trip coach air travel on American Airlines, courtesy of Empress Travel. The Dream Getaway at BRACO VILLAGE includes all meals and beverages plus use of all water sports facilities with instructions, and resort facilities including tennis (night and day), bicycles, and fitness center. Estimated value of Grand Prize: $3,700.00

Grand Prize bookings must be made through Empress Travel, and travel arrangements and resort accomodations are subject to availability. Grand Prize trip must be taken within 12 months of date awarded. Blackout dates may apply. Winner will be responsible for any expenses involved in traveling to the nearest airport serviced by American Airlines. The winner and his/her guest must each have a valid passport or a photo I.D. and proof of citizenship. Once travel arrangements are made, no changes will be allowed. All expenses not mentioned are the sole responsibility of the winner.

Three (3) First Prize Awards:

a) The Touch of Enchantment "A Year of Flowers" mailed monthly to winner's home. Estimated value of First Prize: $350.00

"A Year of Flowers" First Prize arrangements will be made by Bantam Books marketing department for winner. Shipments will be made once per month to one address.

b) The Silver Rose Charm, custom created for this sweepstakes, in sterling silver. Estimated value of The Silver Rose First Prize: $300.00

c) The Mermaid "Weekend Getaway" for two. Estimated value of The Mermaid First Prize: $325.00

The Mermaid Weekend Getaway First Prize arrangements will be made by Bantam Books marketing department for winner. Weekend must be taken within 12 months of date awarded. Blackout dates may apply. Winner will be responsible for any expenes involved in traveling to "Weekend Getaway" Package. The winner and his/her guest must each have a valid passport or a photo I.D. and proof of citizenship. Once travel arrangements are made, no changes will be allowed.

Ten (10) Second Prize Awards:

A package consisting of 3 Bantam backlist paperback romance novels and one 100% cotton, One-Size-Fits-Most "Romance Readers Never Go To Bed Alone!" nightshirt, custom-created for this promotion. The three paperbacks will be chosen by Bantam marketing for the winner. Estimated value of Second Prize: $28.00 each.

ELIGIBILITY

3. Entrants must be 18 years or older at the time of entry. There is no limit to the number of entries. Entries must be received by Bantam no later than SEPTEMBER 1, 1997. The winner will be chosen in a random drawing by the Bantam marketing department from completed entries received and the winners will be notified on or about OCTOBER 1, 1997. Bantam's decision is final. Each winner has thirty days from the date of notice in which to accept his/her prize award or an alternate winner will be chosen. Odds of winning depend upon the number of entries received. No prize substitution or transfer allowed. Only one prize per entrant; one prize per household.

4. The winner and his/her guest will be required to sign an Affidavit of Eligibility and Release supplied by Bantam Books. Entering the sweepstakes constitutes permission for use of the winner's name, likeness and biographical data for publicity and promotional purposes, with no additional compensation.

5. **Prize awards are subject to the rules of entrant's employer.** Employees of Bantam Books, Bantam Doubleday Dell Publishing Group, Inc., Empress Travel, American Airlines, Braco Village Resort, their subsidiaries and affiliates and their immediate family members are not eligible to enter this sweepstakes. This sweepstakes is open to residents of the U.S. and Canada, excluding the Province of Quebec. Canadian winner would be required to correctly answer an arithmetical skill testing question in order to receive his/her prize. Void where prohibited or restricted by law. All federal state and local regulations apply. Taxes, if any, are the winner's sole responsibility. In the event that these prizes become unavailable, Bantam Books reserves the right to substitute with prizes of equal value.

6. For the name of the prize winners, available after December 1, 1997, send a stamped, self-addressed envelope entirely separate from your entry to BANTAM BOOKS ROMANCE READERS NEVER GO TO BED ALONE! SWEEPSTAKES WINNER, Bantam Books, 1540 Broadway, Dept. JL, New York New York 10036